A ROSSLER FOUNDATION MYSTERY

# THE 10TH CYCLE

A THRILLER

HUMAN HISTORY IS ABOUT TO CHANGE ...
FOREVER

JC RYAN

# The Tenth Cycle

## A Thriller

## A Rossler Foundation Mystery

## By JC Ryan

This is the first book in the Rossler Foundation Mystery Series. Want to hear about special offers and new releases?

Sign up for my confidential mailing list www.jcryanbooks.com

# Your Free Gift

As a way of saying thanks for your purchase, I'm offering you a free eBook which you can download from my website at www.jcryanbooks.com

## MYSTERIES FROM THE ANCIENTS

### 10 THOUGHT PROVOKING UNSOLVED ARCHAEOLOGICAL MYSTERIES

This book is exclusive to my readers. You will not find this book anywhere else.

We spend a lot of time researching and documenting our past, yet there are still many questions left unanswered. Our ancestors left 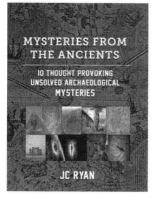 a lot of traces for us, and it seems that not all of them were ever meant to be understood. Despite our best efforts, they remain mysteries to this day.

Inside you will find some of the most fascinating and thought-provoking facts about archaeological discoveries which still have no clear explanation.

Read all about The Great Pyramid at Giza, The Piri Reis Map, Doomsday, Giant Geoglyphs, The Great Flood, Ancient Science and Mathematics, Human Flight, Pyramids, Fertility Stones and the Tower of Babel, Mysterious Tunnels and The Mystery of The Anasazi

Don't miss this opportunity to get this free eBook now.

**Click Here** to download it now.

# Table Of Contents

# Prologue

**10th Cycle year 25,990 A city near the present site of Giza, Egypt**

The Supreme Council of Knowledge had been in session for more than two hours and the mood between the twenty-one elders was somber, although what they heard excited some.

Aleph, first among the members, listened attentively as Zebulon, their youngest, made his request. The nineteen Chosen who ranked between the two listened in various mental states, some supporting, others dismayed. Zebulon, a genius and excellent orator, was making a compelling argument, succeeding in convincing the elders that he had a worthy cause.

Concluding, he said. "We have made our world a better place since we received it nearly 26,000 years ago. Why should we not pass the benefit of our knowledge on to Those Who Come After? Our world will end soon, in about ten years if my calculations are correct. We have nothing more to prove or achieve, our time has come and gone. Let us be gracious about it. A new civilization will be built on the ruins of ours. Why should we not give them the best chance to build it even better than ours? A chance to break the cycle of destruction? They are our children and descendants. We owe it to them. I beg you to consider wisely." Zebulon bowed and sat down.

All eyes were on Aleph as he made his answer. "Why would we undertake this task? It has ever been so, God has decreed it. Civilizations are born, they live and grow and they are destroyed. This is the tenth Cycle. Those Who Come After in the eleventh must once again learn wisdom in their own Cycle and in their own way. You defy the natural order!"

"With respect, Aleph, show me in the holy writings where God has decreed we may not reveal our knowledge to Those Who Come After." A gasp went up as nineteen pairs of eyes flew to

Aleph expecting to see his rage. Instead, they saw him in deep thought.

He looked at Zebulon. "Very well, you have spoken well, and have convinced me. If the rest of the members agree, you may gather the information and build your Library of Knowledge of the Tenth Cycle." The nineteen members nodded their heads in agreement.

Aleph looked around, confirming he had the support of everyone, and continued. "The Council will bear the expense of what you described to us. But there is one very important condition. You must devise and encode the message in such a way that it is time-locked to Those Who Come After. They will first have to achieve a high measure of intelligence and civil behavior before they can read it. Only when they have advanced to the point where they can read and understand the message will they be ready to make use of the information you will leave for them to improve their world. If you fail to do so, it might cause them much more harm than the good you intend for them."

The other nineteen members nodded their heads in agreement again.

"Thank you, Aleph and learned elders. I will follow your wise counsel with great care and precision."

Zebulon bowed in affirmation and turned to leave the conference chamber. There was no time to waste. According to his calculations, the Cycle would end in less than ten years. Despite the engineering capabilities of a 26,000-year-old civilization, it would take at least eight years to build the massive structure he planned, a pyramid, shaped and constructed to withstand any natural disaster he could imagine. Within its measurements and placement would be a sign for those who could see it, that a great accumulation of facts, history and scientific discovery was contained within. In turn, the key to unlock the treasure-trove would be encoded, requiring both intelligence and persistence to locate and read it. In this way, he would cleverly time-lock the knowledge and wisdom of the Tenth Cycle of humanity.

# Chapter 1 - Near Kabul, Afghanistan, July 2009

Daniel Rossler and two of his friends from ISAF headquarters in Kabul, Afghanistan set out early in the morning on Daniel's birthday, July 8th, on the A1 toward Jalalabad some one-hundred and fifty klicks and three hours or so to the east. IEDs, or Improvised Explosive Devices had made this stretch of road one of the most dangerous places in the world.

Daniel, an irrepressible 26-year-old journalist embedded with the Marine unit, matched his comrades' skill for skill except in armed combat. As a journalist, he was neither expected nor permitted to carry a weapon, though his upbringing in the North Carolina Mountains had included skill with a hunting rifle. Now, his preferred physical activities were hiking, swimming, and the occasional impromptu wrestling match with the two friends in the Jeep with him today or other opponents from their unit. At six-foot-three, his wiry frame was perhaps a little lighter than most of his heavily-muscled Marine opponents, but his quick thinking and unconventional moves allowed him to win more often than he lost.

"Hey, Sarge," Rossler yelled over the noise of the vehicle on the highway. "Isn't this the road that the Taliban keeps bombing?"

"You afraid of a little rebel IED, Rossler?" the sergeant retorted.

That effectively shut down any further discussion on the matter. The one thing Daniel couldn't allow was his Marine friends thinking he was a wuss. Traffic was unusually light this morning, which should have warned the three friends, especially the Marines. Instead, they were elated to be making such good time during the early hours before the heat of the day set in.

Seeing the well-populated area on both sides of the road

for the first fifty klicks, Daniel wondered at the logic of the Taliban rebels who harassed travelers along this road without regard to loyalty. Anyone could be killed by an IED, even Afghan citizens making their way to market, or children.

He was aware of the joint task force squads that had been specially trained to sweep for and dispose of the deadly items, though. Daniel felt as safe on this trip as he did anywhere in Afghanistan, which was to say, not very. Nevertheless, today's mission would provide good background for his next column. It was important work, and Daniel was good at it.

Daniel didn't realize he had stopped watching the road ahead until he heard Sgt. Ellis shout, "Look out!" He found himself in mid-flight as the Jeep swerved violently, and then overturned beside the road, pinning Ellis and the driver, Sgt. Pierce, and throwing Daniel clear. He was trying to sort himself out to stand when shots rang out from further up the road.

"Shit!" Daniel cried, hunkering down into a rapid belly crawl toward the Jeep where his friends lay injured a couple of yards away. With bullets kicking up the sandy dirt all around him, Daniel reached the relative safety of the Jeep more in rage than in fear. Finding Pierce conscious but injured, he said, "What the hell?"

"IED," Pierce answered, wincing in pain. "Didn't see it until Ellis hollered, had to swerve to miss it."

"Who's shooting at us?" Daniel asked.

"Oh, I don't know. The Taliban maybe?" Even in pain, Pierce was acerbic, causing Daniel to wish he hadn't asked such a stupid question.

"How are you doing? What hurts?" he asked.

Pierce said, "Think my arm is broken, maybe leg too.

Mostly I'd like to get this hunk of metal off me."

Daniel surveyed the way the vehicle had come to rest on Pierce's leg, noticing that a fortuitously-placed rock had kept the vehicle from resting heavily on the leg, though it would still need a couple more inches to clear the leg and foot. Sgt. Ellis was unconscious, his head resting on a larger but flatter rock, and both legs pinned by the frame of the windshield. One looked bad, like the frame had acted as a cleaver. Daniel couldn't tell if the lower part was still attached to Ellis' body.

"Where's your weapon, Pierce?" Daniel asked anxiously. While he and the two Marines were relatively sheltered by the bulk of the vehicle, sporadic automatic weapons fire told him the rebels were still out there, and would probably come looking for anything they could pick up unless they knew someone would shoot back.

"Racked between the seats," Pierce ground out between clenched teeth.

"Hold on. I'm going to try to get you and Ellis out from under this thing, and then I'll grab the weapons."

Daniel quickly surveyed what they had in the Jeep that could be used as a lever, or at least a prop, without finding much that he thought would be useful. They did have a large metal lockbox, which Daniel found a few feet from the rear of the vehicle. Retrieving it, he shoved the box under the center of the vehicle to prevent it shifting further - he hoped. Bullets were flying overhead and hitting the Jeep sporadically. If the Jeep crushed the box, they'd be in worse shape than before. Then, with no other choice, he asked Pierce if he would be able to scoot out from under the vehicle on his own, if Daniel could lift it a few inches.

"I'll try," Pierce answered.

Daniel wormed his way into the gap, shoving his head and shoulders under the frame and pushing until his body was lifting one side of the Jeep, while dragging the box in with him to solidify his gains. He had managed to lift the vehicle only a couple of inches when Pierce said, "I'm loose."

Leaving the box in place, Daniel backed out, hoping to find that he'd also made enough progress that he could drag Ellis out. When he went to look, he paled at the damage he could now see. Though he swiftly used his belt as a tourniquet, it appeared Ellis could be in trouble if help didn't arrive soon. However, there was nothing else he could do but pull him out from under the vehicle before it shifted again and finished the job of severing Ellis's leg. With little more to be gained in lifting the Jeep higher, Daniel stood, then half-crouched to get purchase on the injured man, pulling him to safety as bullets flew by his now-exposed head.

Both of his friends now released but too injured to help, Daniel retrieved their Colt SMGs and fired a few shots back in the general direction of the gunfire just to let the bastards know there would be hell to pay if they dared to come closer. He could only hope that a friendly military patrol would come along before he exhausted his ammunition. With that in mind, he quickly reconnoitered to see if he could determine the exact location where the shots were coming from. About three hundred yards away he could see a structure, and nothing in between. Well within *their* effective range, but to his advantage was that if they were to attack him and his friends they would have to approach over open terrain with no protection. He would have the cover of the Jeep and would be able to pick them off one by one. He fired a few shots toward the building to scare them and let them know that he knew where they were. He would wait until they approached before firing more shots, and just hope there weren't too many of them coming at the same time. With adrenaline pumping through his system, he waited.

Half an hour passed, during which time he'd been forced to fire a short burst to keep two insurgents off them. Then, a rumble that signaled a vehicle approaching from the direction of Kabul caught his attention. It was followed shortly by automatic weapons fire and the gun fire from the building going quiet very quickly.

The sound of American voices, yelling out "Yo, jarheads, you all right?" brought him up from his post.

"Got two wounded here. Who are you guys?"

"Task Force Paladin. Looks like you started to do our job for us out here. Who the hell are you?"

Daniel didn't take offense. He wasn't in uniform after all. He stood to his full height and walked toward the Army squad to explain what had happened.

## Chapter 2 - Newsroom Of The NY Times, Mid-April 2013

Thunderous applause greeted the last of the four announcements of Pulitzer prizes awarded to the Gray Lady's reporting for last year. So-named because of the tradition of having a higher-than average ratio of verbiage to images, the venerable paper almost always pulled in several Pulitzers per year, and this year was no exception with four won. It wasn't the highest number of the coveted prizes the Times had won, missing the record seven of 2002 by nearly half. Still, it was cause for celebration.

Daniel Rossler applauded along with the rest of the crowd, who thronged the newsroom floor and lined the glass safety barrier of the upper floor. As a science feature reporter specializing in archaeology, he probably couldn't expect a Pulitzer, not unless he broke a story that somehow changed human knowledge. Chuckling and shaking his head, Daniel told himself he had probably missed the boat when his previous assignment ended.

His physique still showed the rigorous training that he had received in tandem with the Marine battalion with which he was embedded in the Middle East. At times, Daniel missed the adventure and the adrenaline rush of battle, though he shouldn't have been a part of it. His willingness to put himself in the line of fire, though, had paid off when both Marines whom he'd helped that day near Kabul survived their injuries. For that, he had received a letter of commendation from the battalion commander when he left the assignment.

Rossler was a modest man, though he appreciated praise as much as anyone. He had been embarrassed when his friend Owen had found the reference online and read the letter aloud to the newsroom. 'Mature, brave and composed in the face of difficult and life threatening conditions...' and '...would have been proud to have commanded him as a Marine...' High praise for an outfit that prided itself on being better than all others. But the truth was, aside from that occasional nostalgia for adventure, Daniel was happy that the only loud noises he usually heard around here were cars backfiring on cold days in the city and the crash of a vehicle collision now and then.

Mindy, the archaeology desk executive assistant, watched from a few yards away as Daniel's face reflected the pride he felt in the Times for the Pulitzers. Mindy took every opportunity she could to stare at Daniel's face, because it was a very pleasing one, not only to her, but to the other women in the office. Everything just seemed to work together, though no particular feature, except his sincere blue eyes, stood out. He was fit, that was clear from his trim body, casually dressed most days. His face was almost chiseled, with a jaw line that betrayed no hint of fat, a firm chin and straight nose. His brown hair, often tousled carelessly, looked as if it would be soft if she ran her fingers through it.

Mindy blushed as she recalled her first clumsy attempt to get his attention by inviting him to join her for a drink some night. He had been sweet about it, saving her from the embarrassment of a public rejection. "Sure, Mindy, let's do that sometime." But, although he treated everyone with respect and received their respect in turn, he never, ever dated the women from the office. Mindy had learned that later. His friend Owen Bell said it was because he didn't want rumors to start about the girls, and that it was a strict policy that he, Owen, did not subscribe to, if she'd like to go out with him.

Unaware of Mindy's scrutiny, Daniel turned back to his computer monitor to finish the article he was reading. There may be a story, there, but it would require quite a bit of research to be publishable. A Brazilian archaeologist claimed that his study of South American cave art suggested that people had inhabited the region 18,000 years before it was previously thought. After reading the introductory paragraphs again, Daniel leaned back into his chair and considered the implications.

The dull roar of hundreds of people working in an open room served as white noise while Daniel finished the Brazilian's article and began some research to determine if the story he vaguely sensed was there. More than once a hunch like this paid off in major stories, so he had learned to go with his gut. Daniel needed a story, preferably one that he could back up with the appropriate documentation that would interest the readers, and most of all that would pass the scrutiny of his editor, John Kingston.

Before he settled on this story, though, Daniel turned to another article he'd seen in ArchaeoScience Journal. This one might be too controversial, though. The trick was to make John think it was his own idea and to assure him there would be no controversy in his own article, that it would be balanced and fair. Controversy had become Kingston's worst enemy.

Daniel knew his secret. John was at the top of his career ladder. In his mid-fifties, Kingston could expect no further promotion, as younger men and women of greater ability held those spots. He had lost interest in the job, although he still went through the motions. But, in his spare time, and occasionally on company time, he was writing a novel in the hope that it would afford him an early retirement. Until then he wouldn't rock the boat, nor would he allow his reporters to do so.

Daniel made a few calls, gathered some references and skimmed the articles. Meanwhile, he prepared his approach to his editor, crafting it to match what he knew of Kingston's interest and concern. Unlike his fellow journalists, Daniel's philosophy was that you can catch more flies with honey than by hitting them over the head with a baseball bat. His ability to persuade people to his point of view was legendary and bore out his philosophy to perfection.

~~~

The title of the ASJ article that had caught his interest was, "**Who Built the Great Pyramid and Why**?"

Daniel had skimmed dozens of similar stories, but had paid little attention before. Interested in archaeology from a young age because of his grandfather's profession, he had studied ancient Egypt and her archaeological treasures as a boy. The claims that the pyramids, and specifically the Great Pyramid at Giza, were older than scientists said, or could not have been built in those times, and especially the speculation that 'aliens' built it, had always struck him as silly, on a par with his friend Raj's conspiracy theories. But this article was a peer-reviewed piece from ArchaeoScience Journal. ASJ was a well-respected scientific quarterly; they didn't print trash.

As Daniel skimmed the Great Pyramid article, he went on high alert. Much of the data was over his head at first reading, especially the mathematics and the discussion of the precision of measurements. But if he could dig in and understand it, this might be his story. The facts alone about the Great Pyramid were astounding. Current accepted archaeological evidence about its origin put the building of it at almost forty-six hundred years ago, some five hundred years before the invention of the wheel, which begged the question, how did the builders move those blocks of solid granite? The quarry where the blocks had been cut from the living rock was over five hundred miles away! Telekinesis, maybe? Daniel muttered under his breath, "Anyone who believes in telekinesis, raise my hand." Smirking, he let his hand rise slowly off the keyboard, but in all honesty could think of no better answer. He read on.

Considering he had already dismissed any mode of transportation that may have existed at the time, it was a bit of an anticlimax to learn that each of the blocks weighed between two and an astounding seventy tons. Curious, he stopped reading to research whether even the most powerful modern crane could lift those stones, much less transport them five hundred miles. What he learned was very confusing, involving the mathematics of weight versus distance from the counterweight. Deciding he'd get expert help on that question, he gave up looking for the answer; it was ridiculous anyway, since ancient Egyptians clearly had no access to modern cranes, and if they had, would still have had no wheels to move them. His head began to hurt; math wasn't his strong suit.

Never mind how the blocks had been transported and then lifted into place, the article went on, what about the precision of the cuts and measurements? The structure had been built solid, the blocks fitting together so tightly that not even a sheet of paper could be inserted between them, but no mortar had been used except that which held the original facing stones onto the pyramid. That was another mystery in itself. Apparently, although the composition was known, to this day scientists had not been able to duplicate the mortar.

The passages and chambers were then cut out after the pyramid was constructed. But, they didn't follow the plans of other pyramids of the time. Once again, Daniel found himself entangled in a bewildering set of facts about measurements. All he could clearly understand was that the precision not only in the cuts of the stones, but also in every aspect of the pyramid, from its placement with regard to the Earth's poles to its measurements, required knowledge that wouldn't be discovered or established for thousands of years. In fact, taken as a whole, it was as much as anything a microcosm holding what were, at the time it was built, the secrets of the universe, everything from the circumference of the earth to the speed of light.

Now Daniel was deeply intrigued. Unable to stop reading, even though he could understand only half of what he read, Daniel began to suspect that this was a far more interesting story than the one he had started to research. He started jotting down names of experts he could consult for a better understanding of those areas where his knowledge was weak. Regretting his inattention in his math classes in high school and college, Daniel resigned himself to a crash course. What was the significance of this business about Pi and Phi? He would have to dig into all of it.

# Chapter 3 - Wurzburg, Germany, mid-April, 2013

In the ancient city of Wurzburg, Germany, a chilling conversation was taking place in a half-ruined refuge castle. Near the edge of the bombing that destroyed ninety percent of the city and took countless lives on March 16, 1945, it had been passed over during the restoration of more important historic buildings. The Bronze-age fortress was dank, ill-lit and thought to be uninhabited, but the four people who were meeting thought nothing of all that. Their secrecy was the greatest concern. Meeting in such a place would not have been expected of persons possessed of their wealth and power, much less the demi-gods they considered themselves; therefore, the discomforts were to be endured with no complaint. Besides, it had been used for this purpose for untold centuries.

The three men and one woman had gathered around an ancient stone table, each seat named for one of the four quarters of the Earth, as were the members. Now, of course, with modern communication and travel, their projects tended to move quickly, rather than in decades or centuries as in former times. They typically met via their own private and ultra-secure satellite videoconferencing facility. However, once per quarter, they went through the ancient motions for the sake of history. Their seating arrangement around the rough stone table was as set as was the stone itself; clockwise, from Septentrio at the head of the table in the North position, Oriens in the East position at his left, then Auster in the South position, the role traditionally filled by a woman, and finally Occidens in the West position at Septentrio's right hand. All wore masks, as was traditional, along with heavy robes that not only obscured the identity and body of the wearer, but served as a barrier to the piercing cold of the castle in summer and winter alike.

It had been so since the beginning, each generation

naming a descendant from the next to take the place of any member who chose to exit the earthly plane for one of the four corners of heaven, according to their names. The four current members of the Orion Society were as mad with their power as any of their predecessors, and highly anxious to find the answer that had eluded them concerning their ascension to heaven prior to death.

One of the current projects, that one long-standing and requiring the patience of generations, promised to provide, if not answers, then at least clues. The other was undertaken for financial reasons. Septentrio indicated that Auster should make her report first, as her project was the simplest at hand.

"The rumors we've investigated are at least partially true. You will recall from our last meeting that we had reports of a team of archaeologists finding an ancient ruined city deep in the Brazilian rain forest, and that it was said the city was full of gold artifacts. Naturally, we questioned the literal truth of the rumor, but as you know, Brazil does have large gold reserves, and there are some areas where many Brazilians make their living panning for gold. At this time, we have questioned the leader of the archaeological team. He was very vague about the location, but we have been able to ascertain that there is indeed a ruined Inca city in the Mato Grosso plateau.

"More importantly, it appears that an abandoned underground mine nearby shows signs of massive gold reserves. We are in the process of courting this man's greed in order to take over the exploration and exploit the mine. I estimate that we will be able to quash the rumors and any reports the members of the team might otherwise bring back, as well as begin mining operations, within the next three months." Auster's tone suggested that she considered her project a great success already. Septentrio affirmed it.

"Excellent work, Auster." However, he could not resist issuing a warning, "I don't need to tell you that the members of the team must disappear in ways that cannot lead back to us."

"Of course not, Septentrio. I will take care of the matter."

Septentrio had a small contribution before the meeting was adjourned. "As you all know, we maintain a data-mining operation to flag items posted to the internet that are of interest to our projects. We also investigate anyone who might be taking a more than passing interest in these items.

"It has come to my attention that someone whose IP address leads back to a journalist at the New York Times has, over the past few days, heavily researched facts mentioned in an article that ArchaeoScience journal published regarding the age and technology of the Great Pyramid. It is too early to say if anything will come of it. I will keep a close watch on this through my contact at the New York Times and report as usual.

# Chapter 4 – The Babysitter

By seven a.m. on the following Monday morning, Daniel was at his desk on the newsroom floor. The room was half-empty, but the information machine for a news outlet of the size and diversity of the Times was a twenty-four hour a day operation. The Gray Lady never slept. Daniel was one of the most dedicated employees, routinely receiving stellar performance reviews because of it. Daniel would not put out an article that wasn't well-researched, well-vetted, and well-documented; a matter of personal pride as well as professionalism.

He had three hours to pull out and document more claims from the article to add to his editorial presentation, which already contained an overwhelming array of facts and figures to prove that the stones could not possibly have been moved from the quarry with contemporary methods. Daniel was so engrossed in his study that he almost missed his planned nine-thirty cutoff, to give himself time to go over his presentation to Kingston one more time. He hurriedly brought up his presentation and looked through it, searching for holes in his logic, details that might bore Kingston and shoot down his story, and opportunities to plant the suggestion in Kingston's mind that he had helped shape the story.

Point one was that a respected, peer-reviewed journal had published an article questioning the status quo on scientific research of the only remaining Wonder of the Ancient World.

Point two was that there was a wealth of information on both sides; one supporting the questions the articles raised and one ingeniously refuting them, so Daniel would have plenty of fodder for a series of six to eight articles.

Point three gave John some startling and thought-provoking facts about the Great Pyramid that readers would be eager to know more about.

And, point four was the wealth of mathematical coincidences Daniel had read about, but not yet studied in detail. For that, he would need expert help, but as the article pointed out, 'coincidence' is not an accepted scientific conclusion.

Was it enough? He would know shortly, as the hour had arrived. Daniel knocked softly on the frame of Kingston's open door, reflecting that Kingston must be a little interested. Normally, the door would be closed, giving John time to blank his computer screen if he happened to be writing his novel when someone knocked. Daniel took it as a good omen, and walked in confidently at John's invitation.

"What's got you so fired up about this story that you're emailing me over the weekend?" was Kingston's opening salvo. Daniel would have to make his answer good.

"John, you know my readers are more interested in Egyptology than any other archaeological subject, right?"

"Yes, so? That's kind of a dead subject."

Daniel gave the obligatory chuckle at John's witticism. "Maybe not so dead. I came across an article in ArchaeoScience Journal that raises questions about the construction of the pyramids, specifically the Great Pyramid of Giza. It's pretty compelling stuff."

"Oh, save me, you aren't going to claim that aliens built it, are you?"

"I'm not enough of a crackpot to claim that. I'm not going to claim that anyone in particular built it. But I think there's plenty of evidence that it couldn't have happened as scholars are currently claiming. Can I show you some of the details?"

"Whatever. But don't waste my time."

"Sure, John. Okay, first, you already know that I've studied the engineering, and discovered that it's a pretty well-accepted fact that we couldn't even build that thing now, with modern engineering techniques. The ideas that scholars accept as fact are ludicrous. I want to know why they keep up the smokescreen. Then, the design is unique. It's the only one in Egypt that has passages going up and down both, and the only one that has a Grand Gallery."

"So?" John interrupted. "Maybe Cheops had a more creative interior designer?"

Another obligatory laugh, and then Daniel went on. "How about this, then? What it doesn't contain, and never has from the time of modern study, is a mummy or any other type of human remains. Nor are there any hieroglyphics, paintings or cartouches with the pharaoh's name. So, why was it built in the first place? All those pharaohs built their tombs to have some sort of everlasting life."

Now, John began to look intrigued. "That is a good question, and it's something I didn't know before."

About mid-way in the presentation, the facts and the concept as Daniel slanted it caught Kingston's imagination and he began to pose the questions exactly as Daniel intended. Daniel started making the assumptive close.

"When will you want me to start on the research? I figure I can get enough for the first couple of articles by the end of the month, and have it wrapped up by the end of May for June publication."

"Oh, come on, Daniel, you can work faster than that. This is an important story, and I don't want you to sit on it. Drop everything else and work on this. Let me know if you need my advice on anything. And show me what you've got, say, every couple of days. I want to guide my story from the beginning, so it turns out right."

Daniel's face had an earnest expression as he shook Kingston's hand, thanked him and eagerly agreed to keep him informed. But inside, his grin was ear to ear. He hadn't lost his touch; John was putty in his hands.

What Daniel hadn't counted on was interference. He hadn't been back at his desk for more than twenty minutes and was still organizing his to-do list, when Kingston's instant message popped up on his screen. "See me immediately."

What was this? Had Kingston changed his mind so soon? Daniel grumbled under his breath, but got up immediately to return to John's office.

"You wanted to see me?"

"Yes, but this won't take long. I've arranged for you to meet with an old friend, Professor Allan Barry. He has agreed to take a look at the research you've done so far. If it turns out you've done a thorough job, he'll help by making sure what you write has scientific merit, all the proper documentation, that sort of thing. Maybe even appoint someone to work with you on the research. If you leave now, you can be there by afternoon. Take your time, spend the night and come back tomorrow.

Daniel was bewildered. Take his time, spend the night? Where was he going?

"Thanks, John. But who is Prof. Barry?"

"Can't believe you don't know, and you call yourself an archaeology journalist! Professor Allan Barry is the director of the Joukowsky Institute for Archaeology and the Ancient World, in Providence, Rhode Island. Surely you know of it."

"Oh, yes sir, of course. But I didn't recognize the director's name. My bad."

"Well, get going! You don't have all day."

Daniel moved with alacrity. He had been a little resentful that Kingston had made this move without consulting him, but the more he considered it, the more he agreed. It would be great if his articles had the rigor of a scientific paper. The last thing he wanted was to stir up controversy, and it wouldn't hurt to have a research assistant, either.

Daniel signed out of his workstation and raced home to grab a change of clothes and a bite to eat before hitting the road for the three-hour drive by one p.m. He would make it easily in time to meet with Prof. Barry this afternoon, and would leave his laptop with the research and presentation for the man to examine overnight. With any luck, by mid-morning tomorrow he'd be heading back to the city, with Prof. Barry's blessing and perhaps an assistant to help with the research. Sweet!

~~~

Professor Barry wasn't at all what Daniel expected, in appearance or demeanor. Based on the name, Daniel had visualized a tall Scot, with red hair and a bluff manner. Instead, Barry was not tall, and was dark of skin and grizzled of hair and beard. Daniel would have pegged him for Jewish or Middle Eastern, if he had seen him before hearing his name. On the other hand, his rumpled suit with suede patches on the elbows fit the stereotype perfectly, as did Barry's abrupt speech and short manner. Suppressing his curiosity about the anomaly his name represented, Daniel thanked Barry for seeing him.

"Nonsense, John Kingston is an old and valued friend. Anything I can do for him is my pleasure."

"Thank you, then, in John's behalf. I assume he told you about the project?"

"A little. Seems you've found an intriguing article in ArchaeoScience Journal, correct? And you want to explore it in depth and in layman's terms for your column in the Times?"

"That's correct. Did John mention the topic?"

"Something about the construction of the pyramids. You realize this has been argued to death?"

"Yes, sir, but this article brought out all the facts and coincidences that leads to the conclusion that the established theory is not, cannot be, correct."

"John asked me to keep my mind open, so I'll hear your evidence."

As Daniel once again went through his presentation, complete with multimedia-enhanced slides and his well-formed analysis, Barry began to sit forward in his chair and frown at the screen. Once he muttered, "Yes, yes, nothing new here."

Occasionally, he would hold up his hand and ask a question, halting the slide show. Or, he might ask to stop for a minute and scribble something on a notepad, frowning and muttering under his breath. He seemed to be doing calculations in longhand. In any case, he didn't explain, merely waved at Daniel to continue the slide show.

At the end of the presentation, Barry peppered Daniel with questions and objections, only a few of which he could answer.

"What makes you think you can prove anything that generations of scholars have failed to prove?"

"I'm not out to prove anything, Prof. Barry. The aim of my articles will be to raise the questions for laypeople."

"Young man, all this will accomplish is to create

controversy. We already have the most logical answers. You'll have the conspiracy theorists cropping up with that hogwash about aliens again. When you ask unanswerable questions, it leaves gaps. Science hates gaps."

"Yes, sir, I understand. But, what if it leads to more study, and more plausible answers are found? Surely you can admit that the first question alone, that of transportation and placing of the stones, doesn't have a believable answer. By my calculations, one of those massive blocks would have to have been placed every five minutes for the pyramid to be built in the twenty years that scholars claim. We can't even do that now."

"Er, yes, that does seem to be a valid question."

"May I show you the original article?"

"I suppose. ArchaeoScience Journal, you say? Hmm, there must be something to it, then."

"Yes, sir. Otherwise I wouldn't have paid any attention."

Prof. Barry turned his scrutiny on Daniel. "No?"

"No, sir. My grandfather is Dr. Nicholas Rossler. Perhaps you've heard of him? He taught me where to find information that can be trusted."

Barry's bushy eyebrows had risen in surprise. "Nick Rossler is your grandfather?"

"Yes, sir."

"Well, why didn't you say so? Fine man, fine scholar. Why are you wasting your time with journalism, young man?"

Daniel seized the opportunity. "I don't have the focus that Grandpa does, sir. I'm interested in archaeology in a general sense. That's why John thought I'd need the help of someone who could guide my research, I guess. He's very interested in this story, and because he'll receive much of the credit when it's published, he wants it to be right."

Daniel could not have hit on a more persuasive argument. Barry's demeanor changed, the frown dissolving, the corners of his mouth turning upward. He appeared to be thinking carefully, nodding as his eyes darted around the room.

"Yes, I suppose it will do no harm to investigate these matters more closely. And I can see that it would be a good idea for someone with professional credentials to oversee your research. I'll assign someone to the project; however, anything you publish must receive my prior approval."

Now it was Daniel's turn to lift his eyebrows. Oversee my research? Receive Barry's approval? He would have to quash that notion, but his better judgment told him that now was not the time. He would establish the working relationship when he met the person Prof. Barry had in mind. As far as receiving Barry's approval, he'd let John deal with his friend.

"Thank you very much, sir. I'm sure John will be grateful. When can I expect to hear from your assistant?"

"You're welcome. I'll speak with her tomorrow morning first thing. Can you stay to meet her?"

"Oh, yes, John told me to take my time, spend the night if necessary."

"Splendid. By the way, I wouldn't call Dr. Clarke my assistant if I were you. She is a brilliant researcher. In fact, she may not think much of this assignment, but I'll deal with that. Where are you staying?"

"I'm at the Renaissance Providence downtown."

"Expect Dr. Clarke's call, say around ten a.m.?"

"Yes, sir, that will be fine."

After Daniel left, Barry left a message for Dr. Clarke to see him as soon as possible, then dialed again, this time long-distance to Langley, VA. After several rings, a voice mail greeting barked nothing more than "Leave a message."

He was ready. "It's Barry. We have another one. Journalist researching the Great Pyramid, doubt if anything will come of it but will monitor. Will send details on journalist and the babysitter I assign him later."

~~~

"Really, Professor, you can't be serious!"

"I'm quite serious, my dear."

"Why is this so important to you, sir, if I may ask?"

"I have my reasons. One of which is maintaining good relations with the editor of the archaeology section at the New York Times. They can influence grants, public opinion of our institution and how much attention our research projects receive. It's good business."

"But, sir, my own research."

"This should not affect your own research. I doubt it will take much time, and it's just temporary. And now, if that's all, I'll leave it to you to contact him this morning. He's staying at the Renaissance downtown, and he expects your call around 10 a.m."

Sarah Clarke suppressed her annoyance with difficulty. This demand was infuriating! But, Barry's vote was important at her tenure hearing next year and she already knew that a university was a political workplace. She would have to make the best of it. Sarah stood to go, not trusting herself to speak again after her dismissal. She marched briskly to the door, and took extra care to close it gently.

Honestly, couldn't Prof. Barry have at least consulted her schedule before making that appointment for her? She would have to take control of how this, this *journalist* impacted her time. She had better things to do than babysit a reporter.

~~~

Daniel found himself at loose ends after leaving the meeting with Prof. Barry at around five p.m. the previous afternoon. After an early dinner, Daniel thought to check his email. While he had the laptop open, he Googled Dr. Sarah Clarke, thinking perhaps he could be better prepared for the meeting. He wasn't prepared for the beauty whose picture came up. Was there ever a more perfect face, or a more brilliant smile? Daniel gazed at the picture on his screen for several minutes, noting the perfect skin, the lovely long dark hair and warm brown eyes. His head buzzed with an unfamiliar energy, which eventually coalesced into a thought his quirky brain instantly translated into a Looney Tunes character with its heart bursting out of its chest and shouting va-va-va-VOOM!

After a few moments spent in reverie about how closely he would be working with this woman and whether his policy against dating colleagues was applicable, Daniel set aside his baser nature and began to read with interest that Dr. Clarke had received her PhD with honors a little more than a year before, her dissertation shedding new light on Egyptian mythology.

Daniel jotted down a few notes to set the information in his memory, so he could appear well-prepared. Then he allowed himself to gaze at the picture again. If she had a personality to go with those looks, he might get a bonus out of this. He appreciated women as much as the next man, and despite his loftier standards, was not unaffected by looks. He just didn't like to be a caveman about it.

~~~

By the time the phone rang in the hotel room at precisely ten a.m. the next morning, Daniel had determined to take advantage of John's instructions to 'take his time'. While he was here, he would attempt to meet with Dr. Clarke and persuade her to see his side of things. Her voice on the phone was as warm as her brown eyes, further cementing the attraction for Daniel even before he had met her. He maintained his professionalism, though, as he asked to meet with her before he left town. As if it were an afterthought, he asked if she would like to have lunch with him, assuming it didn't interfere with her lecture schedule.

Sarah was at first reluctant, but, taking into account that he had been courteous enough to give her a way out, accepted after all. This Daniel Rossler had a nice voice, and he hadn't been pushy. Maybe he wouldn't turn out to be the run-of-mill jerk reporter that she had imagined. Nevertheless, she would have to be firm about the working relationship. Agreeing to meet him at Fat Belly's Providence, which she assured him had good food at modest prices and an atmosphere that would allow them time for their meeting, Sarah ended the call with optimism. She intended to make short work of this assignment.

At the appointed time, a carefully-groomed Daniel was already waiting and watching for the attractive woman he expected from his online research last night. She sailed in on a breath of spring air precisely one minute late. Daniel's breath caught in his throat. In person, she was even more lovely, her body slender but shapely, and her eyes sparkling. The reality was so much better than the picture that Daniel kept his composure with difficulty. Only his strict self-discipline and his upbringing kept him from looking her up and down and emitting an appreciative wolf whistle. Dr. Clarke's smile did indeed light up the room. He stood to greet her, impressed with her firm handshake, and then seated her in a booth, thinking he may have to do a column sometime on the concept of love at first sight.

"I hope a booth is okay, I thought it might give a little more privacy. The subject of my story is confidential."

"That's fine. Just what is the subject of your story? Prof. Barry was a little vague."

"Why don't we leave that until after we order? It's a bit complex, and I want to do my best to help you understand what I'm after."

"Very well, but you must understand Mr. Rossler, that my time is valuable. In fact, I must be on campus for my next class in only an hour."

Sarah was discreetly giving Daniel an appraising look, and thinking that for an annoying assignment, at least the man was easy on the eyes. But, going on personal experience, it would be better to keep this on a professional level. Her eyes flicked to the menu just as Daniel's came up to look at her.

"What would you recommend?"

"Excuse me?"

Daniel lifted his menu slightly.

"Oh, you mean recommend to eat? Everything is good here. I'm partial to the pulled pork, but it's messy."

"Messy it is, then. And what will you have?"

Sarah couldn't help the small smile that played around her lips. It was impossible to dislike this guy, despite her annoyance at being saddled with him. "Oh, I'm having the pork."

"Two orders of messy, coming right up." Daniel was confident he could charm her into at least liking him, if not the assignment. At the moment, that seemed to be more important to him than the assignment anyway. Down boy, he thought. Keep it cool. She didn't seem to be the type of girl who could be rushed off her feet, and that wasn't his style anyway.

Their orders for food and drink settled and the server dismissed for the moment, Sarah tried again.

"Mr. Rossler, I'm sure you know that with my class and research schedule, I have no time to waste. Please tell me what this is all about."

"Okay, Dr. Clarke. At its essence are facts brought to my attention by an article in ArchaeoScience Journal regarding the mystery of the construction of the Great Pyramid at Giza."

"Oh, no, not that again!" Why would Prof. Barry have even given this the time of day?"

"Please, Dr. Clarke. I'm beginning to understand that this is a touchy subject. The last thing I want to do is write a speculative story that stirs up controversy. Have you read the article I mentioned?"

"No, it isn't really my area of interest, although of course I respect the journal. What does it say that got you interested?"

"Well, at first I was interested because they brought out some facts about how the construction could not have happened, and I verified them. That got me curious about how it must have been done, but the article was neutral on that subject. It merely raised the questions. The more I read, though, the more questions I had. My job is to bring archaeology to the layman in such a way as to make him think, ask himself questions, and hopefully find some answers if I can provide them."

"And what is your expertise, to think you can find those answers?"

"To be honest, my degree is in journalism. But, I've been interested in archaeology since I was a boy. My grandfather is a noted archaeologist, Nicholas Rossler."

If Daniel hoped Dr. Clarke would recognize the name as Prof. Barry had, he was disappointed. But, it wasn't surprising. His grandfather had been retired for fifteen years, since she was barely a teen. The name didn't mean a thing to her, obviously.

"Why did Prof. Barry involve me? What is it that you want from me?"

"He didn't tell you?"

"No, he was quite vague."

"My editor, John Kingston called him. Evidently they're old friends. Prof. Barry seemed to want to make sure that the article was well-vetted, so as to reflect well on John."

"How curious. Do newspaper articles typically require scientific oversight?"

There was that word again, oversight. Time to put the kibosh on it. "No, not at all. I rather had in mind that you would help in the research, make sure I steered clear of crackpots for my expert opinions, that sort of thing."

"I see."

When their lunch was done and Sarah indicated her need to hurry to her next lecture, they made plans to meet again the next day to iron out how they would proceed. She still betrayed both annoyance and reluctance, but at least she was cooperating. Daniel stood as she got up to leave, and asked her to please leave the check to him when she started to reach into her purse.

"Thank you. I'll see you tomorrow." Her voice, though the words were curt, betrayed some warmth already. Maybe she was just a nice person, but Daniel wanted to think he had made some inroads on forming a friendly relationship. He watched her as she made her way to the door, for once allowing himself the luxury of gazing on a most pleasing and shapely backside and pair of legs, then was embarrassed to be caught as she turned at the door and waved. Was that a mischievous smile curling her lips? When Sarah was all the way out the door, Daniel gave a happy grin, a fist pump, and a heartfelt "Yes!" to the amusement of several people around him.

~~~

Energized both by the acceptance of his story idea and the opportunity to work with the lovely Sarah Clarke, Daniel threw himself into the research, carefully documenting his sources as he built a database of facts, speculation and potential answers. For the first couple of weeks, he and Sarah had a Thursday morning Skype conference to give her an overview of what he'd researched and have her systematically knock down his conclusions. It was frustrating professionally, but on a personal level he was stunned to realize he looked forward to just seeing her. When her smiling countenance appeared on his monitor, he dared hope that she even looked forward to seeing him, though it didn't stop her from ruthlessly destroying his logic.

Daniel's growing attraction to Sarah led him to make a trip to Providence over the last weekend of May. He had all his facts, and he had questions. Unfortunately, he was no closer to finding the answers that were a prerequisite for publication with the blessing of the Joukowsky Institute. Without that, Kingston would be reluctant to publish as well.

Nevertheless, Daniel's research had convinced him that there was some sort of message being conveyed with all of these facts, almost like a flashing neon light saying 'look here'. Maybe he was looking at the sign instead of what it pointed to, he decided, not realizing he had hit the nail on the head.

He considered the weekend a success when he persuaded Sarah to see him on Saturday evening for a date, rather than a research meeting. As was his habit, he was the perfect gentleman, sensing that a woman like Sarah couldn't be rushed. Conveniently, an open-air concert in a local park was on tap, so after a pleasant dinner, they listened companionably to light classical music, before Daniel escorted her home.

On Monday they met at her office to look at everything he had produced so far and also report to Prof Barry. That's when she burst his bubble.

"Daniel, you have to admit that all you have here is a rehash of the original article. Sure, you've documented the claims, but there are no answers here. I'm sorry, but I simply have no more time for it."

Daniel's voice was tight as he risked the next question. "What about me? Do you have any more time for me?"

Sarah's eyes flew to his. "What do you mean, Daniel?"

"I mean, I value our friendship. Can we stay in touch? Is that too much to ask?"

In truth, Sarah's thoughts had too often turned to Daniel already. She had to admit he was different, not only from her stereotype of a journalist, but also from any man who had caught her interest. He admired her intellect, unlike her former fiancé. Fit, good-looking, articulate and thoughtful, he was someone whose friendship she valued, too.

"Of course not, Daniel. I'd like to stay in touch."

Daniel had been holding his breath for her answer. Now it whooshed out of him forcibly, causing Sarah to raise her eyebrows.

"I live in my own little world," he explained. "They know me here."

Laughing, Sarah pushed at him hard enough that he had to catch his balance. "Only call me if you can refrain from those terrible jokes."

"I'll do my best, ma'am," he returned with a mocking smile. She had no doubt she had just given him incentive to coin even more of them.

But, the more Daniel thought about the waste of time and the questions he would still like to answer, the more he determined that this would become his 'pet project'. Maybe that Pulitzer wasn't such a long shot after all. As he prepared to discuss it with Kingston when he reported that the story couldn't be written yet, Daniel made sure to make some well-targeted remarks about the valuable contact he had made in Sarah, as well as her indication that she would look favorably upon introducing him to others at the Institute for interviews and articles about their latest research, including the paper that would be her ticket to tenure next year if her hopes panned out. The latter point was a bit of an exaggeration, but he had no doubt that he could make good on the claim. The bonus, of course, was that he would be able to have a good excuse to continue to see her. This much Daniel knew: Sarah was open to that. There was no other way to interpret what she had said.

# Chapter 5 - Mathematics Is A Language

Throughout the next month, Daniel subtly courted Sarah with calls and a couple of visits and hikes around Providence. His willingness to poke fun at himself and his circumspect treatment of her charmed Sarah. After a painful breakup with the former fiancé who didn't appreciate her accomplishment in attaining her PhD, Daniel was a breath of fresh air. Sarah warmed to him and they were soon enjoying a lighthearted relationship that nevertheless hadn't progressed to anything physical, though it tested Daniel's resolve. He'd give anything to know if she would respond to a kiss, or his arm around her.

Early in July, Daniel saw that his calendar had a notation for a lecture by Dr. Ben Zacharias titled '***The Language of the Pyramid***.' Daniel had read papers by Dr. Zacharias, world-renowned for his theories on the mathematics of the Great Pyramid. This was not to be missed, and he thought Sarah might enjoy it as well. He gave her a call, inviting her to attend. He had told her that he still had an interest in the Great Pyramid, and she indulged his occasional mini-lectures on his discoveries.

When she said yes, he casually offered her a choice; he would get her a hotel room, or she could spend the weekend with him in New York. In his guest room, of course. Their relationship had not yet progressed so far as even a kiss, but Daniel's natural reticence was beginning to wear thin around the edges. He had hope that she would view this as a date, not research. To his delight, she opted for the guest room.

Sarah drove to New York, arriving at mid-morning on the day of the lecture. She looked forward to the lecture, but even more she looked forward to seeing Daniel in his natural habitat. It promised to be fun, as well as enlightening. She was rather overwhelmed when Daniel ushered her onto the news floor. She wouldn't have believed such excellent writing could come out of the vast, noisy, anthill the newsroom resembled. Daniel explained that the noise receded into white noise when he was working, and it was more distracting when it stopped, assuming that ever happened, than when it was in full voice.

Daniel wondered if it was his imagination that their passing created a stir. He stopped by Owen's desk to introduce Sarah, and received confirmation in the sparkle in Owen's eyes as he greeted Sarah.

"Pleasure to meet you! When you get tired of this mope, I'm available." Sarah laughed lightly, while Daniel did his best to glare at his friend. As usual, he was completely unaware of the glances from his female colleagues, some of which would have surprised him. More than one woman that morning narrowed her eyes and took a long, assessing look at the beauty on his arm. There would be conversation about the couple later, among hopefuls for his affection, but his nickname among them was 'Clueless'.

Daniel looked around for Raj, and spotted him hanging back, apparently trying not to call attention to himself. Typical behavior for Raj, but not necessary under this circumstance. He motioned Raj forward and introduced him to Sarah, who flashed her brilliant smile and dazzled poor Raj as she had everyone else who saw it. She caused quite a stir in the deli, too, where Daniel was a regular but never came in with a woman unless it was in a group.

Daniel and Sarah settled into their seats in the lecture theater a few minutes before the distinguished scholar made his appearance. Daniel switched his cell phone to record and placed it on the edge of the stage in front of his first-row seat. When Sarah took a small paper notepad from her purse, preparing to do it the old-fashioned way, he leaned over and whispered to her.

"Nostalgia isn't what it used to be."

"What? Oh, my notepad? Well, it's good for other things, too." She whacked his arm with it to make her point, then stifled a giggle.

Assuming an air of injury, Daniel suppressed the urge to take her in his arms and steal a kiss, but the moment had passed. Dr. Zacharias was being introduced.

Dr. Zacharias began with a statement, "Before the turn of the last century, Josiah Willard Gibbs said, 'Mathematics is a language.' Indeed, it has been called the universal language. As we explore the mathematics of the Great Pyramid today, consider whether the message is just that; a message from the builders of the Great Pyramid."

Daniel's interest was piqued. He had been approaching his questions from the stance that if he could solve the riddles involved in the construction, he would have the answers that would give his theory credence among Egyptologists and other archaeological scholars. What if that had been the wrong approach all along? Daniel listened as Dr. Zacharias cited fact after fact that begged for explanation.

Beginning with the fact that the Great Pyramid is precisely located in the center of the land mass of the earth, could it be a coincidence that the curvature built into the sides of the pyramid exactly match the radius of the earth? Daniel could see that Sarah was taking rapid notes, but these were facts he already had stored in his database. He listened closely as the noted speaker went on with another quote about mathematics being a language.

"Mathematics is the language with which God wrote the universe. Galileo Galilei said that. Can we doubt it when we see that two facts intersect in the language of the Great Pyramid? The first is that the estimated weight of the pyramid, multiplied by ten to the eighth power gives us the earth's mass. Can it then be a coincidence that twice the perimeter of the granite coffer, multiplied by the *same* ten to the eighth power, gives us a number exactly equal to the sun's mean radius? Is this not a message that the builders of the Great Pyramid knew of the relationship of numbers that we did not know until centuries later?"

Daniel could hardly contain his elation. Here was an expert that was raising the same questions and anomalies that he had catalogued. Not only that, but Dr. Zacharias was posing a theory that would account for it; it was a message! But, what message? And who had left it? Hoping the answers would be forthcoming, Daniel quickly made a note on his iPad; 'It's in the math'. He was so engaged in the revelations as they came, that he almost forgot even Sarah, equally engaged, at his side.

As Zacharias went on, methodically cataloging the mathematical facts, it boggled the mind. When Dr. Zacharias suggested he pause the lecture for a break, Daniel's mental sigh of relief was almost audible. It was humbling to think that he had all these facts, or most of them, and had not thought to put them together in this way.

"What do you think so far?" Daniel asked Sarah, as they settled into their seats again after having gone in separate directions to restroom facilities.

"I think there are an awful lot of wild coincidences," she said.

"Are you serious? You think this is all coincidence?"

"No, quite the opposite. I think it's too much to be coincidence. I hope he has some answers soon, I'm dying of curiosity here. I mean, what are the chances if a tornado were to hit a scrap yard, that it would assemble a complete Boeing 747, in perfect flying condition, complete with pilot and passengers?"

Daniel's eyes lit up at the hint that Sarah was catching his obsession, not to mention that she seemed to finally get his sense of humor. He laughed too loudly, drawing stares from the people around them. Sarah rolled her eyes at him and then winked. Daniel's eyes widened. Was she flirting with him?

Sarah's sharp mind would be an asset in his quest, no doubt about it. Something told him, though, that if Dr. Zacharias had answers, he would have led with them, and saved these facts to back it up. He hoped he was wrong. Excusing himself for a moment, he went in search of the professor who arranged the lecture and gave him a note for Dr. Zacharias, asking for an interview after the lecture.

Intermission over, Dr. Zacharias took the stage again.

"'For the things of this world cannot be made known without a knowledge of mathematics.' I think by now, we can all agree with Roger Bacon, can we not? Without a knowledge of mathematics, we would not be aware that there is perhaps a message in the Great Pyramid, one we have yet to decipher. We would not know of these parallels, fact piled upon fact that attempt to grab our attention and say 'look, we have something to say to you, pay attention'."

By the time the lecture was finished, Daniel had collected a headache, numerous incoherent notes, several new facts, the notion that Sarah was more engaged in the story than ever and a conviction that the math held the answer. Dr. Zacharias, as Daniel expected, had not put forth a theory that could account for all this. If he could get away with that, why couldn't Daniel get away with publishing a story that raised questions it couldn't answer?

"What did you think?" she asked. Daniel replied truthfully that he didn't see how Dr. Zacharias could get away with listing the facts and pointing out the coincidences without reaching a conclusion, while he couldn't.

"Oh, but he did reach a conclusion."

"What? I didn't hear one!"

"Then you weren't listening. His conclusion was that the math in the pyramid is a message. It's up to someone else to decipher it."

Daniel grumbled that the difference was minute, but he couldn't articulate why his story was similar in intent to Dr. Zacharias' message, without Sarah shooting down all the similarities he could name. She was doing it in such a cute way that he couldn't be mad, and it became a game, with him bringing up ever more ridiculous similarities, and Sarah grinning more broadly each time she countered him.

Dr. Zacharias was a few minutes late for their meeting, and Daniel was beginning to wonder if he had been stood up when the man rushed into the staff lounge apologizing.

"Many students wanted more answers," he said. "I may give another lecture soon."

"That would be very interesting, Dr. Zacharias," Daniel said. "I'd like a few more answers myself. First, I need to make a confession."

Dr. Zacharias' eyebrows went up in question, and Daniel hastened to explain.

"I will use some of what we talk about today, as well as the notes I took during your lecture, in a column soon. But I had an ulterior motive in asking to speak with you. May I explain?"

"I suppose you'd better, since you got me here under false pretenses." The sting of the words was taken away by Dr.

Zacharias' broad smile. He was a good sport.

"May I introduce Dr. Sarah Clarke, of the Joukowsky Institute?"

"Dr. Clarke, I'm pleased to meet you. I read your dissertation. Brilliant work."

Sarah couldn't help but smile at the man, whose stunned expression betrayed his sudden attraction to her. Daniel smirked. At least he wasn't the only one to fall head over heels in love every time she turned on that 150-megawatt smile. He observed as the good doctor visibly pulled himself together, no doubt reminding himself that he had a wife, not to mention children and grandchildren.

"If I may..."

Dr. Zacharias dragged his attention from Sarah to listen politely to Daniel, who began to explain his predicament. Reluctant to admit that the story had already been killed, he mentioned the difficulty of pulling the facts together in such a way as to not ruffle the scientific community. As he stated it, his goal was to put forth a theory that contradicted the current accepted facts, while providing answers to the questions that the loss of the current theory would pose. As Daniel spoke, the other man grew more animated and could hardly contain his need to speak.

"Mr. Rossler, you must abandon all that, it is a smokescreen."

"Smokescreen? Are you saying that the anomalies are deliberate attempts to keep scientists from learning the truth?"

"I would hesitate to put it in so many words. One never knows who might be listening. But I can tell you this, the answer is in the mathematics."

"That's why we were so fascinated by your lecture, sir. What else can you tell us? For example, what will be the subject of your second lecture?"

"I have been considering that. Of course, I can't afford to be labeled a crackpot, but there are some very interesting discoveries coming out of Giza that few seem to be talking about. My only conclusion must be that the information is being deliberately suppressed."

Daniel sat back, the answer to one of his questions clear now. All along, he wondered why the scientific community couldn't see the problems that to him were as plain as the pens in their pocket protectors. So they did know! And what could be the secret that an entire community of egotistical researchers would keep secret? He was about to find out.

"In 2008, a Brit named Andrew Collins discovered, or rather re-discovered, a system of caves under the pyramid complex at Giza," Zacharias said. "There's some back-story to it, and I'll give you the sources so you can get the full impact. But the bottom line is, Collins discovered some catacombs that led into a vast underground system, and the Secretary General for Egypt's Supreme Council of Antiquities flatly denied that it was true. However, he then took a team to investigate, and over a year later was forced to admit that it was true."

"What does all this mean? What did you mean when you said the answers are in the math?" Daniel asked.

"It's the only thing that makes sense. If some ancient civilization was trying to leave a message for future generations, mathematics would be the only reliable language. Suppose Atlantis did exist, and suppose they knew that a disaster would destroy their civilization. Would they want to leave a record? Would they leave it someplace where the disaster couldn't touch it? I'm not saying this is the case. I'm asking, what if? The discovery of this cave system has some interesting possibilities, but rather than hamper your research with my theories, why don't I give you the sources and let you research it for yourselves. If you dare."

Zacharias hadn't meant it as a challenge, only an observation that Sarah's career may not be able to afford to go there, either. But Daniel took it as a gauntlet thrown down in front of him. His chin went up and his eyes took on a stubborn look.

"Oh, I dare, all right. Nothing could stop me. Dr. Zacharias, thank you for the tip."

"You're very welcome. I would be most interested in what you discover."

"May we call on you for help if we get stuck?"

"Certainly, as long as you leave my name out of it. And speaking of my name, about this 'interview'…"

"It won't mention any of this, you have my word on it. You've been very helpful, sir. Thank you."

"Don't mention it. And I mean that literally," Zacharias joked.

After he walked away, Sarah turned to Daniel. "I liked him."

"I did, too, but man, I hope this doesn't lead us to Atlantis. That would be almost as bad as aliens."

"What do you have against aliens and unknown civilizations?" she retorted. "It could explain a lot."

Daniel stared at her, aghast, until he perceived she was joking. Then he answered in kind, "Oh, I don't know. I guess I'm afraid they'll take my job."

"There is that."

It was too early for dinner, and too late for Daniel to return to work, so they decided to head for his apartment and talk some more before having dinner. Daniel had in mind a romantic Italian restaurant, where he intended to hold her hand, ply her with good red wine, and maybe steal a kiss.

Sarah had undergone a radical shift in attitude about the project as she listened to Zacharias' lecture. Mathematics, although not her field of study, was something she could understand. After all, it figured largely in cracking the hieroglyphics code she used in her dissertation to bring new light onto Egyptian mythology. Without it, her work would have been speculation, but with it and with the help of a savant cryptography student who was scary-smart, she had made translation strides that surpassed the work of the past century. It was indeed brilliant work, if she said so herself. However, it flattered her that Dr. Zacharias knew of it. Now, she justified her intrigue with the project by telling herself that it was a way to stay close to Daniel.

# Chapter 6 – The Italian Job

Speaking of Daniel, whose physical attributes occupied more of her thoughts than comfort dictated, she wondered if he was now showering in cold water. He had been in there for a very long time. He was a mystery to her; although he was clearly attracted, he was as circumspect as a Victorian suitor. She would just have to find a way to respond to his tentative advances that would encourage him further. After all, those Victorians could be pretty naughty behind closed doors. The thought alone animated her, and Daniel emerged at that moment to find Sarah blushing.

*What's that all about?* He wondered.

By mutual consent, they tabled the discussion about the pyramid mystery while they ate dinner. Sarah was enchanted with Daniel's choice of restaurant, a small room with just four tables and no menu. Daniel had discovered it shortly after he arrived in New York, and by now was an old friend of the owner. He had called ahead, telling Luigi that he was bringing a date, and to do him proud. Now Luigi was attempting to do just that, seating them at the most secluded table, but not before parading them through the small dining area so that his other customers could cast admiring glances on the couple.

A lovely couple they made, too. The woman was exquisite, and Luigi had to admit that his wife's small crush on Daniel had to do with his looks as much as anything else.

Daniel was aware of the stares of the men, though he overlooked those of the women. All his attention was on Sarah, who looked more radiant than ever. She took his breath away. How he would get through a romantic dinner without betraying how much he wanted her was a problem. Fortunately, Luigi helped by bringing out course after course of delicious Italian delicacies that even Daniel hadn't tasted before.

They started with carciofini e funghetti, which turned out to be an appetizer of artichokes and mushrooms. Luigi insisted on pairing each course with a glass of wine, making Sarah laugh and say it was lucky they'd be walking home to Daniel's apartment. Daniel lost count of the courses after the first three, and everything was perfect. By the time the dessert came, both were a little tipsy, and it seemed the perfect time for Daniel to take her hand.

Sarah's eyes softened as she looked at their entwined hands and said, "Daniel, I've enjoyed today so much. Thank you for inviting me."

Encouraged, Daniel stroked the back of Sarah's hand with his thumb and said, "It's been my absolute pleasure. I hope we can do more of this."

If Sarah realized that there was a double meaning when he said 'this', she didn't remark on it, only smiled her remarkable smile and said, "I hope so, too."

When at last Luigi accepted that they had reached their limit, he boxed up the tiramisu and sent them on their way, first waving off Daniel's proffered credit card.

"Daniel, my friend, you have earned this meal by bringing your bellissima donna – such a beautiful woman – to my little ristorante. Thank you for letting me gaze upon her lovely face."

Both proud and protective, the full force of Daniel's attraction to Sarah hit him in that moment, and he finally admitted what he had been hiding from himself. It wasn't just a physical attraction, although heaven knew that was there. He could love this woman, if she gave him half a chance. So, that's why they call it 'falling in love'! Daniel had the peculiar sensation that he had fallen over a cliff, but was floating in mid-air. With wonder that he hadn't realized it before, he tucked her hand into his elbow and strolled down the street, keeping his feet firmly on the pavement despite his tendency to float.

The brisk winter air cleared their heads somewhat, but for separate reasons, neither wanted to take up the pyramid discussion again when they got home. Daniel was looking for an opportunity when kissing Sarah would be a natural thing to do. Sarah was thinking about how fond she had grown of Daniel, and what that might mean. She agreed when he suggested they watch a movie before turning in, and they settled together on the sofa, his arm around her, to watch a romantic comedy.

When the movie got to a point where the hero didn't dare kiss the girl, Daniel said, "Oh, just kiss her already!"

Sarah turned to him and spoke softly, with an enticing smile, "Why don't you take your own advice?"

Daniel didn't need a second hint. He tilted her chin with a gentle finger, looked into her eyes long enough to see the invitation there, and dipped his head to taste her lips for the first time. It wouldn't have surprised him if he had heard an angel choir at that moment. In fact, his ears *were* ringing with some kind of music.

Sarah's lips were warm, soft and tasted faintly of the wine they had shared earlier. Kissing her was more intoxicating than the wine and he lost himself for a few minutes as he let the kiss linger. When at last it ended, Sarah put her head on his shoulder and they looked again at the TV, although both of them had lost track of the movie. When the movie was over, Daniel asked, "Would you like to go to bed?"

Sarah's expression betrayed surprise at the directness of the question. What should she answer? Actually, she thought she might like that very much; it had been too long since she had been with her ex-fiancé. But would Daniel think she was too forward if she just said 'yes'? "Um,"

Daniel realized his mistake when he saw her face. "Oh, hell, Sarah, that came out wrong. I meant, are you ready to turn in? In the guest room?"

Slightly disappointed, but relieved at not having to decide, she laughed. "Oh. Yes, I'm tired."

Daniel walked her to her door, ventured another kiss to say goodnight, and left her there. As he closed his own bedroom door, he mentally kicked himself. The question was already out there, why had he supplied the answer? What if she wanted...? No, a woman like Sarah needed to be courted. He would have to be satisfied that she had kissed him in return, with every evidence of pleasure. He could wait.

For her part, Sarah was kicking herself for her hesitation. She didn't get Daniel's reserve. He gave every evidence of liking her a lot, but he was either the world's most patient man or he had been raised with the manners of another age. Like Victorian. Maybe her signals weren't strong enough?

The next morning, Sarah seemed a little shy with him at first, but Daniel maintained his cheer as he put the coffee on to brew and tried unsuccessfully to get a breakfast of sausage, scrambled eggs and toast all on the table at the same time. Fortunately, Sarah came to his rescue, buttering toast and pouring orange juice, in a sweetly domestic pas de deux that had them both thinking they could get used to this. But, neither said it.

## Chapter 7 - Message In A Bottle

Back at work, Daniel struggled with a sense of unreality. Since the last time he sat at this desk, his world had shifted profoundly. He was having trouble focusing on his next column, and decided to write up his interview with Dr. Zacharias. Dancing around the Atlantis references was proving more difficult than he thought it would be. The lecture was interesting, but the possibilities of the new information were so enticing that it kept creeping into his narrative. He had been at it for four long hours, with only about two thousand words to show for it, when Owen came by his desk and asked if he was going to lunch.

"Wow, is it noon already?"

"Yeah, man. What's got you so out of it? Didn't you even see Alison from the fashion desk parade down the aisle here in a polka-dot dress that didn't even cover her ass?"

"Hmm?" Daniel's attention had turned back to his story and he hadn't heard the question.

"Alison. Ass. And legs down to there."

"Owen, grow up. Who cares?"

"I care. It made my day! I think she wants me."

"Good for you. Did you want to get some lunch or not?"

"Sounds good to me."

Daniel liked Owen, a lot really. He was a good friend, but sometimes his blatant sexual references were just over the top. Daniel hoped they could get through lunch without being arrested. To ward off more of the same, he mentioned Dr. Zacharias' lecture over a foot-long meatball sub.

"Heard a great lecture on Friday. Dr. Ben Zacharias, do you know of him?"

"Oh, yeah, the 'math is language' guy. He's pretty hot stuff in my field."

"How so?"

"Well, you know he's got this theory that the ancient world used mathematics to communicate with us today. Actually, more than a theory, it's pretty much accepted."

"I didn't know that."

"It is among astronomers, anyway. The stars are another thing that's been pretty constant over the millennia, other than where they are in our sky, of course. But somehow, ancient astronomers were able to predict the movement, and it had to be math that helped them do that. They were more accurate than you'd believe, in spite of their primitive tools."

"Do you think the ancients actually left messages for us? Or were they just leaving records?"

"I'm not sure there's agreement on that among scientists. But look, we did the same thing."

"What do you mean?

"We sent a message, like a message in a bottle. Have you ever heard of one of those washing up on shore? It happens fairly often."

Now Daniel was a little lost. Who was 'we'? And what message in a bottle? Owen was in full lecture mode, though, so maybe it would become clear in a minute.

"Some of them travel hundreds of miles, I saw a story about it on TV just last week. People have been doing it for ages, and it's crazy. The one on TV turned up over a hundred and eighty years after it was thrown in the ocean. Think of the journey it took! It makes me want to get inside a bottle and see where I end up."

"Suffocated or at the funny farm, no doubt."

"That's right, scoff. But you're the one who brought it up."

"Me? I still don't know what you're talking about, message in a bottle. What did you mean 'we did the same thing'?"

"Voyager, man. Remember? The space ships we sent out to explore the Universe back in 1977? They put some gold records in the capsules, in case there's intelligent life out there. Sound recordings and stuff. And pictures of what we look like, you know, I think they put Da Vinci's Vitruvian Man on it, and some math formulas. Even if they can't figure out anything else, the math has to be universal."

Daniel had forgotten about this, but now he remembered. There was even more on the phonograph records than Owen was babbling about. As he recalled, they contained information about topics such as our location in the solar system, mathematical definitions, the physical unit definitions we use, our solar system parameters, chemical definitions, our DNA structure, diagrams of male and female human anatomy and cell division, a diagram of conception, a fetus development diagram and much more. And, if he remembered correctly, it was meant not only for intelligent extra-terrestrials, but for future humans as well, should it come back to Earth in the distant future. Like Owen said, a message in a bottle, which might be washed up on the same shore from which it was cast.

Daniel's excitement had grown as he thought about it, until in an uncharacteristic gesture; he seized Owen's shoulders and planted a kiss in the middle of his forehead. "Owen, you're a genius!"

"Jeez, man, get off! Don't be doing stuff like that in

public!"

Lifting his eyebrows, Daniel's arch reply was, "You'd rather we were in private?"

"NO! Get away from me, you pervert!"

Daniel couldn't help it, he threw back his head and laughed, drawing stares from their fellow diners. "I owe you one, Owen. You've given me a brainstorm."

"Well, you gave me a heart attack. Settle down, before someone comes after *you* from the funny farm. What brainstorm?"

"You know I've been working on the Great Pyramid at Giza, trying to figure out a way to write a story about all the things that can't be true about how it was constructed, right?"

"Yeah, so?"

"Dr. Zacharias' lecture got me thinking about it maybe being a message somehow. You just made it clear, that's what it has to be – nothing else makes sense."

Now it was Owen's turn to be a little confused, but he sensed Daniel was on the right track. His agile mind seized on the name Zacharias now, and the biblical name triggered something else he thought might be helpful.

"Have you ever heard of the Bible code, or the Torah code?"

"No, what's that?"

"People have been playing around with possible codes in the holy books for a long time, and they've found some things that could be messages. They even made a movie about it, The Omega Code."

"Oh, I saw that, now I remember."

"Yeah, so some scholars have written about it in peer-reviewed journals, and they claim it couldn't have happened by chance."

"There are more things in heaven and earth, Horatio, than you could ever find even with the help of a super-computer."

"Oh, man! Not Shakespeare! Twist anything else around, but leave the bard alone, man, that's sacred ground."

Daniel just grinned. He had a lot to research this afternoon, so he could tell Sarah during their regular Skype session. What a wonderful invention, Skype. He didn't miss her as much as he would have if he couldn't see that sweet face any time he wanted. But before any of that could happen, he needed to finish his article.

"Are you through stuffing your face?" Daniel asked Owen. "I need to get back."

~~~

Back at the office, Daniel pounded out the remainder of his story about Zacharias. Satisfied that he had turned in an honest day's work, he Googled 'bible code' and spent the rest of the afternoon chasing down every hint he could find about secret messages, whether from reliable sources or the fringe lunatics. He'd sort it out later.

What he learned was fascinating, beginning with the long tradition of seeking coded messages in the Bible, or the Torah. Even Sir Isaac Newton had believed that such a code existed, but in fact, Jewish priests and Bible scholars from the more distant past had a tradition of seeking interpretation of their world in the holy books. There were even a couple of words to describe the results; exegesis and eisegesis, meaning, respectively, insightful and false interpretations. The thought crossed his mind that it might not be possible to determine for sure which was which, except perhaps with hindsight.

Then there were the factual data, for example, that by selecting every fiftieth letter from the Book of Genesis, you could spell the word Torah. What meaning to attach to such a message was open to interpretation, but many people agreed that it could not have happened by chance, especially in view of the fact that the same exercise practiced in the Book of Exodus produces the same result.

Seeking further enlightenment, Daniel read of the history of such studies, culminating in the 1980s, when a mathematician at the Hebrew University of Jerusalem became interested in the discoveries of an Israeli schoolteacher and brought the power of a computer to bear on the subject. After writing a software program for it, the equidistant letter sequence, or ELS, was employed to find many messages. A group of religious scholars including the mathematician later published findings in the scientific journal Statistical Science with an article that gave strong statistical evidence that information about certain rabbis was coded in the Torah years before those rabbis lived.

Some proponents of the discoveries held that it was extremely unlikely such evidence could have happened by chance, like the word Torah appearing in two separate books of the Bible; others said of course it could, and served up example after example of similar sequences from both Hebrew and English texts.

After that, Daniel learned, controversy arose as to the validity of the method when applied to any other text, holy or not, as the Torah was unique in having been given to mankind directly from God and in exact letter-by-letter sequence in the original Hebrew language.

His head spinning, Daniel took a break at mid-afternoon and pondered whether this was useful to his quest or not. Of course, whatever his thoughts, he would run it past Sarah for her opinion, too. They were a team, after all.

As he mulled over the statistical aspect, Daniel thought of the aphorism attributed to Mark Twain. There are three kinds of lies: Lies, damned lies, and statistics. While he didn't go that far, Daniel knew it was possible to manipulate statistics to mean just about anything. He needed to know more about the computer software and the statistical methods used. After a cup of coffee and a stale donut he found in the break room, Daniel returned to his task with new questions.

What it all had to do with the potential message in the Great Pyramid was another question altogether. Fascinating as the Bible Code information was, Daniel couldn't relate it to the math in the pyramid, other than as an ancient example of using mathematical code to send a message across the centuries. But, it was compelling enough to make him read the first book in the Bible Code series all through his bachelor dinner and up until the time to call Sarah. As Daniel set up his laptop for the call, facts and speculation spun in his head like a kaleidoscope.

How could he convey all of this to Sarah in a rational way? It seemed fantastic, and he wasn't convinced. But every time he tried to shake it off as a man with a fertile imagination taking advantage of some wild statistical coincidence, his mind dredged up a fulfilled prophecy. It reminded him that the same things had happened with Edgar Cayce's prophesies, too, although some of that could be attributed to vagueness. It was enough to make you wonder, and enough to drive you insane, he decided. Maybe Sarah could straighten him out.

~~~

At nine p.m., their agreed-upon call time, Daniel sent Sarah a text. 'RUR?'

She sent back 'RUR?' After a second, he realized she was asking what he meant.

'RU ready?'

'RWA'

Did that mean what he thought it did? 'RWA?'

'Ready, willing and able ;).'

Daniel's eyes widened at the innuendo. Then he roared with laughter. Great. She was ready, willing, able, and three hours away. He sent back, 'What RU wearing?'

Sarah giggled. This was fun. It took her a minute to think of a reply that would have a double meaning. Then she sent, 'I'm getting ready for bed, wearing something special just for you.' And scrambled for her room to find that high-necked, long-sleeved flannel nightgown that kept her warm on cold Rhode Island winter nights. 'Give me 1 min.'

Daniel had heard of sexting, but he thought that was for teenagers. His heart was pounding in anticipation. He gave her exactly the one minute she asked for, then called.

As always, the moment he saw her face, Daniel's heart skipped a beat. Her smile short-circuited his brain every time, and he stammered as he greeted her.

"Hi, B-b-beautiful." Then he noticed what she was wearing. The look on his face was priceless, and her musical laugh rang out to see it. A combination of hope, confusion and disappointment washed over it, before he schooled it to a salacious leer.

"Nice! Sexy nightgown."

"Nice save, you flatterer. What did you think you were going to see?"

"I take the fifth. Amendment, that is. Although if you do that again, it may need to be a fifth of Jack Daniels."

"Ha, ha, smarty-pants. How was your day?"

"Better, now that we're talking. How was yours?"

"Hey, one of my students turned in a brilliant essay today. I may have to change research partners," she teased.

"Don't even think it! You'll give me heart failure."

"I'm kidding, silly. I'm all yours." Daniel hoped she meant that in the way he took it. Even in the granny nightgown she looked delectable.

"I got some interesting insight today, can I run it past you?"

"Sure!" Serious now, Sarah listened intently and watched his face over the jerky connection as he told her about his discussion with Owen, and his subsequent research. Daniel tried hard not to sound too gullible as he related the Bible code predictions, and must have succeeded, because she responded as if she took it seriously.

"That's interesting, Daniel, but..."

"I know, but how does it relate to the Giza mysteries. I've been thinking about that. I want to dig into these books and into Edgar Cayce's predictions, to see if there are any parallels. It may just be a wild goose chase, but if there are, then is it possible that Cayce really was onto something in his visions of Atlantis? Remember, Dr. Zacharias seemed to think there was a link there with the caves under the pyramids."

"What could it all mean?"

"I don't have a clue, but if we don't chase it all down, we'll never know. Sarah, the questions won't leave me alone. I almost feel like I'm the one the pyramid builders meant to reach with their message. It's not a story or even a hobby now, it's a quest."

"Daniel, are you sure that's healthy? It sounds to me like it's becoming an obsession."

"'Without obsession, life is nothing'" he quipped, one of his favorite aphorisms. "Can you say you aren't equally obsessed?"

"Hmmm, no, maybe not."

"Then I don't see any alternative but to chase down every lead, no matter how crazy it sounds."

"I guess you're right. But something about all this is beginning to bother me."

"What's that?"

"Why hasn't anyone else ever put it together?"

"I know, but you could say that about any great scientific discovery. Why didn't anyone ever think about why things fall until that apple hit Newton on the head?"

"Silly, that's a myth."

"That's not the point. Gravitational pull and the acceleration of gravity existed long before Newton came along and observed it, then made the breakthrough that we now accept as a universal law of physics. No one ever put that together before, either. At least, not that they reported or wrote down."

"That brings up another question."

"What this time?"

"What if someone has put it together before now? Why

would they conceal it?"

"I don't know. Maybe they're writing it up for a scientific journal as we speak. What difference does it make?"

"What if the answer is dangerous?"

"In what way?"

"Think about it Daniel. What message would be important enough to make sure someone would understand it centuries later?"

"Oh, I don't know. Maybe the end of the world?" He tossed it off facetiously, but then he saw her face change.

"Maybe that indeed."

Now who was buying into conspiracy theory? He wanted to ignore it, but his heart clenched at her worried expression.

"Hey, where did that come from?"

"That brilliant essay I mentioned? It discussed some of the hieroglyphics found in the other pyramids of the Giza complex." She paused, struggling to throw off the superstitious dread that came over her when she thought about it again.

"Yeah?"

"They referenced the Book of the Dead. Daniel, it's creepy. Here are these texts in the very pyramid complex we're studying, and they talk about Atum dissolving the world someday and returning to his primeval state."

"What do you mean, dissolve?"

"Atum's primeval state is described as being within the waters of chaos. He said only Osiris and he, the creator, will exist."

"What's the significance of Osiris?"

"The God of the Afterlife. My student did a brilliant job of postulating that the text referred to a destruction and rebirth of the world, similar to the Flood stories. You know, Noah and the Ark; the Epic of Gilgamesh."

"Oh, yeah. Wow, Sarah that could be a lead we should pursue."

"Daniel, what if it's all true?"

"Honey, be realistic. That's all mythology, but wouldn't it be cool to tie it together, find the message in the Great Pyramid to help us figure out what happened to Atlantis, if it really existed? I had forgotten that all the ancient civilizations had flood stories. Must have been some really rainy years back then."

"It would certainly make the scholarly community sit up and take notice."

"Why don't you take the lead on that part of the investigation? I'll work on the Bible Code and Cayce stuff."

"Okay. Daniel?"

"What, sweetheart?"

"I'd give just about anything for your arms around me right now. Good night." Sarah signed off and was gone, leaving Daniel to stare at the screen in open-mouthed astonishment. He'd give just about anything for the same circumstances, himself.

# Chapter 8 – Satellite Videoconference Wurzburg, Germany

Septentrio called the meeting to order, then spoke into the silence. "It is time to inform you that I have been monitoring the development in the United States that concerns us." The others leaned forward, for Septentrio's project was to learn of any research into matters that could provide information on rediscovered ancient wisdom, especially the secret of ultra-longevity. They had been waiting for news since the first mention of this research in April.

"For some time, I have been in contact with one of our operatives regarding the research project into the Great Pyramid mysteries that I mentioned at our last regular meeting. The researchers are a journalist named Daniel Rossler and a woman who is assisting him, a Dr. Sarah Clarke. There has been no significant progress at this time, but the research has taken an interesting turn."

"Do we know these people who are watching them?" Oriens questioned.

"Yes, they have proved useful in the past, and they are in a unique position to monitor this subject. A John Kingston, an editor at the New York Times who happens to supervise Rossler, and Prof. Allan Barry. You'll remember Barry from previous attempts at this research under the auspices of the Joukowsky Institute. Kingston was astute enough to involve him at first presentation of the story idea."

Heads nodded around the globe. With no further information given, it was clear that patience would be required. No matter; they and their predecessors had been patient for centuries.

"What progress has been made?" Auster, ever willing to

undercut her fellow Orion Society members by innuendo, let her tone express her skepticism and impatience.

"We have continued to monitor Rossler's IP address for relevant searches. Just this morning, there was a shift in focus from the facts concerning the pyramid's construction to some sites that explore mathematics as language and others that seem to have something to do with encoded messages in ancient texts," Septentrio answered mildly.

"We have always thought that the mathematics contained the message," Auster said impatiently.

"And yet, no one has been able to break that code previously. Perhaps these researchers will have better luck." Septentrio's patience with Auster was at an end, so his repressive tone cut off further discussion.

"I will keep you informed as developments occur," Septentrio said. "If there is no further business, this call is at an end."

"Wait," said Auster. "I have something."

"Yes, go ahead," Septentrio said.

"Our efforts to suborn the leader of the gold exploration effort in Brazil were unsuccessful, but he has died from an unfortunate accident, leaving our own man in his place," Auster reported. "We are one step closer to learning the location of the abandoned mine."

"And the accident?" Septentrio queried.

"Has been satisfactorily explained to the authorities. No repercussions will reach us," she assured him.

"Very well. Is that all?"

Hearing no further discussion, Septentrio ended the call.

# Chapter 9 - A Passionate First Move

After achieving what felt like a breakthrough with their decision that the key was the math, Daniel worried at the problem like a terrier with a toy, to no avail. They had some math facts, certainly. Daniel had a feeling that the technique of skip-sequence coding that he'd found in the Bible Code books had some merit, but they had nothing to which to apply it. He was at a standstill again, and frustration turned to exasperation with the whole project. He had columns to write, including the cave-art column that he'd set aside months ago. The only bright spot in his weeks were the times he and Sarah Skyped. They were developing a light-hearted, teasing relationship that he cherished, almost as much as he cherished the idea of holding her in his arms.

Every time they chatted on Skype, Sarah searched Daniel's face, until she had memorized every fold and freckle. Their connection, and her physical attraction to him, had grown so strong over the weeks, and yet Daniel had made no move beyond some kisses. She wondered what was going on behind that handsome countenance. Daniel knew she had been engaged. He had hinted he was no virgin, either. What was holding him back? This week, they were planning on her visiting him in New York again, maybe taking in an off-Broadway show. Sarah thought she might have to take matters into her own hands, so she packed a red silk teddy, one of the guilty pleasures she kept in her lingerie drawer for special occasions. Not that there had been any since her fiancé left, but a girl could hope. If she had anything to say about it, this weekend would be a special occasion. She only hoped that she could manage it with some finesse.

At last, Friday afternoon arrived again and with it, Sarah. Daniel had left a visitor pass for her at the reception desk, not knowing when she would arrive. Cell phone reception was lousy in the building, so they arranged that she would just come in and get him when she got there. Sarah circled around, putting her finger to her mouth when she was spotted by people to whom he had introduced her. The first he knew of her presence was when a pair of cool hands covered his eyes and a breathy whisper tickled his ear.

"Guess who?"

"Oh, man, did the guys send me a lap dancer again?" he quipped.

Slapping him lightly on the shoulder, she said, "Guess again."

But, instead of guessing, he stood and took her in his arms for a long kiss. As the catcalls started, she blushed and pulled away. Public display of affection was all right in its place, but she thought the newsroom of the New York Times probably wasn't that place.

Sarah had some shopping to do, and Daniel was willing to trail along. She thought about torturing him by dragging him to a lingerie department, but decided against it. It would be better to surprise him with the teddy than give him any hint of what was to come. With quite a while left to work before their dinner reservations, they went to his apartment after her errands were done, to discuss where they were with the research.

A strange, almost electric buzz seized Sarah as they walked through the front door. It was as if she were standing in a different plane, watching herself interact with Daniel and observing how he reacted, making a judgment about her decision. With difficulty, she pulled herself together, literally, and with effort focused on what he was saying.

Daniel had opened his laptop on the kitchen counter and was tapping keys as he spoke.

"...the only language shared universally, and I mean that literally, regardless of culture, religion, or gender. Pi is still approximately 3.14159 regardless of what country you're in. Adding up the cost of a basket full of groceries involves the same math process regardless of whether the total is expressed in dollars, rubles, or yen. With this universal language, all of us, no matter what our unit of exchange, are likely to arrive at math results the same way."

Oh, he was talking about math again. Her quick brain caught up, pushing aside any thoughts outside this discussion, for the time being. And she could agree. Very few people, if any, are literate in all the world's tongues - English, Chinese, Arabic, Bengali, and so on. But virtually all of us possess the ability to participate in the shared language of math, at least to some extent. Why was he giving her this lecture?

"So, I've decided all this other stuff..." he gestured at the bubbles of data on the left side of the mind map that organized his information, "...is irrelevant. Once we understand the message, this will all become clear. And to understand the message, we have to focus on the math, just like Dr. Zacharias said. Are we on the same page?"

"Yes, Daniel, I thought we had already established that."

"Here's the thing. We don't have enough math to provide a code. We're missing something." Sarah had heard this before, so she merely nodded. Daniel flashed a smile at her and went on, "Okay. What I think we need now is to bring in a mathematician, someone who can spot the pattern in all these measurements. I'd ask Dr. Zacharias, but I've emailed him and he hasn't gotten back to me."

"I know a mathematician. Mark Simms. The guy's brilliant."

"What's his field, specifically?"

"Actually, it's the history of mathematics and civilizations. He studies the parallels in mathematical thinking as it evolved in different ancient civilizations. Fascinating stuff, although it's over my head. He's the one who introduced me to that cryptography student I told you about."

"Brilliant! Sounds like what we need is right up his alley."

"I'll talk to him when I get back next week, show him what we've got and see if he can spot anything off the top of his head."

"Fantastic! Oh, damn, look at the time! We're going to have to hurry for our dinner reservation. Do you need to change?"

As a matter of fact, she did. That teddy was going on as underwear, and over it a soft dress that hugged her curves, in a tasteful red silk that flattered her coloring. The softly-draped neckline dipped just low enough to hint at hidden treasure. Almandine garnet earrings set in silver and a pair of Jimmy Choo ultra-high-heeled red sandals completed the outfit. When she appeared in the living room, he literally staggered at the vision she'd created. Thinking wildly that he wished he had some nitro pills around, because his heart was going to explode, all rational use of his vocabulary left him. All he could think to say was, "WOW!" When she smiled at the implied compliment, Daniel thought he had truly died and gone to heaven. Did angels wear red? This one apparently did.

Daniel and Sarah returned to his apartment much later that evening, wined, dined and flushed from a conversation that Sarah kept titillating with innuendo. He wasn't sure he could restrain himself from caveman behavior when they got behind closed doors. Showing her in, he turned to close and lock the door, then turned back and found Sarah standing so close that he almost collided with her as he turned. Her warm brown eyes had flecks of gold in them; he could have lost himself there for hours. She kept them steadily on his as she moved into his arms, murmuring, "Make love to me, please, Daniel."

He searched her face for any sign of lingering doubt, finding none. With a moan of long-repressed passion, his lips first found her throat, then, still encircling her with his arms, nuzzled lower, to the enticing curves hidden by silk. Sarah's hands tangled in his hair as she held him to her with a sudden fierce desire to melt into him completely. "Please, Daniel."

With her second plea, Daniel stood and swept Sarah into his arms, carrying her to his room and depositing her on his bed, just like the caveman he had feared being only moments before. His hands were gentle, though, as he removed her shoes and fumbled to find the fastener for her dress.

"Let me help." Sarah stood and with one movement stripped the dress off over her head. The vision he beheld made Daniel forget to breathe. There could be no mistake, she had to have planned this - that teddy proved it. For a moment that felt like an eternity he was frozen, paralyzed by the emotions flooding his mind and body. With shaking hands, he reached to unwrap the rest of the gift she had for him, barely noticing that she was unbuttoning his shirt as well.

# Chapter 10 – The Consequences

Sarah woke, realizing slowly that the restraints holding her still were Daniel's arms, and that they were sleeping curled into each other, with her head on his shoulder and her leg thrown over his. Her body tingled as full memory returned. Could their lovemaking have been as good as she remembered? Waves of memory-induced pleasure washed through her, making her wriggle even closer to him. When he spoke, a bubbling laugh forced its way to her throat.

"Woman, are you trying to kill me? Be still, or you'll face the consequences."

She wriggled in his arms again, hoping the consequences would be what she thought he meant.

Afterward, Sarah climbed into the shower behind him just as he was washing his hair. With strict admonishment about where it was permissible to touch, they managed to get out of the shower with no more consequences, as she was now calling their lovemaking. Daniel could hardly believe that his whole world had changed overnight. It was brighter, somehow, and Sarah was more carefree. His heart constricted every time she smiled or laughed. He felt like a rooster, wanting to crow his triumph to the world. Instead, he kissed Sarah whenever he caught her within arm's-length.

"Sweetheart, I've got an idea," he said, after they'd had coffee and bagels at his favorite coffee shop. "How would you feel about a road trip? My grandparents live less than two hours from here. I think you'd like Grandpa; he's a retired archaeologist. I'd like to run some of this past him, get his take on it. And Grandma would love you. What do you say?"

"I guess that would be okay. Where do they live? Would we just go for the day?"

"They live in New Jersey, and the name of the town always cracked me up. Little Egg Harbor Township. You need a legal-sized envelope if you're going to mail something, just from the length of that name. Did you bring anything to walk in, or just those crazy red sandals?"

"I've got my hiking boots in the car. I never know when you're going to drag me out on a muddy trail," she laughed.

"Let's stay overnight then." Forestalling her first protest, he said, "I promise they won't think it's an imposition. I don't visit often enough, and they're likely to tie us up to keep us from leaving anyway."

Sarah's family was the same way. Rolling her eyes at his hyperbole, she said, "At least call them and warn them we're coming."

~~~

They both avoided the topic of mathematics on the drive, knowing it would be the main topic of conversation with Nicholas, instead exchanging memories of their families and tacitly knitting their lives together. Daniel wasn't certain how Sarah felt about forever, but he was already committed. It may be too soon to talk of marriage, though.

Thinking along these lines, he didn't realize it was coming out of left field when he reached for her hand across the console.

"Sarah, last night was...it was incredible. Thank you."

"No, thank *you*, trust me," she laughed. "I can't believe I could keep my hands off you as long as I did. Think of all that wasted time."

"I don't know, I guess I thought, I mean, what if it was too soon? I didn't want to insult you or scare you away."

"Daniel, I'm not as easily scared as you might think. What did you think, I'm an orchid or something that would turn brown if you touched me?"

He turned his head to face her fully. "A priceless jewel, far out of my league."

For a long minute, she gazed back at him, searching his eyes for irony. There was nothing to say to that, it was so sweet. She leaned forward and kissed him. Then, unable to stand the tension that was suddenly between them, whispered, "Watch the road, honey, or we won't get another chance."

~~~

When they arrived in Egg Harbor, both of the old people met them at the door. Bess enfolded Sarah in a hug, which Sarah returned with as much affection as she received. Nicholas slapped Daniel on the back and offered his opinion.

"You sure know how to pick 'em, boy. You told us she was smart, but you didn't say she was beautiful!"

"I did, too!" Daniel defended himself.

Bess sided with him, saying, "Oh, yes he did, you old coot. He just didn't have the ability to do her justice."

Sarah was blushing furiously, and Nicholas took her arm. "Don't let us intimidate you, honey, we're just pullin' Danny's leg."

"Danny. Oh, that's so cute, he never told me he went by Danny."

"Well, he doesn't now, and I may be in trouble for telling you. But that's what we called him as a boy. Danny boy."

After lunch, the young couple and Nicholas settled in the living room to discuss their progress since Daniel had last called and updated his grandpa. Daniel started by relating the change of focus after the Zacharias lecture, but was soon deep into the side information that was proving intriguing. After he talked about the Bible code, and ruefully admitted he was looking into the Edgar Cayce visions regarding Atlantis, Sarah chimed in with her flood story findings. At this, Nicholas perked up. He had some information to share.

"How much has Daniel told you about my research?" he asked.

"Only that your specialty is in the Native American and ancient tribes of the desert Southwest," Sarah answered. "And something about the mystery of the sudden disappearance of the Anasazi from the Mesa Verde site."

"True, true. But here's something he may not know. Were you aware that the Hopi have a tradition of a flood destroying the Third World, and the more righteous people being saved by Spider Grandmother, who sealed them into hollow reeds to ride out the destruction?"

"No, that's fascinating! I've found flood stories from the Far East to the Mediterranean, but I never would have thought to look for them in a desert environment."

"Perhaps I should tell you more about the geography of the region. It was once covered by a vast inland sea, which, come to think of it, could have been the remnant of the flood the Hopi remember. All that's left now is the Great Salt Lake, in Utah."

"Of course! Actually, I'm from Colorado, and I knew that. Just didn't think of it."

"So, where does all that leave you in your research?" Nicholas asked.

"We're going to focus on the message. We spent the last

week trying to make sense of the why of it. But I think that if we could only decipher the message, the why and even the how should become clear."

Nicholas thought for several moments, then agreed. "That sounds sensible. How are you going to proceed?"

"Sarah has a friend whose specialty is the history of mathematics and how numeracy developed in parallel civilizations. We're going to ask him if he wants to help, and see if he can spot a pattern in the mathematical coincidences in measurements of the Great Pyramid. I think there's probably a link with the astronomy, too," he added.

"Without a doubt," Nicholas agreed. The three talked all afternoon, stopping only for Sarah to help Bess with dinner.

~~~

They were about to put dinner on the table when Sarah, prattling on about Daniel and his quirky sense of humor, said, "I just love him! He's adorable."

Bess put her hand to her mouth, and tears started in her eyes. "Oh, honey, I hope you do. He loves you, you know."

"I know he's fond of me."

"No, dear, he loves you. Head over heels, completely smitten, trust me, I know Daniel. Didn't you know it too?"

Sarah's voice went quiet, her heart too full to spare much oxygen for speaking. "I didn't. But I'm so happy to know it now. I can't imagine life without him."

Bess hugged her. "Well, hopefully you won't have to. Has he said anything at all about his feelings?"

"A little. There hasn't been much time. We only last night... Never mind. TMI."

"TMI?"

"Too much information."

Bess laughed, delighted. "I'll have to remember that one. You keep me posted, honey. If he doesn't do the right thing soon enough for you, just let me know. I'll take care of it."

Now it was Sarah's turn to laugh. "I'm glad you're on my side. But I'm not sure what 'the right thing' is just yet. Let's give it some time."

"Your call, dear. Any time you say, I'm ready, willing and able to light a fire under that boy."

Sarah burst out laughing, to Bess's bewilderment. In the living room, the object of Sarah's affection tilted his head, a silly grin spreading across his face to hear her laugh. Daniel was delighted that Sarah and his grandma were getting along so well. Little did he suspect that at that moment, Sarah was explaining their texting shorthand to Bess, who laughed even though talking by typing into a phone had never made much sense to her. Why didn't they just talk?

Meanwhile, Daniel and his grandfather were working to put into some kind of logical order the points Daniel wanted to show to Mark Simms. He decided it was best to go from the simple to the complex, pointing out relationships between them where he could, although Simms would probably spot them immediately.

Therefore, he started with Pi. One of the facts about the Great Pyramid concerned the ratio between its perimeter and its height being two Pi. Taken by itself, it was easily dismissed as coincidence. However, as they had already discussed exhaustively, taken with all the other mathematical references, maybe it wasn't. The trouble was that at the time of the purported building of the Great Pyramid, the value of Pi had not been precisely determined. The earliest written approximations of the value were in fact over fifteen hundred years later, in Egypt and Babylonia respectively.

Daniel couldn't help but wonder if that date would have been extended dramatically if the builders of the Great Pyramid had left any records about it. Whatever the case, the fact remained that the value of Pi is so ingrained in the sciences that it was probably the most widely-known mathematical expression in the world, even among the general public. Musing about this fact, and about it being found in such diverse disciplines as cosmology, fractals, thermodynamics and even electromagnetism, Daniel unconsciously voiced a joke he had employed back in high school.

"Pi are square, but I like round pies better."

His grandfather's groan brought him back to the task at hand.

"Sorry, Grandpa, that was an accident. I'm trying to cut down."

"I think we've exhausted the subject of Pi, unless Bess has one of her famous cherry rhubarb creations for supper. Shall we move on? What's next?"

Before he could go on, Bess called them to come to dinner, and the discussion was tabled for the moment. Daniel's eyes sought Sarah as soon as he arrived in the same room with her. Finding her with high color in her cheeks and more beautiful than ever, he went to her and kissed her cheek.

"Is it that hot in the kitchen? You look a little, I don't know, flushed maybe."

Sarah shook her head at him, and refused to meet his eyes. His grandmother looked a little odd, too, gazing fondly at him as if he had said or done something special. Were the women in his life ganging up on him? He pulled Sarah's chair out for her and helped her seat herself, causing her to remark that he might be the last gentleman in the world. At that, Nicholas cleared his throat and ostentatiously pulled out Bess's chair. Bess rolled her eyes at him as he leaned over her. "Thank you, darling."

~~~

After dinner and clearing away the dinner dishes, Bess declared that she was tired of being left out of the deep scientific discussions that were going on and threatened to show home movies of Daniel if he didn't agree to some other entertainment. That was enough to get Daniel's compliance. Nothing could have been more embarrassing than home movies, unless his mother had sent a copy of that picture of him as a baby, lying flat on his back with nothing on but a pair of socks and looking every inch the male that he was. Nope, even a rousing game of pinochle beat that. Some hours later, the grandparents were ready for bed. Daniel told them to go right ahead, but that he and Sarah would sit up for a while longer. Bess gave Sarah what seemed to be a significant look, making her blush. Daniel wondered if Sarah had been telling tales out of school.

Once Nicholas and Bess had closed their bedroom door and were safely out of earshot, Daniel started tickling Sarah, demanding to know what she had told his grandmother. Gasping and laughing, trying to get away from his unremitting assault, Sarah denied telling Bess anything. She wasn't ready to tell Daniel she loved him, unsure whether she could do so before he had declared himself or not. A look of bitterness crossed her face as she thought of her ex-fiancé. Daniel, misinterpreting it, stopped tickling immediately and put his arms around her.

"What's wrong, sweetheart?"

"Nothing, dear. A passing thought, nothing to do with us. So, are we really going to sleep apart?"

"Yes, unless you want Grandma asking when the wedding is planned."

"Oh. Yes, I guess that would be awkward."

"It's only tonight, hon. We'll drive home tomorrow, and we have tomorrow night, if you want to."

"Yes, please. Goodnight, Danny."

"I can't believe you just called me Danny." She was already halfway down the hall, and now ran for her door as if her life depended on it, with Daniel in hot pursuit. Giggling, she closed the door just as he reached her, but then opened it again for a goodnight kiss that curled his toes. It was going to be a long night.

Daniel lay awake for hours in the single bed in another guest room, physically frustrated and too stimulated intellectually to find sleep. Turning to his obsession instead of counting sheep, he began to mentally list his facts. The strategy worked; long after midnight, he began to drift and garble the math equations. Slowly, he dropped off to sleep, having inadvertently primed his brain for a breakthrough.

At three a.m., he sat bolt upright and said aloud, "Wait, I was wrong! It *is* the why we should be looking for!" Unable to stay in bed, Daniel got up and paced as he searched for the subconscious thought that woke him. Eyes shining in the dark, he spoke aloud, but barely above a whisper to avoid waking the household with his *Eureka!* moment. "They built this impossible construction. We still don't know how, but it doesn't matter, they did it. They showed us in the measurements and placement how much they knew about math and astronomy, and the earth. The point isn't that they knew, but that they were showing us! Why?"

Realizing he was babbling to himself, Daniel clutched his new idea to him like a stuffed animal and climbed back into bed. That had to be the key - *Why?*

At breakfast the next morning, Daniel dominated the conversation, unable to wait any longer to share his thoughts. "So, suddenly I woke up, and the idea was swirling around in my head. What if the medium *is* the message? What if they did all this not to keep a secret hidden, but to draw attention to the fact that the knowledge was there?"

Sarah and Grandpa exchanged a look. "I'm not sure what's different about your theory, Daniel," Grandpa said carefully.

"Look, it was a way of showing off. The first generation of people who come along and figure that out are the ones worthy of the knowledge."

"What knowledge?"

"Okay, wait. Let me think. They did it because they could. It's like that story about the Swiss sending the Japanese the tiniest spring in their tiniest watch and saying, 'Beat that.' The Japanese sent it back, and the Swiss didn't see any difference, so they started bragging. Then the Japanese said, 'Look at it under a microscope.' Lo and behold, they had drilled holes in it and inserted screws. Just because they could, and to make a point."

Now the other three were staring at him as if he had grown another head. Sarah broke the impasse. "And what was the point, Daniel?"

"The point was, if we can do this, think what else we can do."

"But, where does that leave us with the pyramid?"

"Remember, we started with the anomalies in the construction, not just how did they do that back then, but why was it different? All the math and astronomy, that was to say, 'look what we've done, what we can do'. But the Great Gallery, the upward-sloping passageways, those mean something different. I'm guessing there is a message in there, and it's not just a single message, but maybe the sum of their knowledge."

"Daniel, I know that by 'they' you mean the builders, but who were they? The Egyptians of 3500 BC didn't know these things, am I right?"

"That's the thing. It had to be a civilization that existed before the Egyptians. That pyramid is older than anyone believes, I'd bet big bucks on it."

"Then where are they? What happened to them?"

"I don't know. Maybe one of your famous floods. Or *the* Flood. But just think what the pyramid is. It's a library, and all we have to do to gain entrance and discover all that knowledge is break the code. Maybe that will tell us who they were and what happened to them."

Grandpa was lost in thought. Now he lifted his head and said, "Like the Anasazi at Mesa Verde. They left tracks but no one has been able to read them. Yet."

~~~

Despite the protests that they hadn't stayed long enough, Daniel and Sarah left around noon to get back to New York before pitch dark. Their trip home was productive, as Daniel handed Sarah his iPad and asked her to help him finish his outline for her friend Mark Simms.

He continued where he had left off with his grandfather, detailing the further expressions of the relationship between Pi and Phi in the pyramid. Sarah thought about the numbers for a while as Daniel fell silent, no doubt searching his brain for other mathematical facts to list. Then she asked, "Could the pyramid have been based on only one of these numbers?"

"I think so. Even on only an approximation of them. Something that size has some leeway and still achieves a high degree of accuracy. I think I read somewhere that Pi can be approximated with integers, as a ratio of 22/7. When you parse that out, you end up with a number that differs from Pi by something like four hundredths of one percent. Same with Phi, only you have to start with the ratio of its square root, which is 14/11."

"Who dreams up this stuff?" she said.

"I don't know. Idiot savants?"

"Oh, Daniel, don't use that term. It's demeaning."

"Sorry, love, didn't mean it that way. I meant the nerds who have nothing to do all day but play with numbers. Like the monkeys and the typewriters, sooner or later they're bound to come up with something meaningful." He was still teasing, but Sarah had lost the train of thought. He called her 'love'.

As the miles passed, they worked on the presentation Sarah would give Mark Simms until she deemed it finished. There would be no time to work on it further before she left, as she was determined to have another romantic evening to tide her over until they saw each other again.

They arrived at Daniel's apartment in time for Sarah to prepare a light dinner on Sunday, followed by a very cozy evening just cuddling on the sofa. They weren't talking much, but Daniel loved the weight of Sarah's head on his shoulder, and the sweetness of the kisses they exchanged now and then. Daniel tightened his arms around Sarah and vowed to himself he'd never let her go. She was his to love and protect forever. They just hadn't yet worked out the details.

Near midnight, Daniel realized that Sarah had fallen asleep on his shoulder. He touched her hair and whispered, "Sweetheart, it's late. Would you like to go to bed?" He wasn't sure she was awake when she answered.

"Yes, my love. Please take me to bed. With you." Once again he carried her, laying her gently on the bed and removing her shoes. He wasn't sure what to do about her clothes. Certain she wouldn't be comfortable sleeping in them, but hesitant to take liberties, he settled for removing his own shoes. She stirred as he sat on the edge of the bed.

"Daniel, come here." Rolling to her side, he kissed her.

"What is it, sweetheart?"

"My sexy nightgown is in my suitcase. Would you get it for me?"

Now that he knew her humor, he fully expected to find the flannel gown she had worn on their 'sexting' date, and wasn't disappointed. Nor was he disappointed when he turned to find her lying in the bed, sheet and blanket thrown aside, naked. A sharp intake of breath made her open her eyes.

"What are you waiting for, Danny?"

"For my heart to start beating again," he answered as he started toward the bed, tearing off his t-shirt on the way.

Sarah was reluctant to leave the next day, nor did Daniel want her to. But duty called, her lecture was at two, so she had to be on her way. After a breakfast of coffee and a Danish at the coffee shop on the corner, they said a lingering goodbye at her car. Daniel said, "This has been the best weekend of my life, sweetheart. You're incredible, and I'm the luckiest man alive."

Sarah lifted her hand to his cheek. "I'll count the hours until we're together again. Daniel, we have something special, don't we?"

In answer, he tightened his arms around her and gave her a kiss that weakened her knees. "Oh, yeah, baby. Very special."

# Chapter 11 – A Message In The Blocks

Although Sarah wasn't completely convinced of Daniel's new theory, she could not budge him from the notion. As a scientist, she wasn't comfortable with his 'gut feelings' as he called them. He told her that a journalist lived and died by instinct. She decided to go along with the slant Daniel was now putting on it when she presented their material to Dr. Simms. If math was the language, Simms could probably read it. Then the answer would be clear.

Sarah's meeting with Simms on the following Wednesday went well. She knew Mark as a sweet man, happily married and nearing retirement age. When she met with him in his office, his eyes lit up at her entrance.

"Sarah! What a wonderful surprise to hear from you, my dear."

"Oh, Professor Simms, I'm so sorry to have neglected you all this time."

"Nonsense, my dear. You have your life to lead. Catering to a doddering old man like myself has to be low on your priority list."

"Doddering?" she scoffed. "There is nothing doddering about you. How is Martha?"

"Fine, my dear, fine. Not sure what she's going to do with me underfoot when I retire. I need a project to keep me busy and out of her way."

"Funny you should mention that. I have one I'd love to get your opinion on."

"Really? What could that be?" Sarah knew he was thinking about the gap between their disciplines, but she plowed ahead.

"It would be easier to show you, sir. May I set up my laptop? I have a little PowerPoint."

"Certainly! How intriguing, a formal presentation. This must be very important."

"It's very important to a good friend of mine, and I've become interested too."

"Judging from the color that just flooded your cheeks, I'm guessing this good friend is a man, and maybe more than a good friend?"

"Can't slip anything past you, can I? I told you there was nothing doddering about you." Taking on a severe expression, she pretended to be annoyed. "Now, pay attention, and stop changing the subject."

With a hearty laugh, Simms feigned obedience, "Yes, my dear."

When the slides had run their course, Sarah turned the lights up to find an intense look on Simms' face. "What do you think, sir?"

"First, if we're going to work together on this, you'd better call me Mark. Next, I think I need to meet this young man of yours. You say he's a journalist?"

"Yes, sir. He has a master's in journalism from Columbia."

"Good school. Your friend has a good mind. Shame we can't steal him from his newspaper. I've heard some of this before, dismissed it as nothing more than a curiosity to be discussed at a cocktail party. Must say, you've caught my attention. I'd love to work with you on it. Give me something to do so my mind doesn't molder away after I retire. When can your young man be here?"

"I'll call him tonight, set up a time. Will next weekend be convenient?"

"Yes, that should be fine. Bring him to the house, Martha will be happy to see you again."

"Thank you, Dr. Simms. You don't know how much this means to us."

"Mark. And the favor is mutual. This is going to be fun."

While she was on campus, Sarah took the chance that Prof. Barry would be free and dropped by his office to report the new development, as promised.

When she had explained, Barry asked, "Do you think anything will come of this?"

"I have to say I hope so," she answered. "But it may not. It's a departure from what he was thinking before, but that didn't pan out, so I'm willing to explore this with him. We've asked Mark Simms to help us with the math. Do you know him?"

"We've met. Can't say we're well acquainted, different department and all. Thanks for stopping by, and let me know how it works out."

Once more, Barry waited for Sarah to get well away before calling his Langley contact and reporting the new development. He took care to cover his own credibility by saying he doubted anything would come of it, but that his mandate was to report everything.

~~~

Daniel was in Providence the following Friday, so Sarah could introduce him to Mark. The men hit it off immediately. Mark, whose fondness for Sarah was rooted in a professor-student friendship that started in her undergraduate years, scrutinized Daniel and approved of what he saw. The young man had an open, honest face, a firm handshake and a clear adoration of Sarah that shone in every look he sent her way. He would do.

While Martha. Simms kindly made a light lunch for them, Daniel and Sarah brought Mark up to date on everything they had done so far, even the red herrings and false trails they had followed at the beginning. When Daniel started on the mathematical facts, Simms interrupted.

"No need to go into that. Sarah's presentation gave me enough to begin looking into that myself. I'm familiar with Dr. Zacharias' work, and I can see where you were going with it. In fact, I agree. But Sarah says you have a different take on it. Why don't you tell me what that is, and why you think it will be more productive than manipulating the math and astronomy for a code?"

"I can't really explain it. To tell you the truth, it came to me like a bolt out of the blue, but my gut says it's the key. I still think finding a code will unlock what we're looking for. But now I think that's more along the lines of a whole encyclopedia than just a telegram."

"Fair enough. I suggest we continue along the lines of inquiry that you've started, but I'll dig into the history of these equations, see if I can find a common theme that relates to the pyramid. Or, at least a point of origin."

"That sounds like a place to start, at least. We'll add you to our SkyDrive folder so you can communicate your findings to both of us at the same time."

~~~

Later that afternoon, while Daniel was taking a shower after a run on campus, Sarah sat down idly in front of the huge monitor on her desktop, gazing at the jumble of blocks that had occupied her attention for many months now. Her screensaver was a close-up of the entrance to the Great Pyramid. Sometimes like now, when she was trying not to think of anything, Sarah would let her eyes go out of focus and fall upon a pattern; maybe the pattern of tiles in a kitchen backsplash, or a linoleum floor. When that happened, it never failed that her eyes sought the repeat of the pattern and the mindlessness of it would put her in a trance of sorts. It was a great way to relax her brain when she was stuck on a problem of some kind. Now, she did the same thing while staring at the screensaver.

The pattern jumped out at her almost immediately. There, on one side of the passage, three blocks that appeared to be too small for the course of stone they occupied, broken she thought at first. But, exactly opposite were three identical blocks. That couldn't be an accident. Alert now, Sarah refocused. And found more. "Oh my gosh", she said aloud, "Why haven't we seen this before? What could it mean? Daniel!" she called. "Hurry, I have something to show you!"

It was like a blemish on someone's face that, once seen, could not be ignored. As Sarah excitedly pointed out other instances of repeated pattern, they asked themselves if it could just have been design decisions, but Daniel's famous gut feelings were fluttering, no, kicking him in said gut. There was no reason for the pattern, there on the passage from the outside to the inside of the pyramid. Sarah contained her excitement, now that Daniel was here, to provide some balance. Sarah pointed out that she had read somewhere that the different sizes and shapes of the blocks had been chosen to make the structure earthquake-proof, could that be the reason?

"What did they know of engineering that would tell them how to earthquake-proof it?" Daniel demanded.

"They knew of all this other stuff, why not engineering?" Sarah returned calmly.

Daniel took her in his arms, vibrating with the energy of his excitement. "Baby, I think you really have a discovery here. Don't try to talk me out of it." Releasing her reluctantly, he opened his laptop to search for a source of the dimensions of the blocks, those that could be seen or accessed without destruction. He had read something somewhere, maybe in one of the Bible code books, about a method that they could use to test this.

Then he had it. If they could get enough data about the dimensions and shapes of the blocks, it might be possible to input them all into a database; size, shape, location, everything, and detect a pattern or code of which their human eyes were only able to see a hint. And he had just the computer geek to tackle the project. Raj.

"Sarah, do you know whether all the blocks in the pyramid have been cataloged? All that can be accessed, that is, the ones on the outside faces, and in the passageways?"

"I would think so. Why?"

"Can we get hold of that data?"

"I can ask around. I still have contacts in Egypt from my dissertation survey. You didn't answer my question."

"It's just an idea I have. You remember Raj, don't you? You may not know it, but Raj is a computer whiz. I'm thinking maybe he can help us with this."

"So now you're willing to bring in an outside expert?"

"Trust me, Raj is like Fort Knox when it comes to information. He's brilliant with data, but he has this one little idiosyncrasy."

Almost afraid to ask, Sarah raised her eyebrows questioningly.

"Okay, don't freak out, but he's convinced that all that Area 51 stuff is true."

Now her eyebrows went even further up and her mouth dropped. "Seriously? You're going to bring aliens into this now?"

"No, no. Listen. That's just Raj's quirk. Let me tell you what he does for the Times. You know we track all kinds of social media, right?"

"I guess I hadn't thought about it."

"Well, we do. And Raj is the guy that extracts the data and comes up with metadata."

Sarah's brow wrinkled. "And that is, what?"

"It's data about data. Here's an example, Raj can mine Facebook's data and come up with a more accurate prediction on an election, say, than the Harris poll."

"Okay, I don't know what you're talking about, but wow, that's some claim!"

"We've proven it over and over. And it isn't just Facebook. He tracks Google+, Bing, Twitter, all the big search engines, even Amazon and Barnes & Noble, to find out what people are buying to read. How do you think we come up with our Top Ten Bestsellers these days? Raj. He's our secret weapon."

"So where does Area 51 come into the picture?"

"It's his pet project, just like the Great Pyramid is mine. His fondest wish is to find the data that proves the government has been pulling the wool over our eyes for more than sixty years. And he's convinced that if he ever does, his life will be in serious danger. He's as far off the grid as you can get in New York City, and prepared to run for his life."

"I had no idea he was so…"

"Crazy?"

"Yeah. Sorry, I know he's your friend."

"Sometimes a friend has to overlook a friend's quirks. Like I overlook Raj's, and Owen's, and yours."

"Mine! What quirks do I have?"

"Well, you're sleeping with me, you must have some quirk, for that to happen."

"You goof," she said, lightly slapping his arm. "Doesn't take a quirk to want a gorgeous guy who's the world's best lover."

Laughing, he pulled her down to his lap. "I'm crazy about you."

"That must be your quirk."

"So, I'll talk to Raj while you get hold of your buddies in Egypt."

"There's another quirk."

"What?"

"You can switch from lover mode to work in zero point five seconds."

"Lucky for you, I can switch back just as fast."

"Prove it."

With a challenge like that, Daniel was obligated to perform, and more than willing. A consequence ensued, causing a minor delay.

"We don't know yet exactly what it means, but it does feel like a breakthrough." Daniel and Sarah had contacted Mark as soon as they came up for air, and were now at his house showing him what Sarah had found. As Mark watched and listened, Sarah brought up on her laptop the photo she had been staring at when she saw the patterns. Now they literally leaped off the screen at her. Mark grasped the importance almost immediately.

"What are you thinking, that this is some sort of alphabet, or something else? Clearly it's deliberate, and I agree, there can have been no other reason for it. Even earthquake-proofing. That would have been done differently, I think."

Daniel was gratified to have his thoughts validated. Now he interjected, "I was thinking more along the lines of determining whether the ratios in the cuts of these stones bear any relationship to the other numbers in the design of the pyramid as a whole. If so, maybe it's a code. But it's something. We just need to get the data and analyze it, to find out which way to look at it. Or, hey, Raj could look at it in both ways, anything's possible."

"Raj?" Mark's question made Daniel remember that they needed to let him know about the rest of his idea.

"He's a computer whiz I know. Sarah and I thought we could get his help with the data."

"Oh, okay. Is he a mathematics expert too?"

"Only in the sense of how to program a query to extract statistical data. We'll still need your help."

"I can't wait to get hold of whatever he comes up with! This is sounding more and more like one of those puzzles that's just one color. You have to put it together based on nothing but shape, and no two shapes are alike, but almost all of them fit a wrong shape from at least one dimension."

"That's a great analogy," Sarah said. "It does look like a puzzle, doesn't it?"

~~~

On Monday, Sarah spoke to Prof. Barry about Daniel's request for information about the pyramid stones.

"Why in the world would he want that?" Barry asked.

Remembering that Daniel didn't want to give away too much, Sarah hedged, "I'm not too sure, but I think it has something to do with all those number coincidences. He wants to see if the dimensions or shapes of the stones carry the theme through, or something."

Barry gave Sarah an appraising look that gave her an uncomfortable feeling she couldn't identify. At last he spoke.

"I think the University of Cairo has that data, although I'm not sure it's complete. When do you need it?"

"I'd guess he wants it as soon as possible. Will they lend it to us? I was going to get in touch with my contacts in Egypt."

"I'm not sure they could help, though you're welcome to try. But, if I pull the right strings, I'm sure we can get it. I don't know if it's in electronic format, though. We may have to pay to get it copied and sent here. Do you want that to come out of your research budget?"

"Hmmm, it isn't really relevant to my research. Let me ask Daniel what he wants to do. What do you think it might cost?"

"A few hundred dollars, at most. I got the entire Book of the Dead from Queen Mentuhotep of the 13th dynasty copied and shipped for about one-fifty if I recall correctly. Of course, the list of the stones would probably be longer, but not as much as twice that long, I wouldn't think."

"If you don't mind, would you go ahead and make inquiries? I'm sure Daniel will want to go ahead. I can leave my credit card with you if you like."

"That won't be necessary, dear. I'll square it with accounting, and you can pay me back when we know the exact cost."

"How can I thank you, Prof. Barry?"

"Just don't get so caught up in this wild goose chase that you forget your own research. You do have a publication deadline, you know." So that's why he'd given her such a strange look. Well, he'd gotten her involved in this, now he'd just have to live with her decision to follow through.

"Only too aware of it, sir. I'll be ready."

Later that evening, Sarah said to Daniel, "I've spent some money in your behalf, hon." Their Skype calls were getting to be a nightly pleasure, as often fraught with sexual tension as business.

"Oh? What did you buy?" Lowering his voice though he was alone, he continued, "Another of those amazing teddies, I hope. A white one?"

"Don't be silly," she laughed. "Do you have anything else on your mind at all?"

"Not much," he grinned cheerfully. "How can I have anything else on my mind? You own my heart, my brain and my..."

"Daniel!"

"Well, you do. Seriously, what did you buy?"

"I told Prof. Barry that we'd pay for a copy of the inventory of the blocks in the Great Pyramid."

"Oh, okay."

Even though it was late when he and Sarah finished talking, Daniel called Raj to invite himself over. Now that they had a source for the data he'd need, Daniel wanted to go ahead and enlist Raj's help.

The spare room in the apartment was a veritable Area 51 museum. Poster-sized images on the walls purported to be photos of the bug-eyed creatures that supposedly crashed in the New Mexico desert near Roswell and were immediately taken into immediate government custody. One wall was nothing but a huge bookshelf surrounding a TV/DVR combination with VHS tapes and DVDs in the shelves below. Daniel assumed the videos were either documentaries or fictional movies about the incident. Of more interest were the rest of the shelves. Two were crammed with books about Area 51.

Exploring further, he found bits and pieces of metal and other artifacts, turning to question Raj with his eyes.

"Possible debris from the crash," Raj stated. "I picked it up in the desert, can't tell you where. Just know that I wasn't supposed to be in that area, and if the FBI or CIA or NSA knew I had that stuff, I would probably just disappear and you'd never know what happened to me."

Daniel did his best to be respectful of Raj's obsession, having the unique perspective of someone who had a theory he couldn't prove yet, about a mystery that no one else believed mysterious. But, Raj's statement was just a bit over the top. It was difficult to keep a straight face, so he turned back to the shelves, the rest of which were filled with dozens of three-ring binders. He pulled one out at random. Raj rushed to take it from him and examine the label on the spine.

"Okay, you can look at that one."

"Raj, what are all of these?"

"Research binders. I have search bots combing the web for

every story about sightings, the crash at Roswell in 1947, essays and studies, pictures, you name it. Every scrap of information I find, I print out and put in the appropriate binder."

"Good lord, Raj, why? Why not just keep it in your computer?"

"For one thing, I don't want a digital trail, but this is just backup. When online I use proxy servers all over the world which are changing my IP address every few minutes so that no one can track me down. My only exposure is when I print the article, and I do that at public libraries under a false name. Then I scan it into my external hard drive here. The computer it's attached to is never connected to the internet."

"That seems, I don't know what to call it Raj, besides paranoid."

"You've said that thing you say about paranoid many times, Daniel. How does it go? Just because you aren't paranoid doesn't mean someone isn't out to get you? Well, I'll admit it. I am paranoid. This conspiracy is so big, and the American government so corrupt, that I feel I have good reason to believe someone is out to get me. Or would be if they knew what I had, and how close to a breakthrough I am."

Daniel had come with an objective in mind, so he changed the subject.

"Raj, I've stumbled on something that I could use your help with. It's very sensitive, but I know I can count on your discretion."

Raj leaned forward and whispered, "It has something to do with your pyramid? I knew it! Aliens did build it!"

Daniel responded in equally hushed tones, "I don't know about that, Raj, but it's damned sure the Egyptians of 3,500 BC didn't build it. We think we've discovered something that will help us figure out who and why."

"Tell me more, how can I help?"

Well, we think there's a message in the stones, maybe a code, maybe an alphabet. We're not sure yet. Sarah has sent for full data on the dimensions of the stones in the pyramid. It's a big project, Raj, but what we need is someone who can catalog them, both graphically and numerically, and then help us search for the message."

"You keep saying 'we'. Who is interested in this?"

"You know Sarah, my research partner. Me, of course. And a former professor of Sarah's, a mathematician."

"You've told no one else?"

"No one else knows the full picture, why?"

"Think about it, Daniel. Who else could the builders have been, if not the Egyptians? It's got to be aliens, and that's a dangerous subject. You're sure no one's onto you?"

Daniel reflected. How far to indulge Raj's obsession? Finally, he said, "I really don't think so, Raj. I mean, a couple of other people knew I was looking into the question, but it went nowhere at the time, and probably everyone else either doesn't care or has forgotten about the whole thing. It's just my pet project, you know?"

Raj narrowed his eyes. "You're going to a lot of trouble for just a pet project."

"You know how it is, man. A question gets hold of you and won't let you go."

"All right, my friend, we will leave it at that for now. But when the time comes, you know that I know there's more to it.

When do you want me to start working on it?

"Thanks, Raj! We should have the hard copy for the stone dimensions within a week. If there's an electronic file, it will be sooner, but Sarah doesn't think there is."

Raj rubbed the back of his neck. "Where is this hard copy being sent?"

"I'm not sure. Do you want it delivered to you?"

Raj almost yelped as he whisper-shouted, "No! I want nothing to lead to me, certainly not a delivery. When you get it, we'll arrange a way for you to give it to me."

"What if it's several boxes? It probably will be, you know."

"We will make the transfer away from the city, where there is no one to see. That will do."

By Friday, Daniel was on pins and needles. He missed Sarah more every week, and looked forward to weekends like a dying man in the desert looks forward to an oasis. This week, it didn't help that every time Raj passed his desk, he lifted one eyebrow in an 'is it here yet?' question. This morning, he was wrapping up his weekly column and getting ready to leave for Providence as soon as he was finished at his desk. The car was packed, he didn't even have to go home for it. Raj passed by, two aisles over and pretended to cough. Daniel looked up at the sound. Raj was tilting his head toward the restroom in short, jerky movements. Pushing out his breath in a heavy sigh, Daniel got up and sauntered toward where Raj was waiting.

"Any word yet?"

"No, Raj. I'll let you know, okay?"

"What is taking so long?"

"Sarah mentioned that they might need to photocopy the

records, and then FedEx them. I'm not sure whether there's overnight service between Cairo and New York. Might take two or three more days, especially if it's heavy."

"Okay, my friend. I may be out of cell range part of the weekend."

"That's okay, I'll just catch up with you Monday."

"Fair enough."

When Daniel got to Sarah's late that afternoon, though, a pleasant surprise was waiting. Sarah had received an email that the data was on its way, and even better, it was on DVDs, not hard copy. Less bulk to sneak around with to satisfy Raj's natural caution. But Sarah had an even better surprise.

Since it was Daniel's birthday on Monday, Sarah wanted to get him a special surprise. After a lot of thought, she realized that the best gift she could give him was the fulfillment of a fantasy. Accordingly, she'd gone to Victoria's Secret and purchased just what he wanted - a white teddy.

# Chapter 12 – A Lovely Declaration

Daniel managed to signal to Raj that the material was on its way as he passed by Raj's cubicle on the way to lunch on Monday. Although no words were spoken, Raj got up and casually followed him out.

"When do you expect it?"

"Sarah's email said Second Day delivery, so she should get it tomorrow. She'll bring it here on Friday"

On Wednesday morning, Sarah sent a text that the package had arrived. Such a small package for what would potentially be the biggest archaeological find in recent times. He forwarded the text to Raj, feeling like James Bond or some super-spy. Raj passed by casually a few minutes later, and gave him a straight-faced nod. Daniel felt this crazy spy craft thing was a bit much, but whatever suited Raj and didn't make Daniel look like a nut case, he'd go along with for now. He just hated to have to wait until Friday to pass the material along and get Raj started.

Sarah was able to get away early on Friday, so she arrived at mid-afternoon, dressed in a pretty spring outfit and looking so beautiful that it made Daniel's heart race. He wondered if there would ever be a time when he'd be able to breathe when he first caught sight of her. Then Owen made a spectacle of himself and Sarah both by staggering up from his chair and throwing himself at Sarah's feet, clutching her ankles and begging her not to leave him again. The whole newsroom floor was in an uproar in minutes, as Sarah's clear laugh pealed out and others came to see what was so funny.

Sarah was now pleading with him, "Get up, Owen, that's enough. Yes, you were very funny and I'll take you back and love you forever, but you've got to let go of my ankles before I fall down."

It was only Daniel's approach that made Owen scramble to his feet, hold both hands up in a warding gesture, and say, "I had to try, man, just look at her! She's a vision of loveliness."

"That's true, but you're going to be a vision of bloody nose and broken jawbone if you ever pull that again." His tone and expression were much milder than the words would have indicated, though. Sarah was still laughing, along with a few of the onlookers.

Owen had achieved his objective, so he meekly went to his desk, but not without a parting shot, "She did say she would take me back and love me forever. Beat that, you dork!"

Daniel was shaking his head in disbelief when he got to Sarah. "So, you've thrown me over for that clown," he said, smiling.

"I had to - he was about to bring me down to the floor with him."

"If I thought you were serious, I'd have to kill him."

Raj had planned an elaborate charade that included a picnic at a state park outside the city, to which he brought a date. Daniel was stunned to see that Raj's date could have been a supermodel. She was a woman whose features and name suggested she was also from India, but Daniel couldn't see how Raj would have attracted a woman like Sushma. He'd have to watch his friend more closely for clues.

On the Tuesday after the transfer, Raj signaled Daniel to meet him outside. Daniel reflected that they might both have to take up smoking if they were going to meet this way, otherwise it would be noticed. Raj merely told him that he was making good progress.

"I'm thinking the first thing to do is replicate the shapes in graphic files, using the measurements and a precise scale. Once we have the images and the dimensions of each in a relational database, we can apply whatever queries you want."

With about twenty blocks entered, Raj explained that the bulk of the progress had been on Sunday, so Daniel should expect the first one hundred to be completed by the end of the week. Most of Saturday evening had been used in thinking about how to approach the problem and setting up the database, which would only have to be done once. Daniel hoped that the process would become quicker as Raj settled into it. Raj explained that he was selecting 100 blocks from among thousands, but not doing so in sequence, in order to get a better sampling.

True to his word, Raj used every spare minute to enter the data for the first one hundred blocks, finishing on schedule. Raj had made a copy of the database file on a flash drive, which he slipped surreptitiously to Daniel at the coffee shop. Daniel planned to deliver it to Mark with much less drama when he went to Providence Friday afternoon. He managed to ask a few questions of Raj sotto voce.

"Will he need special software to open this?"

"Is he on a Mac or a PC?" Raj asked.

"Mac I think."

"Hmmm, is he computer literate?"

"I guess. What does he need?"

"He won't have a native database program, but he can get an app that will open the files, and even support queries. He should be able to get one from the Mac App Store if he doesn't have it already."

"Okay, I'd better write that down." He made a note in his iPhone. "Thanks, Raj. I'll let you know if we run into any problems."

"Tell him that there's a text file on the drive that will give definitions and ranges for the ID numbers and sequence numbers, that'll help him do queries. And it can all be exported to a CSV file to transfer everything but the graphics to a spreadsheet. Or, if he has Office for Mac, it can go straight into an Excel file."

Daniel had to admit that at this point, he was way over his head in understanding all that was going into the research. He was working on pure gut feeling that this exercise would bear fruit, either in the form of a code they might eventually break, or in a straight message that they just needed to find a way to translate. He wasn't even sure he could articulate what he meant by the difference, only that there was a difference, and they would have to devise a way to determine which it was, as an intermediate step.

On Friday, Daniel arrived in Providence just in time to take Sarah out to dinner. One of these Fridays would be the day he'd pop the question. Not today, though. He was waiting for the stone he had chosen to be set into a band of platinum with five tiny diamonds flanking it on both sides. He hoped it was elaborate enough, but Sarah seemed to have simple though elegant tastes. The stone was very beautiful, as he had taken an independent appraiser with him to advise him on the clarity and brilliance.

Sarah was quiet. While Daniel paid attention to the wine list, she wondered what it was going to take for him to declare his feelings. Without saying it in so many words, hadn't she given him enough demonstration that she loved him? He seemed to feel the same about her. What was stopping him from saying it? Was she going to have to break her resolve and say the words first? Men! Can't live with 'em, can't kill 'em! Damn, now she was making his jokes, too.

Daniel saw the look of exasperation cross Sarah's face, turning from the server after having made his selection just in time to catch her thoughts expressing themselves externally. He tilted his head slightly and crinkled his eyes. Taking her hand, he said, "What's wrong my love?"

Tears sprang to Sarah's eyes immediately, alarming Daniel even more. "Sarah?"

"It's nothing."

"I don't know much about women, but I do know when you say it's nothing, it's something. What is it sweetheart?"

"I can't…"

"Come on, honey, you can tell me anything. Don't you know that nothing in the world could make me stop loving you?"

At this, she broke down entirely, burying her face in his shoulder. "Daniel, that's the first time you ever said you did!"

"What? No, I say it all the time!"

"Not to me. I wasn't sure."

"Oh, baby, how could you not be sure? I love you with all my heart, and all my soul, and I thought I showed you that every day."

Overcome, she wept in his arms until the server, alarmed, came to ask if there was anything they needed. Daniel waved him away, then put his free arm around Sarah to hold her close. "It's okay, baby, I'm sorry I never said it. I'm an idiot!"

Sarah's voice was muffled by his shoulder as she said, "Don't you call the man I love an idiot."

It was Daniel's turn to be emotional, but the physical manifestation was completely different. Grinning now from ear to ear, he raised her face with a thumb and finger to her chin. "You mean that? You love me too?"

"I was just waiting for you to say it first, you idiot."

"Hey!" A deep, lingering kiss followed, both Sarah and Daniel oblivious to their surroundings.

Sarah and Daniel were expected at the Simms residence for breakfast, since Sarah had called to tell Mark that they finally had something for him to work with. Their emotional dinner had given way to the most amazing night in their experience together. Daniel reflected that it even topped their first time, though he would have thought that impossible. With less sleep than optimal, they were both reluctant to get out of bed, but Sarah finally managed to drag herself out and into the shower. Daniel had coffee on when she emerged.

"Why didn't you join me?"

"If I had, there would have been consequences and we would have been very late for breakfast, and that would be rude."

"Good point," she smiled, giving him a kiss on the nose. "Thanks for the coffee. Better grab your shower or we're going to be late anyway."

"Be out in a jiffy. I don't have to worry about putting on makeup and fixing my hair, all that primping you do."

"Primping! Why you…"

Laughing, Daniel scooted for the other room. He knew she seldom wore makeup, had no need for it. And he knew she knew he knew it.

Their breakfast with the Simms was a pleasure. Martha knew as soon as she saw them that something had happened between them. Since they didn't say what, she didn't comment, but couldn't help beaming at them like a proud mother hen as she served poached eggs, bacon and scones with clotted cream. That was a new one on Daniel, and as soon as he tasted the delicacy, he declared himself in love with Martha. Mark raised his eyebrows, Sarah laughed and swatted him, and Martha blushed.

"I'll give Sarah the recipe," she said.

"That'll do," Daniel replied.

While Sarah helped Martha with the dishes, Daniel and Mark went to Mark's study, where Daniel gave him the flash drive and all of Raj's advice.

"Does that all make sense?" Daniel asked.

"Yes, perfect sense. I'm not bad with a computer for an old geezer."

"With all due respect sir, you are not an old geezer."

"Okay, just old."

Daniel gave up, but patted the other man on the shoulder.

"You're never too old to learn something stupid," he quipped as he left. Behind him Mark turned and gave him a puzzled look. What the heck was that supposed to mean? But the data was calling him, so he didn't ask.

# Chapter 13 – Fibonacci Speaks

Mark started by just looking at the data. His neatly-ordered mind could often pick out patterns just by seeing the dataset as a whole. Discerning nothing in the string of numbers that represented the locations of the stones, he turned to devising an expression of the dimensions of the stones as a circumference. Once he had the single dimension expression, he then arranged them in ten columns of ten rows each, using a right to left sequence from the first number at the top left corner, ending with 100 at the bottom right. Nothing. Then he reversed the strategy, using column one for numbers through ten and moving to the right. Performing this exercise four times, once forwards or left to right, and once backwards, that is, right to left, top to bottom and then bottom to top, nothing in the dimensions of the blocks spoke to him.

He didn't really expect anything from the first exercise, but it was the simplest to perform, and an orderly experiment called for trying the simplest first and then moving to the complex. Classes had ended for his last semester of tenure, and nothing remained for him to do at the university except clear out his office and attend the retirement party. He filled his time instead with hour after hour of patient trial and error, parsing the dimensions to find a ratio between height and circumference and then between width and circumference and finally between height and width.

Nearly a week passed before, on Thursday afternoon, he found a pattern. He called Sarah.

"Sarah, dear, I've got something. When can you come over and see what it is?"

"Mark, that's fantastic! Daniel will be so excited. We should wait for him."

"Could he come tonight? This is definitely something deliberate, something worth being excited for."

"I'll call and ask him. How late can we come over?"

"Just call me when you know if he can come tonight. We'll set a time then."

"Okay, give me a few."

Sarah dialed Daniel immediately. "Daniel, you'll never believe it! Mark's got something. He wants us to come over and see for ourselves. Could you make it tonight?"

"Let me clear it with Kingston, and I'll let you know. But I'll plan on being there no later than nine, if that's okay with him."

"Got it. Text me if that changes."

"Okay. See you tonight sweetheart! I love you."

"Love you, too, and I can't wait to see you."

Daniel wasted no time arranging the time off with Kingston, explaining that they had a breakthrough and a story might come of it after all. Kingston waved him off, saying, "Go, go. No problem, as long as you've turned in your column."

"I'll file it before I leave."

"Fine. Get out of here, I'm busy." Kingston went back to his keyboard. Daniel wondered if that novel was ever going to be finished, but he didn't have time to dwell on it. He hastily proofread his column, then sent it to the editing team and left. He needed to go by his apartment to pack for the long weekend. He was fretting about the waste of time when he realized that the answer was to keep part of his wardrobe at Sarah's. A second set of toiletries, toothbrush and razor, and let's not forget hiking boots, and he would never have to pack for the trip again. He was whistling as he locked his apartment and put his things in the car to begin his drive. Before starting the car, he sent Sarah a text, 'Leaving now.'

She sent a picture of a thumbs up in return. Daniel knew why he felt so light—he would get to see Sarah a whole day early and spend three whole days with her instead of just two.

Hours later, the two of them sat on either side of Mark as he showed them step by painstaking step how he had found results. He still hadn't told them what, and they were anxious to see. Repeating his sequence, first, he ran a query to find the ratio between the height and the width of the blocks, and exported the result to an Excel file. Next, he explained that he was expressing the ratio as a percentage, then dividing it into the circumference of the respective blocks. A column of numbers appeared on the spreadsheet, and Mark waited for the other two to see it.

Sarah saw it first. "Oh my goodness! Those are Fibonacci numbers!"

Daniel thought the term was familiar, but couldn't place it. "What's a Fibonacci number?"

"It's a number derived from the sum of the two previous numbers, starting from zero or one. The sequence starts, from one, 1, 1, 2, 3, 5..."

Then Daniel got it. "So the next number is 8..."

"Very good," Mark said. "Do you notice anything else?"

This time it was Daniel who saw it. "There are only eight numbers. They repeat."

"That's right, and it's amazing that we could calculate this with only one hundred examples. Despite every block being a slightly different size and shape, calculating the ratios gets us only eight different ones, and the same thing happens when we divide the circumference by the ratio as a percentage. Furthermore, the eight unique numbers that result from that calculation are all Fibonacci numbers."

After several moments of excited chatter during which Mark described his process until Daniel's head was whirling, Sarah brought them crashing back to reality. "But what does it mean?"

"I have a few ideas," Mark said. "Let's get some refreshments and I'll run them past you."

They found Martha in the living room reading, and persuaded her to have a drink with them, though she said it would put her right to sleep. A quick glance at his watch told Daniel it was just about bedtime for most people anyway. He made a subtle gesture to his watch, keeping his eyes on Sarah's. Her slight nod told him she understood.

"What's that idea you had, Mark? It's late, Daniel and I should get going."

"Why, just that the Fibonacci numbers have to be significant. Because of the ratios in the structure as a whole, you see. I think the builders were trying to draw our eyes to the fact that there's an alphabet here. We can't see all of it, because we don't have enough data. But I'd be willing to bet that if we arranged these Fib numbers by location of the blocks they came from, we'd see something that looks random but is actually some representation of a written language."

Daniel stared at the numbers in awe as Mark rearranged them according to the location of their blocks. It was like watching an animation of a Scrabble game, as the numbers that represented letters slid into their respective places one by one. It was easy to see that there were gaps. "We need the rest of the blocks."

"Yes, we do. Obviously ten letters isn't enough for an

alphabet. Do you know what language this code would have been in?"

Stricken, Daniel and Sarah admitted that they hadn't thought to question that it would be in Arabic.

"We're going to need a linguist, aren't we?"

Sarah and Daniel were still celebrating when they returned to her house. After one more glass of wine, they took the celebration to bed, where Daniel took great care to make sure that Sarah knew just how much he loved her. The next day, they dutifully reported to Prof. Barry that with Mark's help, they had discovered something that could be important, though they didn't specify what, citing their need to make sure it panned out first.

<center>~~~</center>

Daniel also called Raj on Friday to tell him the good news. Raj, however, as soon as he had heard enough to guess what was coming, stopped him.

"Wait! Not over a cell phone."

"Come on, Raj, you're kidding. No one is paying us the slightest bit of attention. Let me tell you."

"If you want me to keep working with you on this, you'll either go to a pay phone to call me or better yet, wait until you get here and show me."

"But..."

"That's the deal, my friend. Take it or leave it."

"Okay, I'll see you on Monday if I don't call first."

"That will work."

Daniel turned to Sarah, who was lingering over her last piece of toast and a second cup of coffee.

"I think Raj has gone off his freakin' nut."

"Well, you said he was a little crazy. What did he say?"

"He wants to communicate only through pay phones, in case our cell phones are bugged. Or, wait until I can tell him in person. Or he won't play anymore."

Sarah snorted when Daniel mentioned bugged cell phones, and was now mopping up spewed coffee.

"I suppose you'd better indulge him. Do you want to go find a pay phone, or wait to see him in person? You won't leave early to do that, will you?"

"No, sweetheart, nothing is going to tear me from your side before Monday morning. Let's just go about our weekend, and if we happen to see a pay phone, we'll do that."

"That sounds lovely. What shall we do? I've no classes today, and I can run by my office and put a note up that office hours are canceled."

"Super! Let's drive out into the countryside, maybe have a walk in the woods, and a picnic. Hey, have you ever thought about..."

"Not on your life, mister. All I need is to be caught *in flagranté* in public. I'm not that adventurous."

Daniel pretended to pout, but in truth he wasn't all that adventurous either. It was fun to get her riled up, though. She was never more beautiful than when her color was high from laughter, embarrassment or passion. It was his mission in life to keep one of those in play at all times.

Though Daniel and Sarah found plenty to do over the weekend, they never did spot a pay phone. Admittedly, they could hardly have expected to find a pay phone in Sarah's bedroom, where they spent the bulk of their time. Daniel couldn't get enough of Sarah's willing sensuality. Her soft curves welcomed his body like no other woman, ever. Sarah had shown him in every way that she was as hungry for him as he was for her. He couldn't wait until the time when, he hoped, they would be together every day. This weekend love affair was taking a toll on his nerves.

In any case, he wasn't able to get the discovery to Raj until Monday evening after work, by which time Raj had entered a few more of the blocks.

"Raj, why all the paranoia and spy craft stuff?"

"I have told you, my friend. Government agencies are aware of my interest in extraterrestrials, I'm sure of it. If they discover by listening to my phone conversations that I am on the verge of a breakthrough in this matter of aliens having built this pyramid, there's no telling what they will do."

"Raj, we don't have any notion that aliens built it, we think it was an older, more advanced civilization that has disappeared in some way."

"Precisely. Alien civilization."

"Not necessarily."

"Daniel, do not be naive. A civilization that advanced would have to have come from beyond the stars, it could not have developed in such a primitive world."

"Okay, let's say for the sake of argument that you're right. Does it make any difference to our work here if we agree to disagree?"

Raj inclined his head, giving himself time to think. "No, I suppose not."

"Then let's do that. I won't tell you I think you're stark

raving mad, and you won't assume or mention aliens, and we'll get along just fine. Agreed?"

Although a slight frown crossed Raj's face at the phrase 'stark raving mad', he nodded. There would be no more talk of aliens until he could prove his theory, although he had no doubt at all.

"So, you wish me to finish as soon as possible just the passageway stones?"

"That's right. We're going on my hunch that the message there gives the key to what's inside."

"All right, then, I will do one side and then give you the report. If the other side is identical, I can just replicate the records."

"I'd hate to miss something because our eyes are fooled by very close but not identical stones. Go ahead and do one side first, but please do the other individually. It could be important. I mean, I'd hate for one side to say, 'Take out the 3rd stone on the thirtieth course of the pyramid to find a great treasure.' And the other side to say, 'Just kidding. The treasure is really behind the 4th stone of the fortieth course."

Now Raj was laughing, his pique over Daniel not taking his extraterrestrials seriously forgotten. He continued the joke, "Or, 'Just kidding, there's a deadly poison in the air pocket there. Don't do that.'"

"Yeah, that would be a real bummer," Daniel chuckled. "Don't do as I say, if you do, you're done for."

~~~

The following day, Raj appeared at Daniel's desk with a cup of break-room coffee that he offered to Daniel. Without another word, he headed back to his own area. Daniel couldn't understand it, it wasn't typical Raj behavior, but he wouldn't turn it down. Even sub-par break-room coffee was better than no coffee. His eyes were on his computer screen when he finished it, so it was a little while later, when he picked it up to throw it in the wastebasket that he realized there was a message printed on the insides of the cup. Daniel slowly rotated the cup as he read the words.

"We must not be seen meeting, but come to the Little India restaurant at eight o'clock tonight. R."

What the heck? Had Raj found something of significance already? Daniel had told him of Mark's process, so he could have replicated it and already have something to tell them. He sent Sarah a text, saying only 'Call will be late, explain later.' Raj's paranoia was beginning to affect Daniel. He was reluctant to send anything across open airwaves that might let a listener know what he was doing at any given time. When he realized what was happening, Daniel gave a light chuckle and waved off the adrenaline that suddenly washed through him. All this cloak and dagger was becoming too easy to buy into.

Daniel knew the Little India, from previous outings with Raj. Indian wasn't his absolute favorite food, but he enjoyed Indian cuisine now and then. He arrived at eight and was trying to decide between chicken tikka masala and vindaloo when Raj slipped into the booth on the other side. At least, he thought it was Raj. The apparition was dressed as a woman, with a blond wig over a patently Indian face.

"Raj, what the..."

"Shh, my friend. Call me Sushma, it is safer."

"Does she know you've stolen her clothes?"

"She loaned them to me and helped me create this

disguise. Clever, yes?"

"That's one word for it. Okay, Sushma what is all this about?"

"I have come to warn you. You must take precautions and take this seriously. You and your Sarah could be in danger if you don't."

"Seriously, what's happened since yesterday to get you this riled up?"

"People I know are talking about increased surveillance. It may not about us, specifically, but because of it we are all the more vulnerable."

By now, Daniel had serious doubts about his friend's mental stability, although he did make a pretty cute girl. But, they needed Raj, so he would play along.

"Okay, what should we do?"

"Get your data off of any computer that accesses the internet. Keep it on flash drives and be sure to eradicate all traces of it on the hard drive after you use it. If you have only one computer, don't let it be connected to the internet when you are manipulating your data. Be careful of Wi-Fi; disable automatic connection so you won't forget. Be very circumspect in what you say to Sarah or her colleague and what they say to each other over your phones, whether they are landlines or cell phones. Watch your text and instant messaging. Daniel, our lives are far too open for anyone who wants to read them like an open book. You must be hyper-vigilant."

Now, there was a ten-dollar word for a man who spoke English as a second language. Raj was so sincere that Daniel was caught up in his intensity.

"Okay, I'll let the others know. How should I do that,

email?"

"Heavens no! The best way would be in person, but if you won't be seeing them for the next few days, send a letter by FedEx. NOT the postal service—FedEx." Raj handed Daniel a flash drive, which he said not to connect to a computer until it was disconnected from the internet. "There is a document here that explains the best way for us to communicate from now on, but it will take me the rest of this evening to set it up. I will give you the information you need when I see you at work tomorrow, and you will tell the others in person.

Raj's method for communicating among the research team was to set up a series of free email accounts using randomly generated numbers and letters for the account names and passwords. Those he intended to list in the first account, in the Drafts folder, to be saved in a secure place by each member. The messages would never be sent, but instead would remain hidden in the email accounts' Draft folders, accessible to read by anyone with a password, but leaving no trace otherwise. It was a method that had been used successfully by spies in the recent past without detection. They would use each account for only a week and then move to the next, unless they had reason to believe one had been compromised, in which case they'd send a text saying 'Next!' to each member of the team. Raj would close each account as it was retired.

"Okay, I'll do that. Raj, you've got me worried."

"That was my intention, my friend. I fear others are far more interested in your work than you believe."

## Chapter 14 – Double Crossed

Allan Barry was a bitter man. He'd been relegated to an administrative role at the Joukowsky Institute, which, though it had attracted a remunerative side job in providing information to his shadowy employers, left him out of the loop academically. As he neared retirement, he realized that he hadn't put away the sums he would need to retire in the style he desired. But Dr. Sarah Clarke had just handed him the remedy to that problem.

When Sarah and Daniel had left after hedging about their potential breakthrough this morning, Barry decided to think for a while before reporting to Langley. His conclusion was that if the brilliant Dr. Clarke thought there may be something to Rossler's theory, there probably was. Accordingly, he formed a plan to grab a bigger piece of this particular pie. Executing it would require advance knowledge of what was happening, and it seemed that much of it was happening in the home office of Dr. Mark Simms. He made a call to a colleague in the secret organization he worked for, this time to New York City.

"Impes, Barry." When making these calls, it was always best to use as few words as possible, even if he had no indication that listeners overheard.

"Go," was the terse reply.

"Have you ever given any thought to … Oh, never mind. Probably not." Barry was suddenly nervous that he couldn't trust Impes. Maybe it wouldn't be good to ask him on an open phone line whether he'd like to steal the secrets for themselves and sell them to the highest bidder.

"Say it," Impes directed.

"I think a project I've been working on with our employers may break open soon, but I may be in a position to get there first.

I think maybe I can break the code they're interested in. But if I do, I'd like a bonus. A big one."

Impes considered the implications, not only of what Barry had said, but how he said it. Was the man actually offering to partner in a double-cross of the Orion Society? If so, he didn't realize just how dangerous his masters were. Now the question was whether to report it that way, or whether to let Barry think he was going to go along with it, then kill him and report the find to Septentrio himself.

"Let's hear your plan," he said. He could decide on the best course of action after he heard what was on offer.

After that, Barry reported to Langley just what he'd heard from Sarah; progress of some sort had been made, but she was hesitant to say exactly what until it proved newsworthy.

Before the day was out, Martha Simms noticed that her home phone wasn't working. She used her cell to call the service provider and was gratified to see that they were paying attention to customer service these days. Within an hour of her report, two service technicians in a phone company truck had arrived and checked the phone lines throughout the house. When they were done, her phone worked as well as ever. Such nice young men they were, too. By dinnertime, she'd forgotten all about the incident.

In New York, a team of listeners was assigned to monitor the conversations of a soon-to-be-retired mathematics professor. It was a boring and seemingly senseless assignment, but the team was paid no matter what did or didn't go on, so they did their jobs. No one was at home during the day but the old woman. She had nothing better to do than talk on the phone with her cronies. On the off chance that these conversations concealed coded communications, every word was noted and analyzed for its relevance to certain subjects.

The night-time hours were a little more interesting, though the listeners had little to no desire to eavesdrop on the bedroom secrets of a couple of folks in their sixties. One, in his forties and already thinking he needed a boost, was encouraged to learn that there was, in fact, life after fifty.

Only when the visitors arrived did the listener on duty perk up his ears, recording what he picked up though it made little sense to him.

From a complex near Langely, VA, Daniel and Sarah's internet searches continued to be monitored, as they had been from the beginning. The only thing new was several searches on the term linguist. It was Sidus who put it together that the breakthrough must have given the researchers some notion that they had hit upon a code of sorts. His report to Septentrio resulted in an order to begin tracking their whereabouts at all times via their cell phones. Langley called on NSA contacts to follow that order.

# Chapter 15 – The Keyboard

Sarah and Daniel were at Raj's apartment on the first weekend in October, deep in discussion about the numbers.

"I added new fields to the database, with the calculations your colleague applied to the data. Now we are able to see the result as soon as I have put the raw data into the record," Raj was saying. As he typed, a dizzying array of numbers in rows and columns marched across the screen. A few more keystrokes, and the data arranged itself into a chart, showing the final calculation in colored numbers. Sarah and Daniel looked closer, to notice that the different colors always represented the same number, red for five, green for eight, and so on. The sequences, clearly Fibonacci numbers, went no higher than thirty-four.

"How many of these blocks have you finished, Raj?" Daniel asked.

"All of them in the passageway, both sides."

"And yet, not counting zero or the repeated one, we have only eight numbers, the highest being thirty-four. Could we have been mistaken about the message? It doesn't seem like enough."

Raj said, "You know, it looks like we have discovered the keyboard and the screen of a computer, but where is the computer?"

Daniel and Sarah saw it almost at the same time, but Sarah found her voice first. "That's it, it's a sign, but it's only pointing to the alphabet, it isn't the alphabet itself."

"Why do you say that?" Raj asked.

"Because, there aren't enough letters, if we assign a letter to each number. No alphabet has so few."

"Then, how will we discover where it's pointing?"

Daniel took over, having grasped the same idea. "Look, the numbers up to eight are expressed everywhere in the pyramid, all the angles and measurements, everything. That was the builders saying, 'look at this, we've left you a message if you can interpret this'. Now we've got three more numbers in the sequence, thirteen, twenty-one and thirty-four. I don't know of any alphabet, ancient or modern, that had so few as thirteen characters, so I think it's just that they chose Fibonacci numbers to get our attention and then point to the alphabet; the thirteen has no significance. I can't see any, at least at this time. But twenty-one, and thirty-four, now we're getting somewhere. We just have to find the alphabet that has one of those numbers of letters, and we'll know what language they were speaking."

The men turned to Sarah, the closest they had to an expert on ancient languages. Raj asked, "So, what language is it, Sarah?"

"Don't look at me! I don't have a clue. I do know that Sumerian is the oldest language we know of."

"How many letters does it have?"

"I don't know, not my field. For all I know, they used pictographs instead of letters."

Daniel sucked in his breath, gaining the attention of the others. While they looked at him curiously, he gathered his thoughts. Then he gave a slow shake of his head. "We may have been going at this all wrong, thinking in terms of modern writing, where we use these symbols to mean a sound. What if these builders did use pictographs to express their language in writing? It would fit the times. Their spoken language and written language could be completely different, and unless we can find another Rosetta Stone, we could be screwed." Daniel slumped in his chair. They had come so far, only to hit a dead-end.

"Wait," Sarah said, "It isn't all that bad. We just don't

know enough. You said it before, we need a linguist. Daniel, don't give up!"

Raj, who had also slumped when Daniel pointed out their difficulty, rallied. "Yes, Daniel, do not give up. I will work on the stones from the Great Gallery next. Maybe there will be another clue."

Slowly, Daniel gained control of his sudden depression. Forming a steeple with his hands and pressing them to his lips, he gave Raj a silent nod of thanks. Sarah moved closer to him and put her arm along his shoulders, allowing him to pull her into his embrace.

"Guys, thanks. This means, wow. This means a lot to me. I can't believe I'm the one to give up, and you guys aren't letting me. Sorry."

Raj reached out his hand, and Daniel unwrapped his right one for a handshake, but Raj instead clasped his forearm. "We will see this through, never fear my friend. We are too close to give up."

"So what do we do now?" Daniel wondered.

Sarah answered. "I think it's best for Raj to do as he suggested, continue getting the database populated with at least the Great Gallery stones, and then if we haven't found the key yet, maybe those in the inner passageways, and possibly the chambers. But the Great Gallery is intriguing. It's another anomaly. No other pyramid that I know of has one. I think it's another attention-getter."

"You could be right, but what about the language?"

"I already said it. We need a linguist. Let's talk to Mark, see if he knows anyone."

Raj objected. "We cannot have too many people to keep

the secret."

"There won't be any secret unless we get a linguist to help us crack the code. I'm sure Mark knows someone who is trustworthy."

Although Raj continued to make dire predictions, he eventually had to bow to the majority. Nevertheless, he treated the other two to yet another long lecture on computer and communications security, and made them promise to adhere to his recommendations.

On the way back to Daniel's apartment, Sarah asked, "What do you think Raj would do if we sent him a text saying Code cracked, they're onto us, run?"

Daniel guffawed, "He'd probably have an accident and have to change his drawers."

Sarah giggled. "I don't want to do that to the poor man, but seriously, what is his problem?"

"I'm beginning to believe someone is after him."

Sarah smacked Daniel on the shoulder, "Don't you dare start getting me paranoid."

He laughed. "Would it make you cling to me and say 'Oh, Daniel, save me!'?"

"Oh, probably. You goof."

"I honestly don't know, Sarah, but my theory is that he has enough contact with conspiracy theorists to have a raging case of conspiracy paranoia. But it won't hurt to go along with him."

"Except that I have to dig that darned flash drive out of its hiding place in my sugar canister every time I want to use it." Sarah was referring to one of the three copies of the data that Raj had prepared, given to each of them as a backup, and then told them to hide when they weren't in use. Though everyone but Raj thought it was overkill, it was easy enough to go along with him to keep him happy.

"There is that. Maybe you should get a bushel of kidney beans, like Martha."

"Where did you hide yours?" Sarah said.

"I'm not sure I should tell you."

"Do I have to strip search you to find it?"

"Yes, please."

"Funny man. Where did you hide it?"

"Oh, all right. There aren't many places in a small apartment to hide something. I taped it to the back of my underwear drawer. There's a trick to getting the drawer out of its slot, so anyone searching probably wouldn't be able to, without destroying the chest. And if that happened, we'd know it."

"Clever. They might search the bottom, but not the back."

"Exactly. Listen to us discussing this possibility like it was something that might happen," Daniel said.

"I know, crazy, huh?"

"Let's change the subject."

"Okay, what do you want to talk about?"

"Let's talk about that threat to strip-search me," Daniel leered.

Sarah smiled a wicked smile. "You'd like that, wouldn't you?"

"What man wouldn't, if you were the one performing the search?"

"Oh, now flattery might get you somewhere."

"You fascinating, gorgeous, intelligent, sexy woman, what would you say if I told you I had hidden something you would be interested in, somewhere on my person?"

"I'd say I just might have to strip-search you."

"Oh, goody. You wouldn't happen to have hidden something somewhere on your person, would you?"

"I guess that's something you're just going to have to find out."

# Chapter 16 – A Serving Of Alphabet Soup

Daniel was winding up his explanation about what they had discovered and the problem he saw with it. Sarah looked at Mark expectantly as he stared at the floor, letting the information sink in. Finally, Mark raised his head.

"Look, I think you've jumped to a conclusion that isn't necessarily warranted. I'd like to propose that we do a few tests before we involve a linguist, especially since you say your friend is opposed to it. What do you say?"

"I'd be interested in hearing your reason for thinking our conclusion isn't warranted. If we can avoid a can of worms like an unknown pictograph language, I'm all ears."

"Okay, so here's what I'm thinking. We're assuming that this was an advanced civilization, more ancient than that of ancient Egypt, and also more advanced, maybe more than even we are. Does that give a fair assessment of your thinking?"

"Yes, I believe we're on the same page," Daniel answered.

"Then, what is to prevent them from having a more advanced written representation of their language? I mean, maybe we can assume that one of the ancient languages grew out of it, after whatever disaster made them disappear. But maybe the written language didn't survive," said Mark.

"That's an intriguing thought. Like, if we had a world-wide nuclear holocaust, all traces of our written language would disappear, but the survivors would still speak it, although they might be too busy trying to survive to think about teaching their kids the alphabet." Daniel was tapping his chin with his forefinger, his brain trying to fill in the blanks.

Mark said, "Exactly."

"Okay, suppose that is our working premise. What's next?"

"I think we have to assume that there is in fact an alphabet hidden somewhere in the numerical codes we've discovered. Let's go a little further, and say we assume the language represented, resembles an ancient form of Arabic, like Sumerian. That would be logical, as the survivors of their disaster would, as you say, still speak the language, albeit an evolving form of it, just as all language evolves." Mark was wound up, talking faster and faster as his theory took shape.

"So, we're looking for a language resembling Arabic. How many letters does Arabic have?"

"Twenty-eight, if I'm not mistaken. But, look, there could be diacritical marks and punctuation marks as well. If we include those, it wouldn't be a stretch to say the 34 that you say is the highest expression of the blocks Raj has done so far..."

"Represents an alphabet that we can eventually understand, at least phonetically," Daniel finished his thought.

"Right," confirmed Mark.

Sarah spoke up now, having mentally left the conversation as soon as the words Arabic and Sumerian were spoken. "You know, if I remember correctly, Arabic used to have more letters. Some have been dropped over the centuries, and when other languages developed out of it, others were added in the different languages."

Mark and Daniel both gave her their full attention. "Sweetheart, I didn't know you could read Arabic."

"I can't, not really. I learned that much in one of my undergraduate anthropology classes, I think."

Daniel said, "So, we should go ahead and bring in a linguist, one who specializes in Arabic."

"Wait," Mark interjected. "I disagree. I think we should

examine what we have for patterns first, see what we can come up with on our own. Maybe we'll see it has nothing to do with Arabic. I don't want to start a linguist with a misleading premise, otherwise it will take longer to find the right fellow."

"That's a good point, Daniel," Sarah agreed.

"Ok, then what should we do?"

Of course it was the mathematician who came up with a simple but elegant solution. "Let's say the alphabet is actually in the size and shape of the stone; that is, each stone represents a distinct letter, even though they were clever enough to leave a clue in the ratios to show us what alphabet to use. Or at least they thought so, not realizing maybe that by the time their message was seen, many diverse alphabets would have developed. Let's set that speculation aside, because it doesn't matter what they thought, the key is, they have written a message in the blocks themselves.

"So, what we need to do is assign a letter, and I'm suggesting it be one of the letters in the Arabic abjad, to each block, beginning with the top left block and repeating all the way to bottom right. If I remember correctly, that's the way Sumerian was written. We'll have to find out where those extra letters that Sarah mentioned belonged in the sequence, and if there are letters that sound different if they have an extra dot or tittle, we should include those."

"What's a tittle?" Daniel asked.

Mark drew breathe to answer but Sarah cut him off. "Long story, you can look it up later. Suffice it to say it's a diacritical mark, something that changes the sound of the letter, like a Germanic umlaut."

"Oh, okay. Funny word."

Mark said, "May I finish? This sequence will have to be put through all its iterations, starting with each of the thirty-four letters or symbols we come up with at the top right corner. Then we need to repeat the process from left to right and bottom to top just in case."

"Why not do the same thing reading down in columns instead of across in rows?" Sarah asked.

"We should, with the same process; right to left, left to right, top to bottom, and bottom to top."

"How about diagonal?" Daniel's question was meant to be a little sarcastic, as he contemplated the painstaking work involved.

"Good point," said Mark, causing Daniel's mouth to drop in disbelief. "Yes, have him do that, too."

"Have who do what?" Daniel asked, confused now.

"Raj. I'm thinking that he could write a fairly simple computer program to run through the data and show us the translations. We'd be able to see in moments whether any direction gives us actual Arabic words. If not, we'll select some other ancient language, one of the precursors of the Indo-European group perhaps. But my money is on Arabic, or more precisely, Sumerian language expressed in the Arabic script."

~~~

The NSA listener thought it would be best to report immediately that he'd heard what might be a code word at the home of the math professor. Fibonacci number. That plus the discussion of alphabets and ancient languages was intriguing enough when you didn't know what was going on. Assuming correctly that the person to whom he would make his report would know more, he took care to make his call before the end of his shift early in the morning on August fourth. Then he got a day off before his next shift.

Impes thought for a moment before taking action. Should he report this back to Barry, or report immediately to Septentrio? Intrigued by Barry's innuendo, he decided to let it play out a little longer. His directive to Barry was simple: Find out what the significance of the Fibonacci numbers was.

<center>~~~</center>

When Daniel spoke to Raj, after an elaborate charade where they made sure they weren't followed before meeting up, he was happy to hear that Raj thought he'd be able to write a program for their purpose within only a couple of hours. They made arrangements for Daniel to come to Raj's home, properly disguised, to see the results the following day.

When he arrived, Raj was in high spirits, spouting his usual logorrhea about aliens. Aware that calling him down for it would be of no lasting benefit, Daniel let him run his course until he calmed enough to talk about their data.

"Raj, can you show me what we've got at this point?"

"Sure! You know, we used an identifier for each block for relational queries, right?"

"Umm, yeah. Although I'm not sure I know what relational queries are."

"Don't worry about it. So, I wrote a little program to run inside the database program and deposit the block's image and an image of the sequential Arabic letters into a report. The result is a chart for each iteration. Then another program puts the Arabic letters together into one long string. Your linguist should be able to recognize if there are any words in the string, kind of like those find-a-word puzzles."

"Okay, I get it. Wow, that wasn't as much trouble as I thought it would be."

"No trouble at all, my friend. Do you want to see it running?"

"Sure! Have you run all the iterations yet?"

"No, only the top left to right bottom one, but it works perfectly. Let me show you."

Once again Daniel watched as the screen filled with symbols, only this time it was Arabic letters that meant nothing to him. He assumed they meant nothing to Raj as well, and was therefore surprised when Raj pointed out a short sequence. "This is the word for 'person' or 'human being'."

Daniel stared at Raj. "You know Arabic?"

"No, not really. I have read Nizar Qabbani in translation, and this word is a particularly beautiful shape, is it not?"

"Still waters run deep, Raj. So you read Arabic love poetry. I wouldn't have ever guessed."

Raj blushed. "Sushma is more woman than I can handle without help," he admitted. "Qabbani writes more than just love poetry. It is quite erotic." Blushing more deeply, he ducked his head. "Too much information," he quipped.

"Not at all! I'm going to have to look that up. And don't think you're going to get away with dropping that little bombshell without an explanation!"

On Friday morning, Raj walked by Daniel's desk and casually dropped something at his feet. When a few minutes had passed, Daniel dropped his pen and bent to retrieve it, along with the object that Raj had dropped. It was a black flash drive, and Daniel had no doubt that it contained the reports for all of the iterations of data strings Raj was running all week. He sent Raj a one-word text, 'Complete?' An image of a fist with the thumb up appeared in response. Great! Now they were getting somewhere. As was his usual practice, he filed his column by noon and then set out for Rhode Island, his heart singing and body tingling at the thought of seeing Sarah soon.

<p style="text-align:center">~~~</p>

On Monday, Sarah found a note on her office door that Professor Barry wanted to see her. She cataloged the possible reasons mentally, and reviewed her primary research project, which was due for publication soon. She was on track, so if this was Barry's concern, she would be able to reassure him. In due course, she presented herself at Barry's office door.

"Come in, Sarah, thank you for stopping by."

"You're welcome," she said, automatically. "How can I help you?"

"I just wanted to have a little visit. You've been making yourself scarce."

"Have students been looking for me, sir? I am keeping regular office hours, and I've missed no lectures."

"Relax, Sarah. I didn't call you in to have you on the carpet. I just haven't seen you around much, that's all. How's your side project with that Rossler fellow coming?" Barry's nonchalant manner put Sarah on alert. Always before, he had waited for her to report, and had acted as if he were interested in the latest developments.

"It's going, though very slowly," she said. "We thought we had something in the measurements of the blocks, but it hasn't panned out." It was the truth, if only partially. It hadn't panned out, *yet*.

"Well, keep me posted, will you?"

"Of course, Professor. You know of course that the Times is no longer interested in publication?"

"Perhaps I could be of assistance if you make any interesting discoveries. John Kingston is an old acquaintance. I may be able to persuade him, if the report is worthy of the university's name."

Very interesting, thought Sarah. Aloud, she said, "Thank you, sir. I'm sure Da.., I mean, Mr. Rossler would be grateful."

Now Barry was saying something else. Sarah brought herself back to the here and now.

"...good reports about your work," Barry was saying. "I want you to know that, assuming your project is on track and you'll publish on schedule, I'll be supporting you at your tenure hearing."

"Thank you, sir! I appreciate your support."

"You deserve it, my dear. Now, don't be a stranger, and keep me informed about both of your projects."

"Yes, sir. Thank you again, sir."

Sarah stepped out of the office after her dismissal, lost in thought. What could have triggered Barry's closer interest in the pyramid project? She would have to report this oddity to Daniel, and hear his thoughts.

When she had left, Barry did a little thinking of his own. Why hadn't she mentioned the Fibonacci numbers?

# Chapter 17 – The Great Pyramid Speaks

A week passed before Mark had news for them. Daniel and Sarah stared in awe at the large screen on Mark's desktop on Saturday afternoon. There, at last, was vindication for Daniel's obsession and their long search. Mark's friend had sent back word that indeed there was a message, and what a message it was! Before discussing the meaning of it, Mark said his friend had told him it bore a striking resemblance to a very ancient dialect of the Arabic family of languages. He thought it was more ancient still, and asked if they had more data, as it needed lots of work. But, he was pretty confident that the message went something like this:

**[Unknown word] traveler/person/human/man from future. [Unknown word] critical/important/significant [Unknown word] telling/story/message [Unknown word] read/browse/assimilate/learn all/ [Unknown word] everything/all here/in this place/at this location [Unknown word]**

Daniel pumped his fist in the air. "I knew it! My god, we're the first to ever see this message from at least three and a half thousand years ago! How cool is that?" He danced around the furniture in Mark's office, swinging Sarah along with him in a waltz of some creativity. For her part, Sarah couldn't stop smiling and now and then a giggle escaped her as Daniel narrowly missed some object that would have ended their dance in disaster. Finally, Daniel danced over to Mark, and let Sarah go only to throw his arms around the older man and lift him off his feet.

Mark was chuckling as Daniel set him down. "Here, now, none of that. You can sweep the lovely Sarah off her feet, if she'll let you, but have a care for an old man's dignity."

Daniel's answer was to pick him up again and give him a resounding kiss on the cheek.

"Don't you see? We've done it! We can turn it over to the experts now, let someone who knows what they're doing translate the rest of it. It's finished! We were right all along!"

Mark and Sarah exchanged a more sober glance. Sarah said, "Um, Daniel? Hang on, honey, it isn't finished."

Daniel stopped prancing around to look at her. "What do you mean?"

"For one thing, this isn't nearly enough. We aren't even sure what it says. Remember our talks when all this started? We've got to validate this with more. Mark, would your friend join our group? Help us translate more of the message?"

"Maybe. Sarah's right, Daniel. We're not ready to go public. How much more has Raj done in getting the blocks from the Great Gallery entered into the database?"

"I'm not sure. He stopped that to write and run the program that got us this."

"Let's get more data to analyze, maybe get my buddy on board, and see if we can get some more before we announce it to the world."

"Okay, if you guys say so. I'm still stoked."

"Of course you are! Now, let's see if we can figure out what this means."

After more discussion, they came to the consensus that the message said something to the effect of 'Person from the future. Here is an important message. You must learn everything about it.' With Daniel still figuratively bouncing around the room like Tigger, the other two couldn't help but join in his enthusiasm. The only thing that marred their elation was that Martha was once again out, attending her garden club meeting all afternoon. So their toast was just among the three of them this time.

Despite Mark's protestation that Martha would hate to miss them and would want them to stay for dinner, Sarah demurred. They had dropped in as unexpected dinner guests on Martha often enough, but doing it to her when she had been out all day was not an option. Instead, they went to a little pub where Sarah sometimes met her graduate students for fish and chips and a draught beer. Remembering that she had told Daniel about it before, she said, "This is where you can get that wonderful IPA I told you about."

"Great! That ought to go down well with fish and chips."

After their meal, they decided to play a game of pool, which turned into two because Sarah beat Daniel at the first game and he wanted a rematch. After the second game, there was a tie to break, so they played a third. At the end of that game, Daniel ran the balls in, one after the other, but scratched on the eight ball, handing Sarah the game by default. He thought it was a perfect outcome. So did some of Sarah's acquaintances, who had greeted her when she came in and were standing on the sidelines watching the game, flagrantly taking her side and cheering whenever she sunk a ball or Daniel missed.

"I see the way you are," he teased her as he opened her door for her at the car. "That was a totally unfair match, you had all the partisans."

"You'll just have to bring your own partisans next time," she grinned. "But I warn you, I'm a great pool player."

"You're great at everything you do, my sweet."

"Everything?" Her brow was lifted, enticingly.

"Everything," Daniel said, leaning over to kiss her as he buckled his seat belt.

~~~

They were in bed and sound asleep when the racket at the door startled Sarah awake. She sat up abruptly. "Daniel, someone's at the door."

Groggy, he answered, "Huh? What time is it?"

She turned to look at the bedside digital clock. "Good heavens, it's two a.m.!"

"Who the hell?"

Just then, the pounding started again.

"Ms. Clarke? Open up, police."

Now the pair looked at each other in alarm. Sarah scrambled out of bed and grabbed her housecoat, rushing to the door while Daniel struggled to get his pants on.

Sarah no sooner cracked the door open than two police officers shoved their way into the room, causing her to cry out in alarm. Daniel came racing down the hall, prepared to do battle. He glared at the officers.

"What the hell is all this? How dare you scare her? You'd better have a good explanation…"

One of the officers held up his hand. "I have a warrant for the arrest of Sarah Clarke and Daniel Rossler, on suspicion of murder. Are you Ms. Clarke and Mr. Rossler?"

Sarah's face went white. "M-m-murder!" she stammered. "Wh-who…" Daniel was stunned. This couldn't be happening. What the hell was going on?

The officer was still speaking. "You have the right to remain silent. Anything you say can and will be used against you in a court of law. You have the right to an attorney. If you cannot afford an attorney, one will be provided for you. Do you understand the rights I have just read to you? With these rights in mind, do you wish to speak with me?"

Sarah opened her mouth, but Daniel spoke first. "No, we do not wish to speak with you. We want an attorney. In fact, we want two. Sarah will tell you the name of hers. I will have to speak with my office at the New York Times before I can contact mine."

Sarah was looking at him with confusion. "But, Daniel, we've done nothing..."

"Shh, Sarah. Trust me, this is best." Turning to the officers, he said, "I assume you'll want us to come to the station, and then we'll be given a phone call to contact our attorneys, is that correct?"

"Been through the drill before have you?" the second officer smirked.

Daniel raised an eyebrow. "Any idiot knows that much from TV, but as it happens, I've done enough reporting on the criminal beat to know exactly what our rights are." After giving the officer a significant look of warning, he continued, "May we get dressed?"

"One at a time. You stay here with us while the little lady gets some clothes on." To Sarah, he said, "If you care for this guy, you won't try to run. It wouldn't go well for him if you did."

Indignant now, Sarah flashed him a look of contempt, then turned and marched down the hall. She would follow Daniel's lead, but when this all settled out, heads would roll. She was so angry that she didn't realize the officers hadn't told her who she was supposed to have murdered.

Daniel and Sarah rode in silence in the back of the squad car. Because they hadn't resisted arrest, and because they had already asked for lawyers, the officers were circumspect in their treatment and allowed them the courtesy of not being cuffed.

Sarah kept glancing at Daniel, hoping for a signal regarding her unanswered questions, but after whispering to her that she must answer no questions of any kind until her lawyer was with her and that there was nothing to fear in the verbal bullying, he kept his eyes straight ahead. Their hands were tightly intertwined, though, and she knew he was aware of her glances, because every time she did it, he squeezed her hand. It was very comforting, made her think that everything would be all right.

The ride was surreal. Barely able to think from being awakened from a sound sleep and the impossible events since being awakened in the middle of the night, Sarah was bewildered. The one question she wanted to ask, but dared not because Daniel had told her not to speak, was, who was dead?

When they got to the police station, Daniel and Sarah were separated without even being allowed to kiss. Their fingers clung to each other until the last possible second, as the officers pulled them in opposite directions. A last desperate glance behind her told Sarah that Daniel was standing tall and implacable. It gave her the courage to do the same. She was taken to an interrogation room and told to sit down. Then the officer left, without another word.

For a few minutes, Sarah sat, tense and shaking, expecting at any moment that another angry policeman would come and ask her questions. Or maybe, there would be two, a good cop and a bad cop. One would offer her coffee, and the other would slam his hand on the table to scare her and yell in her face. When neither of those things happened, Sarah succumbed to her weariness and slumped over her crossed arms, her head resting on her forearms, and closed her eyes. Maybe she could sleep a little. But the question circled in her brain; who was dead? Why would she and Daniel be suspects?

In another room, a preternaturally alert Daniel was also

waiting for interrogators. He, too, had wondered the same things that puzzled Sarah. But his reporter's analytical mind had the answer, he thought, and it was a disaster. Nor could he ask directly to confirm his suspicions, because that would only add fuel to the fire. If he seemed to know who, it would look as if he were guilty.

Instead of dwelling on it, Daniel went over every action he and Sarah had taken since leaving Mark's house. Was it enough? His guess was that it would depend on when the murder occurred. Next, his thoughts went to Raj. He hoped Raj was okay, and he knew he needed to get word to him. When it came time for his phone call, he would kill two birds with one stone, call Raj and ask him to get in touch with the Times. Daniel wasn't sure that the Times would defend him against a murder charge, but he was fairly confident they would send someone to check out the situation. First things first, though. He had to find a way to confirm who was dead.

~~~

Daniel was still on hyper-alert when two plainclothes officers entered the room. One introduced both himself and the other man to Daniel, and then spoke in a mild voice. "Do you want to tell us what happened?"

Daniel answered, the only thing he intended to say until a lawyer was with him, "Why don't you tell me what happened?" The officer regarded him for a moment, his face neutral. The other man melted into the background as Daniel focused on the one who had spoken.

"Professor Mark Simms was killed sometime this afternoon, stabbed multiple times. His office was ransacked. His wife found him when she came back from a garden club meeting. Naturally the poor woman called us. We know you were there this afternoon." The succinct story had no less impact on Daniel than would a hysterical and detailed account. Mark dead. As he suspected. Thank god Martha was all right, although how she would be all right after the death of her beloved was beyond Daniel to consider at the moment. He shook his head.

"I'll talk, but I want to consult my lawyer first. May I have my phone call?" His manner was calm, although the officers could see that he was laboring under some emotion. If it was guilt, the fastest way to get a confession would be to let him consult his lawyer and try to work out a plea bargain. Maybe he would give up the dame, maybe not, but there didn't seem to be any downside in letting him make his call.

~~~

Daniel dialed Raj's number from memory. It was past three a.m., no doubt the call would panic his paranoid friend, but at this point, panic may not be the wrong choice. Raj answered before the second ring had finished. "Yeah."

"Raj, it's Daniel. Are you awake?"

"I am now. What the hell, Daniel?"

"I don't have much time. Simms has been murdered. I'm under arrest but I haven't been booked yet. Call the office and get them to send a lawyer to Providence for me, precinct number four. Then get rid of your phone, I had to call from their system." Under 15 seconds, too short to trace the call. He slammed down the receiver. Raj would come through, or Sarah's lawyer could help him if not. But at least Raj had warning. Now he was prepared to wait. He raised his hand in a signal that he was done, and the officers came back in, this time trailed by another man in plain clothes, who introduced himself as James Jones. *Very creative*, Daniel thought.

"Are you ready to speak to us now, Mr. Rossler?"

"I'll wait for my lawyer, like I said already." Daniel let his heavy sarcasm convey his displeasure. "I might add that if I learn you have treated Dr. Clarke badly in any way, even made her feel bullied, I will use every resource at my disposal to bring the full disapproval of the New York Times down on you. You'll wish you were lucky enough to have a patrol beat in Southeast LA when I'm finished. Now, would you gentlemen care for a game of Texas Hold'em while we wait?" His sardonic grin expressed his opinion that he'd won this round.

The officer who had been silent until now snorted, earning a look of reprimand from his partner. Jones answered for all of them, with equal sarcasm. "I don't think so, but thank you for offering. If you don't want to talk about Simms, tell us about your research. What are you working on?"

Daniel regarded him appraisingly. "What part of I'll wait for my lawyer' did you not understand?"

He could only hope that his abrupt manner earlier had clued Sarah not to say a word, about anything, too. Taking a page from Raj's book, he didn't trust this Jones guy, and everyone knew you couldn't trust the cops. The defiant set of his chin let the others know that they would get nowhere until Rossler had seen his attorney. Without another word, they filed out, locking the door behind them. Daniel decided he might as well get some sleep, and in an unconscious mirroring of Sarah in the other room, crossed his arms on the table, put his head down on them and closed his eyes.

~~

Sarah wasn't having any luck sleeping. Fear for what was happening to Daniel, apprehension about who was dead, and anxiety about what she should say or do kept her from actually falling asleep, even though she kept her eyes closed against the too-bright fluorescent lighting. When the door opened, she jerked up with a gasp. Two officers came in. *Oh, so it's to be good cop, bad cop*, she thought.

"So, we've got your boyfriend's story, want to tell us your side?"

Sarah was baffled. Her side? She had no idea what they were talking about, but she did know that Daniel would lay down his life for her. He would never have thrown her under the bus for a crime that neither of them had committed. Straightening her spine, she gave the officer a flat, schoolmarm look and deliberately pressed her lips together.

Undeterred, the officer fired questions at her. "When was the last time you saw Dr. Mark Simms alive? Where were you between six p.m. and eight p.m. yesterday evening? What did you guys do with the knife?" With each question, Sarah's eyes grew larger and expressed more distress. Tears had started with the first question. *Oh, no. Mark. It couldn't be Mark.* An alarming thought crossed her mind and without thinking she said, "Martha? Is Martha okay?" The officers exchanged a look. That sounded like a genuine question. This woman was either a consummate actress or she hadn't had anything to do with the murder. But her question signaled a crack in the wall of silence.

"What do you think? Is she or isn't she?"

Sarah began to cry in good earnest then, holding her hand to her mouth to prevent the sobs from escaping.

"Please," she choked out.

"She's fine, except she's pretty shaken up over finding her husband stabbed multiple times and his office ransacked. She gave us your name. Want to tell me why she would do that?"

Sarah's eyes flew to his. Martha accused her of harming Mark? How could that be? She shook her head rapidly, to clear it, but the officer took it to mean no, she didn't want to talk. This pair was proving to be a tough nut to crack, but a small doubt about at least the woman's guilt crept into his mind. Maybe she would cover for the boyfriend, but he didn't think she was involved first-hand. Didn't matter though, accessory after the fact carried the same penalty. If her boyfriend were convicted of first-degree murder, she too would spend the rest of her life in prison unless she gave him up and told the truth.

"Your boyfriend has already called for his lawyer. Maybe you'd better call yours, too, before he makes a plea bargain that isn't, shall we say advantageous? To you."

The thinly-veiled hint wasn't lost on Sarah, but she trusted Daniel. Still, the sooner she contacted her lawyer, the sooner this misunderstanding could be cleared up. Sarah nodded, and a phone was brought in and plugged into the wall jack. "May I have a phone book?" she asked. Her lawyer wasn't a criminal attorney, of course, but he was the only person she could think to call locally. However, she didn't know his number by heart. It didn't occur to her until the greeting kicked in that of course no one would be at the office yet. Not certain that she would be given another call, she left a message that she was at the police station and needed help. Hopefully, someone would be in before too many hours and her lawyer would either come to her rescue or send someone that specialized in this sort of thing.

Her task complete, Sarah turned her thoughts to Martha. Tears streamed down her face as she remembered the love between her older friends. Martha alone. It didn't bear thinking of. Sarah wasn't worried for herself or Daniel, being just a little naive about the criminal justice system. Neither she nor Daniel had killed Mark, so this would be straightened out soon. But

Martha - Martha would have to live the rest of her life without Mark. Fresh sobs broke through as she thought of the loss of her friend. Mark had been like a second father to her. Who would want to kill him?

~~~

It was only an hour later when Daniel was awakened by the door to his interrogation room being opened. He sat up quickly, shaking free of any lingering grogginess. Now the two officers, the James Jones character and another man filed in, overcrowding the small room. The man he hadn't met before held out his hand for a handshake.

"I'm attorney Robert Jeffs, and I've been sent here by the Times. For now, I'm your lawyer."

"Am I glad to see you!" Daniel said, more relieved than he would have guessed he would be.

Jeffs turned to the other three men and said, "I'd like to consult with my client in private, and then we'll come to a decision about talking with you gentlemen."

With a curt nod, the lead investigator, a Sgt. Jackson gathered his colleagues and left. Daniel had qualms about the room being bugged, but Jeffs assured him that anything the police learned through a dirty trick like that would not be admissible in court.

"I don't expect it to get that far," Daniel said. "Have they told you anything about why I'm here, or about the crime I'm accused of?"

"I know the basics, but why don't you tell me what you know, and I'll fill in if necessary."

"They've told me that our friend Mark Simms was murdered sometime yesterday afternoon or evening. We were with him in the afternoon, until about five. He was alive when we left him. Then we went out to dinner. Sarah saw some friends, so I think we will be able to present an alibi there. Then we played a couple of games of pool, and went home around nine p.m. We must have gone to bed around eleven, and the cops woke us up at two."

"Sarah is…"

"My girlfriend. I stay with her on weekends, so when I said home, I meant her place."

"What is your business with Mark Simms?"

Here Daniel did not want to be quite so forthcoming, especially if there were listeners he couldn't see. "He's a friend of Sarah's. We've gotten close over the past few months. This is devastating news. I need to be with Sarah, and both of us need to see about Martha, Mark's wife. She's okay?"

"Yes, but how did you know?"

"I didn't, but no one said anything about her, so I assumed."

"All right, Mr. Rossler, I see no reason not to talk to the officers. I'll be there with you, and if they ask something improper, or pose the question in an ambiguous manner that could be detrimental to you, I'll tell you not to answer. Unless I miss my guess, we'll have you out of here before too much longer."

"Thank you. Can you find out if Sarah is okay?"

"I'll see what I can do."

Jeffs called the officers back in, and they stood uncomfortably as Jackson asked his questions. First, he made a point of putting a digital recorder on the table. "Okay if I record this?"

"Please do," Jeffs responded.

"Where were you yesterday between three p.m. and seven p.m.?"

"Until about five, we were with Mark Simms at his residence. Then we went to dinner."

"Don't you think that's a little cold? You just went to dinner after stabbing the man?"

"Don't answer that. Officer, is my client accused of the murder or not? If so, this interview is over. If not, then I take serious offense to your question. My client will not be intimidated by you; I want to make that very clear."

"Okay, you went to dinner. Do you have a receipt, does anyone at the restaurant know you? Can you prove where you were until about seven?"

"Yes, sir. All of the above. We went to a little pub where my girlfriend is known, had dinner and played a couple of games of pool. Both the proprietor and several of her friends should be able to confirm we were there."

"Then what did you do?"

"We went back to Sarah's, listened to some music and then went to bed."

The officer spoke to Jeffs. "I'll have the recording transcribed and ask your client to look it over and sign it. Do you have any objections?"

"Not as long as the transcription is accurate. I'll stay here with him to confirm that it is."

"Suit yourself."

"Who was the man in black? He looked like a spook." Jeffs asked Daniel.

For the first time since his rude awakening hours before, Daniel snorted with amusement.

"Your guess is as good as mine, but that's a possibility. Calls himself James Jones, asked me to talk about what I'm working on in my research. He gave me the impression that he worked for some government agency."

"What are you working on?"

"If you don't mind, I'd rather not say. I didn't kill Mark, a better time of death estimate after autopsy should make it possible to prove it, and that's that."

"So what interest does the spook have in it?"

"I don't know, but when we get this straightened out, I intend to find out. Would you mind checking on Sarah now? I don't know whether her lawyer has arrived, and I don't want them questioning her without one."

"Smart man. I'll check, but I can't represent her. It would be a conflict of interest."

"That's okay. I just want to make sure she's represented when she talks, and that they aren't scaring her. Poor Sarah, she's really going to take Mark's death hard."

"I'll be back in a few after I find out what I can."

"Go ahead, I'm not going anywhere."

Jeffs located the investigators and asked to see Sarah.

"Are you going to represent her, too?"

"No, but I'd like to be able to reassure my client that she's okay."

"What do you guys take us for? We're not giving anyone the third degree. But, I'm sorry, you can't talk with her. Best I can do is show you through the window that she's okay."

"I'll take that. Who is the enigmatic and silent man in black over there? What's his interest in this?"

"Name's James Jones, and he's Federal. I didn't catch the agency name."

"That's hard to believe. Didn't you check his credentials?"

"Nope. Word came down from the Captain to cooperate with him, is all I know."

"What has he said to you?"

"Wouldn't tell you if he had said anything, but as it happens, he's said jack squat. Just asked Rossler what he was working on."

"May I peek in at Miss Clarke now?"

"I'll take you."

Jeffs was led into a large dark room adjacent to the interrogation room where Sarah's head was once again on her arms. The officer entered the interrogation room and woke her up, saying, "Miss Clarke, someone is interested in knowing that you are okay. Would you please raise your head, face the mirror, and state your physical condition?"

Sarah did as he asked, saying "I am fine, although I'm tired. Please tell Daniel I'm not saying anything until my lawyer gets here. I would like some water and the ability to use the women's room, though."

The investigator said thank you, told Sarah he would send a female officer to accompany her to the ladies' and that he would get her a bottle of water. Then he left her alone again and returned to Jeffs.

"Satisfied?"

"Yes, I'll let my client know that you're treating her well. She's his girlfriend, you know."

"Figured it was that when we found them both at her place, in bed. Hot little number, isn't she?"

Jeffs' cold stare curbed the investigator's interest in discussing Sarah's sex appeal. He returned to Daniel's room and was let in.

"She's fine. Said to tell you she won't say anything until her lawyer is here."

"I did the right thing, didn't I? Refusing to talk until you were here to see it went the way it was supposed to."

"Of course. And if they release you before her attorney gets here, I'll be free to help her too if she wants."

"That would be great, thanks!"

Sarah's attorney arrived a little after eight, having been alerted by his assistant that she had left a message in the wee hours of the morning. It was true that he wasn't a criminal attorney, but he knew enough to keep her from incriminating herself until one could be arranged to defend her. He didn't for one minute believe that his client could be guilty of a major crime anyway.

Shortly after his arrival, he and Sarah had their consultation and the officers repeated the questioning that Daniel had endured, minus the provocative question that had angered his attorney. The stories were identical, except that Sarah was able to name the proprietor and those of her friends who had seen them throughout the evening.

After a consultation with their Lieutenant, the officers told Sarah and then Daniel that they didn't have enough to book them, but they should remain in town until further notice while their alibi was checked. Daniel's attorney agreed to drive them home. On the way out, the mysterious James Jones appeared and matched them step for step, again asking Daniel about his research project. Daniel stopped, bringing all of them to a halt.

"Who are you? And why are you so interested in my research? I'm a journalist, I don't have to tell you anything about a story I'm developing, and I won't unless you give me a damn good reason why I should."

"Mr. Rossler, I have reason to believe that you're investigating something that has nothing to do with a story. It would be in your best interest to talk with me about it."

"I don't think so." With that, Daniel strode on, pulling Sarah in his wake by the hand.

Sarah held it together as long as they were in public, and in the car with Daniel's lawyer, but the moment the front door closed behind them, she broke down. Sobbing in Daniel's arms, she asked, "Why, Daniel? Why would anyone kill Mark? Honey, we've got to go to Martha. They have no children! She'll need someone."

Daniel agreed, but before they went, he wanted to talk with Raj, if he could reach him. He asked Sarah if she could throw together something to eat, while he tried. Operating on only a few hours of broken sleep, he was desperately in need of coffee, and besides, giving a woman something to do was the best way to keep her mind from helplessly circling questions with no answers. Daniel was afraid that the answers they would receive were not going to be pleasant.

# Chapter 18 – Just Because You Are Not Paranoid

Raj must have rid himself of the cell phone Daniel called him on that morning, because he didn't get an answer or even a voice mail greeting. The only way to reach him now, unless he called them, would be to leave a message at one of the hidden email addresses.

Then, he called John Kingston.

"Boss, I'm in a bit of a pickle."

"So I hear. What's going on, Rossler? Do you need a leave of absence?"

"I don't think so, at least not yet. But I'm not supposed to leave town until they corroborate my alibi. Just wanted you to know why I'm not at my desk."

"I don't need to tell you that this is not the type of publicity The Times wants, Daniel."

"No, sir, I understand. But it is a misunderstanding, and it will be cleared up soon. I've done nothing wrong."

"Keep me posted. Unless I hear differently, I expect you back at your desk by day after tomorrow."

"I'll do my best, sir."

Sarah then called Barry, to ask him to send a teaching assistant to post a note that her lecture for today was canceled. Once they had taken care of obligations and choked down a piece of toast with their coffee, they dressed more appropriately and went to comfort Martha. It hadn't occurred to them that the house was a crime scene, but they were unable to get closer than two blocks away. A female officer who was guarding the perimeter kindly radioed someone inside the house, who relayed the news to Martha Simms that friends wanted to see her. It wasn't long before she appeared, walking slowly and bent over, as if she had aged twenty years. Sarah's tears started again as soon as she saw her friend. A police officer accompanied Martha to the perimeter and checked their identification before he allowed her to approach them closely.

"Ma'am, are you sure you want to see these people?"

Martha's eyes flashed as she answered with a stronger voice than Daniel expected, "Of course I want to see them! I told you they are our friends and that they had nothing to do with this."

Without another word, the officer stepped aside and allowed Martha to rush toward the pair. Daniel let Sarah take the lead in hugging Martha, but put his hand on her shoulder.

Sarah was sobbing, "Martha, I'm so sorry, I'm so sorry!" Daniel considered it fortunate that the officer had withdrawn far enough away that he couldn't hear that. He might consider it a confession.

At last, Martha stood away from Sarah's arms and gave her a severe look. "I'm sorry. I never would have given them your names if I thought for a minute they'd accuse you! They asked me who might have seen Mark after I left, and I told them maybe you and Daniel. I was so stupid!"

"No, Martha, of course you had to tell them about us. They would have found out sooner or later anyway. Honey, can you speak about it? What happened?"

"I came home from the garden club meeting, half expecting you two to still be there. When I walked into the house, everything was dark, no lights on even in Mark's study. I called out to tell him I was home, but there was no answer. So I went to his study, and, and, and…" Unable to go on, Martha broke down in sobs again.

Sarah put her arms around Martha again and said, "Don't honey, you don't have to say any more. I'm so sorry."

Martha lifted her head and made a visible effort to calm herself. "There's something you need to know. Mark's study was ransacked, and his computer was taken. I'm not sure it has anything to do with what you all were working on, but I can't help but wonder. Mark had no enemies. Please be careful, and if you have any information that will lead to the killer, please tell the police."

Daniel held Sarah's gaze over Martha's head. If what she thought was true, then they had indeed killed Mark, they just hadn't wielded the knife. Sarah's stricken face told him she had the same thought. But, what had they discovered that could possibly be worth killing for? Or did someone think they knew more than they did? One thing was certain. Martha and Raj both needed protection, and they needed to get to the bottom of the mystery, before anyone else got hurt.

~~~

By late afternoon, enough of their alibi was established and corroborated that the investigating officer let Daniel know he was free to leave town. It took every ounce of willpower he had to actually leave Sarah behind. He begged her to come with him, terrified for her safety now, but she was adamant that she had to carry on with her obligations if she hoped to get tenure. She promised to be careful, and showed him a handgun she kept in her bedside table. Daniel was both shocked and impressed.

"Why didn't I know you packed a gun?"

"It never came up, Daniel. Are you upset?"

"No, of course not, especially if you know how to use that

thing. But you're going to have to keep it with you. Do you have a carry permit?"

"I know how to use it. Daddy taught me. Remember? I'm the tomboy. I'm actually a crack shot. I don't have a carry permit, though, and even if I did I still couldn't carry it on campus."

"I want you to apply for a permit on an emergency self-defense basis. And I don't care about campus rules, I want you safe."

"Daniel, I'll be okay. I'll get a security system installed tomorrow. Please don't worry."

"My love, I would die if anything happened to you. And if I thought it was because of something I got you into, it would be by my own hand."

"Daniel, don't ever say something like that again. I got into this because I'm just as curious as you are. And now I'm pissed off. They killed my friend. I owe it to Martha to see it through, and to find the killers if we have to."

"Don't do anything crazy, Sarah. If anyone approaches you about the data, give it to them. Call the police if you feel that something is wrong. I'm going to talk to Raj, and then I'll be back as soon as I can."

"I'll be careful. Daniel?"

"Yes, sweetheart?"

"I've been thinking about that James Jones guy."

"What about him?"

"Could he be NSA or CIA, one of those, that's interested in your research?"

"Now you sound like Raj."

"Well, maybe it's true. Maybe they're interested in the pyramid, too. Someone must be. It's an open secret that you've been looking into a code or something. Prof. Barry knows, John Kingston knows, and all those experts you interviewed. What if they thought we had found out something important?"

"I think we have found something important, but darned if I know what it means or why it would be important to a spy agency."

"I still think that James Jones is a spy. I can't shake the feeling."

"You could be right. I'll bring it up with Raj, get his take on it."

"Okay, honey. Go, and be safe. I'll be waiting for you to get back."

Daniel got to New York late, and took care to examine every inch of his apartment for evidence of intruders. Only when he was satisfied that no one was there now and probably hadn't been, did he close the blinds at his windows and slide the drawer out to feel for the flash drive hidden on the back. Finding it just where he expected to, he breathed a sigh of relief and sent Sarah a text. 'Home safe, everything fine.' She would understand, he hoped, that it meant their information was safe. They couldn't afford to worry about anything the killer might have taken when they took Mark's computer. It would have been highly insensitive to ask Martha if she had checked her beans, and of course they weren't allowed into the house. Their fingerprints and other trace evidence all over the place were already proving to be a hassle for the CSI team.

The next morning, Daniel found Raj at his desk, giving the impression that he had no cares in the world. But, when they met for lunch, Raj was very agitated. It took quite a while for Daniel to reassure him that no one but he and Sarah knew of Raj's involvement, now that Mark was dead. True, Mark had known, and it was possible he had talked. But Daniel thought it more likely that the killer hadn't asked about Raj, only about Sarah, himself, and the data. He was more interested in security going forward, and he apologized to Raj for not taking it as seriously as he should have.

Daniel checked in with Kingston after lunch, only to be unceremoniously waved out of the office after a terse, "Glad you got that cleared up. Better get to your column."

It seemed to Daniel as if his real life were being lived in a dream, wherein he went to work, wrote his column and went home again, while on the side, a completely different life was playing out. Everyone was going about their own business, unaware of his drama, while within that drama, life and death events were taking place hidden from all his friends and co-workers.

He was on edge, worried about Sarah being alone and deeply disturbed that his research had stirred up something sinister. Not to mention that it had probably gotten Mark killed. Owen's pranks annoyed him now, as unrelated to his sharp focus as a yapping dog at his feet would be. After the second time he snapped at the man, Owen snapped back, "Who tied a firecracker to your ass?" he said, stomping away angry. Daniel didn't have time to regret it, but knew he would have to mend fences with his friend sometime.

That night, he took his computers and drove a circuitous route around the city to be sure he wasn't followed. At last, he arrived at Raj's door and stepped inside, anxious to know if he had been hacked.

To Daniel's dismay, and Raj's even greater consternation,

the evidence figuratively looked like a public transportation map. Both on his hard drive and on his online accounts, Daniel's accounts showed multiple access points of long-standing. Anxiously, they checked Sarah's login, especially to the SkyDrive account they had started with. It, too, had been tampered with, and the spying wasn't all recent. As they tracked the digital intruders, they developed a calendar and traced back to the first illicit entry they could find.

Wracking his brain for incidents important to the project with corresponding dates, Daniel realized that one of them was immediately after Sarah had last spoken to Prof. Barry. He remembered that she had an odd feeling about that meeting. Could Barry have something to do with it? Barry had asked pointed questions that Sarah didn't feel comfortable answering. And now she was in Providence by herself, with no way to know of their suspicions.

"Raj, I have to call Sarah and let her know about this."

"I highly recommend you do not."

"She could be in danger."

"Her phone could be bugged. For that matter, so could yours. You must get rid of it."

"Not until I've warned her about Barry."

"All right, but call from a pay phone, or a throwaway cell, for god's sake. Otherwise, you could lead them right to us."

Once, Daniel would have dismissed Raj's paranoia as ridiculous, but too many weird things were happening. He went out to find a place where he could buy a prepaid phone with the fewest minutes possible, as well as another with several hundred minutes. When he dialed Sarah's number, his message was prepared.

"Sarah, don't talk, just listen. Your phone may be bugged and I have important news. Go to an internet cafe. Check for messages," he said, placing an emphasis on 'messages' so she'd know he was talking about the hidden one at the shared email account.

"Okay." Sarah knew from Daniel's abrupt sentences that his directions were both important and urgent. She left her house immediately and drove to campus, where she parked her car and then dodged in and out of almost deserted buildings until she must have lost anyone who might have been following her. Then she headed to an all-night internet cafe close to campus, to follow Daniel's directions. Since Daniel had said her phone might be bugged, she left it at home.

Daniel gave Sarah a fifteen-minute head start and then went looking for an internet cafe himself. Since he had used his prepaid phone to call Sarah's number, it was now useless. He would leave it in a trash bin somewhere, but the other one would be usable for a while. He was getting anxious when, after nearly an hour had passed since his call; there was still no return message in the Drafts folder. Daniel was ready to jump in his car and race to Providence when, checking one last time, he found a message. 'I'm here. What's happened?'

'Computers compromised. Disconnect all your devices from internet. Get prepaid phone and call me at 212-555-1246. Be alert, you may be followed.' Daniel hated to entrust that number even to a private message in a hidden email account, but he had to be able to communicate directly with Sarah, or he would lose his mind.

'Understood.' With a sigh of relief, Daniel left the store and got on a bus for a short tour of the city. After leaving the bus and getting on a second one, he was a sure as he could be that no one was following, so he made his way back to Raj's place to talk some more and crash for the night.

Raj was impatiently awaiting his return, and highly agitated over a second shock. He had continued to trace the incursions into Daniel's computer, and had discovered an IP address that belonged to the New York Times. Someone from the paper had been spying on Daniel, since April! Daniel was an even-tempered man, seldom flew into a rage, but this was beyond his ability to remain calm. Not given to displays of temper, he went into a slow burn that threatened to break out into violence to Raj's possessions. After looking around wildly for something to punch, he settled for punching the sofa. At least he couldn't break that. When he had regained control of his temper, he asked Raj, who was watching him with trepidation, whether they could narrow it down.

"Perhaps. But it would be better if we had an idea who it could be."

"Only two choices that I see, the first two people I told about the pyramid story. John Kingston and Owen Bell. And if it's Owen, I'll never trust my judgment about people again."

"Oh, no, surely not Owen!"

"Check John Kingston first. I'd lay money it's him. Can't think of any reason for Owen to do it, at least none that I'd want to think of him."

A few minutes later, they had the confirmation: John Kingston had been freely roaming the memory of Dan's laptop since the pyramid story emerged. Why? Daniel struggled to remember the details of their first meeting. Kingston had been indifferent when he first pitched the story, but then hadn't he had an abrupt change of heart?

Now Daniel recalled that it had been only a few minutes

after his pitch that Kingston called him back and told him he had arranged a collaboration with Barry. He mentally kicked himself for welcoming that idea without protest, but if he hadn't, he wouldn't have met Sarah. The chain of events led to the death of Mark Simms, so he couldn't go down that road. We never know when a seemingly minor event will lead to big changes, he realized. And we can't be responsible for the consequences of an innocent decision. So, why did he feel crushing guilt over Mark's death?

Raj interrupted Daniel's thoughts then, with a question about the flash drives with the data and their equations on them. As far as Daniel knew, Sarah's was safe and he doubted that Mark's had been found, unless he was using it when the intruder came in. His was in his pocket. Raj wasn't happy about that.

"If they come after you, they will search you and find it."

"I was more worried about a search of my apartment, but you're right. What should we do?"

"Leave it with me, and bring Sarah's to me as well. If you can find out about Mark's and it is still at his house, bring that one also. I have a safe place for them. From now on, we must work only face to face on this. But before you move forward, I suggest we figure out who is after this work."

"I meant to talk to you about that. One of the people who tried to question us at the police station was dressed in plainclothes, looked like the ones in the Men in Black movies. Called himself James Jones."

"Daniel, that sounds like NSA, or something even more secret. What did you tell him?"

"Essentially to go piss up a rope."

"I must talk to some of my acquaintances. What are you

going to do?"

"I'm not sure. I could take a leave of absence from the Times, but then Kingston would know something was up."

"When is Dr. Simms' funeral?"

"I don't know if they've even released the body."

"Call in sick tomorrow, and go take care of Sarah. When you know the date of the funeral, take leave for that. We should know more by then. Do you have a copy of the Hitchhiker's Guide to the Galaxy?"

Raj's question was such a non sequitur that Daniel reacted physically, twisting his head and thrusting it forward while frowning.

"Do you know the meaning of the phrase 'one time pad'?" Raj asked.

"I think so. It's a type of cryptography, yes?"

"Yes. This will be an adaptation for our circumstances." Raj pulled out his copy of the book he had mentioned and made Daniel note the edition and publication date. "You must get the exact same book. When I send you a message, it will be in groups of numbers with a hyphen between each two-number code. The first number is the page number, and the second is how many letters to count to reach the letter I want you to use. But you must shift the letters like this: starting with 'a' equals eight, if the letter you count to is an 'a', count eight letters up, and write down 'h'. And so forth; 'b' equals nine, 'c' equals ten. Do you understand?"

"No one could break the code you're using unless they know the book and the key, even if they intercept your message. Yeah, I think I get it."

"It will take them a while, anyway. This will be only for long messages, or something where we have to use the word pyramid, or anything having to do with your research. Short cryptic texts will be fine, as well as short phone calls. But you must change phones often. Whenever either of us changes phones, send a message with the new number through the email accounts, but only through an internet cafe. For everything else, use your regular phones so that anyone listening won't know you're suspicious. Bring your computers to me and I'll run a virus and malware checker that looks normal but will wipe out their ability to get in again."

"Raj, are you sure all this is necessary?"

"Did you believe me before Simms was killed?"

"No."

"If you had, perhaps he would be alive still."

Daniel's heart sank. Raj was right. Too little, too late, he would nevertheless follow Raj's lead from now on.

~~~

The next few days were surreal, as Daniel arranged for a few personal days, citing a bad sinus infection as the reason. He couldn't escape the feeling that something bad would happen to Sarah if he didn't go to her, but was almost as anxious about leaving Raj. Deciding that he couldn't protect everyone, and that Raj was well-versed in staying out of sight, he followed his heart. Without returning to his apartment, he left for Providence the following morning after his conversation with Raj.

Sarah was torn between thinking that none of this could be happening to them and wanting to cling to Daniel. As a practical matter, she had disconnected both her desktop and her laptop from the internet, but doing the same with her computer at her university office proved difficult. She settled the matter by backing it up to an external drive and then avoiding its use. Whatever had been of use to the people who hacked it was compromised already, but she would give them no more.

"What about your tenure hearing?" Daniel asked.

"I'm playing it by ear," Sarah answered. "It's coming up in two weeks, and I'm ready, but I have a feeling that you and I are going to be busy trying to get to the bottom of this, or trying to survive."

Daniel, who had his arm around her, clutched Sarah to him. "Getting to the bottom of it. Surviving. There is no 'try', only do or do. Yoda said that."

With a faint smile that broke his heart because it was only a pale imitation of the one he loved, Sarah said, "I think Yoda said only do or do not."

"You should know by now that I never quote anything straight."

"True. I love you, Daniel."

"I love you, too, and we are going to be fine. We'll get through this."

Sarah called Martha from the phone in her office, not wanting to compromise her pre-paid, and learned that the funeral was planned for Saturday, as Mark's remains had been released that afternoon. Knowing they were still 'persons of interest', Sarah asked if the autopsy had pinpointed a time of death. Martha didn't know, the information had not been released to her, so Sarah called her lawyer to see if they could find out. An hour later, a return call confirmed that it had been established as between six and seven, based on the digestion of a sandwich that indicated he had been alive at least until six. The relief was palpable. Daniel and Sarah had a solid alibi for that hour, and several afterward. They no longer had to worry about the police, but the shadowy figure of James Jones was still on their minds.

~~~

Daniel spend his 'sick' days following Sarah from home to school, sometimes at her side, sometimes at a distance to see if he could spot surveillance. When he received no word from Raj, he sent a text. 'Doing okay?'

'Check email' was the answer. Daniel left Sarah at home with instructions to keep her gun at hand, and searched out an internet cafe on the opposite side of town. There he printed out a long ciphered message from Raj, and then took it home to decrypt it using the copy of Hitchhiker's Guide that he had fortunately found at an off-campus used book store. The message said: Too much to tell you in message. Can you and Sarah come this weekend? Rather than go back to the store for a long answer, Daniel sent a text, 'After funeral Sat. See you 6.'

~~~

Martha asked Daniel and Sarah to sit with her at the chapel and again at graveside, having no children or other relatives to support her. Her quiet dignity during the moving service was an inspiration, and she greeted well-wishers afterward with dry eyes and a gracious smile. Her exhaustion was apparent afterward, though, as the couple accompanied her back to her home, now cleared of the crime scene tape except for one strip that sealed the study doors. Martha's garden club had decked the living and family rooms in flowers, and members were in the process of laying out a buffet meal in the kitchen. Mark's students, fellow math faculty and other friends, as well as Martha's friends, dropped in for a few minutes or to partake of the meal, as they felt appropriate. Sarah kept an eye on Martha, who had rallied and was thanking each guest for their thoughtfulness. It wasn't unlikely that she would collapse at any moment, so Sarah stood by to pick up the pieces if and when it happened.

Daniel had spotted Sgt. Jackson among the attendees at the graveside service, and now looked for him at the house. Finding him in the kitchen with a large plate of food, Daniel took the opportunity to speak to him.

"So, I understand the time of death clears Sarah and me, is that correct?"

"Apparently. For the moment anyway."

"Then is Sarah free to leave town? I need to get her away from all this. I'd like to take her to New York with me."

"That should be okay, as long as she leaves word with us where she'll be. You should, too."

"We will. Thank you."

Daniel left the officer staring after him. It wasn't often that a suspect thanked him. He was beginning to like both of these people, despite the guy's prickly interactions with him. They seemed to have just been at the wrong place at the wrong time.

When the last of the guests had left, and the remaining food was put away, Sarah helped Martha into bed and told her to stay put.

"Take some of that food with you, dear. I'll never eat it all."

"Daniel and I have to go to New York tonight, hon. We'll take some of it when we come back, if you want. You rest. Some of your garden club friends will be back in the morning to check on you, okay?"

"Thank you, dear. I don't know what I would have done without you and Daniel here."

Sarah returned to the kitchen, where Daniel was eating a slice of apple pie. "Let's see if the flash drive is here."

They dug through the container of kidney beans where they last knew the drive was hidden, with no success. They had to believe that the data, including the translation of the initial message, was now in the hands of the bad guys. But who were they?

Carefully locking the door behind them, Daniel and Sarah left the house. At the end of the driveway, the police officer materialized from behind a large clump of pampas grass, holding his hand up as if he wanted them to stop. Daniel rolled down his window.

"Speak to you for a minute?"

"I guess."

"I assume Mrs. Simms is still alive?"

Daniel's face instantly turned red, and he reached for the door handle. This cop had just pushed the button on his last nerve, and it was time to teach him a lesson. Sarah, perceiving what was about to happen put her hand on his arm to stop him. Meanwhile, the cop realized his mistake.

Holding up both hands to placate Daniel, he said in a more conciliatory tone, "Wait, sorry. Occupational hazard. Do either of you have any idea who might have done this, or why? We're drawing a blank."

Still angry, Daniel snapped. "I don't, but I have a theory."

"What's that?"

"That your friend James Jones knows more than he's

telling you. Ask him." With that, Daniel rolled up the window and drove off, leaving the officer with a thoughtful look on his face.

# Chapter 19 – You Must Get Out of Town

Three hours later, they were at Daniel's apartment, since it was too late to call on Raj. Daniel sent him a text. 'Here.' Raj sent back 'Looking forward to our picnic tomorrow noon, fav place.' So, he wanted to keep Daniel away from his place. That made sense. Daniel told Sarah they were going to picnic with Raj the next day, and maybe he'd bring Sushma for camouflage. He was happy to see her spirits lift, but hoped that what Raj had to say wouldn't depress her again. After getting into bed beside her, he pushed her hair back from her face and gave her a tender kiss.

"It will be okay, sweetheart. It will all be okay."

In answer, Sarah turned and clutched his body to her. He felt her tremble and put his arms around her in turn. The only way he knew to reassure her that he was there for her was to hold her close until she fell asleep. It had been a long day. He wanted to make love to her, but decided she needed her rest even more than he needed the physical release. He kissed her tenderly and said, "Go to sleep, sweetheart."

The next day, a Sarah that was more like herself than she had been since the rude awakening in the middle of the night last Sunday dressed in a pretty sundress, ordered a picnic lunch from the deli on the corner, and put on a brave face. Daniel's heart was going to burst if his love for her grew any stronger. He couldn't stop touching her, squeezing her arm, trailing a finger softly along her jaw line, tugging on a lock of hair until she turned for a kiss. If the shadow of Mark's death and the uncertainty about their immediate future hadn't been there, Daniel would have been the happiest man on earth.

Their conversation with Raj would have made other picnickers very curious, if they hadn't chosen a spot that was isolated from anyone's hearing. Raj had indeed brought Sushma, who had in turn brought her little poodle along to take for a long walk while the others talked. What Raj had to tell them was a serious wake-up call. He still hadn't heard from all his contacts, as getting in touch with them sometimes took a circuitous route around obscure foreign domains. But from what he had heard, he urged the two to leave their respective homes for a while and lie low. There was talk in some circles about someone stepping up inquiries among pyramid conspiracy enthusiasts. His prognosis for how long their make-shift encryption would last was discouraging.

"You have to understand, Daniel, that these people have computing power that will be able to crack even AES encryption in a matter of hours. Our government has made it difficult in the extreme to legally distribute programs that will encrypt even to that level, and our cipher is nowhere near that powerful. All they would have to do is read one of our messages and then perform trial and error runs on computers that would put a Cray supercomputer to shame. It would take days, perhaps, but not a week."

"So you think we should make ourselves scarce until you find out more."

"Yes, I do. What makes it even more alarming, is that if it is our government that is after you, they could easily make you disappear, but recent developments mean that even more nefarious groups may know of the government's interest."

"How so?"

"You know there has recently been a major security breach, yes?"

"Seems like there's always a major security breach."

"True, but what you may not realize is that this time it's compromised US spying operations globally. Our operatives are at risk, not only from governments that are not our friends, but also from international criminal elements. Any of them might become aware of you, and your value."

"Wait a minute," Sarah objected. "What value? We don't know anything of any value."

"They may not realize that yet. They may think you've cracked the pyramid code that people have been trying to decipher for hundreds of years. That may even be why they killed Mark, because he refused to give them the key. Until we know what it is that they think you know, your lives may be in danger."

A chill washed over Daniel as he took in Raj's logic. As whacked-out as it sounded, nothing could erase the fact that Mark was dead, their data was compromised, and their safety was in question. He exchanged a long look with Sarah and she nodded. It was decided, then. They would get out of town. It only remained to decide where to go.

As Daniel and Raj continued to discuss how to continue to communicate without endangering Raj or giving away what they were up to, Sarah got an idea. "Daniel, we could go to my dad for help."

Surprised, Daniel asked, "What could he do that we can't do ourselves? Besides, it might put him in danger."

"What he does is classified, so I don't know exactly, but I do think he could help. And he'd be upset if he knew I was in danger and hadn't come to him."

"Well, I don't want him mad at me!" Daniel said. "Give him a call and see if we can come."

"No need to ask, but I'll let them know we're on the way. We need to get somewhere to buy plane tickets."

Raj spoke up then. "Wait. Don't fly out of New York.

Anyone tracking you is watching passenger lists out of here and could have someone ready to pick up the surveillance when you get there. And Daniel's right, that could also put your family in danger. Where does your dad live?"

"In Colorado. A little mountain town outside Denver. Driving there would take over a full day, even if we drive straight through."

"Then your best bet is to drive to someplace like Pittsburgh, say. Somewhere where neither of you has any connections. Get on a plane there. Pay cash, and preferably use a small carrier."

Daniel was sure that was overkill, but he wouldn't insult Raj by saying so. "We've got some planning to do. First, we're going to need a lot of cash."

"I already thought of that." Raj handed Daniel a fat envelope, which proved to be full of $100 bills. Daniel could only stare at the money blankly. Sarah took a peek, let out a small cry and clapped her hand over her mouth, her eyes flying to Raj. That broke Daniel's trance, and he asked, "Raj, we can't take this."

Raj shrugged, "I've got a few of these stashed away. Don't worry, it's mine, earned legally, and you can pay me back when you can, if you can. Take it, my friend, you're going to need it, and it's untraceable."

Daniel gripped Raj's forearm in a gesture of gratitude and friendship, unable to speak. Sarah threw her arms around Raj and hugged him hard, until Sushma, who had taken in the last part of the conversation with growing amazement and alarm, finally said, "Hey, that's my guy. Hug your own." The jest broke the intense mood, and caused all four of them to laugh.

After much discussion, they decided to keep Sarah's laptop

and flash drive with them, so they could more easily explain to her dad what they had discovered. Raj ran a few diagnostics on it and did find traces of snooping. He installed a program that would block any further attempts. However, he told her, she should still not connect it to the internet unless absolutely necessary. And even then, the flash drive must not be in it at the time.

The three of them agreed that they must go forward with the translation at any cost, since not knowing was at least as dangerous as knowing. During this discussion, Raj asked for the name of the linguist who had translated the first part. Sarah and Daniel looked at each other with consternation written on their faces. Mark hadn't said the man's name. Getting in touch with him through the University could prove dangerous to him, if it hadn't already. They would have to find another, but getting to Denver and her father's advice was first on the priority list.

Daniel and Sarah then took their leave of the others, Sarah hugging Sushma fiercely and whispering, "Take care of Raj, hon. He's very important to us."

# Chapter 20 – We Have Been Watching You

Denver International Airport was as familiar to Sarah as her childhood home, but Daniel was startled by the fantastic shape of the roofline. Made of Teflon-coated fiberglass in peaks to resemble the Rocky Mountains to the west, it was lit from within to create a surreal glow. He wondered if Raj had ever seen it, and whether the thought of alien construction might have crossed his mind. They boarded the shuttle train to the terminal with relative ease as the lateness of the hour meant fewer passengers than usual. Sarah's dad had insisted on coming to pick them up, even though it was late and Daniel thought he might want a rental car at his disposal. Ryan swept away all his objections, though, and Daniel considered it prudent not to argue with the protective dad from hell. Sarah just shook her head at him when he expressed the thought, and mildly suggested he not use that phrase in the presence of the man. He assured her that it was just his little joke, that he had the utmost respect for her dad.

Sarah spotted her parents waiting for them at the rail that separated the huge main terminal from the arriving trains. She raised her hand to signal them just as her dad also spotted her, and broke into a little trot to make her way around the railing and into his arms, with Daniel trailing a little behind her at a more sedate pace. One bear hug and one group hug with her mom joining in later, Sarah turned and drew Daniel to her.

"Mom, Dad, this is my Daniel." Her smile was radiant as she said the words.

"Of course it is," her dad observed. Grinning, he held out his hand for Daniel to shake, which he did with a firm grip.

"Well, I want a hug," said Emma. Daniel was happy to oblige. Here was a living picture of the woman Sarah would be in twenty or thirty years, and the thought took his breath away. He needed the pace of their lives to slow down a bit so he'd have a chance to properly propose to her. Daniel wouldn't rest until he knew Sarah would marry him. She would be just as beautiful as a grandmother as she was today; her mom's beauty proved it. His smile was genuine as he hugged the older woman.

"Let's get your luggage," said Ryan. Daniel was bone weary, but alert. However, Sarah was beginning to droop. Their day had started before eight a.m. in Manhattan, and it was now two a.m. in Denver, twenty hours later. Emma persuaded Sarah to sit in the back seat of the car with her for the forty-minute drive to Boulder where they lived. Maybe she could nap. That would give Daniel a chance to begin the explanations that Ryan would need before they would be able to form a plan.

As they drove away from the terminal, Daniel started right in on the story, skipping everything that he knew Sarah had shared already. Ryan knew that their research involved the Great Pyramid at Giza, and some odd coincidences that made Daniel wonder if the Egyptians of 3500 BC had actually built it. He knew they were looking for an elusive code hidden in the construction methods, the measurements or something, but the events of the past couple of weeks had moved too fast for an update. When he heard that a linguist had actually been able to decipher a message, he was astounded.

Glancing into the back seat to find that both Sarah and Emma had nodded off, he said quietly, "Sarah said that the man who was working with you was murdered last Sunday."

"Yes sir, our friend, Mark Simms a mathematician, was murdered. But he didn't decipher the message. He calculated the values and sent them to someone in the linguistics department. It was that guy who deciphered it. I'm afraid he's in danger, too, but we don't know his name."

"How can that be?"

"I guess we were so excited by the message itself that we didn't think to ask. And Mark was killed before we did think of it."

"You don't know how much he might have said before he was killed, or whether Sarah is in danger?"

"Sir, I'm operating on the assumption that everyone who had anything to do with the project may be in danger. But keeping Sarah safe is my first priority."

"I'm glad to hear it. What's your plan?"

"If you don't mind, sir, I'd like to have Sarah involved in that conversation, and we're dead tired. Can we sleep on it and take it up in the morning? I'm sure we weren't followed here."

"That sounds sensible. We're almost home anyway."

Four sleepy people made their way into the house, where Emma told Sarah her old bedroom was ready for her, and showed Daniel to the guest room. He would have liked to be able to hold his Sarah and make her feel safe as she went back to sleep, but he respected her parents too much to blatantly sleep with their daughter in their house. He just hoped Sarah felt safe because she was at home. Morning was going to come much too soon, in any case, so he made himself as comfortable as possible in the strange bed and dropped off instantly.

Ryan had spent about half an hour thinking about the situation before going to sleep. His judgment of Daniel was that he was a solid man, not given to flights of fancy or bombast. If Daniel thought there was genuine danger, he, Ryan, would proceed accordingly. He had a few ideas along those lines, but he wanted to discuss it, both with Daniel and Sarah and with his brother, before he did anything. Ryan set his alarm for eight a.m. It wasn't enough sleep, but on the off chance that Daniel and

Sarah had left a trail, they needed to be prepared.

When his alarm went off, he left Emma sleeping and knocked softly on Daniel's door. Ryan approved when it was answered immediately. Good, the boy was awake and alert. His opinion, already high, notched up a bit.

"There's coffee in the kitchen if you want it. I'm going to wake Sarah."

"Yes sir, thank you."

Daniel had both his and Sarah's coffee ready when she appeared trailing Ryan. "Thank you, honey."

He risked a chaste peck on her cheek, though he wanted to hold her tight and kiss her properly. "You're welcome, sweetheart. Mr. Clarke, I didn't know how you like yours, I'm sorry."

"No need to be sorry, of course you didn't. And please, call me Ryan."

Fortified with their coffee, Ryan signaled that he would like to talk outside. The crisp October morning held just a hint of fall but the snow-covered peaks nearby spoke to the imminence of winter. Sarah, who had come out in her nightgown, robe and slippers, went back into the house for a shawl to throw over her shoulders. When she returned, Ryan spoke first.

"Sarah, how much of Daniel's story did your mom hear last night?"

"I'm not sure, Dad. I think just the part where he reminded you of everything I had already told you. She went to sleep before I did, and I was asleep before we hit 87." She was referring to the highway between the airport and Boulder.

"Okay. Until we figure this out, please don't alarm her. She knows something's wrong, but not the extent of the danger."

Daniel interrupted, "So you agree that there is danger."

"Absolutely, and I'm afraid even you aren't aware of what you may be facing. I suggest we have breakfast, and then we should go visit your Uncle Luke, Sarah."

~~~

When they went back inside, Daniel called the office, since he was already late for work and wouldn't be making it in.

"John, I need another couple of days."

"You're pushing it, Rossler. What is it now?"

"You remember about Mark Simms, right? Sarah Clarke's friend that got killed and we got picked up for it before they checked out our alibi? He was buried on Saturday, and I have to stay a few more days to support Sarah and also Martha Simms, the widow, who has no family."

"Ok take a few more days, but I'll see you on Wednesday.

Thank you, I'll work from here so my column won't be late, okay?"

~~~

After the breakfast, which was heavy enough to make Daniel want to go back to sleep, but delicious for all that, he and Sarah cleaned the kitchen and then they were ready to go. Ryan had been pacing for the past fifteen minutes. While they cleaned the kitchen, Sarah filled Daniel in on her Uncle Luke and Aunt Sally, for whom she was named.

"They never had any children, so when my sister and I visited they spoiled us shamefully," she said, smiling fondly at the memories. "It was always exciting when they took us to the Smithsonian or the Baltimore aquarium or the National Zoo."

Daniel was puzzled. Sarah was talking about people who lived near Washington, DC. Luke had to live nearby. Seeing his confusion, Sarah explained that her uncle had been employed by the government, something to do with Foreign Affairs, she thought, although she wasn't clear on exactly what he did. On retirement, he and his wife had moved to the area to be nearer Luke's only family, his brother.

Now he lived on a little hobby farm, about fifteen miles out of town. He and Sally led a quiet life, gardening, raising chickens and keeping a couple of cattle, a few pigs and some horses for riding. Uncle Luke always said that when the zombie apocalypse happened, he'd be ready to head for the hills and be independent. Daniel snorted when she said 'zombie apocalypse'. He didn't think she paid any attention to pop-culture stuff like that. His Sarah never ceased to amaze him.

Meanwhile, Ryan had called Luke and told him that Sarah was in town and would like to see him. Exercising caution that would have made Raj proud, he didn't mention any of the trouble. Luke said he and Sally would be overjoyed to see their niece and her friend. He made a joke about making him disappear if he wasn't up to snuff, and Ryan laughed with him, but then said he was sure this one was a keeper. They made arrangements to have lunch and then spend the afternoon there, pending Emma's approval. Ryan had no doubt that she would approve, once he was able to bring her in on the real reasons for Sarah's visit.

In due course, they arrived at Luke's farm and introductions were made all around. Sally offered coffee, and Daniel was particularly grateful. He and Sarah were operating on less than four hours' sleep, not counting the cat naps in the plane and on the way to Boulder from the airport. Ryan waited only until he could see that Daniel had finished his coffee before he suggested that Luke show them the newest foal. The three men made their way outside, while the women stayed behind to gossip. Sarah wanted to see the foal, but she knew Aunt Sally was dying to ask her about Daniel.

"He's a dreamboat, honey," Sally said, smiling fondly at her favorite niece.

"That he is," Sarah agreed.

"So, how did you meet him? What does he do? Tell me everything."

Sarah was certain that her mother would have already told Aunt Sally much of what she wanted to know, but she was more than happy to talk about Daniel.

"He's a columnist for the New York Times, in archaeological subjects, and that's how we met," she said, going on to explain the original story project and how she became involved.

"So how did it go from that, to you two being involved?"

"Well, the more I worked with him, the better I liked him. He tells these outrageous jokes. Quips, really. Like, he'll start out with a well-known saying, and by the time he's finished it's all twisted around and makes a weird kind of sense that just makes you laugh."

"Oh, I love a man that can make me laugh. That's what has kept Luke and me together through thick and thin, even when it got rocky."

Sarah's mother looked surprised and interjected, "I didn't know you and Luke ever had problems. Why didn't you tell me?"

"Oh, Emma, it was all about his work, and you know I can't talk about that."

"Of course."

This exchange piqued Sarah's interest greatly. "You mean, Uncle Luke's work is classified too?"

"Yes, dear, some of it. But that's all behind us now. Since his retirement I haven't had to worry about that. Tell me more about Daniel."

Sarah prattled on, talking about Daniel's interests that intersected with her own, especially the hiking they both enjoyed. She also told what she knew of his family, and that she was sure he was closer to his paternal grandparents than to his own folks, though he seemed to love his parents. She talked about his grandfather's career, and how sweet his grandma was. By the time she wound down, Emma and Sally felt they knew him almost as well as Sarah did. And they liked him, very much. He seemed perfect for Sarah.

"I hope he's good in bed, dear. Otherwise he seems perfect."

Sarah was thunderstruck. Of all the subjects to bring up, this wasn't one she would have expected, especially from the normally circumspect Sally. Sarah wouldn't have answered, but she noticed her mom was looking at her expectantly.

"Really, Mom, Aunt Sally. You can't expect me to answer that!"

Emma said, "I'm sure Sally feels the same way I do, honey. We just want you to be happy."

Her cheeks flaming, Sarah muttered, "I'm happy, okay? Jeez."

Sally laughed and said, "I knew it!" To Sarah's utter amazement, the older women shared a high five. She just hoped Mom wouldn't blab to Dad. He and Daniel were getting along so well.

While the women were having this interesting conversation, Ryan brought Luke up to speed with a succinct recitation of the events that brought Sarah and Daniel to the area. Luke had a lot of questions, but to Daniel's surprise, they centered not around his research or the message they found, but around the police questioning, and especially his observations of the mysterious James Jones. It worried Daniel that Luke's face took on more and more concern.

"Luke, I can't help but see that you're worried about this. Mind telling me why?"

"I have some ideas about who that might be, but I'm going to need a few days to run it down. Suffice it to say, I'm certain you were right to come here, and that there is some danger. I can't say more."

Daniel gazed at him steadily, trying to read what was behind the mask of Luke's poker face. He was about to ask a specific question, when Ryan said to Luke, "I think he deserves to know."

At a nod from Luke, Ryan explained. "My brother is ex-CIA. If he thinks he knows who this Jones character is, chances are its black ops stuff."

"I was afraid of that," Daniel responded grimly. "Rather, that Jones wasn't on the level. Sarah said that you were involved in something classified, Ryan, but she didn't mention her uncle's background."

Luke broke his silence then. "There was never any need for her to know. She was just a little girl, and then I retired. I was an analyst, and I still do a little consulting. Obviously I don't know everything about what's going on today, but I have some contacts. I think I can find out."

"I'd be grateful," said Daniel. "We can't keep running, this is disrupting Sarah's life too much. She has a tenure hearing at the end of the semester."

"What about your own work?" said Luke.

"Don't worry about me, I'll work it out. But we have to make things safe for Sarah. I'm so sorry I got her into this mess. Thank goodness she has a light teaching load this semester, so we could cover for her being gone for a couple of days."

Ryan put his hand on Daniel's shoulder. "From what I can see, son, she walked into it with eyes wide open. No one could have predicted this. You did the right thing by bringing her home, and we'll help you keep her safe. But, you'd better stay safe, too. She'd never forgive me if we managed to protect her and not you."

"Thank you, sir. That means a lot to me."

Luke observed this exchange with satisfaction. He was happy for his niece that she had found a good man to love and who loved her. Now he spoke up. "What's the plan? Do we need to tell the women?"

Ryan said, "I think we have to. Everyone needs to be careful for the next little while, even out here in Colorado." Daniel sincerely hoped that he hadn't led trouble to the door of these people. Not only were they Sarah's loved ones, but he liked them a lot himself. They headed back to the house, without ever getting to see the foal.

They found the women setting out a lunch fit for an army. Daniel remarked to Sarah that they'd better get some hiking in if her mom and aunt insisted on stuffing him full of delicious food like that. Sarah arched her eyebrow at him and responded that he wasn't being held at gunpoint to take such large helpings.

"A reporter marches on his stomach," he quipped.

Luke waited until lunch was over and cleared away before signaling that they should all join him in his study. Sally frowned at his manner, as he had turned very serious and was making small talk that had nothing to do with his actions as he herded them in. The last thing he did before joining them was open and then close the back door, as if they had gone outside. Now Sally was on alert. This was too much like old times, including the small device on his desk. What was going on? She didn't have long to wait.

Ryan began. While Sarah booted the laptop that she had brought in unnoticed earlier, Ryan once again summarized the project. When he was done, Sarah demonstrated the technique that had resulted in the message being translated by the linguist. Emma and Sally attended carefully, although they were still clearly puzzled by Luke's behavior. After they exclaimed excitedly over the message, Luke took over the narrative.

"Shortly after their colleague and friend Mark Simms showed them the message, he was brutally murdered." He had to pause while Emma and Sally cried out. "They were implicated because they had been there only minutes before," this time Emma moaned, overcome with belated fright for her daughter. When she had brought herself under control, Luke continued. "Fortunately, they had an alibi and were cleared, but we have reason to believe that the message or whatever other message lies coded in those stones, is of interest to someone who doesn't mind killing to keep it from being made public."

Sally had grown very quiet, knowing what this would mean, but Emma's little scream of protest took her husband to her side to comfort her. Determined, Luke plowed on. "I'm going to call in some favors, see who this James Jones character is, and get whatever information I can from the division that studies ancient history for modern implications."

At this, Daniel looked at him sharply. This was new to him.

"Yes, Daniel," Luke went on. "Very likely this group has been monitoring your research. They know there's information that has been lost over time, and periodically it turns up. If it would be dangerous to the US for others to discover it, they're tasked with covering it up." Daniel's jerk of surprise didn't faze him. "They keep track of researchers and archaeologists to get warning when anything like this turns up and looks like it might lead to more. I have no knowledge of how they make sure it doesn't get out these days, but as I said, I have some contacts that can probably help us."

"What's our role in this?" Daniel asked.

"I think the best thing would be for the two of you to go back to work and pretend that you have given up the research. If you want to work on it, make sure you do it in such a way that your tracks are covered. I'll give you some pointers before you leave. Meanwhile, I'll look into it and get back to you."

It wasn't an entirely satisfactory plan as far as Daniel was concerned. For one thing, it left Sarah on her own with no physical protection. He said so.

"Sarah's an excellent shot, and if I'm not mistaken, she still has a pistol I gave her on her eighteenth birthday," Ryan remarked.

Sarah made a 'told-you-so' face at Daniel, who was still not certain he approved of a gun anywhere near his beloved, even if it were hers.

In the end, they decided it was the only practical solution. If they disappeared from work, not only would it raise suspicion among the very people they hoped to avoid, but their funds would soon run out as well. Besides, it would only be a few days, they thought, before Luke could get some information.

~~~

Later, back at Ryan and Emma's place, Ryan put Emma to bed with a headache tablet and then once again summoned the young people to a conference outside. Swearing them both to secrecy, he revealed his business to them. Although he didn't have one at hand, his company manufactured a counter-surveillance device that was small, portable and powerful enough to disrupt listening devices at a distance of about ten yards in circumference. Luke had used his that afternoon when letting the two older women in on the secret. Daniel's sense of humor warred with his need to be serious and not offend Ryan, but eventually overcame his ability to behave. "Like a cone of silence?" he asked.

"What?" Ryan's voice revealed he didn't remember the series.

"Like Maxwell Smart," he explained. "He and agent 99 had a cone of silence. Okay, I guess you had to be there," he added, abashed. Then Ryan's memory kicked in and he laughed.

"Not exactly, but good analogy." He went on to tell them that he would pick one up from his lab the next day for their use.

Their plan was to spend just the next day in Colorado, and get Sarah back to her classroom in time for her Tuesday lecture. That should give Luke time to reach out to his contacts and maybe it would all be over after that.

# Chapter 21 – The Langley Connection

Luke wasted no time in putting out feelers among his friends who were still actively on duty in the CIA. Without going into detail, he called each one, made small talk, and then as if it were a bit of a joke, asked if they had heard anything unusual about aliens, pyramids or Atlantis lately. Most took it as a joke and laughingly told him no, nothing that the nutcase conspiracy theorists hadn't beaten to death already. Only one responded seriously. "Not on the phone," he said.

With that corroboration that something may be on the radar of the CIA, Luke made plans to fly to Washington, DC for an in-person talk with his friend. He left on a red-eye flight that would get him in early on Monday morning, while Daniel and Sarah were still in Boulder, hoping to be back before they flew out the next day.

Luke arrived in DC at midmorning, and a taxi deposited him near the George Bush Center for Intelligence in Langley, VA, CIA headquarters. Finding himself back in his old stomping grounds made him slip easily into the field craft that had kept him safe during his years as an active agent. Even when he had 'come in' and become a desk-bound analyst, he practiced hyper-awareness of his surroundings. Thus, he was both annoyed and alarmed when his contact failed to show up at the planned meeting place.

After more than half an hour, Luke decided that something had kept his contact, and that he should just have lunch and make another call. Just in case, he would buy a throwaway cell phone, but even so he couldn't risk more than a few seconds on the call. He knew as well as the next man that all calls to CIA headquarters and even to the employee's personal cell phones were monitored.

Luke chose an open-air deli for his lunch, a favorite from

his years in the area. It was close enough to GBC that he could monitor the comings and goings from the main entrance. Of course, there were other entrances, and exits, but this was the most convenient to street traffic, and therefore the most likely to be used by his contact. Nevertheless, an hour later he still hadn't seen the man. It was time to secure transportation and a place to stay for the night. Given the circumstances, he called Sally and told her not to expect him home for several days, asking her to pass the message to Sarah. This looked to be more complicated that he had at first believed.

Two days passed with the same frustration. He had called the man he was there to see on his personal cell phone in the afternoon on Monday, saying only his phone number without the area code. A few minutes later, his man called from a pay phone.

"Sorry, Luke, I got tied up. Try it again tomorrow?"

"I'll be waiting."

But the following day was another no-show. This time, the call came in only half an hour after the planned meeting time.

"Not sure I'll be able to get together. Something's going down."

"Our subject?"

"Not sure. I'll call."

And with that cryptic message, Luke had to be satisfied until the next call came in. At least he now had a rental car, and could cruise around town, maybe see some old friends that had nothing to do with the CIA. On the morning of the third day, he called several friends to see if they were available for a visit, or to have dinner with him. He was between calls when the new cell phone rang. His friend sounded out of breath.

"No time. Forget this, can't talk. Go home."

The call was disconnected before he could protest that he couldn't forget it, couldn't go home, because it involved his niece. The instant redial reached a number that had been disconnected. Frustrated, he considered throwing the phone across the room, but decided it may still come in handy, so he curbed his temper. He would have to start over to find someone who could tell him something.

As Luke pulled into traffic later that evening, he was looking forward to seeing his old college roommate for dinner. When he had called that morning, Jack's wife Cindy insisted that he have dinner with them. Luke had been the best man at their wedding, and their long friendship had kept the two couples close over the years. As frustrating as this trip had been for the purpose of information gathering, at least he would be able to see his old friends.

He had booked a flight home tomorrow, since he was stymied at every attempt at finding someone to talk to him about Daniel and Sarah's research, or about the murder of her colleague. Bitterly disappointed at his failure, what he needed now was a chance to think about something else—anything else—for a few hours.

At the first red light he encountered, his calm was shattered by a quiet voice in his ear. "Hello, Luke."

"Holy shit!" he exploded. "Son of a bitch, who are you?" The light had turned green and the motorist behind him had already honked impatiently. Without waiting for an answer, he drove forward and pulled over. The face that he could now see in his rearview mirror was as familiar to him as his own.

"David!"

"Keep driving, Luke, and don't look back."

"Got it. What are you doing here, trying to give me a heart attack?"

"You're slipping, pal. You didn't look in the back seat."

"You've got me there. Seriously, David, what the hell?" Although his heart rate had returned to normal, Luke was annoyed, both with himself and with his old friend and colleague. Surely there would have been a safer way to get in touch with him. Luke thanked his lucky stars that David had at least waited until they were stopped at a traffic signal, otherwise there might easily have been a traffic accident.

"I hear you've been asking about something on the down-low over at the Shop." David's voice held a slight question, as if he was waiting for Luke to confirm or deny.

"Where'd you hear that?" Luke's neutral tone of voice belied his consternation that his inquiries had caused talk.

"Doesn't matter. Listen, I think I can help you, but you've got to keep this under your hat. No talking to anyone but me, got it?"

"Got it."

"Good, now listen, don't talk."

Luke suppressed his almost automatic 'okay' and waited. David's voice was hypnotic as he began.

"Luke, we think we have a mole in the division that looks into all this X-Files type stuff. You knew that we did that, right?"

Luke did have an idea that a division of the CIA was tasked with investigating every new lead, no matter how far-fetched, that had security implications for the United States. He had heard some crazy rumors, such as they were experimenting with remote viewing and psychic control. As unbelievable as it was, the movie

'Men Who Stare at Goats' was based on a true incident that was later repeated and brought about a huge study of paranormal powers. What it had to do with the Great Pyramid, he didn't know, but hoped to soon find out. He nodded.

Receiving the non-verbal affirmation, David went on, "I can't emphasize enough that if your questions come to the notice of the mole, it could jeopardize you and your wife, as well as our investigation. You talk to no one, and I mean no one, except me."

The veiled threat to Sally got Luke's attention in a way that little else could. He cocked his head, in a signal that he needed more.

"You're wondering what this has to do with your niece's research?" Luke jerked, causing the car to swerve. How did David know anything about Sarah, even that she was his niece?

"I can see you're startled, so I'll explain. We've known for a long time that there is information hidden in ancient texts and other places, lost to the world. Some of it is dangerous in the extreme, and when it turns up, we have to suppress it. I think you were at least partially aware of that." David paused for Luke's nod.

"To keep abreast of discoveries, we have informants and in some cases undercover operatives in all the best archaeology departments in the world. Needless to say, we're aware of the buzz in academic circles about anomalies and coincidences in the Great Pyramid at Giza. We agree with Daniel Rossler that there is a message hidden there, and in fact we've been aware of that for years. But despite our best efforts, we haven't been able to crack it." Luke was no longer capable of being shocked that David also knew about his niece's boyfriend. But this information was going a long way toward explaining what they had gotten themselves into. How to get them out of it was high on his priority list. He continued to listen without speaking as David went on.

"What you may not know is that we believe there are many such messages, from pyramids in the New World to the moai on Easter Island and other such monuments. But, we have reason to believe that the message in the Great Pyramid holds the key to all the others. It's of critical importance to us to discover what that message says first, so that if it's a national security issue, we can suppress it, or at least keep it out of the hands of the bad guys. Does that make sense?" Once again, Luke only nodded, not wanting to stem the tide of no doubt classified information that was reaching his ears.

"Okay. So it should also make sense that we flag everyone for domestic surveillance who starts asking questions about the Great Pyramid, whether academic, student or reporter. We monitor their phone conversations, internet activity, email, everything. It all goes to our friends and neighbors, the NSA, for execution and interpretation. Your niece and her boyfriend have dropped off the grid, after some very provocative communications. Want to tell me about that?"

"Why don't you tell me? You seem to have more than I do anyway."

"Very well. Your niece's department head is one of our undercover operatives. She may not know, but he's not only an expert in his archaeological field, but also an expert linguist. Shortly after he reported a breakthrough in her research with her boyfriend, a known associate of hers was killed and she was considered a suspect for some hours, along with Rossler. As I said, we believe there is a mole in the department, and that he's looking to find the answer first. Your niece is in danger."

For the first time, Luke was unable to suppress his need to speak. "Do you have any suspects?"

"Not specifically. We do know of an organization that seems to parallel our research, but they're too slippery to pin down. Sometimes, we discover that something we want to quash has already been suppressed by someone else. They don't leave tracks, more like holes where something is supposed to be. We do think they aren't good guys."

"That's terrifying, man," Luke exclaimed.

"Tell me about it. At various times, we've suspected mythical organizations like the Illuminati, all the way to big pharma and oil companies. They're well-established, well-funded, and elusive as hell. We can't even discover anything that's illegal. Whoever they are, we now suspect that one of them is also one of us."

"So, what does all this mean for Sarah? Can the Company protect her?" Luke's agitation was beginning to get the best of him. This was bigger than he had suspected, too big for Ryan and him to handle on their own.

"Not much. If they see us sniffing around her, they'll know their cover is blown, at least partially. The best I can do is meet with your niece and her boyfriend discreetly, give them some pointers, and try to convince them to let this go. It will have to be arranged carefully, though. In person only."

"I understand. Give me a day to see them, set something up. How can I reach you?"

"You can't. I'll text you on your new toy."

With a chill across his shoulders, Luke knew that his throwaway phone was already compromised. But David seemed to think it was safe to use, so he would follow instructions. David was an old and trusted friend, and would never betray his trust. After all, he had saved the man's life twice when he was still active. David was saying something about dropping him off. Oh, at a Metro station. Fine, and also fine that he should continue his evening as planned. Only a few minutes late, he pulled into Jack and Cindy's driveway, prepared to feign a carefree retirement when they asked him what he was up to.

~~~

Back in Providence Sarah paid Martha a visit to see how she was doing.

"I'm fine, dear. Of course I miss Mark terribly, but he wouldn't want me to pine away. You know that."

"You're right, Martha. He'd want you to be happy."

"I think happy might be a stretch, for a little while. But I'll get there. By the way, Sarah, there's something I need to give you." Martha handed her a small black object. Sarah looked at it in wonder. The flash drive! Why in the world hadn't Mark given that up? Then she realized that he probably would have been killed anyway. It had been such a senseless attack. One thing was certain, though. If they hadn't gotten what they were after, the bad guys would still be after Daniel and her.

~~~

Luke changed his flight arrangements at the airport the next morning, hoping to catch the next commuter shuttle to New York. From a pay phone, he called Sarah and asked her to meet him there and bring Daniel. Then he called Sally to let her know he would be delayed one more day and sat down to wait for the flight. He would arrive in New York before Sarah, as the flight was less than an hour, but it would give him time to replenish his wardrobe, which hadn't been packed for this long a trip. Engrossed in his planning, Luke was completely unaware that his face betrayed his worry, and that a watcher took note of it.

It was a weary and bedraggled uncle who greeted Sarah with a hug at the Little India restaurant where Raj and Daniel usually met. Daniel took in his appearance and grew concerned, but Luke waved it off as jet lag. Raj had declined to join them, and Daniel couldn't blame him. As far as they knew, Raj's involvement had not been discovered, and there was no reason to risk discovery now. They would fill him in later. After placing their late lunch order, Daniel and Sarah gave Luke all their attention.

It took Luke a while to get through the information David had shared, punctuated as it was with Sarah's little cries of dismay. Both of them were thoroughly shaken when he told them that their actions had been observed by the CIA from the beginning. Daniel muttered something about Raj being right all along, who could have thought that?

They took the news even more badly that they were now possibly targets for some shadowy organization that apparently had all the resources and power they needed to get whatever they wanted. Simms' murder took on a newly sinister cast, as if it hadn't already been bad enough. Daniel was almost beside himself with rage when he put it together that his editor had put not only him but also Sarah in harm's way by involving him with Prof. Barry, who then involved Sarah to keep an eye on him. Luke and Sarah calmed him with difficulty, Luke because he didn't want to call attention to them in the restaurant, Sarah because she recognized the murderous intent in Daniel's eyes from the policeman incident.

"What now?" Daniel demanded.

"I think you should meet with my contact, David, and listen to what he says," Luke said calmly.

"Is he going to tell us to stop the research?"

"He may. Or, he may want you to turn it over to his

department. Either way, I hope you'll do what you must to remain safe, and especially to keep Sarah safe."

Abashed, Daniel drew Sarah closer to him in the booth. "Of course. Sarah's safety is the top priority."

"But, Daniel," she said. "We're so close."

"Maybe we can take it up later, sweetheart. This is too much to deal with. I can hardly take in how close we've already come to disaster. What if Martha had been at home when they came for Mark? What if you had been there? I can't risk it."

The stubborn set of her mouth told Daniel that Sarah hadn't yet uttered her last word on the subject, but for now she was quiet.

"Luke, thank you for digging this up for us," Daniel said. "We'll take it from here."

"All right, but give me your cell phone numbers so that David can get in touch with you."

After exchanging cell phone numbers, the three finished their lunch and then Daniel and Sarah dropped Luke off at LaGuardia for his well-deserved trip back to Colorado and Sally's arms. Since it was already Thursday afternoon, Sarah had come prepared to spend the weekend. They would see Raj, have a nice evening, and then Daniel wanted to finally show Sarah Black Rock. They planned a hike and picnic lunch for the next day.

By mutual consent, Daniel and Sarah avoided the subjects of pyramids, spy agencies, murder and mayhem for the rest of her visit. Until Luke's friend David called, they would do nothing more on the pyramid research, although Raj continued his data entry and rendering tasks. Saturday morning dawned warm and sunny, a beautiful day for a hike. They picked up their usual picnic lunch at the corner deli. By nine a.m., they were on the road toward

Cornwell, where he had last hiked with his friends almost a year ago. Daniel reflected on the events of the past six months as he drove.

Without a doubt, it had been the most intriguing, frustrating and yet the happiest few months of his life. No matter what else happened, even if he had to give up the quest to interpret the message of the pyramid, he had Sarah. Meeting and falling in love with Sarah was the most important thing that had ever happened to him, or ever would. A surge of adrenaline poured through him as he thought of the life they would make together, and he reached for her hand. Sarah looked over at him, then. He could feel her loving gaze on his face as he negotiated the curves in the road. With her by his side, he could be happy under any circumstances.

Later, the two would stand at the summit of Black Rock, taking in the grandeur of the valley below and the mountains further in the distance, and know that their love was perfect. There would never be another man for Sarah, nor another woman for Daniel. Yet, in the midst of their happiness, was the sorrow for Martha's grief, and the knowledge that someday, hopefully far in the future, one would be without the other. All they could do was vow to make every day until then count.

That philosopher and poet of ancient China, Lao Tzu was right when he said, "If you are depressed, you live in the past. If you are anxious, you live in the future... If you are happy ... You live in the present."

# Chapter 22 – The Linguist

Thoroughly shaken by everything that had happened and all they had learned in the two weeks since Mark's death, Daniel took Sarah to Raj's to talk about what they should do before she left. In his pocket was the small device, about the size of a cellphone that Ryan had given him for this type of meeting. Because it was classified, he said nothing to Raj, but he had it switched on before they knocked on Raj's door.

To his surprise, both Raj and Sarah advocated continuing the research. Raj put his arguments forth with more passion than Daniel had ever seen him display.

"My friend, we must not let the forces of evil deter us. We are too close to learning the secrets that have been hidden for thousands of years. Don't you realize what it would mean to my research? A final confirmation that we are not alone in this universe, that ancient visitors have helped us along!" Sarah nodded her head as he spoke, until he got to the part about extraterrestrials. She wouldn't go that far.

"Honey, we've already had this conversation, right after Mark's funeral. We agreed then that it's more dangerous not to know than it is to know. At least we'll understand what they're after," she said. "And what's more they still don't have the data which they were looking to get from Mark so the only place they can get it is from us."

"But, we don't have a linguist," Daniel protested.

"I have an idea about that, if you agree. There's no reason to believe anyone would suspect your grandfather of conspiring with us. What if we asked him if he knows of anyone, or could find someone through his cronies?" Sarah was only a little concerned about danger to Nicholas and Bess. Not at all, really. A retired archaeologist shouldn't be a threat to anyone, and maybe he even knew of a linguist without having to ask around.

"All right, suppose for the sake of argument that he did know of someone, and that they agreed to help us, even though the last guy that saw a translation of only part of the message got murdered," Daniel said, pausing for effect. "What would we do with it once we had the whole thing? Who can we trust not to kill us for it? Sarah, Raj, it's too dangerous."

"I disagree," said Raj. "Before, you were not taking me seriously and did not take adequate precautions. Now you must be even more clever." Daniel thought about the device in his pocket. With it, he could communicate in person without fear of being overheard. Maybe this would work after all.

"We need to see Grandpa in person, then, Sarah. We can let him in on the email ruse when we do, but we can't risk any talk over the phone. My grandparents are old and vulnerable. I can't risk them, either."

Sarah said, "I understand. Hey, I don't have a class until Tuesday afternoon, do you want me to go with you? We can make it a day trip this time, and I'll spend the night back here with you, then get an early start for Providence Tuesday morning."

"I guess that would work."

On Monday morning, Daniel and Sarah set out for Little Egg Harbor, arriving mid-morning. Bess answered the door, and gave a little scream of surprise and pleasure to find her grandson and his girlfriend on her front porch. With rain threatening, she drew them inside and called for Nicholas.

"Hi, Grandpa," Daniel said, as the old man came out of his study.

"Well, I'll be damned, look who's here!" Looking from Daniel to Sarah, his analytical mind, keen as ever, took in their tense posture. "What's happened?"

"A lot, Grandpa, and we need your help. Can we sit down and talk?"

Bess immediately offered coffee and cookies, and Sarah went to help her in the kitchen while Daniel settled his grandpa in his favorite chair. "If you don't mind, let's wait for Sarah, and I guess this concerns Grandma, too," Daniel said.

As soon as the women were back with the tray of refreshments, Daniel brought his grandparents up to speed on recent developments, absorbing Bess's cry of dismay when he got to Mark's death. A white-faced Bess pressed her lips together and listened grimly along with her husband as Daniel explained what they'd learned since. He fell silent after stating that he and Sarah felt it was best to go on.

Nicholas observed them keenly from under his bushy eyebrows. "You need a linguist," he stated, simply. Daniel wasn't surprised that Grandpa had cut to the chase. He knew that quick mind as well as he knew his own.

"Yes, Grandpa, and we're hoping you know one. Here's the thing. We can't ask around, because we don't know what they're doing to watch us. For all we know, it could be just our phones, computers and houses, but we have reason to believe it's more sophisticated. I don't want you to have to ask around much, either. Rossler isn't that common a name, and I don't want you or Grandma in danger. But we thought you might know someone off the top of your head. We couldn't call to ask you, so that's why we're here." Daniel added, "Although I'm always glad for a chance to see you and Grandma."

"Good save, boy," Grandpa growled, amused. "As a matter of fact, I do know one, and a brilliant one at that. Do you think it's safe for me to call him?"

"Grandpa, I don't have a clue. For all I know they're tracking all the linguists in the country. I guess it would be safer if you didn't."

"Then we'll do it the old-fashioned way. Can you and Sarah stay for lunch? While Bess gets it ready, I'll write a letter of introduction for you. You can drop in on him, he's usually at home. Retired, like me."

"That's perfect! Sarah, do you mind..." Daniel began.

"Of course not, darling. I'm going to visit with your grandma and help her in the kitchen. You and your grandpa can handle this one on your own."

Daniel was so happy to see the conspiratorial twinkle in Sarah's eye that he didn't even question what mischief she and Grandma might get up to if they were alone together.

Sarah trailed Bess into the kitchen and stood out of the way while Bess puttered around, deciding what to serve. Once she settled on chicken salad and biscuits, Sarah offered to cut up onions and celery for the salad. Bess handed her a sharp knife and cutting board and started mixing up the biscuit dough. "So, what did you want to talk about, Sarah? Has that boy been good to you?"

Sarah laughed. "I should have known you were just as sharp as Nicholas. Yes, Grandma Bess, he's been good to me. I love him so much, and he says he loves me..."

"But?" Bess questioned.

"But, he hasn't said anything about marriage. I don't know where this is going," Sarah said, a small frown marring her lovely face and soft expression.

"I told you before that I'd help if I could," Bess said. "Do you want me to put a bug in his ear?"

Sarah laughed again at the old-fashioned slang. "Maybe later, Grandma Bess. For now, I just wanted to get it off my chest."

After lunch, the pair left amongst admonitions to hurry back for a longer visit. The letter of introduction was safely tucked into Daniel's laptop case. They planned to visit the man, Sinclair O'Reilly, that very afternoon if they could make good time back to New York. Before they arrived in the city, though, Daniel took a call on his cell phone that forced a change of plans.

# Chapter 23 – You Are In Danger

"Am I speaking with Daniel Rossler?" the voice asked. Daniel didn't recognize it.

"Who's calling?" Daniel answered cautiously. His tone made Sarah look at him with concern.

"I'm a friend," said the unknown voice. "Luke Clarke should have been in touch about me."

"Oh," said Daniel, relieved. "You must be David. Sorry, we're a little paranoid. Yes, this is Daniel."

"Can't say that I blame you, and yes, I'm David. Now that we have the introductions out of the way, I'd like to set up a time to meet with you and Dr. Clarke. Is she with you right now?"

"She is. We're on our way back to the city. She has to leave for Providence early in the morning, though. What did you have in mind?"

"I thought we could have a quiet dinner, and I could fill you in on some things that may be significant to you. In turn, maybe you can give me some help."

"Dinner sounds fine. I'll take the rest under advisement until we've heard what you have to say. Where shall we meet?"

David named a restaurant in Manhattan and provided the address, which Sarah wrote down as Daniel repeated it. "Seven o'clock okay? I know it's early, but I've got to catch the last shuttle back to Washington afterwards."

"Seven's fine. We'll see you there." Sarah was questioning him with her eyes when he disconnected the call. "I hope you don't mind I didn't check with you. I figured you were as anxious to meet with the guy as I am, right?"

She answered, "Yes, of course. So, we're meeting him for

dinner? Will we have time to get back to your apartment so I can change first?"

"I'm sure we will."

Seven o'clock found them in the restaurant's waiting area, where David spotted them when he walked in a moment later. He introduced himself and offered his hand to Sarah, who shook it warmly. Daniel didn't much care for the way the man's eyes took in Sarah's charms, but he shook the guy's hand anyway. He should be used to the effect that Sarah had on men by now. In fact, he was. He just didn't like it much. Once again he reflected on his need to put his ring on her finger and claim her as his. Soon, he hoped. But not while all this stress and tension was in their lives. He wanted her to be nothing but happy afterward.

David had made a reservation, so they were shown directly to their table, a small four-top set in a private alcove. It was the perfect place to talk, though Daniel made sure his cone of silence device was in his pocket and turned on before David got there. He knew from Luke's report that the CIA or NSA were watching them, but if any other bad guys could listen, he wanted to keep his meeting with the CIA agent on the down-low.

The three perused their menus and ordered, after which David brought up his reason for wanting to meet with them face-to-face. "Luke and I go way back, did he tell you?"

Sarah smiled at him and said that her uncle had spoken highly of him.

"I told him some things in confidence that concern you, and unless I miss my guess, he would have told you all of it, even the classified parts. Am I right?"

Daniel and Sarah looked at each other, deciding whether telling the truth would get Luke in trouble.

"Never mind," David said. "It doesn't matter, because I'm going to tell you myself. You guys are in danger." David proceeded to tell them exactly what Luke had said, including the fact that David thought there may be a mole in the CIA department that was watching them.

"I've got two objectives, and frankly the first is the most important to me. But because I think you can help and because Luke is an old friend, the second is important enough."

Seeing their confusion, Luke went on. "It's my job to find that mole. I need some way to flush him out, and the fact that Luke came to me for help to protect you guys gives me a perfect way to do it. If you're game, I need you to continue your research."

## Chapter 24 – By the Fires of Hell

Septentrio gazed at the wall-sized screen at the man who was making his report. Dressed all in black, Impes even affected the wraparound aviator shades that the stereotype dictated for a CIA operative, although this man was assuredly not CIA. Septentrio's lip curled. His man needed some discipline, and the next time he or his team screwed up in this manner, he, Septentrio, would provide it in person.

"May I ask why you initiated an operation without authorization?" he said coldly.

"Sir, I was laying a trap for a traitor in the organization…"

"Did it require you to kill the researcher? His death has seriously compromised the *authorized* operation." Septentrio brushed aside the man's excuse, which was unlikely. No one would dare harbor traitorous intent. Septentrio's reputation for punishment of error was too terrifying to consider it.

"No, sir, but…"

"No buts! So he resisted, you tortured him and killed him and you only got a piece of paper with a half-done translation? No data on his computer or on a flash drive or anything? What a fucking mess you have created! Why was it necessary to kill him before you had all the information, you idiot? This is what happens if dimwits like you take matters into your own hands!"

Septentrio didn't have any qualms about killing. What angered him was the fact that he did not give the order for this and on top of that, the premature loss of someone who was key to finding the final answers he sought. Although the man, Rossler, and his woman instigated the research, it had gone nowhere until they enlisted the help of the dead man. Now it appeared it would be delayed while they found another linguist to translate, if this whole untimely operation did not scare them off the whole thing completely.

His fists clenched under his desk. Septentrio would like to wring the necks of the stupid thugs Impes had sent to get the information. It was a clear violation of protocol; Impes should not have interfered without authorization. Now they had lost a key researcher, and they'd soon have to do something about Impes. But, it was possible he could still be of use. For now, he would live.

"I want you to stand by. Sidus will report to me when the original researchers have brought on someone else to help with the translation. This time, I want the man alive, with the data. Do not act until Sidus directs you to, and by the fires of hell, you'd better not botch it."

'Yes, sir. Sorry, sir." Impes sounded sincere, but who could tell from that impassive face what his thoughts were? Could he be mocking the most powerful man in the world? Surely he wouldn't dare. Deciding it was his imagination that a tiny bit of irony crept into Impes' eyes, Septentrio waved him away.

"Dismissed."

On the other side of the Atlantic, Impes breathed a cautious sigh of relief, still schooling his expression and moderating the depth of his sigh, in case the connection were somehow still active. When he was recruited by a member of Septentrio's vast network of operatives, he'd had no idea of the scope of the work. But, as a minor member of a minor branch of a Cosa Nostra family, he'd overstepped his boundaries once before, and had an urgent need to first disappear from his home city and then have his appearance modified forever. The offer from the recruiter had come at a very opportune time.

Impes wasn't a stupid man, just lazy. As his shadowy

employer sent more and more assignments his way, he gathered hints from here and there, information dropped from other associates and victims, until he had amassed enough information to know who he was dealing with. That, he kept to himself, for they were a dangerous group. So dangerous that even major families were afraid of them. But, he parlayed his knowledge into a plan.

For each assignment involving making someone disappear, whether dead or alive, he would do it so cleverly, yet with such flair, that he would eventually come to the notice of the top levels of his organization. He had confidence that he would be made a capo, or whatever the Orion Society's equivalent was, then. Eventually, he dreamed of becoming one of the four prime members of the Society himself. It was unfortunate for him that his homework fell short of informing him that those were hereditary positions. Now his only objective was to escape with his life and perhaps enough money to enjoy it.

Impes was feeling rather savage about the dressing-down he'd received, and, like all bullies, decided to take it out on someone else. He called the two operatives who'd been responsible for Mark Simms' death to report to him at a warehouse on the outskirts of the Bronx. Before he killed them, he would question them about any trace evidence they might have left at the Simms house.

Two days later, two bodies washed up on a deserted stretch of shoreline on Long Island Sound. They wouldn't be found for days, and by that time, they wouldn't be recognizable. Even if they had been, though, with their teeth all removed and their eyes gouged out, a firm identification would be impossible without their fingers, all of which were elsewhere in a landfill.

After dealing with the idiots who'd botched the Simms operation, Impes called Barry. "He's upset, and I don't need to tell you what that means. We need to come up with something solid as soon as they make a move. Be sure she's still reporting everything."

"Shouldn't we bug her house, too, Impes? If she knows why Mark was killed, she's going to be careful what she tells me, and on her phone to talk to Rossler. I think we need more direct information."

"Since when were you in operations, Barry? You let me handle that part, and just make sure she keeps you informed."

# Chapter 25 - 8 Sides To It

Sarah had gone home on Tuesday morning as planned, with the information that David had given them ringing in her ears and the promise of an undercover agent watching her at all times for her safety. Daniel had objected at first; he wanted to be the one to protect her, and was ready to quit his job to do it. But, David had convinced him that he and his team would do a better job, since they were professionals. And that Daniel should remain on the job where the resources of the Times could help with the ongoing research. His arguments were compelling.

As he'd told Luke, David also told Sarah and Daniel that he had faith there was something to their theory. He'd seen secret after secret ferreted out and either given to top-rated companies to develop for the good of the US economy, or suppressed because they were simply too dangerous for anyone to have them. The conversation was so intense that at times, Daniel wanted to ask about Area 51, just so he could tell Raj, one way or the other. On the other hand, he'd promised Raj not to reveal his interest in anything to the CIA. Accordingly, he didn't mention Raj at all.

Daniel had caught some of Raj's paranoia about government agencies, so he was leery of David and the CIA, even while accepting the help and protection of the agency. Somewhere he remembered hearing the phrase "Keep your friends very close to you; keep your enemies even closer." If the CIA were the enemy, he and Sarah would be crawling right into their enemy's lap. However, he'd keep his own counsel about his misgivings, and give the appearance of total cooperation.

David made it very clear that they were to communicate only with him; not the protection detail if they spotted them, and definitely not the reception desk at Langley. He gave them each a card with his private cell phone number so they could reach him at all times. Then he warned them that for their own safety as well as his, he would be very deep undercover and that they should only contact him in case of dire emergency.

"I don't want to try to tell you how to conduct your research," he'd finished up, "but it is of grave importance that you be the ones to translate the message first. From what you've told me, there are likely to be others working on it with the same data you used to get as far as you did. Do you have another linguist to help you?"

"Not yet. We have a name, but we haven't spoken to him yet," Daniel said.

"We think it's only fair that we tell him how dangerous it could be," Sarah added. "So he may not agree to help."

"Let me know if you need me to help find one. We have resources as well. Leave a message at the email on that card," David said.

Then he departed, leaving Sarah and Daniel to enjoy a more leisurely dessert before going back to Daniel's apartment.

With a glass of red wine in her hand, Sarah sank into Daniel's sofa with a sigh.

"What's wrong, sweetheart?" Daniel asked.

"Do you mean, aside from Mark being murdered and us finding out that everything we've put on our computers since the beginning of this has been under someone's scrutiny? And aside from the fact that we may have put Raj, my dad and uncle, your grandparents and soon any linguist we employ in as much danger as we put Mark in? Besides all that?" Daniel had never heard her so negative and depressed. He put his arm around her.

"Yes, honey, besides all that. We're dealing with all that,

other than Mark, and we can't change that. I would have thought that getting protection from the CIA would help."

"It does, Daniel, but I just feel all out of sorts. I can't put my finger on it." She sunk into him, relishing the warm arm around her, and put her head on his chest.

"Sweetheart, maybe I know what's wrong," Daniel said, running his hand down her arm and back up. Her hand on his leg was tantalizing, and it had occurred to him that he didn't remember the last time they'd made love.

"What?" she asked.

"This," he said, tilting her face to him and kissing her ardently. His heart was racing as he deepened the kiss and wrapped his free hand around to run his fingers through her hair. What a sweet armful she was! She must have missed this, too, because she curled into him and pressed into his chest like a kitten seeking shelter. Then her hand crept upward on his leg. Drawing back from the kiss to look into her eyes, Daniel sent a wordless question. Wordlessly, she answered by untangling herself and rising from the sofa. She pulled him along with her, and started down the hallway to his bedroom. It wouldn't be long before everything was all right again.

On the way to Providence the next morning, Sarah felt more like herself than she had since that terrible morning the police had woken them with the news that they were suspects in Mark's death. It made her wonder how Martha was doing, and she felt guilty that they'd been so busy they hadn't seen Martha since right after the funeral. She made plans to drop by after her class this afternoon.

Meanwhile, Daniel had gone to work as usual, and as usual was having lunch with one of his friends. Today it was Owen, Raj having declined citing a big project. However, it was understood that Daniel would meet Raj for a drink and an update later this evening. Conscious of his CIA minder, he didn't want to visit Raj at home. Owen had forgotten his pique over Daniel's ill-temper of the week before, and was prattling on about something interesting he'd discovered, but he often did that. Daniel had learned to feign interest and let the chatter flow around him. Today, though, it had something to do with the Great Pyramid, so Daniel returned from his own thoughts to pay attention.

"The really cool thing," Owen was saying, "is you can't see it with the naked eye or from the ground. It wasn't discovered until someone thought to take pictures from the air. Even then, the light has to be just right, but when it is, voila! Eight sides."

Daniel had collected so many facts about the pyramid that he sometimes forgot some of them until reminded. This was one of them. Instead of the typical four flat sides, the Great Pyramid had eight, but it had been forgotten in the mists of time until an aerial photo had been taken at just the right time. It was now known that at dawn and sunset on the spring and fall equinoxes, a shadow appears in such a way as to divide the pyramid in half, and the concavity that divides each side on the center line is revealed.

Something about this fact nagged at him, but he couldn't bring it to mind. Later tonight, he'd have to use his new technique of thinking about a problem intensely while he was trying to go to sleep, and see if his subconscious supplied an answer. But first, he needed to bring Raj up to speed. Daniel had a feeling Raj wasn't going to like the CIA's involvement.

~~~

Raj's instructions about where to meet him were in the hidden email drafts folder when Daniel checked just before he left for work. Raj wanted him to take evasive action in case he was being followed, and Daniel didn't have a secure way of signaling that he was indeed being followed, but by a CIA protection detail that he wanted there. Torn between exposing Raj by leading the protection detail to the little dive where they were to meet and losing his safety shield, Daniel's military-trained buddy code kicked in. He'd evade surveillance this time, and warn Raj what was going on. After that, Raj could call the shots about meeting him.

Daniel had seen plenty of spy movies, and Raj's instructions could have been drawn from their plots. There wasn't a much better place to lose a tail than near the Times. He walked to the 42nd Street Port Authority bus terminal, went in one door and hurried to the men's room, leaving by a different door than the one he came in. Then he ducked out of the bus terminal and flagged down a taxi, which he had drop him at Saks on 5th Avenue. After several more evasive moves, Daniel thought that if he hadn't lost his tail by now, it wasn't going to happen. He flagged down another taxi to take him to the bar where he expected to find Raj disguised in his girlfriend's clothes again.

To his surprise, Raj was in his own clothes, and waiting for him behind an enormous plate of Buffalo wings. "Have some," he invited Daniel.

Daniel ordered a draught IPA and dug into the wings. Raj said, "What is so urgent to tell me?"

"You're not going to like it, Raj, but Sarah's uncle went to some trouble to find out what's going on and get us some help. I didn't know when we left your place to go to Colorado that Uncle Luke is ex-CIA."

Raj reacted physically, almost jumping back from the table, though he stayed in his chair. "No CIA, Daniel!"

"No, listen, dude. This guy is on the level. He told us what and why all those hacks to our computers were about. Did you know they keep track of research like ours in the interest of national security?"

Raj answered bitterly, "I know they surveil people they have no business to do, and that people disappear when they get too close to the truth. I have told you this, Daniel. Why would you allow them to get close to you?"

"To tell the truth, Raj, we didn't have much choice. You yourself showed us that we've been watched from the beginning, and we suspected it was by more than one group. Now we know. This guy, David, has put protective details on us...wait, sit down!"

Raj had jumped up, knocking his chair to the floor and drawing the ire of the bartender. "I didn't lead them here. Please, Raj, sit down and let me finish."

Reluctantly, Raj picked up his chair and sat down, with a stubborn expression on his face. "I warned you," he repeated.

"I know, Raj, and that's why I took care to lose my tail before I met you. I wanted to let you know that I had one, so that you'd be even more cautious. We haven't told anyone but Mark of your involvement, and I suspect he took that to his grave. I can't protect Sarah by myself, I needed help. If you want out, I'll understand, but I hope you'll stick with us. We'll do everything in our power to keep your name under our hats," Daniel had known the extent of Raj's paranoia about government agencies, and he'd been prepared for anger, but this was more than he'd bargained for. He didn't know what they'd do if Raj bowed out now.

"My friend, you have put me in a very bad position. I see no alternative than to continue, and then to disseminate what we find as widely as possible so that the CIA will have no power over us. But if my contacts get wind of it, it will undo years of trust-building."

"I'm sorry, Raj, I really am. What can I do to make it up to you?" Daniel's contrition was sincere; he did want to make his friend feel better about the circumstances.

"Locate the truth about Area 51, and help me expose it," Raj said, with only a trace of humor. He knew that Daniel didn't believe there was anything to expose.

"If it's out there, buddy, I'll do it," Daniel declared solemnly.

"What's next, then?" Raj asked.

"I need to talk to the linguist Grandpa's introducing me to, see if he'll help. If not, we need to find someone who can, without tipping the bad guys that we're looking."

"So, you are convinced that it is not just the CIA interested in your research?" Raj asked.

"Pretty much, yes. From what Luke and now this David has told us, we stirred up interest among what could be international criminal cartels. And, like you, we feel that the only protection is in exposure. We're going to move forward with all possible speed."

Daniel was so busy smoothing Raj's ruffled feathers that he forgot to mention the hunch he couldn't quite bring into focus about the pyramid's eight sides. He only remembered that when he was ready for bed, but this time his trick didn't work. He actually woke up the next day not remembering he'd even been puzzled about anything.

Sarah wanted to be in on the interview of Sinclair O'Reilly, the linguist suggested by Nicholas, so Daniel curbed his impatience to wait for the weekend. He only checked out the man's address so he'd know how to get there on Saturday morning when Sarah could go with him. She'd spent so much time in New York lately, that Daniel began to wonder if he could persuade her to move here permanently after they were married.

That reminded him to check on the progress the jeweler was making with the ring he'd ordered. It was pretty special, if he did say so himself. He only hoped she'd love it as much as he did. Owen had him half-convinced that if she didn't like the ring, she'd say no to the proposal. That would be a disaster. Nothing would be right in his world until she'd said yes.

# Chapter 26 – The Irish Connection

On Saturday at ten a.m., Daniel and Sarah knocked on Sinclair O'Reilly's door and introduced themselves.

"I hope we aren't disturbing you Dr. O'Reilly, but we're here on a matter of some urgency. May I present a letter of introduction from my grandfather, Nicholas Rossler?" Daniel's speech was so formal that Sarah wasn't sure she was standing by her Daniel. She glanced at him admiringly.

O'Reilly's eyes lit up at the mention of Nicholas. "Of course! I thought you looked familiar, young man. Should have put it together right away. Your grandfather and I go way back. Would you care to come in?"

Daniel ushered Sarah inside and followed, as they were admitted to a house redolent of scones and other delicious aromas.

"I was just about to have a mid-morning snack. Could I interest you in a scone?" O'Reilly was younger than they'd expected, assuming a contemporary of Nicholas. However, as he explained while passing cups of fragrant tea to the couple, he'd actually been Nicholas's student as an undergraduate.

Daniel told himself he should stop trying to visualize how a person would look by their name. Instead of the Irish leprechaun he'd expected of Sinclair, the man was a tall, ascetic-looking academic with iron-gray hair and piercing brown eyes. He had a look of intense interest in the world, whatever was before him, which at this moment was Sarah. Clearly charmed by her looks and gentle manner, he was doing his best to impress her.

When their unexpected repast was finished, O'Reilly suggested they retire to his office where he would read the letter from Nicholas. He raised his eyebrows when he was finished and sent his acute gaze to each of the couple in turn.

"Fascinating," he said. "Nicholas assures me you are quite serious and that you do not expect to find aliens at the bottom of this mystery."

Daniel smiled faintly, "It would be really ironic if we did, after all the protesting we've done that we don't believe it. But no, no aliens in our theory."

"Suppose you tell me what your theory is," O'Reilly said.

Daniel began patiently to tell his story again, beginning with the anomalies of construction and moving on to the remarkable coincidences, if that's what they were, in the measurements, the positioning and the astronomical facts. As he cataloged the facts, O'Reilly nodded periodically as if he'd known of them before.

At last, Daniel was at an end of the recitation, and paused for comment.

"You've done a very thorough job of putting all these facts into logical order, Mr. Rossler. May I ask if you've drawn any conclusions?"

"You may. We've not only drawn a conclusion, we've corroborated it."

This statement caused O'Reilly's eyebrows to rise quizzically. "Indeed."

"Yes, sir. If I may go on…" Daniel then summarized how they'd hit on the idea of a message, and, in a neutral tone that belied the bombshell he was about to drop, said, "We have a partial translation of what we believe is a greeting from the passageway leading into the pyramid."

O'Reilly leaned forward in an almost violent motion. "The

devil you say!"

"It's true, sir. Before I go on, I must tell you that the price of deciphering that message was the death of a very good friend. We believe we're into something quite dangerous, and for that reason we feel full disclosure is imperative if we ask you to work with us."

O'Reilly betrayed surprise again, and then leaned back, his long fingers tented in front of his chin. "Very well. I trust you will reveal the message to me only if I agree to work with you."

"Sir, we feel it's best for your safety," Sarah injected.

"Thank you for your concern, Dr. Clarke. Please, tell me what happened to your friend."

Daniel took up the narrative again, telling of Mark's murder shortly after he'd revealed the translation to them. He then explained that they didn't know who the translator was, only that it was someone at the Joukowsky Institute who had not come forward, apparently in fear for his life.

"So you see, we are at a standstill without a linguist. We have the data, we have the technique, but we haven't pinned down the language, other than that it appears to be an ancient form of Arabic," Daniel concluded.

"I have to tell you, Rossler that you couldn't have hit upon a more enticing subject. I've been very bored since my retirement and the passing of my wife. I'm inclined to agree to work with you. But before we discuss that further, do you have any idea of who would have killed your friend?"

"We've been contacted by the CIA, who have frankly told us of their interest. Our contact also mentioned that there are criminal organizations who would be desperate to get their hands on something as explosive as our theory of a more ancient civilization and their advanced knowledge. Other than that, nothing specific."

"Hmmm. Nicholas may not know it, but as a hobby, I've picked up some knowledge in that area that may be helpful. Tell me, who is helping you with the data?"

Daniel was cautious, but if the project were to move forward, the two men would eventually have to work closely together. On the strength of his grandfather's trust in Sinclair, he mentioned Raj by first name only.

"I wonder if it's the same Raj…" Sinclair mused. "Bet it is. I know he's a data analyst."

Daniel was confused. "Wait, do you mean you knew of him before I brought him up? How?"

"I knew of a data analyst named Raj from my association with a group of Area 51 enthusiasts."

Daniel and Sarah could not have been much more shocked if Sinclair had stood on his head and declared his belief in men in the moon or Martians. They looked at each other significantly and then turned to Sinclair for an explanation.

"Don't worry, I have no illusions that there are a colony of extraterrestrials being held prisoner by our government. I sort of backed into the group, based on my belief that there is something going on at that location that the government isn't telling us. From my research about the time it started, I suspect it has something to do with fissionable material, but that's as far as I've thought about it."

Heaving a sigh of relief, Daniel said, "Yes, that sounds like our Raj. He does believe the alien story, wholeheartedly. But that's his only crazy notion, other than being paranoid that the government would somehow make him disappear if they knew he was researching the reason for the secrecy."

"I wouldn't call that a crazy notion, son. You'd be surprised what we think and what we know is going on behind the scenes, not only in our country but worldwide. Some of it is an open secret, like the NSA and CIA illegally spying on American citizens. Other stuff is deep, deep underground."

"Like what?" Daniel asked, intrigued. "Do you know who would be after this pyramid code, besides the CIA?"

"I've heard rumors of a small group of super powerful families who control world-wide wealth," Sinclair answered. "I'm thinking it's them."

"Everyone's heard of that," Daniel scoffed. "You mean the Illuminati."

"No, I don't have an opinion about that group, if in fact they still exist. I'm talking about a group that call themselves the Orion Society. There have been strange disappearances among my acquaintances, and from the pattern it appears to be one group behind most of them. There's always a plausible but unprovable story about it. Only a couple of times has someone let slip the name of the group, and then that someone has disappeared for good."

Chilled, Sarah scooted closer to Daniel on the sofa. "Do you think they're the ones?" she asked Sinclair.

"I wouldn't be surprised. And if they are, you're going to have to be even more careful than you already are. They are ruthless and very, very determined to have whatever they set their minds on. If you dig deeply enough, you hear that they've been around for centuries, and may have been behind some incidents that affected the entire world."

Daniel was looking skeptical, which Sinclair, intent on

Sarah's face, didn't notice. "Like what?" Daniel asked. Now Sinclair looked at him and saw the doubt. "Well, how about the assassination of Archduke Franz Ferdinand of Austria?"

Shocked, Daniel blurted, "But that was some group called the Black Hand."

"True, but who was behind the group? What other actions did they take, and where are they today? Even though the history is fairly clear, you know the old saying that history is written by the victors? Who were the victors in this case?"

"The Allies, of course."

"Think again, son. The victors were those who profited from the war, arms dealers among them. Big military suppliers, financiers, and large corporations. As always."

Daniel had the peculiar impression that he was talking with an older Raj, but he had to concede that what he had learned in high school and college history classes wasn't always the whole truth. This was something that would bear investigation, and fortunately he had the time to do it when they got home. He would start with the information that Sinclair seemed willing and able to give them, and try to sort out fact from fancy.

"Thank you for bringing that to our attention. Our IT specialists has ties with virtually every conspiracy theorist on earth. I'll see what he can dig up about them."

"Excellent! Please pass the information on to me. I find it quite fascinating. All right," said O'Reilly, rubbing his hands together. "Let's say I'm in. Tell me what you know of my field, and what specific progress you've made."

Daniel began to bring Sinclair up to date on their progress, letting him know also what they had learned about proto-language construction and reconstruction of unknown languages, as well as what their IT specialist hoped to do with heavy-duty computing power. Sinclair was impressed with Daniel's grasp of the basics, and with the understanding of the absent computer whiz. He made a few suggestions regarding the program that Raj was busy writing even now, and gave Daniel a list of languages to feed into it, including those using the Linear A and Linear B scripts, particularly Linear A. He explained that the language was still unknown, but was thought to be a pre-Hellenic version of Greek. He also gave Daniel a quick history of how more than a dozen languages developed in the area. Sarah was particularly fascinated by all this, and loved hearing the private lecture by a leading scholar.

When the linguistics discussion had been exhausted, Sinclair brought up the subject that Daniel and Sarah were already working on, the turmoil that their findings would undoubtedly cause. He mentioned that he'd been surrounded by such controversy all his professional life. After a quick glance at Sarah to confirm his desire to be completely honest with this man, Daniel began to explain what they were doing about the issue.

"We've started organizing our ideas around what schools of thought will be destroyed by this new information," he began. "We think the best defense is a good offense. We're working on a white paper to release at the same time as we make the announcement about what we have found." Detailing their process, he continued by listing the arguments against evolution, the first subject they had addressed.

Sinclair said, "It's interesting that you should bring that up first. I've questioned evolution from my professional perspective, as well. In a way, the scientific process mimics what neo-Darwinists tout as the evolutionary process, but there is a very different result. That alone should make anyone question evolution."

"How do you mean, sir?" Daniel asked.

"I know you've come across papers that promise to bring into question current thinking, as a journalist. In fact, that's what got you questioning the pyramid facts, am I right?"

"Yes, of course," Daniel answered.

"Then you know what happens to new ideas. First, the findings are published, but before they can be published in a respected journal, they must be submitted for peer review. Anything that's too far out of line is dismissed out of hand. If it has too much merit for that, the peers start massaging it and explaining it until it fits with established 'fact'." Sinclair described quotation marks with his hands in the air as he said the word fact. "If a scientist wants to have his work considered seriously, he'll do that part for himself before submitting it for peer review. Not to do so is to invite professional suicide."

Daniel understood the point very well, had made the same observations himself, in fact. But he didn't get the connection with evolution, and said so.

"Think about it. Let's say there is a favorable mutation. It's going to happen in one individual, and very likely be subsumed in the larger gene pool before it can make a difference to the genome in general. So one individual ape ancestor gets the ability to more efficiently manipulate a tool. Will that help him dominate, or will he be ostracized by the community? Very likely the latter, which would mean that his genes wouldn't be passed on.

"But, if not, if he dominates instead, what good is it if he can't convey that ability to the rest of the pack? He would have a few offspring, sure, but how many would inherit that particular trait? To make a difference in that way would require a much longer time span than the evolutionists have to work with. It's like peer review, do you see?"

Sarah had followed the conversation silently, but now broke in. "That's something we haven't put in the mindmap, Daniel. That, and environmental pressure, another argument that the evolutionists put forth. And it's a very good point, because their reasoning is circular."

Again, Daniel asked, "How do you mean?"

Sarah was so excited by the ideas that Sinclair had given her that she began talking with her hands as she explained. "Okay, some of them say that evolution was the result of environmental pressure. Not talking about humans, now, environmental pressure would be, say, that some animals developed thicker fur as they responded to an ice age. But, realistically, wouldn't that kind of pressure kill them off before mutations would allow them to grow thicker fur? Or would they have just willed themselves to grow it thicker?" The sarcasm in her last remark made Daniel and Sinclair smile, but Sarah was on a roll and continued in the same vein.

"So, for some unknown reason millions of years ago some of the apes decided to leave the jungle and move to the plains where there was no food or protection for them. Then, when they got there they decided it would be great to walk on two legs rather than four and then they started shedding all their hair on their backs, even though being away from the protection and shade of the jungle they would actually need more hair on their backs to protect them from the sun. Unless they planned all along to make clothes for themselves, as soon as they started using tools like awls and needles. Oh, and by the way, they also decided to change their diet dramatically and start eating meat and other animals that required them to invent weapons to hunt with, instead of eating the bountiful fruit, leaves insects and roots and vegetables they left behind in the jungle. It makes no sense whatsoever!" Out of breath, she paused and for the first time noticed the stunned look on Daniel's face, and the look of amusement on Sinclair's.

Going on, Sarah said, "But what I meant by their logic being circular is, they have to account for why the new and improved species became dominant, because as Sinclair observed, the gene pool would more likely have absorbed a beneficial mutation before it could become widespread. Unless the mutated population was isolated until cross-breeding was no longer possible." She sat back in triumph, expecting Daniel to make the logical leap that finished the observation. Instead, he and Sinclair looked at her, obviously expecting more.

"Don't you see? How could they be that isolated?"

"Maybe there's a mountain range that's impossible to cross," Sinclair said, playing the straight man although he had already seen where she was going with it.

"Then, how did the isolated population get there in the first place?" Sarah smiled, knowing that Sinclair had anticipated the argument.

"Well," Daniel said, "it looks like we need to update that mindmap with a few more arguments against evolution, among other things."

Sinclair thought of something as they were preparing to leave. "Would it be possible for me to work directly with this computer genius you've enlisted?"

"He's quite paranoid, but I'll try to persuade him," Daniel answered.

"Given everything you've told me, I believe he's probably wise to be paranoid. And very clever to have come up with this secret way of communicating. Let me know his answer that way, and I'll stand by to do my part when he's finished the database."

"Thank you sir, again, for agreeing to help. We will keep your involvement under our hats until it's time to publish, and then you'll get full credit along with Sarah, and me."

"I appreciate it, son. But please, if we're going to be colleagues, call me Sinclair."

~~~

On Saturday afternoon, Daniel sent Raj a message through the email drop that they had information he needed. He knew that Raj was still agitated about the CIA minders, so he left it to Raj to figure out a way to meet that wouldn't reveal him to the operatives. The scheme that came back made Daniel howl. He was to go to church the next day. Not a Southern Baptist church, in which he'd been raised, but a Catholic church. After the service, he was to enter a confessional and wait for Raj to speak to him. Even funnier to Daniel than him going to confession was Raj, a non-practicing Hindu, as the priest. But, he had to admit it was clever. At least he wouldn't have to call him Sushma this time.

At the appointed time, Daniel and Sarah left for the mass and took their seats near the front of the chapel, assuming that their minders would not approach too closely lest they be seen. Sarah appeared to enjoy the service more than Daniel did. During the times of prayer, though, he sent sincere expressions of gratitude for Sarah and her safety, and pleas for continued safety.

After the service, Sarah engaged one of the priests in conversation, while Daniel made his way to the indicated confessional. He really wondered how Raj was going to pull this off, but he needn't have worried. He'd barely settled himself in the cramped space, when a person he couldn't see well made a movement suspiciously like the sign of the cross. Daniel began to wonder if he'd entered the wrong confessional. Then Raj's lilting accent in a strong whisper came through. "Daniel?

Daniel breathed a sigh of relief, and, in a moment of irreverence relieved his tension by saying, "Forgive me father, for I have sinned."

Even in a whisper, Raj's displeasure was evident. "Do not blaspheme, Daniel. We have been granted this favor by people who would be offended by your levity. Have some respect."

Surprised, Daniel expressed his apology. "You're right, Raj. I apologize."

"You have news for me, my friend?"

"Yes. We've made contact with Grandpa's linguist friend. He's in. He'd like to work with you directly if possible, and he also gave us some more information that I'd like you to run down if you can."

"Only if it is absolutely necessary will I meet him in person, Daniel. This is already far more dangerous than we thought when you began. What other information did he give you?"

"The name of a criminal organization that may be behind the attack on Mark. I don't know how seriously to take it, because Sinclair indicated there were probably a number of them. The Mafia might be one for all I know. But he named one called the Orion Society. I was wondering if you could find out something about them, like whether they'd have any interest in our research." Daniel's throat was beginning to hurt from the whispering, but he didn't know how close his babysitter was, and this was something he wanted to keep quiet, along with Raj's identity.

"I will make inquiries. Did you give this linguist access to our secure communication?"

"Yes," Daniel answered.

"I will prepare a message to let him know I can meet him if

necessary. Is there anything else?"

"No, Raj, except that you're a damned devious guy."

"Daniel, may I remind you that we are in a house of God?"

# Chapter 27 – We Can't Hear You

Septentrio was indulging himself in a now rare display of temper. In his youth, such displays often destroyed objects in his home or office, or sent his wife or son to a hospital emergency department for treatment of suspicious accidents. However, in his old age, his physician had told him that he must curb his temper or face a stroke. Calming medications usually helped, but this time he feared he was losing control of his most important assignment. First one of the key researchers had been killed, and now there were problems in monitoring communications between the remaining two.

All email and most text messaging had ceased between the primary researchers. Their cell phones were frequently turned off or left at home when they traveled, so that their whereabouts were unknown. And now mysterious silences were cropping up in conversations in the female's home.

It hadn't taken long to locate the person named Raj that had been mentioned in the Simms home just before he was killed, once Impes had turned over those transcripts. Further investigation revealed that he had long been interested in the Area 51 mystery, but was nowhere near the true answer when he became involved with Rossler and Clarke. It appeared his only role in their research was that of data mining, therefore he was of no importance. Nevertheless, with great difficulty because of his extreme paranoia, listening devices had been deployed in his residence as well, to no avail. Every time Septentrio's considerable resources reported Rossler or Clarke at Sankaran's residence, the same mysterious silences occurred there.

It was maddening and unacceptable. His response was to throw objects around the room and kick those that landed on the floor until he was exhausted and breathing hard. Only then did he have a brandy and school his voice to call his top operative in the US, code-named Sidus.

"We are extremely displeased by the way this project has gone, Sidus.

"No, sir, I'm on top of it. It's just that there hasn't been any progress. I can put some pressure on them to move it along, if you'd like."

"If I'd like..." mocked Septentrio in a sneering tone. "Of course I'd like, you imbecile! Do I have to tell you everything! And while you're at it, find out why they go silent at times. Sometimes the transcripts show a gap of twenty minutes or half an hour with not so much as a clearing of the throat. They have to have some sort of jamming device, and it's the most effective we've ever learned of. I want it. Don't make me wait too long for either of these items, Sidus."

"Yes, sir. I'll get right on it. No, sir, I won't make you wait."

Septentrio allowed himself one last display as he slammed the receiver of the antique gold telephone set into its cradle. It really felt good to let go once in a while. Since he was still in a savage mood, he sent for his son. Time to put some backbone in the boy. Too bad he hadn't managed to do so in the fifty-six years since his son's birth, but he wouldn't live forever, and time was running short to mold him in the traditions of the Society.

~~~

Sidus regarded his cell phone dispassionately as he considered how to accomplish his assignments. His employer was exacting and demanding, but he was paid well in offshore accounts that he never touched. That was for his retirement, which would take place under a different name and appearance, in a small out-of-the way place where nubile young women were willing and nothing else ever happened. He had no illusions that he would be allowed to retire peacefully otherwise. He knew too much about the Orion Society.

He considered all his options for pressure, before placing a call to Barry.

"What can you do to put pressure on Clarke?" he asked without preamble.

Barry recognized the voice instantly, and said, "Let me think a moment. Well, I could move her tenure hearing up, so she maybe wouldn't be prepared."

"No, we don't want them to suspect you are anything but supportive." This with no irony at all, though he had reason to believe they already suspected.

"I'll give it some thought and get back to you," Barry said, beginning to get an idea that he wanted to execute himself, with Impes.

"Make it quick. I'm getting flak from above, and I don't like it much." Sidus considered it too easy to make flagrant threats, so he used sinister hints to do the job.

"I will."

~~

Now Barry called Impes, who, when he heard Barry's voice, flipped on a recording device to protect himself. It hadn't escaped him that Septentrio didn't believe in his story about a traitor. If he didn't give Barry up, he'd take the blame for any further problems, and he'd need evidence.

"What can I do for you, Barry?"

"Sidus wants me to put pressure on Sarah Clarke," Barry answered.

"So? What did you have in mind?"

Barry lowered his voice, as if that would hinder anyone overhearing what was traveling across the airwaves. "I still think they know more than they've told me. Sidus doesn't want me to tip my hand, but I've thought of something you could do."

Once again, Impes was faced with a decision. He'd been told directly by Septentrio not to do anything without Sidus ordering it. On the other hand, Sidus had more or less ordered this, even if it was indirectly. "What is it?"

"Rossler has a grandfather, an archaeologist who was prominent before he retired." He didn't want to specify what he had in mind, hoping for deniability, but he knew how Impes operated. He could rely on the man to take the hint and run with it.

"So, if some threat of harm were to come to the old man, you think they'd give up the rest of what they have?" Impes clarified.

"I'm sure of it."

"What's the geezer's name?" Impes asked.

"Nicholas Rossler. Sorry, I don't know where he lives," Barry answered.

"We can find him. I'll get on it."

# Chapter 28 - Don't Upset The Marines

Bess Rossler was in the kitchen as usual early on the morning of September 18, preparing dough for biscuits to serve for breakfast. As she'd done every morning Nick was home for over fifty years, she started the coffee, then turned back to the counter to drop the biscuits onto the cookie sheet. Next, she started a few strips of bacon and got the pan ready to fry eggs before placing the biscuits in the oven. Satisfied that Nick's breakfast would be ready in about ten minutes, she went down the hall to wake him.

As soon as she had left the kitchen, the man who had been watching through the window signaled his partner at the front of the house, and both quickly picked the old locks. Slipping in from both sides of the house within seconds, they took their places, one in the kitchen next to the door where he could grab the old woman as soon as she returned, and one concealed behind the doorjamb on the other side of the hall, ready to overpower the old man when he went to the aid of his wife. Their directions were to fulfill the mission with as little violence as possible, not because their employers abhorred violence, but because if they damaged the hostages, they would no longer be of use.

Their plan went off without a hitch. Bess barely had time to squeak in surprise before her captor's hand effectively cut off further communication by the simple expedient of covering her mouth and pinching her nostrils shut at the same time. He whispered fiercely to her, "Don't scream and I'll let you breathe."

With her faded blue eyes wide in fright, Bess had the presence of mind to nod and go limp, allowing her captive to release her nostrils, though he kept his hand over her mouth.

"Good girl," he said approvingly. "Behave and everything will be fine." He then walked her over to a kitchen chair and bound her there, with a gag in her mouth.

At the same time, the other intruder had grabbed Nicholas, who at over six feet was still brawny and strong for all his years. Struggling to control him, the intruder found himself slammed into the wall and pinned by Nicholas' big body, his breath knocked out of him with a whoosh.

"Bess!" shouted Nicholas, alerting the other that his partner had failed to secure the old man. He rushed to help, and finding them entangled where he couldn't get a purchase, delivered an expert chop to the old man's neck karate-style. Nicholas dropped, unconscious.

~~~

When he awoke, Nicholas was puzzled at first, not remembering what had happened earlier that morning. He was bound to a kitchen chair, with Bess weeping silently beside him, also bound to a chair. The odor of burned bacon and biscuits flavored the air, along with the aroma of coffee. His neck hurt, and something was wrapped around his mouth, preventing him from asking Bess if she was okay, other than being tied to the chair. It was a bewildering state of affairs, like nothing that had ever happened to him in his 80 years.

When she saw he was conscious, Bess drew a ragged breath and sighed deeply, then blinked slowly at him. He thought she was trying to tell him something, and wondered if she would remember enough Morse code that they could communicate. Pausing to get the sequence in mind, he blinked out U OK? But she didn't know the letters, though she did appear to understand it was Morse code he was trying to get across with short and long blinks. She nodded and then shook her head, so either she was unhurt but not okay, or she understood that it was Morse code but didn't understand his message. Before he could think how to resolve it, a stranger came into the kitchen.

The man was of medium height but displayed an impressive build, even disguised as it was by parachute-style clothing. A black balaclava hid his features. Seeing the man did more to snap Nicholas into full understanding even than realizing he was tied to a chair. It was frustrating, being gagged. He'd like to ask the man what he wanted. Not that they had anything of intrinsic value. While he and Bess were comfortable in their retirement, they didn't have expensive baubles lying around, nor a lot of cash. He only hoped that when the robbers discovered their mistake, it wouldn't cause them to take it out on their persons. Best to remain calm and wait for more information for now. If only he could reach out and hold Bess's hand.

Bess was also watching the man warily, and if he'd been able to read her thoughts, he might have been given pause. For a woman nearing eighty herself, and very petite, she was feisty for all that. If he gave her a chance to get at her iron skillet, she'd show him a thing or two. She lowered her eyes when he looked at her, lest he read her murderous thoughts in them.

The intruder spoke, interrupting the couple's musings. "Tell us what you know about Daniel Rossler's research." Bess's eyes went wide and then flew to Nicholas, who was shaking his head.

"Mmmmph," he said, reminding the man that he was gagged and couldn't answer the question. The second intruder came in then, and told the first that he hadn't been able to get the computer booted up, because it had a password. "What's the password?" the first asked Nicholas.

Irritated at the man's stupidity, Nicholas frowned and shook his head, which both strangers took to be a refusal. The first backhanded him across the face, causing Bess to cry out, muffled though it was. With a trickle of blood running from his cut lip, Nicholas tried again. "Guh."

The second intruder had watched the exchange with disbelief. "You are a fucking idiot," he said to his partner. "How's he supposed to answer with that gag in his mouth?" He moved to Nicholas to remove it, and then for good measure removed Bess's. "Be good, now. One scream and it goes back on. Do you need some water?"

Bess was desperately in need of water, and then of the restroom, but she was so relieved that the second man was being somewhat reasonable that all she could do was nod. He went to the cupboards and found a glass, filled it with water and returned to hold it to her lips. "How about you?" he asked Nicholas.

"Thank you," Nicholas replied. "The password is verde1300, and only the D is uppercase. But you won't find anything about my grandson's research there. We know nothing about it." It was a half-truth. Nicholas had kept no records on his computer, going so far as to wipe out the browsing history so no one could tell he'd navigated to the email server for the hidden accounts. He had no doubt that a forensic computer examiner could find it, but these clowns didn't seem smart enough. On the other hand, he knew rather more than he wanted to right now about the process Daniel and Sarah were using. To protect his grandson, he'd take what he knew to his grave, but he didn't want to leave Bess at the mercy of these thugs. He hoped he could hold out if they decided to torture it out of him.

In truth, the intruders' mission was just to take the old couple hostage. They had taken it upon themselves to get more information if they could. The objective was to get Rossler to volunteer everything in return for his grandparents' safety. Impes was even now contacting Rossler to let him know of their predicament. Nicholas was thinking hard, trying to come up with plausible but false information to feed these guys, who he'd named in his mind Clown #1 and Clown #2. It helped ward off the fear that tried to creep in, though he suspected that Clown #2 was a lot smarter than #1. Maybe he should call them Good Thug and Bad Thug instead. The thought gave him a little chuckle that he suppressed. He said to Bess, "Don't worry, honey. This will be over soon."

Clown #1 sneered and tried to make it seem like that was a bad thing, like maybe it would be over because they wouldn't survive, but something told Nicholas that they'd be okay if they could stay calm.

~~~

The phone number wasn't one he recognized, but because the call had come in on his old cell phone, the one that he still used for work, Daniel answered. His senses went on alert the moment he realized that the voice was being electronically enhanced, no doubt for the purpose of disguising it. "We need to talk about your research into the pyramid code," the voice said.

"I don't think so," Daniel answered. "I've abandoned that story."

"You'll still want to talk to me. A messenger will bring instructions. Pay attention or it won't go well for your grandparents," the distinctive echo of a dead line followed that.

"Wait, what? What about my grandparents?!" Frantic, Daniel dialed his grandparents' home from his throwaway cell. There was no answer. Daniel forced himself to remain calm, understanding that going off half-cocked would do his grandparents no good. There was no choice but to wait for the messenger, and then do whatever the voice wanted to ensure their safety. While he waited, he composed a message on his laptop for the hidden email address. 'Something wrong about grandparents. Waiting for messenger with instructions. Protect yourselves.' With no more information than he had, it was the best he could do. Across the room, he saw Raj's head pop up from his cubicle, looking at Daniel.

Daniel shook his head, and deliberately turned back to his computer. Until the messenger got there, he wouldn't expose Raj. Not even then if he could help it. He had only a few minutes to wait. Tearing into the sealed envelope, he read instructions to go to a certain payphone a few blocks away and wait for a call. That was easy enough, and probably safe. Even in New York City, people couldn't get snatched away from phone stands without exciting comment. This person obviously didn't want a fuss, and was careful enough not to want to risk a phone conversation. He stood to go. Risking a glance at Raj's cubicle, he noticed that Raj was looking up and around the room now and then. He waited just long enough to catch his eye, lifted the paper with the message, and ostentatiously dropped it into the wastebasket. He'd leave it to Raj to take it from there.

Moments later, he was striding down the sidewalk, dodging the crowds, on the way to the designated phone. It was ringing when he arrived.

"What took you?" said the same disguised voice.

"Had to make it look like I was going for coffee," Daniel answered, hoping his excuse would be good enough. "What's this about my grandparents? Where are they? What do you want?"

"Patience, Daniel. All in good time. We know you haven't abandoned your research, so don't try to lie to me. What have you discovered?"

"Look, I don't know who you are or what this is all about, but one man has been killed over it already. It's dangerous. We're setting it aside. Tell me about my grandparents."

"I know very well that someone has been killed; I gave that order. Shut up and listen, or your grandparents could be next. Their safety depends on your cooperation, now, and to ensure that, I've embedded a team at their house."

Daniel's blood ran cold at that. He was no doubt talking to Mark's killer! And nothing was as important as his grandparents' safety. He had no choice but to cooperate. A movement nearby caught his eye and he spotted Raj arriving at his side. Spontaneously, he reached out his free hand, and Raj caught his wrist in a gesture of friendship and support. No doubt Daniel's face showed his distress.

"All right, you have it. What exactly do you want?" he said. Raj startled and started to shake his head.

"We know you had some sort of breakthrough in the translation. What did the message say?" continued the voice.

"We didn't get all of it, but we think it corroborates our theory that there's information of some sort coded into the pyramid. We have some of the data to translate it, but not all of it. What do you want, the data?" Daniel answered. Now Raj was violently shaking his head.

"We want everything you have. You'll compile it on a flash drive and I'll be in touch to tell you where and when you can exchange it for your grandparents."

"I'll have it for you within twenty-four hours. It's not all in the same place, it will take a while to compile it. Please tell me you won't harm my grandparents in the meanwhile; they have nothing to do with this."

"That's not entirely true, is it? Your grandfather's been helping you. By the way, who's your friend that seems to have such an objection to our conversation? Is that Rajan Sankaran?"

"How…where are you?" Daniel asked, looking around wildly. At this, Raj's eyes went wide, too, but he stood his ground.

"We know more than you think. Your grandparents are fine; they're at home and under my protection. My team will see to it that they're comfortable, as long as you cooperate. By the way, you understand, don't you, that if I see police or anyone else near your grandparents' house, they're dead and it will be like you pulled the trigger yourself. So you and your buddy there better get your asses in gear. The clock is ticking." said the stranger.

"Wait, how will I communicate with you?" Daniel asked.

"I'll be in touch. Keep both of your phones on. Just make sure that your girlfriend and your buddy there cooperate also." With that, the line went dead again. Realizing that his throwaway phone had been compromised but that he couldn't replace it until this was over, Daniel wondered, *Who are these guys?* Their access to information was as sophisticated as some government agency, if in fact they weren't one of those agencies.

As Daniel hung up the receiver, Raj exploded.

"Who was that? Was he watching? What did he say that made you look around? What's going on, Daniel?"

"One question at a time, Raj. I need some coffee, let's sit down." Daniel's defeated tone made Raj look at him more closely. He took Daniel's elbow and guided him across the street to a bakery, where they ordered coffee and Danish, and sat outside on a street side table.

Raj waited patiently. It was clear that Daniel needed to organize his thoughts, and was laboring under some powerful emotion. Finally, he spoke. "Raj, I'm sorry, but I think your cover is blown. What made me look around like that was the caller asked if my friend who objected to our conversation was Rajan

Sankaran. He was obviously watching." Daniel could go no further, because Raj had jumped from his seat and was pacing in agitation, speaking rapidly under his breath in Hindi. Daniel waited for him to calm himself, realizing that it might not happen immediately. To his surprise, though, after a few minutes, Raj sat down.

"I have known this would happen someday, I am prepared. Tell me the rest, Daniel, and then I must go," said Raj in a deceptively calm voice.

"Okay. I got a call from the same person earlier. He said he wanted to talk about the pyramid research. I told him we weren't doing it anymore, and then he said something about my grandparents suffering if I didn't talk with him. Then the messenger brought me the instructions that you must have read, leading me here." Daniel paused, waiting for comment from Raj.

"Go on. What did he say this time?"

"He said he knew we were continuing, and that we'd made a breakthrough. But instead of wanting us to give him the data, he wants us to give him everything we have. They've taken my grandparents hostage, Raj, I've got to cooperate. Oh, my God, what have I gotten us into?" Daniel dropped his face into his hands, overcome for the moment with the knowledge that some of the people he loved most in this world were in danger because of his obsession.

Raj said, "Come my friend, this is no time to falter. There is a solution, we just have to find it."

Surprised, Daniel looked at Raj, thinking he'd never understood the other man's character quite as well as now. "You're right. Okay, first tell me what you're going to do now. I'm so sorry they found out about you."

Raj shrugged. "I always thought it would be the CIA. You

don't think the person who called you is CIA, do you?"

"I don't think so, but how would I know? I mean, they're already watching us and we've already agreed to cooperate with them. There's no one we can trust, and whoever that was has to have all the resources he needs to track us and compromise our communications. In fact," he said, remembering suddenly, "I'm sure that the person I just spoke to was responsible for Mark's death. He basically admitted it." He explained what the voice had said.

"All right, then I don't see that I'm in any more danger than I was before, as long as I'm prepared to turn over the data and everything I know if they come for it," Raj said calmly.

"And you must, certainly. But, what if they decide they don't want you as a witness? Wouldn't they kill you?" Daniel worried.

"Everyone must die sometime, my friend. No, I don't think they will kill me. But, I have a safe house to go to. I will not be at work for the next day or so, until this matter is settled. Contact me through email, as before. I'll prepare the data for you and let you know where to pick it up when you need it. Good luck with your grandparents." With that, to Daniel's further surprise, Raj got up and melted into the crowds on the sidewalk.

It was time to form a plan to rescue his grandparents; he couldn't trust their safety to the honor of an admitted murderer.

~~~

The most obvious solution was to contact David. Daniel still had his card with the private cell phone number to be used in case of dire emergency. If this wasn't a dire emergency, Daniel didn't know what would be. He got up, leaving his unfinished coffee and Danish on the table, and went back across the street to the pay phone to make the call.

Daniel counted three rings, then the line simply went dead. Frustrated, he tried it again, every five minutes for the next fifteen or twenty minutes, with the same result. Unable to even leave a message, he muttered to himself, "Well, then I'll do it myself, said the Little Red Hen."

He mentally ticked off the tasks he needed to accomplish in the next twenty-four hours. He had to get to Little Egg Harbor, and the fewer people who knew he was on the way, the better. That included Sarah, who would just worry about him. He'd fill her in when it was over. He wanted just two people with him, and their numbers were in his primary cell phone's memory. He was running out of change for the pay phone, and he was going to need new disposables anyway, so he ran to the nearest Walgreens where he could buy some. While on his way, he called Owen and breathlessly told him that he'd eaten something bad at lunch and come down with food poisoning. Would Owen make his excuses? He'd be back to work when he felt better.

Daniel transferred the two phone numbers to the first of the new disposable phones. The first number reached a man who'd been medically retired from the Marines five years previously. Sgt. Ellis and he had stayed in touch after Ellis contacted Daniel to thank him for saving his life. Daniel knew that the man stayed fit, despite his artificial leg. "Ellis speaking," he answered.

"Ellis, its Daniel Rossler."

"Rossler, you old dog! How's it hangin'?" Ellis roared.

"You'd like to know that wouldn't you?" Daniel answered with a smile. If there were time, he'd tell Ellis and Pierce all about his Sarah, but not now. "Hey, buddy, I've got a problem."

"Point me at it, dude, I'll take it *out*," Ellis responded.

"I was hoping you'd say that. But you'd better hear what it is first. This is genuine combat stuff," Daniel answered.

"All the better. I haven't seen action in five years, I'm in desperate need of kicking someone's ass."

As Daniel spoke, giving the background and the current situation as succinctly as possible, Ellis's ebullience turned to concern. He waited until Daniel was finished, and then said, "Typical spook doublespeak. I'm in; we've got to teach them not to fuck with a Marine's family or friends. Where do your grandparents live?"

Daniel couldn't speak for a moment. It choked him up that this hero, this damaged Marine, asked no questions about whether it was advisable to leave it to the cops, or in this case the CIA. 'Teaching 'em not to fuck with him' was exactly what Daniel planned, and he was overjoyed to have Ellis at his back.

"They live in a little township in New Jersey called Little Egg Harbor Township. But there are no big airports nearby. Can I fly you here?"

"I'll meet you at LaGuardia on the first plane I can get. And no, you can't fly me. It's the least I can do. Is Pierce in?" Ellis asked.

"I called you first. He's next on my list," Daniel answered.

"Good choice, buddy! Give him a call and have him meet us there. We can plan our approach on the way to Pullet Egg, or whatever you said."

For the first time since the first phone call, Daniel actually laughed. It was going to be good to see his friends again, doubly good when he needed reinforcements. "Okay, let me know when you're arriving.

His call to Pierce went much the same way. His exact words were, "Those sons of bitches need their asses kicked right away my friend. They need to learn not to fuck with the Marines. I'm ready - just tell me where I meet you and when. Oorah!"

As a precaution against an unexpected communication from Sarah, he sent a text saying he would be busy with a friend that night and would call her tomorrow, hoping she'd read between the lines. Even though Daniel thought Raj was already outed, his habit of sending only non-sensitive communications on an open line was deeply ingrained by now. He wouldn't want someone going after Raj, thinking he'd be there, when instead he was headed for Little Egg Harbor. Her return text said, 'Understand. Love you.'

Only a few hours later, both men were in Daniel's car, heading for New Jersey and putting off talk of old times and what came in between until after their mission was accomplished. Daniel carefully described his grandparents' house, isolated as it was by a large lot in a neighborhood of large lots, with plenty of trees to hide one neighbor from the next. At one point, they switched drivers, so that Daniel could bring up a satellite image of the house and surroundings on Google Earth. By the time they reached the sleepy little town, their plan was in place.

Daniel and Ellis would make their way through the neighbor's yard into the Rosslers' back yard, taking care not to be seen. When they were in place, Pierce would knock on the front door and pretend to be a door-to-door salesman. He would keep whoever answered the door engaged until Daniel and Ellis could storm the back door. It was risky, but Daniel didn't think the bad guys would think of him taking this kind of action, so it was likely they wouldn't be holding guns on the old folks. He'd rush to find them while Ellis kept the remaining bad guys at bay with the weapon he'd checked in his baggage and declared according to

TSA regulations. When he heard anything from the back of the house, Pierce would rush the guy he was talking to and secure him before going to help the others.

The plan wasn't perfect. There was no time for fancy planning or tactics. It was a simple plan but if executed correctly, with the element of surprise on their side, could work. They were bargaining that the bad guy who phoned and his henchmen in the house would not expect anything from Daniel. Particularly since he'd sounded so frightened on the phone. The only thing they didn't know was how many of them were in the house. To learn that, Pierce would do a quick recon when they got there.

They discussed what to do if the captors sent Bess or Nicholas to the door instead of going themselves. They had to take into account that one would probably be watching the exchange, so the plan was similar, except that it involved Pierce taking down a grandparent as gently as possible and covering him or her while the other two secured the house. It would have to do. Both of the ex-Marines agreed with Daniel that under the circumstances, he couldn't count on the bad guys just letting his grandparents go when it was all over. And Daniel knew that his grandfather would fight tooth and nail if he could, so that gave them the advantage if there were only two of the bad guys; maybe if there were three. If there were more, this was likely to go south, but they had to try.

By the time they reached Little Egg Harbor, dusk was approaching. Daniel hadn't ever reached David, and he was unwilling to leave his grandparents in jeopardy overnight if he could help it. He and his friends had agreed that dusk was as good a time as any. It was only slightly less plausible that a desperate salesman would continue his rounds that late, and the long shadows would help disguise the movements of the others. Accordingly, Daniel had Pierce, who was driving, stop a quarter of a mile away. The three friends swiftly covered the distance on foot.

While Daniel and Ellis hung back at the property line, sitting behind the neighbor, Mrs. Baker's, shrubbery to avoid detection, Pierce crawled swiftly down the side yard and soon disappeared altogether. Twenty minutes later he was back with good news. "I saw your grandparents. They seemed to be all right, but they're tied to chairs in the kitchen. I only saw two mutts, both little scrawny shits, but they both had pistols. We can take 'em, no doubt, but we'll have to be careful no one takes friendly fire."

He drew a crude diagram of what he'd seen in the kitchen, so that the others could see where in the kitchen the older Rosslers were bound. A nine millimeter slug could pierce walls and still do harm. When they each understood what they were to do and when, the three put out their hands, made a swift downward gesture with their joined fists and whispered, Oorah! It was showtime.

Without further ado, Daniel and Ellis began making their way from shrub to shrub through the neighbor's yard, working toward the Rossler yard. Daniel thanked whoever had banned six-foot fences in the tiny township that there were no artificial barriers to their progress. Meanwhile, Pierce continued up the street to the Rossler house, several hundred feet to the east. His cell phone vibrated, indicating that the others were in place. Pierce knocked on the door. He waited a minute, then knocked again. They hadn't talked about what they'd do if no one answered, and he was getting worried, when the door finally opened, and a man who looked too young to be Daniel's grandfather regarded him with suspicion. "Yes?"

"Sir, I'm glad you're home. I represent Acme Roofing. We're going to be in your neighborhood to replace your neighbor's roof next week…"

"We're not interested," interrupted the man.

Pierce put his hand on the screen door handle. "But, sir, have you noticed the condition of your roof? You have several loose shingles, and we're prepared to offer a multiple house discount to all the neighbors who…"

"I said, we're not interested." The man stepped back, half turning his back on Pierce, prepared to close the door. Pierce hoped Ellis and Daniel were in place, because he couldn't wait any longer. With a swift move, he snatched open the screen door.

"Hey!" the man said sharply, turning back to Pierce in annoyance. That's when Pierce felled him with a right uppercut to the chin which would have done any heavyweight world champion proud. It dropped the joker to the floor like a sack of potatoes before he could make a sound. Pierce stepped all the way into the house, dragged the guy out of the doorway and shut the door softly. From the back of the house, he heard, "Jack, who was that?" Pierce thought quickly. If he didn't answer, the other one was sure to come looking for his friend, and he had a gun. Pierce strode quickly to the wall, where he waited for the man to come through. Just as he heard footsteps approaching rapidly, the back door burst open, and he lunged at the perp to prevent him from going back.

A gunshot echoed through the house, followed closely by a woman's scream, and then Daniel was there to help Pierce subdue the man he was struggling with. With a swift roundhouse kick, Daniel swept the perp off his feet, where Pierce pounced on him and pinned his gun hand. Daniel wrested the gun from him.

"Get off, man, I can't breathe," said the hostage taker. Pierce slowly disentangled himself, watching for tricks, but Daniel was holding the man's own gun on him. They took him back to the kitchen, where Ellis had stopped to untie the old couple. Now they used the same clothesline to bind the bad guy to the chair, then Pierce took the gun to watch over the other until he regained consciousness. Bess rushed at Daniel, who caught her in his arms and hugged her fiercely.

"Are you all right, Grandma?" He also looked up anxiously to find his grandpa and assess his condition. A trickle of dried blood on Nicholas's lip sent a wave of rage through him, but since the only place to take it out was a tied man and an unconscious man, he suppressed it.

Nicholas had found his voice, and now scolded Daniel. "What were you thinking? Couldn't you let the authorities handle this? I'm glad to see you, boy, but that was a hell of a risk."

Keeping one arm around his grandma, Daniel pulled his grandpa in for a hug. "Hell, Grandpa, I couldn't wait for them. I'd like you to meet two of the finest Marines I ever knew, Sgt. Ellis and Sgt. Pierce. Hey, guys, do you have first names?" His expression was so comical that everyone broke out into helpless laughter at the non sequitur.

"No, man, the Marines take away your first name in boot camp. Ellis and Pierce will do," Ellis said. Pierce didn't get a say because he was still in the front room guarding the unconscious man.

Bess said, "I can't thank you men enough for helping Daniel."

"Least we could do, ma'am. You may not know it, but your grandson here saved our lives outside of Kabul a few years back. Marines leave no one behind, you know. Now we're even."

Nicholas was on the phone to the local constabulary, who would soon on their way to take the two hostage-takers into custody. Before they arrived, Daniel cautioned everyone not to say much, as he didn't know if even the cops in the tiny township could be trusted. They agreed on a half-truth; that they'd dropped in on the Rosslers as a surprise and were shocked to find them taken hostage. Since they were combat veterans, they just acted instinctively to rescue the old folks, and they had no idea why anyone would want to take them hostage in the first place.

Daniel was fairly certain the perps wouldn't say a word, and he was right. When the police showed up, they both asked for lawyers and then went quiet. The officers were far more concerned about making sure Nick and Bess were all right than about any questions about Daniel's and the Marines' role in the rescue. After checking them over themselves, they called a local doctor to come and check them as well. Living in a small town did have advantages sometimes. Because it was late, they even told Daniel and the others that they could come in the next day to give their statements. Then they left with the uncooperative hostage-takers.

~~~

It was later that night when Daniel took another call from David. He was still at his grandparents' house. Grandma insisted on whipping up a supper of pancakes, eggs and bacon, but afterward he had made sure his grandparents were safely tucked into their bed. Then he talked to Sarah and filled her in, absorbing her distress and anger at him for not telling her before. Then he assured her he would be there the next day and wouldn't leave her side until the ringleader was apprehended.

He was trying to get comfortable enough on the living room sofa to sleep when David's call came through.

"Yeah," he said, letting his annoyance be heard.

"Daniel, its David. Have you been trying to reach me?"

"Hell, yes! I had a crisis and needed your help, but you weren't answering the phone, so I had to deal with it myself," he complained.

"Oh, man, sorry about that! I've been having trouble with my phone, just realized I missed your calls. Why didn't you leave a message?"

"Your phone kept cutting me off without giving me a chance. Do you even care what happened?" Daniel's grievance was just, but he realized he needed to dial it back a bit. He still needed David's help. "Look, I'm sorry, it's just, things were a little nuts here for a while." He explained what happened.

David said, "Well, good job then! I'll coordinate with the police there. Glad it worked out. I'll be in touch."

"Wait, David!"

"Yes?"

"The guy that called me gave me twenty-four hours to get him the data. As soon as he realizes his team has been arrested, he'll go after Sarah. You've got to swear to me that you'll keep her safe until I can get there."

"Daniel, don't worry. I'm on it. Sorry I let you down," David said.

Daniel knew he had an important errand back in New York the next day before he headed for Providence. He needed to contact Sinclair O'Reilly with the news. The man could still back out, now that the stakes had been raised. But when he said as much to his grandfather the next morning at breakfast, Nicholas told him he'd bet on Sinclair being all the more eager to help.

"Nothing that boy likes better than a fight," Nicholas said. "He's Irish, you know." Daniel got a kick out of Grandpa calling Sinclair a 'boy', since he had to be at least sixty.

"Well, he ought to like this, then. Our IT specialist has gone to ground in a safe house, our math guy is dead, and now look what happened to you two. We've got to get this done and out, before they catch up with us and someone else dies."

Pierce spoke up then, and said, "I'm not doing much of anything these days, gettin' too fat for my own good. Could you use my kind of help?" Ellis was nodding his agreement.

"Guys, I can't thank you enough for what you've done here, but I think we've got it covered now," Daniel said. Was it his imagination that his buddies seemed disappointed not to have more action?

Once that was settled, Nicholas wanted to talk about what Daniel thought could be so valuable in the pyramid code.

"I don't know, Grandpa. But there doesn't really have to be anything valuable in it, only the idea that there might be. I wish you and Grandma would go somewhere safe until we get to the bottom of all this."

"Where would you suggest, boy? It seems your enemies have some deep resources," Nicholas retorted.

"I was thinking Mom and Dad's," Daniel said. "But if they could find you here, they could find Mom and Dad, too. Can I send you on a cruise?" he asked, only half-joking.

"I've got a better idea," growled Pierce. "How about Ellis and me go with them to wherever your parents live, and make sure all of 'em are okay?"

"You'd do that for us?" Daniel asked. "That would be outstanding, but how would I ever be able to repay you?"

Ellis raised his artificial leg and waggled the articulated ankle. "You already did, buddy. You already did."

It was settled that Pierce and Ellis would drive the older Rosslers to Asheville, North Carolina, where Daniel's parents and two younger brothers lived, and stay in the area, keeping watch outside the house whenever Daniel's mom and grandparents were home alone. Daniel felt a huge relief, knowing that now he didn't have to choose between his family and Sarah in keeping them safe.

After breakfast, they took both cars to the police station to give their statements as instructed the night before. When they got there, though, they were told that the suspects had been moved. Daniel was puzzled.

"Moved? When? Why?" he asked.

"All I know is the Chief got a call in the middle of the night, woke him up and pissed him off. Some bigwig in the state capitol told him to cooperate with a guy that was on his way. About five a.m., in comes this guy dressed like one of those dudes in Men in Black and takes custody of them, leaves without even filling out paperwork. Darnedest thing I ever saw," the sergeant said. It was more excitement than he'd seen in the last five years or more, so he was very talkative about it.

"Let me guess," Daniel said. "Called himself James Jones."

"Yeah, that's the guy!" the sergeant exclaimed. "So, you know him?"

"We've met," said Daniel grimly. "Listen, I've got to get back to New York, can I go ahead and give my statement?"

"Well, that's the thing," said the sergeant, with wonder. "That James Jones fellow said there'd be no need. But if you'll all just leave your names and contact information, if we change our minds, we'll be able to get hold of you."

The five filed out of the station after giving the requested information, and stood outside in the parking lot discussing this turn of events.

"What the Sam Hill was that all about?" Nicholas demanded.

"I'm not sure, but I've run into that James Jones before. Everyone I've talked to about him seems to think he's some sort of government spook. What he has to do with this business I can't imagine. But as soon as I get to Providence, I'm going to see if David has any ideas."

They went their separate ways, then, Daniel hugging his grandparents close and whispering to them that he loved them. Then, standing up tall, he said to the Marines, "Keep 'em safe." Both men spontaneously gave the standard response: Oorah!

# Chapter 29 – Just Following Protocol

Ignorant of the events in Little Egg Harbor, Impes once again considered whether he should throw in with Barry, or curry favor by turning him in. The more he thought about it, the more he thought that the value of the information in the pyramid code was far greater than what he was being paid by the Orion Society. He rather suspected that the same would be true of Sidus, who occasionally relayed orders from the bosses. Impes reasoned that if both he and Sidus stood up to them, the bosses would respect them more and would reward them with more money. But there was no need to let Barry in on it. They didn't need him, they could hire a linguist for less than a third of the profit.

His final decision was to contact Sidus and see if he could play him, get him to agree to hold out for more money. Impes made the call.

"Sidus, I've got information for you. You probably don't know about this operation, because I've been working directly with the big guys on it, but something big is going down. I've got a proposition for you."

Sidus wondered what Impes had done this time, but he was afraid he already knew. He was seriously going to have to kill the man if he kept meddling. "Go on."

"There's a guy at the Joukowsky Institute that's turned us on to a research project that the big guys are interested in. Something about a code. Allan Barry is the professor's name."

With a sinking feeling, Sidus asked, "What's the proposition?"

"I've arranged to take the primary researcher's grandparents hostage. He agreed to report his findings to us before anyone else, to ensure their safety. I figure we can get the information, and sell it to the highest bidder. Of course, that'll probably be Orion, but you never know. And I need your help to take the proposition to Septentrio. That guy scares me, you know?"

As Impes spoke, Sidus's eyes narrowed until they were little more than slits through which he angrily studied his surroundings. "Sounds intriguing. Let's meet in person to hammer out the details."

"Okay, I'll come to you. Shall I meet you there in Langely?" Impes asked importantly.

"No, we shouldn't be seen together. Let's meet outside the Beltway. How about Riverbend Park? Can you be there by nine p.m.?" Sidus answered.

"I think so. I'll text you if I'm going to be late."

"Don't be late, Impes."

At nine p.m., Sidus waited in the empty visitor's parking lot. The park had closed at eight, and there were periodic patrols of the area by local law enforcement. Sidus figured he could wait no more than ten minutes before he'd have to leave and arrange another meeting. This whole thing was very inconvenient, so his temper was high already. At five minutes after, another car approached, but it didn't appear to be law. Impes was here.

"Hey, buddy," Sidus called, when the other man got out of his car. "Jump in, let's go grab a drink."

Leaving his car in the lot, Impes gladly got into the passenger seat and twisted to lock his seat belt in place. He was startled to see an angry scowl on Sidus's face just before his hand came up with a hypodermic that he stabbed into Impes's arm before he could react.

When Impes regained consciousness, he was restrained on

a cloth-covered table with a bright light shining into his eyes. He closed them to get away from the light, only to let them fly open as he felt a stabbing pain in his arm.

"I thought you were awake," Sidus's disembodied voice said. Impes tried to peer around him, but the surrounding darkness was impenetrable because of the blinding light. "I'm afraid you've screwed the pooch, buddy," the voice went on. "Didn't Septentrio tell you to stand down until further orders?"

Now Impes began to be truly terrified. He'd made a terrible mistake in trying to involve Sidus. The only way to get out of what he knew was coming with a minimum of pain was to give up Barry. "It was Barry's idea," he whined.

"If someone told you to jump off a cliff, would you do it," mocked Sidus in a high voice meant to sound like every scolding mother in the world. "Let's hear the whole story."

Impes began to babble, trying to tell it all at once, until the stabbing pain in his arm stopped him. Sidus spoke once again. "Start from the beginning, and tell it in sequence, or by the time you die you'll have no skin left." To Impes's horror, a hand emerged from the gloom, holding a strip of skin an inch long and half that wide, with a few drops of blood on it. Was that what was hurting him? A little more of his belief that he would survive this died, and he whimpered.

Pain! And then Sidus's voice again. "Go on, start talking."

"Barry contacted me that he had a researcher on staff that was getting somewhere on something he thought Orion would be interested in. I wanted to find out what before I bothered you or them, and besides Barry was hinting that he'd like me to help him gouge them for more money for it." Pain! *Oh, shit, why is he still doing that?* Impes thought wildly. He talked faster.

"I tried to get more information from a math professor that was helping them, but my team messed up and killed the guy. I've already taken care of their punishment for that."

"Was that after Septentrio told you to back off?" Sidus asked.

"Yes, but he wanted me to kill them, I'm sure," Impes said eagerly. Pain! *Shit! Was there any skin left?*

"So, after he told you to back off, you still thought it was a good idea to interfere?" Sidus's tone was implacable.

"I'm sorry. I got carried away. Barry told me they were holding back on him. I thought if I could make them cooperate, it would go better."

"You mean, you could get the information faster and double-cross Orion, don't you?" Sidus stated.

"No! That was Barry's idea! I wanted to trap him," Impes said, forgetting that he had already laid the plan out for Sidus. His arm was on fire, and he wanted to end this so he could get medical attention. Now he jerked with anguish as the pain moved to his other arm.

"So, you didn't mean what you said when you offered me the same deal without Barry. Or were you trying to trap me, too?" Sidus asked, anger creeping into his voice.

"No! I mean yes! I mean, ahhhhhhhhhh!" he screamed, as a deeper pain registered, all the more frightening since he couldn't see. But his hand throbbed. Another scream punctuated the air as it happened again. Then he understood. Sidus was clipping his fingers off, one by one. He knew what this meant, and his bladder let go as he faced his death.

"Sidus, for the love of God, kill me first," he begged. But Sidus was angry, and there was no one nearby to hear the screams. Therefore, the process of removing anything that could identify Impes before his body was slipped into the Potomac would happen *before* he died. It didn't pay to anger Sidus, much less his powerful employer.

## Chapter 30 – Full Steam Ahead

Daniel's thoughts circled restlessly on the drive back to New York. The incident with his grandparents had shaken him, and in spite of the fact that he was acting normally, his stomach roiled at the thought of Sarah alone, and the mysterious James Jones character on the scene again. He had lost confidence in the CIA because of David's failure to be there for him when needed.

Arriving at Sinclair's address, he knocked on the door. Sinclair opened the door and his face lit up when he saw Daniel. "Don't tell me the data is all ready already," he deadpanned.

"Not quite, sir. We need to talk. And Grandpa says hi, by the way."

"Come in, then, come in! How is your grandpa these days?"

Daniel began to tell him. When he was done, he held his breath. The last thing he'd said was, "So, if you want to bow out, I'll understand. It's gotten even more dangerous."

Sinclair looked mutinous, and he asked, "Did you tell Nick that you were going to give me an out if I wanted it?"

"Yes, sir, I did."

"And what did he say?"

"That you love a challenge, sir," Daniel answered, not quite suppressing the grin that was starting.

Sinclair's laugh boomed out. "That's an understatement, son. Nothing I love more than laying about with a shillalagh, if the occasion arises. But, it seems to me that the best thing would be for me to get started on whatever you have now, and not wait for it to be complete."

"Thank you, sir. But Raj has gone to ground. I have to wait

to hear from him before I can put you in touch with him," Daniel said gratefully.

"Very sensible. I'll be ready when I hear from you," Sinclair said.

"Um, ready for what, sir?"

"Ready to join him at his safe house, of course. And stop calling me sir. It's Sinclair."

"Yes, sir. I mean, Sinclair. That sounds excellent. I'll be in touch."

Daniel took only long enough to stop by his apartment for a change of clothes before heading for Providence and Sarah's arms. Sarah wasn't surprised to see Daniel on a Thursday, as he'd said he was coming straight to her when he'd finished wrapping up at Grandpa and Grandma Rosslers'. She was so glad to see him in one piece that she flew into his arms.

"Oh, Daniel! I was so worried. Are your grandparents okay?" Sarah peppered Daniel with questions and apologies for yelling at him when he called earlier.

"Sarah, my love," Daniel said after he had caught her to him and kissed her hello. "It's okay, and I'm sorry I didn't let you in on it sooner. Will you forgive me?"

"Oh, you silly man, I already have. I just needed to see you for myself, that you weren't hurt. Since when do you go all Rambo like that?" she babbled.

"Since the assholes got personal," he said. "I'd have done it for you, too, you know."

"Promise me you'll let the professionals handle it if anything like that ever happens again," Sarah scolded.

"Well, I didn't have that choice. David didn't answer his

phone and I couldn't leave them in the hands of the people that might have been the ones to kill Mark," he explained. "Besides, no one could be more professional than those two Marine buddies of mine."

Sarah shivered. "I'm so glad your buddies were able to help you."

"Me, too," he said. "I've got them guarding my grandparents now, and I know they'll be here in a heartbeat if we need them. I've got something else to tell you, but I'm starved, haven't eaten since breakfast. Can we go get something?"

A little while later, over their favorite pulled-pork sandwiches at Fat Belly's, Daniel told Sarah about the strange circumstance of James Jones showing up at Little Egg Harbor to take the hostage-takers into custody, and telling the police that statements from the victims wouldn't be needed. They puzzled over it for a while; who the guy might be, what his interest in these events could mean, before determining that they didn't have enough information to speculate.

As they walked back to Sarah's house with Daniel's arm wrapped tightly around her, both were thinking that they could hardly bear to be apart any more. Hours later, the two held each other close in an intimate embrace. Words didn't have to be spoken for their love and devotion to be conveyed to the other. It was in the tenderness of his caress and in her soft sighs of pleasure.

# Chapter 31 – Get That Information Now

Sidus had a lot to think about before reporting to Septentrio. Whether to tell him that Impes was dead by Sidus's hand; whether to confirm Barry's duplicity and most of all, whether to tell him that Impes had offered Sidus a piece of the pie they intended to steal from Orion. He shuddered. If Septentrio suspected he harbored any such thoughts, his fate wouldn't be much different from Impes's. On the other hand, how else would he have discovered the plot? Sidus put off the decision as long as he could, and then decided to come clean if necessary. Maybe Septentrio wouldn't ask him the last question.

"Speak." Septentrio's voice hinted at something stressful, and Sidus swallowed uncomfortably. Bad timing, the Big Guy was already in a foul mood. But, he'd made the call and there was nothing to do but plow forward.

"It's Sidus," he said.

"Yes, yes, I have caller ID, you idiot. What do you want?"

Suddenly, he knew how to handle it. "Orders," he replied crisply. "I have discovered a plot to steal the pyramid information and sell it to the highest bidder. I've dealt with one traitor, but the other is more high-profile. I want your orders before dealing with him."

"Who?" Was the terse answer.

"Impes, and Allan Barry. According to Impes, it was Barry's idea," Sidus explained.

"So, it was Impes you've dealt with already? Protocol followed?" Septentrio said, in a deceptively mild voice.

"Yes, of course. I extracted all the information he could give me, which wasn't much, and then processed the body according to protocol." Sidus didn't believe it was necessary to inform Septentrio that the 'processing' occurred before the death. He wouldn't have cared.

"Well, it's unfortunate about Barry. The man has been in a position to bring us information about many research projects in the past. But we can't have him suborning our operators. He'll have to go. Be sure you get what information he has now before you kill him."

"Yes, sir. Thank you. I'll get right on it," Sidus said. In fact, he'd already assembled a team. This time there would be no blunders like that of the unfortunate late Impes. Carefully, he went over his plan.

The safe house where they'd take Barry was ready; stocked with food and an isolation room. Four men would guard the house, two at a time, and his best interrogator, a woman, would extract the information, painfully if necessary. It never ceased to amaze him what the gentler half of the species was willing to do, with the proper incentive. Not that his interrogator needed incentive. She was just naturally sadistic. His smile would have been chilling, had anyone been there to see it.

Now to put his plan into action. He made the call. "Take him from home if possible, but take him in any case. If you miss him at home, you'll have to be careful getting him out of the building. You have the plans of the campus showing you where the security cameras are deployed. I needn't tell you that if your faces show up on security footage, you're of no use to us any more, nor what that means. Reigna, you are in charge. I'll leave it to you to make the final plans, but get it done this week."

Satisfied that his best team was on the job, Sidus relaxed with a cigar and an old brandy. The perks of being at the top were many and very satisfying. Later, he'd send for a woman.

~~~

On Monday morning, Sarah found a note from her proctor that Prof. Barry wanted to see her. Knowing his duplicity, the prospect of meeting him face to face was daunting. Could she face him without revealing that she knew the truth? On the other hand, the meeting could very well be about her tenure hearing, due at the beginning of next week. She couldn't afford to ignore his summons. Sarah sent a quick email to Barry's university account, asking if Wednesday after her late afternoon lab would be a good time, to which she received the terse answer, "Yes."

On the same morning, Barry had been gone from his house for less than half an hour when five figures dressed in camouflage that blended in with the pre-dawn gloom made their way silently through his back yard from the alleyway behind. They were so proficient at this exercise that even the skittish Jack Russell terrier next door failed to detect their passing. The first one to the back door tried it, and then swiftly picked the lock, allowing all five to pass within. They expected to find the good professor still in bed, but instead, upon searching the house, discovered him gone.

"Bloody hell," said the woman. "Why didn't we know he was away?" This useless question, addressed in general to the men, met with shrugs. "

"Why don't we check the office? Maybe he's an early bird," remarked the bravest of them. With the woman's reputation, none of them wanted to incur her wrath.

"I suppose we must. What's our backup plan?" The four made themselves comfortable in the Professor's kitchen and had coffee while they perused the map and discussed the building where his office was located, the security cameras and the likelihood of encountering students. Deciding that the halls would be quietest between the tops of the hours, they made a plan and then left to carry it out. They would observe him, learn his habits, and then act.

After patiently observing for two days, the team was ready to act. Between five and six p.m. on Wednesday, they entered his office quickly and closed the door.

"Good evening, Professor."

Barry sat up, startled at the intrusion. "Who are you, and what do you want?" he asked sharply. Without answering, one of them, the woman, stepped forward and with a swift move jabbed him in the upper arm with a hypodermic syringe. "What the hell?" Barry started, before beginning quickly to feel the euphoric effects of the cocaine.

Reigna watched closely without speaking, until Barry's eyes dilated, then called the rest of the team forward for a teaching moment. "Notice that the subject has relaxed and has even begun to smile. This is due to the euphoria induced by the drug's interference with brain chemicals. His eyes are dilated, which signals us he is at his most cooperative. Now we'll inject the sodium pentothal, while he's cooperative enough for us to deliver it intravenously."

"Can he hear us?" asked one of the men.

"Yes, but he doesn't care," Reigna answered. "I gave him a large dose of the coke."

"Won't that and the truth serum together have a negative reaction?" asked another.

"Perhaps. But we will have our answers, and then we'll kill him anyway," she shrugged. "It's too dangerous to try to get him out of here unseen. Lock the door."

In the next half-hour, Barry answered Reigna's questions as well as he could, but he just didn't have enough information to satisfy her. In frustration, she asked him, "Who would know of the progress?"

"Sarah Clarke," he muttered. "She'll be here soon. Ask Sarah."

"What do you mean, she'll be here soon?" Reigna asked sharply.

"Appointment. Six o'clock. Be here. Report everything, bitch. Tired of waiting." Barry's words were slurred, his body beginning to shut down.

"Well, gentlemen," Reigna exclaimed. "It seems we have an unexpected opportunity. Who has a silencer?" One of the men raised his pistol over his head. "Kill him," she commanded.

The man obeyed instantly, shooting Barry in the temple at close range.

"Unlock the door and be ready. Ms. Clarke should be here any minute."

## Chapter 32 – She Is A Killer

Sarah put the meeting out of her mind, knowing that her Outlook calendar would remind her on Wednesday to take her completed paper with her. It was already in the hands of the Cairo University press, and should be published within the next couple of months, as they had received it well and disseminated it to expert reviewers for vetting. That night, she Skyped with Daniel; then there was class on Tuesday afternoon, and patiently correcting her students' translations of the hieroglyphics that recorded the stories of Osiris and other Egyptian deities. By Wednesday, she had forgotten her appointment with Barry, and was looking forward to getting home after the lab. A quick check of her Outlook calendar revealed that her plans would have to be changed.

Sarah presented herself at Prof. Barry's door as soon as she could after ending the lab and putting the classroom to order. The shadows were long, and the building dark already, but Prof. Barry was in, as evidenced by the light streaming from beneath the door. Sarah knocked, and a male voice said, "Come in." Sarah turned the knob and walked in, turning to her left to greet Barry at his desk, but something was wrong. Terribly wrong. Barry was slumped over his desk, blood dripping from a frightful wound in his head. For only a second she froze. A memory of Mark flashed through her mind, and she had time to realize that Barry was dead, but no more than that. Opening her mouth to scream, Sarah felt a blow that seemed to explode the back of her head, and then everything went black.

~~~

In New York, Daniel had a meeting with Raj regarding Sinclair's suggestion that he join Raj at his safe-house, and because Sarah's lab had been later than normal due to a scheduling conflict, they had agreed that Wednesday night's Skype session was a no-go. Raj had been agitated again about the potential of the CIA watching him, and it took Daniel several hours to calm him down. Especially in view of the fact that they probably were watching him because of his Area 51 interest, if what Luke had said was true.

After the grueling evening with Raj, it was quite late when Daniel got home. He therefore thought nothing of it when he didn't hear from Sarah that night, though he missed seeing that smile in his computer screen.

Thursday morning, Daniel got up late and rushed to get to the office, grabbing a donut and cup of coffee on the way. He was walking rapidly into the bullpen when one of the large TV monitors overhead blared a "Breaking News" alert. Everyone in the immediate vicinity stopped in their tracks to look, wondering if they had been scooped on something they should have known hours before, Daniel among them, though his column wasn't normally subject to 'breaking' news.

As he watched, the headline flashed on the screen, "Second Academic Killed in Two Weeks; Murder at Joukowsky Institute for Archaeology and the Ancient World in Providence, Rhode Island" Unaware that his face had gone white, although his many female admirers took note of it, Daniel watched grimly as the story was expanded. The announcer sounded almost gleeful that the story was so shocking. "Professor Alan Barry, found dead in his office this morning, with an apparent gunshot wound to his head. Police have made no announcement as to time of death. Police have issued an all-points bulletin for a Dr. Sarah Clarke, now considered the primary suspect as she was reported to have had a meeting with Prof. Barry for last night, and is presumed to be the last person who saw him alive. Dr. Clarke is missing from her home and office."

As Daniel watched in horror, Sarah's face flashed on the screen. "Dr. Clarke is presumed armed and dangerous. If you see her, do NOT attempt to apprehend her. Call police at 204-555-7272 if you have any information regarding her whereabouts. That's 204-555-SARA. We will bring you updates on this developing story as we have them."

As the rest of the people who had been watching melted away, Daniel remained rooted to the spot, unable to think. Raj spotted him there and shook him by the shoulder. "What are you waiting for, man? You must find her!"

Daniel recognized the symptoms of shock he was experiencing, but he had no time to deal with it. Raj was right; he had to find Sarah. Shaking off the lethargy and assuming he would warm up as soon as he moved, Daniel's first thought was of Ryan and Emma. God help him, but he had to report the loss of their little girl, his Sarah, and his fear that she was in grave danger, since it wasn't possible she was a murderer. On shaking legs, he made his way to his cubicle and dialed the number, failing to remember the time difference.

~~~

Ryan answered, "This better be good. Do you know what time it is?"

Daniel's strangled answer was, "Oh, God, Ryan. It's Sarah."

It took several minutes of shouting on Ryan's part to break through the fog that even now threatened to swallow Daniel. At last, he pulled himself together long enough to explain, adding that he knew beyond all shadow of a doubt that Sarah would never murder anyone, not even a lowdown spy like Barry. His plan was to go to her house immediately, inform the authorities that she was more likely a victim than a suspect. At that, he almost broke down, unable to process that his Sarah might be gone.

Ryan's strong voice snapped him back to coherence.

"Pull yourself together, son. Luke and I will be there as soon as we can get a flight to Providence. We'll call you with our arrival time. Get over there and stand up for my daughter, and for God's sake, don't go off the deep end on the way."

"Yes, sir. I'll see you soon, sir, and thank you."

Daniel kept himself under strict control as he made his way to Kingston's office. For all he knew, the son-of-a-bitch was involved in these murders up to his neck, and he had forgotten that Kingston professed to be old friends with Barry. His sole reason for talking to the man was to arrange for an indefinite leave of absence. At the moment, Daniel wasn't sure he would ever be back, but the formalities had to be observed. He knocked on Kingston's door.

"Come in."

Daniel almost staggered into the room, still unable to shake off the shock that gripped him. Kingston looked at him in dismay.

"Good lord, Rossler, what's the matter with you?"

"S-sir, family emergency. I need a leave of absence," was all Daniel could manage by way of explanation.

"Are you okay?" Kingston asked.

"No, sir."

"Then here, you'd better have some of this." Taking a bottle of brandy and a shot glass from his lower desk drawer, Kingston poured a generous slug and handed it to Daniel, who downed it in one swallow. Would it help? Daniel didn't know, but he figured it couldn't hurt.

"Take all the time you need," Kingston was saying. "Keep

us posted."

The impact of the strong drink so early in the morning did more to shake Daniel from his state of shock than his admonitions to himself to get it together. By the time he strode out the door, he was thinking more clearly and had a plan. He would have to trust himself to drive to Providence; at this point it was the fastest way to get there. Everything he would need was either in his laptop bag or at Sarah's house, so there was no need to go home. He would drive to Providence, seek out the investigators in the case and tell them that there was no question that Sarah was in grave danger, if not already... No, he couldn't go there. She was going to be okay. She had to be okay.

~~~

It was a mercy that the highway patrol across three states were apparently busy elsewhere. Daniel's speed was seldom below eighty mph, and often above, but his headlong flight was not interrupted by such mundane concerns as speed traps. He made the normally three-hour drive in two and was at the police station where he and Sarah had spent a rough night just a couple of weeks ago, by noon. To his dismay, the first person he encountered was Sgt. Jackson, the lead investigator who had been so rude when he investigated Mark's death.

"Why does it not surprise me that you're involved in this? Come to turn yourself in, Rossler? Where's your girlfriend?" The sarcasm was back in earnest, as if he knew that Daniel couldn't afford to take physical objection to it.

"You know you had it wrong about us the first time, Jackson, and you have it wrong about Sarah now. I'm here to help in any way I can. You'd better find her before they harm her, or I won't be responsible for what happens to you." The white-hot rage that the officer's flippant remark generated served to steady

Daniel, whose emotions had been threatening to incapacitate him all morning.

"Is that a threat?" Jackson's misplaced humor was gone, replaced by a cold dislike of the man he considered a thorn in his side.

"It's a promise. Sarah's father and uncle are on the way. What can you tell me so far?" An equally cold dislike of the man before him pulled Daniel's lip into a sneer, but his first priority was Sarah. If he had to work with Jackson, he would hold it together until she was safe. Then, if he had to investigate it himself, he'd find out why this arrogant bastard was in a position to harass innocent citizens, and expose it.

Their mutual dislike established, Jackson took one more shot. "What makes you think I would tell you anything?"

"Because I'm your best bet for solving this before your incompetence gets Sarah Clarke killed."

Daniel received a text while getting what information he could from Jackson, and was forced to cut it short to pick them up at the airport. Luke had called in a favor and in short order obtained the use of a Learjet 75 business-class aircraft. Their arrival was imminent. On the way to the airport, Daniel reflected that he shouldn't have been surprised at the lack of concrete information; Prof. Barry had been found only five hours before by one of his teaching assistants, who had an eight a.m. appointment. When the hysterical young woman rushed screaming into the hallway, the ensuing chaos had created a human traffic jam that the police had to fight through to get to the scene of the crime. That also meant extra manpower had to be called in to interview all the extraneous people in the vicinity, none of whom had any information about the crime, and all of whom were in a state of high excitement about being at the scene.

It was a madhouse, and that the information had reached the news media so quickly was almost certainly because of someone wanting their fifteen minutes of fame. It was Barry's assistant who had supplied the information that he had a late-afternoon appointment with Sarah. Calls to her home and university office were unanswered, and it was quickly established that she was missing. While Daniel sped from Manhattan, police had finished up their interviews, secured the crime scene and sent in CSI for photos and trace evidence. Authorities were in the process of getting a search warrant for her house when Daniel showed up at the station earlier and ran into Jackson.

He had told them that he would cooperate with a search of her residence, to which he had a key, as soon as he returned from picking up her relatives. Daniel hoped to arrive at Sarah's house well before the search team did, so that he could hopefully find her attorney's name and phone number. Even though he knew that she had nothing to do with Barry's murder, his natural caution wanted her represented during the search. Ryan and Luke were waiting at a shuttle stop when Daniel arrived. He stopped the car and got out to open the trunk for their small bags, one of which was a kit bag reminiscent of those carried by the radiomen in the units to which he had been attached in his Middle East days.

"What's in the bag?" he asked.

Luke replied with a fierce grin, "I could tell you, but then I'd have to kill you." The cliché was code for 'none of your business', of course. Daniel accepted it; the less he knew about classified matters, the better he liked it. On the way to Sarah's house, Daniel filled them in with what he had been able to learn; not much. He also explained that they were hurrying to get there before the arrival of a search team, and that he had agreed to the search without a warrant in the interest of not wasting more time. Both of the others agreed, although they also agreed that if they could get her attorney there in time, it would be even better. Known facts covered, the conversation turned to speculation on why Sarah had been taken.

Luke was of the opinion that if the perpetrators wanted her dead, she would have been found with Barry in his office. Daniel felt a small release of his tension. Luke thought she was alive; therefore, she must be alive. That was a start. There was no longer any doubt in any of their minds that this string of crimes had to do with the pyramid research.

~~~

Arriving at Sarah's in record time, Daniel rushed in and went straight for her home office, hoping against hope that she had her lawyer's card in a drawer somewhere. Meanwhile, Ryan and Luke conducted a quick search of their own. Ryan pocketed the gun from her nightstand and stashed all the extra ammo and cleaning supplies he could find in his own suitcase. It was only a precaution, to keep police from jumping to conclusions. A quick examination revealed that the gun had been cleaned since last being fired, and it was reasonable to conclude that Sarah had not casually murdered someone, come home, cleaned the pistol and stashed it in her drawer before disappearing. Then he returned the suitcase to the trunk of Daniel's car. Neither he nor Luke wanted their things to be subject to search, which they would be if they were found in Sarah's house. Ryan returned to the house to discover that Luke was finished with his search and Daniel had fortunately found Sarah's attorney's card in the Rolodex Sarah kept on her desk. Handy that she didn't totally rely on electronic records, since her laptop was now in the hands of the police and her cell phone missing, along with her person.

The attorney promised to be there as quickly as he could,

and arrived only minutes before the police van pulled up. A quick conference with him revealed that Sarah's dad, as next of kin, could retain him in her behalf and that he would be glad to oversee the search. He preferred that the police have a warrant, but since Daniel had already given permission to search the house, he couldn't object to it. While police officers were removing equipment from the van, a bill passed between Ryan and Attorney Leavitt, ensuring that Sarah was officially represented.

Leavitt spoke quickly as the officers approached the door. "No one volunteer a word to these officers. They will ask you, Mr. Clarke, and your brother to leave. They'll also ask Daniel to leave, but they can't force him to, and I'd rather he stay. Daniel, hand me a dollar."

He barely had time to comply when the knock came at the door. "Let them in," said Leavitt. "I now represent you as well. Say nothing unless I give you the go-ahead." Daniel nodded.

Luke opened the door, and Daniel was surprised to see Jackson was the first in. Since when did the lead investigator oversee a search of somewhere that wasn't the crime scene? And then he realized that, of course, the police hadn't established that. Maybe it meant that Jackson had taken him seriously about Sarah being a victim rather than the perp. Jackson was also the first to speak, as the others filed in behind him.

"Rossler. Who are these other people?" Daniel glanced at Leavitt and received a nod.

"This is Sarah's father, Ryan Clarke, and her uncle, Luke Clarke. And this is her attorney, John Leavitt." He made no further explanation, mindful of Leavitt's instructions.

"Why would you think she needs an attorney, if she's the victim as you say, Rossler?" Jackson's belligerence wasn't going to take a rest, it seemed. Once again, Daniel glanced at Leavitt, who answered for himself this time.

"It's my understanding that you consider Miss Clarke a suspect, which is in and of itself plenty of reason for her to have an attorney. I also understand that Mr. Rossler has allowed you to search the house without a warrant. That would not be my choice, but since he assures me that she is likely a victim, and her father has no objections, you may go ahead. But you may take nothing without showing it to me first, and giving a receipt."

Jackson had no choice but to accept the terms or go back for the search warrant after all. Grudgingly, he nodded, then waved his team forward. The search was very thorough. Daniel held his breath as the nightstand drawer was opened. Would there be a trace of gun oil inside? A stray bullet? But the officer moved on without comment. Daniel was relieved that they had already removed the flash drive when another officer used a slotted spoon from Sarah's utensils to plow through all her canisters.

He wanted to talk to Luke about it before he revealed to police that he and Sarah had information that he thought had gotten both Mark Simms and Alan Barry killed. And Sarah kidnapped. Even though Luke had told them that the CIA's interest was benign, and that if they came too close to something dangerous, the Company would offer them a deal, not kill everyone involved, Daniel was now almost as paranoid as Raj. He trusted no one except Ryan, Luke, and Raj. He devoutly hoped that Sarah would have the presence of mind to do whatever would save her life. The only trouble was, he didn't know whether that would be to turn over the formula for the code, or refuse to give her captors any information. That was another thing to discuss with Luke, as soon as they were alone.

The search was finished under the watchful eyes of John

Leavitt, and officers only took the contents of her desk. The large monitor and docking station were of no use to them without the laptop, so they left those behind. Leavitt had looked at the papers they took from Sarah's desk and said that he would want them photocopied immediately, in case the originals were lost or compromised. He asked Daniel to drive him to the police station to see that it was done properly. Then he would take a taxi to his office. On the way to the station, Leavitt questioned Daniel.

"Can you tell me what this is all about?" His curiosity was apparent, but his words weren't urgent. Daniel thought he wouldn't press if refused.

"I need to talk to Luke Clarke before I say anything specific," Daniel answered. "But I think it has to do with some research that Sarah and I were doing. John, I'm terrified for her." The emotion in the last sentence made Leavitt turn and examine Daniel's profile.

"Then I'd suggest you reveal to the police anything you know that may help find her. Whatever it is, it can't be worth her life."

"That's the trouble. I don't know whether revealing it will help or put her in further danger. Thank you for coming so quickly. By the way, why did you have me give you a dollar?"

"That was a retainer," Leavitt grinned. "You got off cheap." Daniel could only shake his head. The loss of Sarah, even temporarily, wasn't what he'd call cheap, lawyer or no lawyer. Dropping Leavitt off at the curb, he hurried back to Sarah's for a long-awaited planning session with the Clarke brothers.

~~~

Daniel and the Clarkes hadn't reached any other conclusions, except that Luke thought it would be best to get in touch with his CIA buddy David and let him know what had happened, assuming he didn't already know. It stood to reason that if the CIA were monitoring Sarah's and Daniel's activities, they might even be able to trace her movements, if she had the presence of mind to keep her cell phone turned on. Assuming she still had it. But, before contacting David, Luke wanted a look at the crime scene. Daniel found no opening to question Luke about David's odd behavior. He had more important things to think about now, anyway. They decided that as soon as they finished their lunch, Daniel would drive Ryan and Luke to the police station to have a conference with Sgt. Jackson.

Half an hour later, Daniel was back at the station with the Clarkes, only to learn that Jackson was at the crime scene. They drove to the campus and parked, Daniel leading the way to the stately old building where Barry and Sarah both had their offices. On the first floor, they found a directory that led them to the third floor, where they found crime scene tape blocking the entrance to Barry's office. However, the door was open and Daniel could see Jackson moving inside. Ryan called out to him, and Jackson came to the doorway.

"What are you doing here? This is a crime scene, you can't come in." Ever the pleasant public servant.

Ryan stated his case. "We'd just like to look around, see if we can spot anything of Sarah's, maybe something the police wouldn't recognize. Officer, I swear to you that Sarah did not commit this murder. We think, we're certain, that she's been kidnapped. If you're a father, if you have any compassion at all, you'll let us take a look. We promise not to touch anything. Your CSI unit already collected all the trace, am I correct?" Ryan's voice was level, controlled, and authoritative, as befitted the CEO of a successful company. To Daniel's amazement, Jackson responded to it with more grace than he expected.

"I guess it can't do any harm. And even though I don't want you to touch anything, take some gloves." He produced a box of them from a table next to the door and held it out for the three to each take a pair. After gloving up, they ducked under the crime scene tape and entered the room, skirting a chalk outline of something small near the door. Daniel knew that the smell of cordite was in his imagination. The murder had taken place the evening before, and too many people had been in and out of the office by now for the odor to linger. But, his stomach lurched as he took in the large bloodstain on the desk and the floor beneath. Barry's blood.

Even if he had been spying on them, the man was now dead, along with Mark Simms. What the hell had they discovered that could have created this outcome? And how could revealing it help Sarah now? Luke wanted to consult with David first, and Daniel had agreed, so he said nothing to Jackson about the research. The others were examining every inch of the large room, while conscientiously keeping their hands away from the surfaces. Remembering the small chalk circle near the door, Daniel went over and knelt on one knee to examine it more closely.

"Luke, look here. Is this blood?" Luke came over and got down to see it more clearly himself.

"Yes, I'm sure it is. Officer? Your team took a sample of this, I'm sure?"

"Of course. We're not the Keystone Kops."

Luke ignored the sarcasm. "I'm almost certain this is Sarah's blood. Look, it's right where she would have stopped if she saw Barry dead at his desk. Someone could have stepped from behind the door and coshed her while she was still in shock." Daniel's heart skipped a beat as he thought of Sarah injured, bleeding. At least this stain was small, perhaps it wasn't very bad. Still, any injury to his Sarah was a stab to his soul.

"How can we find out?" Daniel asked.

Jackson answered without sarcasm for the first time since Daniel met him. "We took some hair from her brush, and we've got her toothbrush. Maybe there will be enough DNA on one of them to match up."

"Would a blood sample from me be of any use?" Ryan asked.

"Could be. Let me call the lab. If so, we can put a rush on it." Jackson's about-face gave Daniel hope that the investigation would now turn toward finding and rescuing Sarah. He almost liked the man for a minute.

Within a few more minutes, the Clarkes and Daniel agreed that they didn't see anything else that could shed light on Sarah's disappearance. Citing Occam's razor, Luke declared that the simplest explanation was that Sarah had walked in on the killer, either before or after Barry's death, and that for some reason the killer had kidnapped her rather than kill her. Jackson admitted that they had no motive, or only a very weak one, for Sarah to kill Barry. He was, after all, the head of the department where her tenure hearing was scheduled for the end of the week. Maybe she had discovered that he wouldn't support it.

"No," Daniel said. "She told me last week that he had said he *would* support it. She said he even hinted at a promotion as well." Jackson's thoughtful expression indicated he was beginning to take the idea more seriously. He locked the office door as they all trooped out and down the stairs to the parking lot. It was now late, the campus almost deserted and the parking lot nearly empty as they made their way toward their respective vehicles. Daniel thought of a question to ask Jackson and looked up from unlocking his door. What he saw made him forget the question.

"Ryan! That's Sarah's car!" There, parked between Daniel's car and Jackson's but in a row one further from the building, was Sarah's car. The three rushed over, catching Jackson's attention. He followed, walking more sedately.

"What's going on?"

"This is Sarah's car," Daniel explained. By this time they had reached the car, which was locked and revealed no trace of Sarah inside except an umbrella that she kept in the back seat for emergencies. Daniel recognized it and insisted, "It's hers. I recognize her umbrella."

Ryan turned to Jackson. "For God's sake, officer, didn't you even look for her car?"

Jackson had the grace to look abashed. "We assumed she was on the run in it. There's an all-points bulletin out for it, but no reports."

"Of course there are no reports, it's been sitting right here since yesterday," Ryan huffed. His patience with the single-minded Jackson was at an end. "What are you waiting for? Pop the trunk." Daniel's blood went cold. If Sarah was in the trunk, it wasn't likely she was alive after all this time. He couldn't stand still as Jackson went to his car and retrieved a lock-pick kit. Instead, he paced back and forth beside the car, with Ryan and Luke watching him as if he might explode. At last, Jackson had the lock picked and was raising the lid. Daniel was afraid to look, but Ryan and Luke peered inside as the trunk lid came up. A relieved sigh from Ryan broke Daniel's frozen state of anxiety. Sarah wasn't in the trunk. In a way, it was almost worse than finding her there, though. Where was she? Who had her? And what were they doing to her?

# Chapter 33 – The Hostage

Her head hurt. And it was dark, why was it so dark? As she slowly regained consciousness, she was bewildered. She was sure her eyes were open, but she could see nothing. Did it have something to do with her headache? A quick frisson of fear went through her as she wondered if she had gone blind. But no, wait. There was something pressing on her eyes. A blindfold? Her mind stopped there, the concept foreign. She was blindfolded. Moments later, she thought to ask herself why. It was difficult to think, to assign meaning to her condition. For now, she knew that her head hurt and she was blindfolded. And she didn't know why. Her memory was a blank, and she realized that she didn't know who she was, either. That was more frightening than the headache and the knowledge that she was blindfolded. In panic, she cried out, "Somebody! Help me!"

It was only then that she realized her hands were tied behind her back, and that she was lying on something hard, on her side. Dimly, she realized that meant she was in some kind of trouble, but she had no idea what it could be, nor memory of how she had come to be in this situation. Her cries growing fainter after several minutes, she dissolved into tears instead. What was going on? Had someone left her here to die alone? A random thought brought her up short. Someone loved her. It was all she knew. Someone would be looking for her. Hope bloomed, and she quit crying. Now she was thirsty. Would someone ever come, bring her some water maybe?

"Someone? I'm thirsty."

She didn't know how long it was, but long enough, she thought, to have gone back to sleep for a while. With no memories to ponder, and no sensory input, she wasn't even sure she had been asleep. Or that she wasn't still asleep, and now dreaming. But she thought she heard a noise.

"Sarah, I have some water for you. Do you think you can wake up now?"

Sarah, she thought. I'm Sarah. That she recognized her name was a great comfort to her. That she knew nothing else was of less importance. Maybe it would return to her. Sarah gratefully sipped at the water through a straw. "Thank you."

"Sarah, we have some questions for you." That was an irony. She had no answers. But they would find that out soon enough. Maybe the questions would help her remember something. She waited, silent.

"You don't want to make small talk, all right. We understand. The sooner you answer our questions, the sooner you will be released. What is the algorithm you used to crack the code?" What? What algorithm? What code? The question made no sense.

"I don't know what you're talking about," she answered, her voice timid. Somehow she knew that it wasn't her normal voice. Normally, she spoke with authority. What did she do, that she had an authoritative voice? And why wasn't it at her command now? She tried again, more firmly. "I don't understand. What algorithm? What code?"

Her questioner didn't answer for a moment, then said with exaggerated patience. "The algorithm that allowed you to crack the code in the Great Pyramid. We know you cracked it. We know that someone has given you a partial translation. What was the algorithm?"

Sarah shook her head, and immediately regretted it, as it set the headache pounding again. "I'm sorry, I have no idea what you're talking about."

Someone else spoke, with more menace. "We have ways of making you talk." Sarah jumped, startled by the second voice. She hadn't known there was more than one person in the room with her. The threat frightened her, and she decided to explain.

"I'm sorry. I don't actually remember anything. I didn't know my name until you said it. Please, why am I here? Who are you?"

A muttered oath followed her claim not to have known her name. Then a whisper. "Why did you hit her so hard?"

"Shit, I didn't know her skull would crack like an egg."

"Do you think she really can't remember?"

"Only one way to find out."

For the next hour or so, the questions came from both men, all asking the same thing in different words, but nothing Sarah could do would bring a memory of what they wanted, or anything else. When one of them said, "Do you want to end up like your friend Mark Simms?" her puzzled frown convinced them more than her protestations.

"Who?"

They left her alone then, and came back fifteen minutes later with a TV dinner and more water. They left her for a long time after the meal, long enough that she was afraid she would have an embarrassing accident if they didn't come soon. When she had reached her limit, she called out. "Please, I need to use the restroom!"

This time she got an immediate response. No sooner had she finished her plea than the door was unlocked. Hands assisted her to stand, which almost caused her to pass out from dizziness and the pain in her head. Without speaking, the person guiding her led her into a restroom, unfastened the button on her jeans and pulled down her clothing. The indignity made her gasp, but the relief was gratifying. When she was done, the hands cleaned her, stood her up and re-fastened her clothes. A flush stole over her as she realized this was probably one of her male captors, but the person hadn't spoken and she couldn't see, so she told herself to pretend it was a woman. There was nothing she could do about it anyway, and at least there had been nothing sexual in the touch. But, if she ever got out of this predicament, she planned to kill him with her bare hands. She refused to speak, and the person led her back into her cage, relocking the door behind him. Her. Whatever.

When there were no further visits after that, Sarah determined to go to sleep, telling herself strictly that she would remember when she woke up. It was not to be, however. She was still asleep when the door opened, and at least three people entered the room, based on the footsteps she could hear. The voice from her first interrogation was back.

"Now, Sarah, you must stop this foolishness and tell us what you know, or there will be serious consequences." For some reason, the word made her smile. That was weird, she thought. Her captors evidently took it as a sign of defiance, because now an unfamiliar voice, that she thought could have been female, almost shouted at her.

"You think that's funny, do you? How funny will it be when we remove your fingers, one by one?"

Sarah blanched. "Oh, my god, please, you have to believe me. I don't remember. I don't remember anything! Please don't hurt me. Let me go. I promise, I'll never tell anyone. Please."

"Perhaps you'll remember if we tell you we have Daniel Rossler. He's refusing to speak, too, but that will soon change. We will show him your little finger. Or, maybe you will talk if we relieve him of a few of his fingers. Or perhaps a hand. He will find it difficult to follow his profession one-handed, I believe."

Sarah was horrified. This unknown man could be mutilated if she didn't talk, but she didn't know anything! How could she convince them?

"Please. I really don't remember, but if you could give me something to help me remember. Photos, maybe. Anything. Maybe I would. I swear, I'd tell you if I knew!" Filled with terror for her own safety and horror that they would harm a stranger, Sarah begged. Tears filled her eyes. "Please."

"Very well. Wait here." Laughing at the irony, the woman, or maybe it was a man with a higher voice, left the room. Sarah didn't know whether her pleas would be honored, or whether the next thing she felt would be a blade on her finger. Her stomach rebelled at the thought and she vomited without warning.

"Goddammit," said a deeper voice. "Why didn't you warn me?" Too terrified to answer, Sarah just shook her head.

The door opened and closed again, and Sarah was alone.

With the isolation, Sarah wracked her brain for any information at all about her life, this Daniel Rossler that her captors thought she knew, or an algorithm. She had an idea what the word meant, but it didn't trigger anything. What did she do for a living? Break codes? Was she a spy? The thought made her feel around in her mouth for a pill that she could bite down on and kill herself if the pain of the torture that was to come became unbearable. No such luck, though, she thought, unconscious of the irony that anyone would consider being able to kill themselves lucky. Her mouth was sour, and her throat hurt. It would almost be worth having the frightening threats shouted at her again if she could get a drink of water. Sarah called out hopefully, "Someone? Could I have some water?" No response.

Exhausted with the effort of remembering, Sarah dropped off to sleep, only to be awakened by the door opening again. A straw was thrust at her lips, and she drank the water greedily. "Thank you."

Then hands were at the back of her head, and suddenly bright light flooded her perception. She squinted against it. When her eyes adjusted, she looked around to find five people wearing full balaclavas in the room with her, including a woman whose build put her in mind of a character in a movie, a mannish woman who was the villain, along with the little girl's parents. *Matilda* flashed into her mind, followed quickly by *Miss Trunchbull*. That she could remember anything encouraged her a little. That it was so irrelevant to her predicament was frustrating.

The Trunchbull woman held out a cell phone, positioning it so she could see a photo. "Does this ring a bell?"

Sarah stared curiously at the man in the image. Handsome, manly face with a firm, square jaw, that seemed to have a kind expression on it. Blue eyes, light brown hair, a little tousled. As far as she knew, she had never seen him before in her life, and said so. The phone was withdrawn, and the woman slid her finger across the screen, evidently looking for another photo. Then it was thrust in front of her face again. The same man, this time full body, standing next to a pretty young woman.

"How about this?" the Trunchbull woman said. Sarah shook her head. Pounding the wall behind Sarah's head and making her jump, the woman shouted into her face. "Don't tell me you don't recognize your boyfriend! There he is standing right beside you."

That's me? Sarah thought. Sadness for the loss of the memory flooded her. *I must have loved him*, she thought, seeing the happy look on the woman's face. *How can I save him?*

Aloud, she said, "I'm so sorry. I don't recognize those people. If you say that's me and my boyfriend, I have to believe you. But I'm telling you, I don't remember. It will do no good for you to hurt him. Even if I remembered him and wanted to save him more than I want to save myself, I can't tell you what I don't remember."

With a frustrated growl, Trunchbull withdrew the phone again and again searched through the photos. Once more, she thrust it in Sarah's line of vision. A pleasant-looking man with a receding hairline and smile lines in his face, standing next to a lovely older woman with blonde hair going to gray and a brilliant smile. Her heart lurched. "My parents," she gasped.

A flash of teeth in the mouth of the balaclava, and the voice revealed triumph. "So, you do remember. Yes, we have your parents, too. And if you don't start talking, you'll be seeing them soon, one piece at a time."

Sarah burst into tears, begging as she had never begged before. "Please, no, please. Give me a chance to remember. I don't know!" She was wailing as the last word came out of her mouth, but the woman was shaking her head as if at a recalcitrant child.

"We don't have time. You'd better have it when I return, or it will be the worse for them. All of them."

~~~

Ryan, Luke and Daniel drove to the police lab where Ryan was to give a blood sample. Sarah's car would be towed to a garage where forensics would go over it minutely, then it would be released if nothing was found to indicate it was part of the crime scene.

Their errand to the lab accomplished, the three returned

to Sarah's house, where Luke made a rapid search for surveillance equipment, finding and removing a listening device in Sarah's land line. After a short discussion, they agreed that trying to keep unwanted listeners from hearing anything was like locking the barn door after the cows were already out, so Luke used the land line to call David. The first thing he said was to warn David that their line wasn't secure.

"Friend," he said, "are you in the clear?"

David answered with caution, "Relatively. Where are you calling from?"

"You remember the young lady we discussed?"

"Of course."

"Her house. Land line. She's in trouble, can you come?"

"I'll text my ETA."

This cryptic conversation took all of 25 seconds. Even if there were highly sophisticated Homeland Security listeners being flagged that Sarah's phone was in use, a trace couldn't be accomplished in that time. Luke could only hope that David's phone was secure enough that a back trace of the line after the fact wouldn't lead to him. On the other hand, he was certain that the only group capable of that kind of effort were the good guys...CIA or possibly NSA. After he said so, Daniel muttered that he wasn't so sure those groups were good guys. Luke couldn't blame him, so he said nothing.

There was nothing left to do but wait for something to break. They hoped to hear about the possible blood sample match before too many more hours passed. Then Luke thought of something else. Was it possible that the campus had security cameras? Surely they would, in the wake of all the mass shootings occurring on college campuses and in high schools across the country. It would be foolhardy not to. A call to Sgt. Jackson revealed that he had just received a call from someone high in the police chain of command that federal agents had an interest in the case, and that he was to give his full cooperation. He sounded a little miffed, confirming the popular fiction concept that there was bad blood between the FBI and local police forces, but when Ryan told him he thought it was CIA rather than FBI, Jackson exploded.

"What are those mothers doing involved in a domestic case?" he shouted.

Ryan held the phone away from his ear until Jackson was through venting. "Your guess is as good as mine, but we think it's time everyone put their cards on the table. We'd like to come in and give you our theory of what's happened here, and why my daughter is a victim rather than a perp. And then we'd like to offer our help in the investigation."

"I'll take any information you can give me," Jackson replied. "But I'm not sure about involving civilians in a police matter. You'll have to take that up with my lieutenant."

"We'll be right over."

Less than half an hour later, the four were seated in a conference room at police headquarters, with a stenographer discreetly taking notes. Jackson started the proceedings by clearing his throat and saying, "Okay, shoot. Depending on what you have to tell me, my lieutenant is standing by to let you state your case. Let's start with Mark Simms." His last sentence was stated in a firm tone of voice, while looking at Daniel. Ryan and Luke also stared at him, leaving Daniel with no choice but to reveal to the police officer what Simms had to do with their research. He began with the background.

"Sgt. Jackson, I apologize for not being totally forthcoming with you when you interviewed us about Simms. We didn't want to believe it had anything to do with our professional relationship, but it seems there's no question now. If you have a few minutes to indulge me, I'd like to start at the beginning."

"That's as good a place as any," Jackson said dryly.

"Okay. It's an open secret that Sarah and I were on the trail of a mysterious code in the Great Pyramid at Giza." This seeming non sequitur had Jackson frowning in puzzlement immediately, but he held his tongue as Daniel went on.

"It started as an assignment for my column at the New York Times," he explained. "Sarah became involved because my editor and Prof. Barry were old friends," he continued. "Barry assigned Sarah to vet my work, make sure the methods of investigation I used and the conclusions I came to, were scientifically sound and defensible. But, after we worked on it for two months and missed my deadline, my editor pulled the plug on the story and I was forced to work on it only on the side."

Jackson interrupted now, "Is there a point to this history lesson?"

"I'm getting to it," Daniel huffed. "Keep your shirt on. So, by this time, Sarah and I had developed a personal relationship, and although we didn't advertise it widely, we were still looking for the key to the code. Along the way, we became convinced that the key was mathematical in nature, so Sarah asked Mark to help us. That's how he became involved."

"I'm still waiting for the point."

Daniel plowed on, unwilling to interrupt his story to have a pointless fight with Jackson. "Long story short, Sarah saw something and Mark found the key to the code. He sent some data to the linguistics department and got a partial message back that tended to prove our theory. There's a lot of information hidden in the stones of the Great Pyramid, and we had only begun to translate it, when Mark was killed. We have reason to believe that someone was spying on us from the beginning. Whoever that is must want that information badly. Clearly, neither Mark nor Barry would give it up, I don't know why. And now they have Sarah." The last was said with such sadness and desperation that even Jackson was moved by it.

"Son, why didn't you tell us this before?"

Eyes blazing, Daniel shook off the unwanted familiarity and said, "If I had thought there was a snowball's chance in hell that it would have brought Mark back, I would have. We took precautions, obviously not enough, but we didn't have any reason to believe that they would kill Prof. Barry. We screwed up. Sue me."

Ryan laid his hand on Daniel's arm, but addressed Jackson. "There's no need to lay blame. Everyone around them except Simms, and people they didn't even know existed, had dismissed Daniel and my daughter as a couple of crackpots chasing an illusion. They didn't know until Mark was killed that they were on the right track and that it was a dangerous secret."

"Dangerous to who?" Jackson said, heedless when Daniel winced at the grammatical error.

Ryan answered. "We don't know, but your instructions to cooperate lead us to believe that the CIA is already working this case. My brother," he said, glancing at Luke, "may be able to tell you more about that." A steady look passed between them, during which Luke must have decided that his niece's recovery was more important than his consulting business. He nodded and cleared his throat, gaining Jackson's attention.

"I'm ex-CIA," he stated simply. "I contacted an old buddy

when Sarah and Daniel came to us after Simms' murder. He's told me only that there is something that interests the government in their research, that they were monitored from the beginning. Yes, I know," he said, holding up his hand to stop Jackson's retort. "They aren't supposed to be involved in domestic surveillance, that's the FBI's bailiwick. Why do you think the agencies hate each other? CIA thinks FBI is incompetent and has no compunction about illegal activity, because they have a way around it. They spy on our allies' citizens and governments and in turn our allies spy on us. Then they trade material. It's been going on for as long as the Company has been in existence, and probably will continue. It's immaterial to our problem."

Jackson was now thoroughly confused, but had no intention of giving up his case, cases actually, to a group of civilians and a spy agency that was acting illegally. "And you see your problem as...?" he asked with his old sarcasm showing through.

"Getting Sarah back," Daniel said first. "Nothing matters to me except getting Sarah back. They can have the key to the code, I don't want anything to do with that damn pyramid anymore. I want Sarah back! Unharmed," he added in a whisper.

Once again Ryan's hand steadied him as he addressed Jackson. "We believe my daughter has been kidnapped and the perpetrator is questioning her. The best outcome would be if she gave them what they wanted and they let her go, but we can't count on that. Her loyalty to Daniel may make her hold out, or the perpetrators might consider her a liability and kill her once they have what they want." Daniel tensed as Ryan said the unthinkable in a calm manner, as if he were unaffected by the possible murder of his daughter. Ryan's hand squeezed his arm harder, and Daniel tried to calm his nerves.

Ryan went on, "We can't just wait and see what happens.

Please, let us help gather information for you. We won't get in your way. Surely you can use another pair of eyes on the security tapes, another person to help interview the students who may have seen something in passing."

Jackson was shaking his head. "You're not trained observers, it wouldn't be the help you think it would."

"There's where you're wrong," Luke spoke up. "I'm a trained observer, and I might claim to be better than you if I wanted to piss you off. As a reporter, Daniel is, too. And my brother is highly detail oriented, as an engineer. I know we can help. Let us talk to your lieutenant."

Sensing that he would get no peace if he didn't at least let them state their case, Jackson led the way to the lieutenant's office, while the stenographer left to type up her notes. When the conversation began to show signs that it would be a repeat of the last one, Daniel could no longer contain his impatience. "While we sit around and beat this thing to death, Sarah may be suffering terrible things! Let's do something!"

Jackson, surprisingly, came to his support. "He's right. Lieutenant, these folks have some unique skills. They say they can help the investigation, and if they hang around here pestering me, they're going to interfere with it. I need you to either say they can help, or lock them up so I can get some work done." Daniel gaped at him. *Would they really lock us up?* he thought. Just then, the stenographer arrived with the transcript of the previous conversation. The lieutenant accepted the papers and scanned them rapidly. When he put them down, he held the gaze of each of them in turn, then said, "Okay, you can help, but under the direction of Jackson here. If I hear you've put the investigation in jeopardy, I will lock you up on charges of interfering with a police matter." Going on a little more kindly, he looked at Daniel. "We'll get your girl back, son."

Because of their experience in observation and interview techniques, Daniel and Luke would join the effort to interview all students and staff that were on campus between noon of the day of Barry's death and noon of the next day. Ryan was tasked with watching hours of security tapes and noting on a data sheet the license numbers of cars passing the cameras at every parking lot on campus. It was a monumental task, but helped by the fact that all approaches were gated and the cars had to first pass through the gates with a clear shot of the license plates.

Ryan was joined by several uniformed police officers to help with the work. Because they now believed a victim was alive but at risk, a massive number of officers were tasked to finish both aspects of the investigation as soon as humanly possible. It was just after six p.m. when the lieutenant had given his blessing to the Clarkes and Daniel being involved in the investigation. It was midnight when Ryan realized that he had let the last few minutes go by without really seeing the tapes. He declared a halt in the interest of not missing a vital clue. He had to have some sleep, even though he doubted that he could get any.

Luke and Daniel had dragged in only a couple of hours before, after staying on campus interviewing passing students for hours. David had arrived around eight, looking like he just stepped out of a GQ advertisement.

After establishing contact with Jackson and his lieutenant, he had set about arranging for police protection for the Clarkes and Daniel, and FBI protection for Emma and Sally in Colorado. It was the last that convinced Daniel once and for all that his research had blundered into something huge. In addition, he had their cell phones fitted with surveillance equipment to trace any incoming call immediately, in case a ransom demand came through.

No one had any hope of that, though. Surely they would

have been in touch within the first twenty-four hours if ransom was the goal. Ryan didn't say it, because he had seen how such a thought made Daniel sink further into depression, but he was afraid Sarah was holding out on the information and that the kidnappers were employing coercion. His daughter had inherited a stubborn streak, a mile wide from him and, not for the first time, he regretted it intensely.

By six the next morning, the three were busy checking and cross-checking all cars that were registered to park on campus against the cars that had entered. There were none that didn't belong. Bleary-eyed and fatigued, they pondered the implications. Then, Luke said, "It's got to be someone from the university." Daniel seized the thought. "Probably from the Institute. Who else would be interested in pyramid secrets?" Luke looked at him and slapped himself with the heel of his hand on his forehead.

"Daniel, who was the linguist that Mark Simms got to translate the code?" Jackson, walking into the room at that moment stopped in his tracks, a thunderstruck look on his face. Ryan held his breath for Daniel's answer. The let-down was palpable as Daniel said, miserably, "We never knew. Mark didn't say, and he was killed before we thought to ask."

Jackson said, "We've got to put all of them under police protection. Whoever it was is next, if they know who it was, and if they don't, they might just be ruthless enough to go after them one by one until they find the right one." Daniel heard this with despair. If Jackson thought the killers were going after linguists, it meant he thought that Sarah was a lost cause.

"Why don't we just ask them?" he said.

Jackson replied, "That's all well and good, but if the perps don't know who it is, they may still go after them by process of elimination. Which one of you wants to go with me to interview them?" Daniel stood up, while Ryan and Luke said they'd each call their wives with an update. They agreed to meet at a restaurant for a delayed breakfast at ten. Daniel tossed his keys to Ryan and then followed Jackson out. David hadn't put in an appearance yet this morning, so Ryan and Luke intended to wait for him and fill him in when he got there.

# Chapter 34 – Held For Ransom

Sarah waited in dread for the return of her captors. Nothing she had tried would bring back any but the most basic memories. She had cataloged what she knew for hours, until sleep overtook her, but it was precious little. Her name was Sarah. She had a boyfriend named Daniel Rossler, whom she couldn't remember despite being shown pictures of the man. She had parents that she loved. In the dark confines of her cage, she moved rapidly through what she might have recognized as the five stages of grief, if she had remembered anything. Isolation was not only figurative; she was literally alone and sensorily deprived, her blindfold replaced at some time during the night when her silent jailer had returned to let her relieve herself again.

Denial was constant. No matter who she was or what she supposedly knew that these people wanted, it was not within her power to believe that this was happening to her. She expected to wake up at any minute. At the same time, she was angrier than she had ever been. Angry at the cruelty of the people who held her. Angry at herself for not remembering what they wanted her to. Angry at the loved ones she knew were somewhere, because they weren't rescuing her. Why weren't they rescuing her? Angry that she couldn't wake up from this utterly impossible dilemma. And if she couldn't wake up that had to mean that it was real, and that she should be preparing herself to die. Another wave of grief washed over her as she realized she wouldn't have a chance to remember her life, would never know happiness with the kind-looking man in the photo. Tears rolled unheeded down her cheeks.

They would come for her; that she was sure of. She would bargain for her life, but she had nothing with which to bargain. And then death. A cessation of this torment, at least. Perhaps by the time they allowed her to die, it would be a welcome respite. If only it wouldn't also put her parents in danger, and the stranger, who didn't deserve to be tortured or killed just because she couldn't remember. She had circled back to anger. The tears now represented frustration. How could she convince them to do something else instead?

All too soon, the noise of the door alerted her to the return of her captors. She waited, tense, for the voice that would let her know who was with her.

"Well, what have you remembered? Quick, now, there's no more time for stalling." Trunchbull. The woman frightened her more than all of the men put together, Sarah reflected. But she must answer, try to buy more time.

"Ma'am, I don't know how to say it any plainer. I would tell you if I remembered. I don't know what I know that's so valuable, but I'd tell you, honestly. If you really have that man, and he knows the secret, tell him I said to please tell you."

"Bah!" exploded the woman. "Come on." Sarah was bewildered at the response, and didn't know if the last had been a command to her or what. She was soon enlightened. A man's voice, to the left of the woman's, she thought, somewhere near her feet.

"I don't think she's faking. We should get rid of her and pick up someone else. That linguist has to know." Sarah started shaking when he said 'get rid of her', and almost missed the woman's reply.

"You're an even bigger idiot than I thought. We don't know which linguist did it. Much as I'd like to bash the bitch's head in for the trouble she's given us, our only choice is to offer her in return for the formula and the computer program they used, if he wants us to release her unharmed. How can we get in touch with her boyfriend?"

Sarah's heart soared. They had lied! They didn't have the man after all. And if he really was her boyfriend, wouldn't he give them what they wanted to get her back? Then it sank again. They were liars, what if they had lied about that? A flicker of hope bloomed. There was nothing to do but hope they hadn't lied about that. They were gone now, the door closing before she heard his response to the woman's question. With as much patience as she could muster, she prepared to wait.

~~~

Jackson dropped Daniel off at the restaurant where he was to meet the Clarkes, telling him he'd be in touch if anything turned up. He had to arrange for police protection for seven faculty members from the linguistics program, though only one had knowledge of the pyramid code. That man had been hysterical when they informed him that Mark Simms' and Prof. Barry's deaths had been related to it. They had to call EMTs and have him sedated, so Daniel still didn't know any more about him than he knew before. He was anxious to tell Ryan and Luke that they had found him, though. Spotting them through the windows, seated on the outdoor patio, he made his way through, indicating to the hostess that he had found his party.

Luke recognized first that Daniel had news, his open face unable to conceal his excitement. "Give. What did you find out?"

"We found the guy that did the translation. He's safe, but he flipped out when we told him what's going on. I didn't get to talk to him anymore. He's at the hospital, under sedation. The rest are getting police protection at home. I'm afraid the University isn't too happy with us. We literally shut down the linguistics department. Where's David? Any news on that front?"

Luke answered. "We haven't seen him yet this morning, but I just got a text asking where we are. I sent him an invitation to join us."

"Good." As Daniel uttered his response, a server approached with a pot of coffee in either hand. "Coffee? Decaf or regular?"

They made their choices and Luke asked for artificial sweetener, which the server said he'd bring right away. As Daniel and Ryan prepared their coffee the way they liked it, Luke spoke of Sarah. "You know, the good news is that her body hasn't turned up." Daniel blanched. "No, look. They had no problem leaving Simms and Barry where they were murdered. They're not going to conceal a murder. If she were dead, her body would turn up. She's alive, I know she is."

It was the first glimmer of hope for Daniel. Unconsciously, he heaved a sigh of relief as the server approached again.

"Here's your Sweet'n'Lo, sir," he said to Luke. "And sir, this is a message for you," handing a folded piece of plain white paper to Daniel. Puzzled at the unusual circumstance, Daniel immediately unfolded the paper and read the message. Ryan and Luke, looking on curiously, saw a display of emotion crossing Daniel's face. Fear, anger, hope, excitement followed one another almost too rapidly to process.

"What?" said Ryan.

With shaking hands, Daniel handed over the message to Ryan, who read it aloud.

"We have your girlfriend. We'll trade her for the formula to break the pyramid code and the computer program you're using to parse it. Keep your phone on. We have your number."

"Wait, when they phone you ask for proof of life" cautioned Luke. "You said yourself that if they had killed her already, her body would have been found," Daniel argued.

Within moments, Daniel's cell phone rang. A distorted voice came over the line instructing Daniel where to be for the exchange, and what to bring with him. The voice also warned him that police presence or surveillance would result in Sarah's death.

Lastly, it said, "Do you have all this? There will be no further contact until time for the exchange."

Daniel repeated his instructions, and heard a click on the line. "Hello?" No answer.

"They hung up." The others had heard him as he repeated the instructions, and all started talking at once.

"Stop!" Luke commanded. Each of them stopped mid-sentence and gave him their attention. "We need to go somewhere else for this conversation." Casting his eyes in the direction of the server, he lifted his eyebrows, and the others nodded. They signaled for the check and paid for their uneaten breakfasts, then left for Sarah's house, where they intended to discuss their options. There was no time to waste, as they had to decide what to do about the demand for a one-on-one exchange with no backup, and then if they decided it was safe to involve the police, they would need to go to Jackson and let him know.

~~~

No sooner had they arrived at Sarah's when David pulled up, explaining that he had been on the way to the restaurant when he spotted them and followed them. He gave a good-natured dig at Luke's ribs and said, "You're slipping, buddy. You didn't even notice you were being followed."

Luke laughed, not bothering to explain that he knew he was being followed, because there was an invisible police presence around the three of them. He assumed David was aware of it. Instead, he filled David in on the ransom demand, saying that they were glad he was there, they could use the help in listing and making a plan for every likely eventuality.

Daniel was not unaware of the tricks and double-crosses that kidnappers could put him through, he just didn't care. He would go through hell and high water to get Sarah back safely. But the others were not so sanguine that the outcome would be as Daniel wished. Luke and David especially wanted to detail what might happen and what Daniel should do in each eventuality. They went over the likelihood that the first meeting place would merely be the starting point, with Daniel being sent from place to place while the kidnappers watched from safety to make sure he wasn't followed by the authorities. David had a trick up his own sleeve for that; he had already arranged for the use of a couple of top-secret surveillance drones in case this very scenario came about. He explained their operation to Daniel, with the Clarkes listening in. He also made them swear on their lives that they were not to talk to any living soul ever about the drones, as it was highly top secret technology and the CIA could not afford this technology in the hands of anyone outside the CIA.

"There will be no need to involve the police. These things will follow you and are undetectable in most circumstances. They're ultra-compact, just big enough to carry a couple of rounds of high-powered ammunition in case a take-down is needed. They're solar-powered and make almost no noise. If anyone does see one, they think it's a pigeon. It's got a camera that broadcasts video via cell tower, so we'll be able to see you at all times and can act to protect you if need be."

Even Luke looked suitably impressed at this news. David then went over how Daniel should drive if he were asked to go to a different place; not fast enough to attract a traffic ticket, but wasting no time in case the kidnappers were timing him to prevent him from contacting followers. After they had exhausted all the twists and turns that the exchange could take except for an abrupt bullet to Sarah's brain—no one wanted to go there—David asked Daniel casually what the exact nature of his part of the bargain was.

Daniel answered that he would need a couple of hours to get it together, the database program with all the data and the algorithms for parsing it, which he didn't have with him. He thought of Raj for the first time in hours. He said, "You guys help yourselves to some food. I have an errand to run. I'll be back as soon as I can." He then strode out of the house without a backward glance, leaving a bemused Ryan and Luke in his wake, along with David, who didn't seem pleased. Driving methodically up and down streets with commercial buildings on them, Daniel finally found a pay phone. He dialed Raj's number, and listened as a succession of whirs and clicks eventually resulted in a ring and Raj's cautious, "Hello."

"Hey, it's me. No names."

"I understand my friend. What news?"

"I've been contacted. I need you to get me a copy of your work that I can exchange for her."

"You're sure she's alive?"

"As sure as I can be. Listen, can you fix it so it looks good but doesn't work right? I don't want to jeopardize her. If they test it before turning her over, it has to look legit."

"I understand. How will I get it to you?"

"I'll charter a plane if I have to. You've only got a couple of hours, can you do it?"

"I will have to, my friend."

Daniel returned to Sarah's house and took Luke aside. "I

need to get to New York and back. Is that jet still at your disposal?"

"Yes, but..."

"It's where the program is. I'll be back in time if I leave right now."

"Go, then. I'll get in touch with the pilot, who should be standing by. See you soon."

Without alerting David, who might have objected to Daniel leaving, or Ryan, who was anxious enough now that the plans were set, without learning of an errand that would take Daniel out of the area, Daniel left and drove to the section of the airport where private planes were hangared, parking in a lot that was reserved for the owners. A man stood on the tarmac, with Daniel's name on a cardboard sign.

Daniel went over and introduced himself, to which the man replied, "I'll be your pilot. Mr. Clarke said to take you to New York. I need to file a flight plan; which airport?"

Daniel thought for a moment and asked, "Is it absolutely necessary to file a flight plan?"

The pilot looked dubious, but said, "Well, I should. But no, it isn't absolutely necessary."

"Then, if you don't mind, let's just take off, and I'll tell you once we're in flight." Daniel marveled at how paranoid he had become, surpassing even Raj, he thought. It probably wouldn't matter in the least if the pilot filed a plan, no one could know who his passenger was, and even if they did, the chances that it would get back to the kidnappers were very low. Still, it couldn't hurt to be cautious, could it? Within a few moments, they were taxiing to the runway and only a few moments later were cleared for takeoff.

Once they were in the air, the pilot's voice came over Daniel's headphones. "Okay, Mr. Rossler, where are we going?"

"LaGuardia," he answered. "As quick as you can."

By the time he reached Raj's place, the latter had finished the false database, altering the algorithm slightly so that the Fibonacci number sequence would be obscured. The data would look good, but it would take a linguist days to determine that the code was scrambled. Hopefully, it would be enough.

And then Daniel was on his way back to LaGuardia for the return flight. Barring unforeseen circumstances, he would make it with an hour to spare. In his pocket was a high-density flash drive with what the kidnappers were meant to believe was the culmination of his research. Until he understood the stakes that was the best he could do.

When he rushed back into Sarah's house, Ryan jumped from his seat. "Where have you been?"

Daniel answered, "Sorry, Ryan. I had to go and get what the kidnappers want. I didn't want to worry you, I'm sorry. Is everything ready? I'll need to leave soon. I guess you'll be here monitoring the video from the drones?"

"Yes, David's been setting it up ever since you disappeared. I think he's testing it now, do you want to take a look?

"Absolutely! If I'm going to trust not only my life to these things, but also Sarah's, I guess I'd better get an idea of how good they are."

The pair went into Sarah's office, where David had set up an impressive array of equipment, including an enormous monitor that had a bird's-eye view of Sarah's bed on it at the moment.

"They're operating inside the house?" he asked.

"Yes, just for a test. They've got a four-hour video capacity, but I didn't want to test them outside yet. What do you think?"

Daniel watched as the camera panned over Sarah's dressing table, picking up images of the pearl necklace she had discarded without hanging it in her jewelry chest, a variety of other items, some as small as a tiny pearl earring. The resolution was amazing. But he wondered how it did at long range.

"It has a high degree of accuracy for its weaponry at 500 yards. The camera can pick up a gun at 1000 yards. Anything smaller and it needs to be closer."

"How fast can it cover the distance between seeing the gun and getting close enough to shoot?" Daniel rather thought he'd like it to stay within the 500 yard range.

"Pretty fast, but we're going to keep both of them tight on you, one looking forward, one looking backward to cover your rear."

For the first time in what seemed like days, Daniel's peculiar sense of humor decided to make an appearance, the stress he was under requiring some relief. "You can always count on the government to do the right thing, after it's tried everything else."

David's baffled countenance was his only reward.

~~~

The time had come for Daniel to leave for the meeting place. A last check of his cell phone was performed to determine that the mobile positioning application was active, allowing David to use the technology he had set up at Sarah's house to track Daniel at all times, even if the drones failed. However, David assured the others that the drones would not fail, and that as long as they remained within radio range, they would even operate within buildings, such as a large warehouse. An internet check of the location Daniel was given revealed that there were several such buildings nearby. Daniel's last caution, from Luke, was to be sure he could see Sarah before turning over the flash drive. However, no one but Daniel and Raj knew that the flash drive was useless, but would fool anyone for a short period of time. He thought the kidnappers might want to test it before exposing Sarah, and he had every intention of allowing that if it was what it took to get her back. He was completely confident in Raj's ability to make the ruse undetectable for at least several days.

In spite of the hours of terror for Sarah and agitation at his inability to do anything, Daniel now felt a sense of calm spread through him. He had been on the fringes of combat before, and he recognized the feeling, one of inevitability. He would do his best to do what was expected of him, and if he failed, he would likely be killed or kidnapped himself. If it ensured Sarah's safety, it was well worth the sacrifice. Unconsciously, he squared his shoulders as he walked to the car.

In the house, watching Daniel walk away, Luke said to Ryan, "That's a good man. Sarah chose well this time."

"I believe you're right," Ryan replied.

Daniel keyed the address he had been given into his GPS, and started out, following the directions of the irritating female voice that he often argued with when he drove. He had left in plenty of time to re-route if necessary to avoid traffic jams and accidents, but his excess of caution was unneeded. He arrived at the meeting place with fifteen minutes to spare. He used the time to visualize Sarah's sweet face and brilliant smile. Without realizing it, he murmured affirmations for her safe return. "I'll see you soon, sweetheart." And "Everything will be okay, I promise." It was a promise to himself and his future as much as to Sarah.

Nothing would suffice except her safety and unharmed return. He prayed that the 'unharmed' part wasn't already too late. On the stroke of six p.m., his cell phone rang.

The long silent wait had keyed Daniel up, so the ring of the cell phone made him jump. Instantly, he was flooded with disappointment. Despite his preparations, he had hoped it would be a straightforward meeting right here, with an exchange, and no runaround. The phone call told him that it wasn't going to happen that way. He picked it up and answered. The same distorted voice from this morning, at least he thought it was the same, instructed him to listen and not speak until told to.

"You will drive to the location I'll give you. You have half an hour to get there or Sarah will suffer the consequences. Do you understand?"

"Yes. What is the location?" He committed it to memory as it was spoken. "How about letting me hear her voice? How do I know she's safe?"

"I'll consider it. You'd better get moving."

With no other choice, Daniel rang off and punched the new location into his GPS. Estimated time to get there was twenty-seven minutes. Daniel tore out of the parking lot as if the hounds of hell were after him, hoping to make up time in case of delays along the way. The kidnappers were taking no chances that he would have time to call in reinforcements. With a nervous eye on the GPS clock that told him his ETA, he swung from lane to lane to avoid being trapped behind slow-moving cars. A few people expressed their irritation with his tactics by honking at him as he passed them, but he ignored it. Normally, he hated people doing what he was doing. Today, he sent them mental apologies, and an occasional muttered 'sorry, dude'. If they knew his errand was life and death, he thought they would understand. Daniel arrived with one minute to spare and breathed a sigh of relief to release his mounting tension. The phone rang.

"Very good, you made it. I have Sarah here. Don't ask her questions, just listen." The distorted voice was the second most beautiful thing he could think of hearing in that moment, and in the next second the first most beautiful thing flooded his ear.

"I'm all right. Please do as they say." It was definitely Sarah, he'd know her voice anywhere. But, why didn't she say his name? Maybe they had told her she could only say those eight words. Those eight precious words. His Sarah was all right. Relief flooded his chest and threatened to leak out his eyes, but he knew he had to keep it together to follow the next set of directions.

The distorted voice was back. "Okay, go back to the original place. You have half an hour."

Now the relief was followed by irritation, but Daniel quickly suppressed it and started the car. He no longer needed directions to get back to the original meeting place, but he punched up "Recently Found" anyway, in order to have a time estimate for pacing. Once again he sped out of a parking lot, this time to retrace his route. As he drove, Daniel reflected that the side trip was probably designed to flush any police presence and ensure the kidnappers' safety. Too bad they hadn't trusted him to follow directions, because it was unnecessary. The police had no idea this was going down. Then he considered the first words of the kidnapper on the second call, 'very good, you made it'. Did they have visual surveillance on him? But, he resisted the urge to stick his head out the window and look above. He had to trust that at least the drones were there. What technology the kidnappers had was beyond his ability of conjecture at the moment.

This time when he pulled into the parking lot, there was only one other car parked there, a black Cadillac Escalade, whereas there had been perhaps two dozen before. So part of the pointless side trip had been to allow time for the place to become deserted. Daniel parked and waited, wondering if Sarah was just a few yards away in the other car. He had just turned off his motor when his cell phone rang again.

"All right, you've done well so far. Continue to follow directions and your girlfriend will be released unharmed. Do you have the item we requested?"

"Yes. It's on a flash drive. I have it here."

"Get out of the car and walk toward the Escalade. Stop when you get halfway there. Keep your arms out to your sides or raised over your head, and make no sudden moves."

Daniel opened his door and, pocketing the cell phone, stepped out of the car with his arms extended to the sides. He began walking toward the other car, leaving his own car door open. When he reached the designated spot, a figure dressed all in black from his feet to the balaclava on his head got out of the Escalade and approached. The figure was probably male, from its gait and build, slender but with the hint of a gymnasts' grace as he walked toward Daniel. When he got closer, Daniel realized that the stranger was almost a head shorter than he. But, he dare not make any heroic moves, since he didn't know how many more were in the car with Sarah. He waited quietly. The figure stopped beside him, careful to stay clear of the line of fire from the car, should there be any. A genderless voice whispered, "Where is the item?"

Unsure why the kidnapper was whispering, Daniel also whispered, "In my side pocket, your side."

The kidnapper reached a small hand into his pocket, and

only the seriousness of the situation kept Daniel from asking Red Skelton's famous question, "Do you feel nuts?" It was difficult to suppress it, and Daniel realized in that moment that his peculiar humor served to relieve his tension at times. Meanwhile, the kidnapper had retrieved the flash drive, and whispered again, "Is this all?"

"Yes," he said. "Will you let Sarah go now?"

"In good time," whispered the figure. Again with difficulty, Daniel suppressed a surge of rage. He was prepared for this, he understood they would examine the flash drive in a computer before turning Sarah over.

"Should I wait here?" he asked calmly.

"Yes. Wait here. Keep your hands away from your pockets. When we are satisfied that this is what we require, your friend will be released."

Daniel had never felt so exposed before in his life, not even on the fringes of a Middle Eastern battle zone. He spread his legs in a stance that would be more sustainable for several minutes wait. Without thinking, he put his hands in his pockets. Immediately there was a report from the direction of the Escalade, and he felt the passing of a high-speed projectile near his right ear. Jerking his hands out of his pockets, he held them high. These people weren't kidding; it would serve him better to remember it and stay alert. Slowly, he lowered his hands, but kept them loosely held away from his pockets. He wouldn't make the same mistake twice. He wasn't sure whether the bullet had been meant to miss him or not. Testing it twice wouldn't be a great idea.

As minutes passed, Daniel curbed his impatience. He refused to worry that Raj's subterfuge hadn't worked. But he did worry a little that the kidnappers wouldn't keep their word and release Sarah. Daniel kept having to turn his thoughts away from doomsday conjecture, that they had killed Sarah right after she spoke to him, that they had no intention of releasing her in the first place, that they would keep her long enough to discover his ruse.

He was well aware that most kidnap victims are dead before the ransom demand is presented. But, he had heard her voice, less than an hour ago. That meant she was okay, right? Or did it just mean the kidnappers had recorded her statement before killing her? Daniel's posture began to slump, not only from the fatigue of holding his arms out awkwardly, but also from the pessimistic thoughts that he couldn't control. When he realized it, he made an effort to straighten up again, and raised his eyes from where he had been gazing at the tarmac toward the Escalade.

The door was opening, and, as if in a dream, Sarah stepped out, blindfolded, and assisted by another figure dressed all in black. Daniel didn't think this was the same person; he seemed bigger. Sarah staggered a little as the figure gripped her arm and started to lead her toward Daniel. He started forward, the natural impulse being to save her from a fall, but the figure that gripped her arm steadied her while holding up his hand in the universal sign for Stop! Daniel froze. It seemed to take an eternity as Sarah stumbled her way toward him, guided and supported by the iron grip on her arm. At last, they were next to him, the kidnapper still avoiding the line of fire, Daniel noticed, while Sarah was directly in front of him. With his jaw clenched, he said, "Permission to touch her."

Sarah flinched, but Daniel had no time to wonder, as the kidnapper thrust her into his arms and ran for the Escalade. Daniel immediately wrapped her in his embrace, saying, "Sweetheart, are you okay? Did they hurt you?"

Before she could answer, a shot rang out and to Daniel's

horror, the kidnapper fell to the ground. "Come on!" he shouted, and dragging Sarah with him, sprinted for his car, expecting a bullet at any second. When they reached his car, he thrust Sarah in through the open driver's side door and pushed her to move over into the passenger seat. Slamming his door, he peeled out with a squeal of tires, stopping only blocks later to still his heart and help Sarah, who was sobbing loudly, still blindfolded, and only now did he notice, handcuffed.

Chaos had broken out in the SUV, with the shooting of one of the kidnappers. Two others jumped out of the vehicle, rifles swinging from side to side as they searched nearby rooftops for the sniper who had shot their colleague. Finding no one, they got back into the car and drove toward the fallen man. He had fallen forward, so they kept a sharp eye on the buildings to which his back had been turned, rifles covering the two who got out to retrieve the body.

~~~

"Shh, shh, sweetheart, you're safe, I've got you." Gently, he worked to remove the blindfold. Sarah blinked at the light, though it was twilight and not strong. Daniel was examining the handcuffs for a way to get them off without a key, when Sarah spoke through her sobs.

"Thank you. Who are you?"

Daniel froze in shock. His eyes flew to Sarah's, which were looking at him in a mixture of gratitude and puzzlement that in turn confused him. "Sarah, it's me! I haven't changed that much in three days, have I?"

No sniper showed, but another bullet rang out, winging one of the kidnappers. Hurriedly, they withdrew into the SUV and the driver circled around to head toward the exit. That was when two more bullets pierced the windows, one on the driver's side, killing him instantly, and one on the passenger side.

She was examining his face curiously, her eyes seeming to focus more as each second ticked by. "You're him, aren't you? Daniel something." His mouth fell open. "They told me I had a boyfriend, Daniel. Are you Daniel?"

"Oh, my god, Sarah, what have they done to you! Don't you remember me?" Daniel's heart was breaking, shattering into a million pieces. His Sarah was safe, but it seemed she may no longer be his. She didn't remember him. Her eyes dropped, unable to bear the grief in his.

"I'm sorry. I think they hit me over the head. I don't remember anything." And then she wept.

Daniel didn't know whether to gather her into his arms or not. Would she be afraid of him? Would it help her remember? God willing, this was just temporary amnesia, but he needed to get her to a doctor right away. He settled for a comforting hand on her shoulder. "Sarah, we're going to figure this out. I'm taking you to a hospital, is that all right?"

Still sobbing, Sarah nodded her head.

~~~

Neither Daniel nor Sarah would know it for some hours, but the Trunchbull woman would never again terrorize a kidnapping victim, nor direct the payment of a ransom in a distorted voice. Two kidnappers remained in the vehicle, one wounded, among their dead colleagues. They were afraid to get out. As the wounded man slowly bled to death, the other considered his options. He was relieved to see Daniel put Sarah in the car and leave, after which he simply walked away, flash drive in his pocket, sirens wailing in the distance.

# Chapter 35 – I Can't Remember You

"Ryan, bring Luke and get to the hospital right away. Sarah's okay physically, but she..." Daniel lost his composure for a moment, upping Ryan's anxiety, then continued. "She seems to be suffering from amnesia. I don't know how deep or how serious, but Ryan," again he took a moment to regain his composure, his voice cracking as he went on. "She doesn't remember me."

Ryan's heart sank, but he rallied for Daniel's sake, "She will. We'll be right there."

Signaling Luke to follow, he went to the room where David was monitoring the equipment. "Daniel just called, he's taking Sarah to the hospital. She seems to have lost her memory. Do you want to go with us?"

David turned a neutral face toward them. "No, I'd better stay here and monitor. Something went wrong, the drones started firing. I'm afraid all the kidnappers are dead."

Just then Ryan called, "Luke, let's go!" Luke left with only a backward glance.

Ryan and Luke arrived at the hospital to find a distraught Daniel pacing in the lobby. He rushed over to them. "They took her to the Emergency Department, but they won't tell me anything because I'm not family!"

Ryan went to the reception desk. "I'm here to see my daughter. Her boyfriend just brought her in, and he says she's suffering from amnesia. I'd like to speak to her doctor."

"I'm sure that can be arranged. The young woman who was brought in with head trauma and fugue symptoms has no identification. Can you prove you are her father and provide ID?" Ryan was on the verge of an uncharacteristic temper tantrum when Luke stepped up and flashed a badge. "This is a police matter. I will personally guarantee that this is the young woman's father. Will you cooperate, or shall I come back with a warrant?"

The receptionist's face went white, then flushed bright red. "I'll call someone to help you right away, sir."

The three waited another five minutes before a tall young Pakistani stepped up to them and said in a musical accent, "Are you the family of the young woman Sarah?"

All three answered "Yes" at the same time, causing the doctor a little confusion. He decided that Luke was the calmest-looking, so he addressed his remarks to Luke. "Your daughter?"

"Niece," replied Luke, and then, indicating Ryan, "His daughter."

"My apologies." Now addressing Ryan, he continued, "Your daughter is fine physically except for a little dehydration and an area of bruising behind her right ear. It appears that someone struck her rather hard there with a blunt object. She tells me she remembers her name and that some people who held her captive for several days showed her a picture of her parents that she recognized, although she cannot tell us her last name. She is resting comfortably, and I will be happy to take you to her for a short visit. I must insist that you do not distress her, though. Due to her condition, I do not want to have to sedate her."

Ryan said, "I understand." Bidding the others to wait, he followed the doctor down the hall. Daniel began pacing again, but Luke put a restraining hand on his arm.

"Settle down, son. We'll get this straightened out so that you can see her as soon as possible." A grateful Daniel nodded, and took a seat to wait.

In Sarah's room, Ryan's heart clenched again to see his

baby girl looking so small in the hospital bed. What was it about hospital beds that dwarfed the patient and made her seem waif-like? Her eyes were closed and Ryan thought she might be sleeping, but when he sat down in the visitor chair, it creaked, causing her eyes to fly open, wide with alarm.

"Shh, honey, its okay," he soothed.

"Daddy?" Sending up a prayer of thanks, Ryan covered her hand with his.

"Yes, honey, it's Daddy. How do you feel?"

Sarah's eyes flooded with tears as she said, "Daddy, I can't remember anything. Where am I? What happened? Why can't I remember?"

Squeezing her hand, Ryan said, "Don't worry, honey. The doctors are going to try to help you remember. Meanwhile, you need to stay calm. You hit your head, that's why you can't remember. But we're here with you, and you're going to be fine."

"Is Mommy here?" Ryan realized then that Sarah's memories were from a much younger time, when she still addressed them as Mommy and Daddy. He would have to call Emma soon, and he'd ask her how old Sarah was at that time. In fact, he'd better arrange for her to fly out, and ask Luke if he wanted to stay and have Sally come out as well.

"No, sweetheart, not yet, but she'll be here soon. Do you want to rest now?" His voice was tender, and Sarah's response was to close her eyes.

"Yes, Daddy, I'm sleepy."

"Okay, darling. When you wake up, I'll be here, or someone else who loves you will be here. We won't leave you. But, I need to call Mommy to tell her you're okay, and get her to come here. Okay?"

"Okay, Daddy."

Ryan left, his mind already swirling with everything he needed to get done. First on the agenda was ensuring that both Luke and Daniel would be given access to Sarah, even though she didn't remember Daniel. He didn't know if she would remember Luke or not, but had hope that the deeply-held memory of the little girl she had been would include her beloved uncle. Next, get Emma on a plane, and Sally, too if Luke agreed. Ryan didn't know much about amnesia, but he figured that if more people were around that she *should* remember, her memory would start to return. Finally, talk with the doctor on what specialists to bring in. He went in search of Dr. Kassar to arrange for permission for himself, Luke or Daniel to sit with Sarah at all times.

Daniel took the first shift, grateful to Luke for being patient. He eased into the visitor chair without waking Sarah, wanting to touch her but afraid to wake her, lest she become agitated and Dr. Kassar kick him out. He gazed at her beloved face, and castigated himself again for not staying with her after Simms' death. His obligation to his employer had put the woman he loved in grave danger, and he wouldn't let that ever be the case again.

As Sarah slept, Daniel's active mind sorted through several items that he needed to take care of. Raj needed to know that their plan had worked and that Sarah was safe. And someone needed to inform the Institute that Sarah had suffered a head injury and would require a postponement of her tenure hearing. It was also time to make a tough decision.

Daniel had had enough. Too many people were dead, and too many of his loved ones had been put in grave danger. Now he might have lost Sarah, who, though he hadn't said so to her yet, was the love of his life. He was grateful she at least was alive and relatively unharmed. But if she never remembered him...well, he couldn't bear the thought of not having her in his life. If she never remembered him from their past, he'd just have to win her again. This time, he'd put a ring on her finger and not risk losing her again. But, to keep that promise to himself, he needed to abandon this cursed search for the pyramid code.

When he called Raj, he'd tell him to stop inputting data and instead erase it. He'd have to call Sinclair and tell him it was off, as well. Grandpa would be disappointed. But there was no choice. Daniel finally pulled his cell phone from his pocket and began making notes after muting the ringer so that it wouldn't wake Sarah if someone called.

An hour later, Luke came to relieve him, telling him in a hurried consultation in the hall that both Emma and Sally were on their way. Sarah's small house had only the two bedrooms besides the room she had converted to an office. He and Sally would get a hotel. Daniel protested that he should, but Luke wouldn't hear of it, at least until Sarah was released from the hospital. They would have to play it by ear at that point, depending on how much she remembered by then. It would break Daniel's heart to leave her side, but he couldn't expect her to sleep in the same bed with him if she didn't remember him. Luke comforted him, saying he thought it would be likely that her memory would fully recover, except perhaps for the attack itself. That she remembered her parents were a good sign, he told Daniel, one that they could build upon. Then Luke went into her room to sit with Sarah, while Daniel went to make the calls that he'd prioritized in his notes.

The first was to the Human Resources department at The Times. He wanted to know how much accrued leave time he had, and was happy to learn it was almost two weeks. He then told HR to expect his resignation soon. In the meanwhile, he would exhaust his vacation days. Still angered that Kingston had been spying on him, he declined to speak to his editor – he would do it later. Daniel had a vague idea that he had enough information about the pyramid to get a book deal out of it. The potential advance, plus his savings, would support him for at least a couple of years. He'd figure out what to do before that time was up.

Ryan came back at that time, bearing Daniel's iPad, so he was able to place a message in the email draft folder for his grandparents, who could pass the message on to Ellis and Pierce that their services would soon be gratefully released. He also composed a letter of resignation, which he intended to present to Kingston's supervisor, Aaron Selleck, along with the information that Kingston had been spying on him, in person.

By the following day, the men were exhausted and getting pretty ripe in the clothes they had been wearing for two days. Dr. Kassar finally persuaded them to go home for a shower and some rest. Emma and Sally were due in on a flight that would arrive just before noon, so they agreed they would go home, clean up, sleep a couple of hours if they could, and then bring the women to the hospital. Dr. Kassar promised to have Sarah alert for her mother's visit.

Promptly at one p.m., Ryan and Emma together stepped into Sarah's room, where she was sitting up and looking quite a bit better for her rest. Her IV had been removed, and she was just finishing a hospital meal. "Hello, honey," Emma said.

"Mom! I'm so glad to see you!" Ryan noted that it was 'Mom' now, not 'Mommy,' and took it as a good sign.

"What do you remember, honey?" Emma asked gently.

"I remember you, and Dad. Uncle Luke was here yesterday, and helped me understand who he was, but I can't remember much else. Dr. Kassar says that a specialist will look at me today and make some recommendations."

"That's good, darling, it's a start." Emma's tone was even, but her eyes were sad as she realized just how much Sarah had lost and wondered if it could ever be regained. What about her career? Would she still remember her studies and her research? And what about poor Daniel? The boy was devastated that Sarah didn't remember him, but he was being very brave and sweet about it.

"Mom, my head doesn't work right. When will I start to remember things?"

Emma was helpless to answer that plaintive question, but tried to soothe her daughter, "Soon, honey. Soon, I'm sure."

The specialists who examined Sarah were of the opinion that at least some of her memory loss was emotional, and that if she could work through her fear, most of it would come back to her. They warned Ryan and Emma that as much as six months to three years of her immediate past might be lost for good; specifically that there was less than a 50% chance that she would regain all of it. Daniel broke down when Ryan gently gave him that news. But, he pulled himself together and vowed to win her again if necessary. A Rossler didn't give up easily, as his Grandpa had once reminded him.

# Chapter 36 – We've Got It

"Did you get it?" Septentrio demanded.

"Yes, we got it," Sidus said with a grim smile. "I take it you'll send a courier around to pick it up?"

"Indeed. Expect someone within twenty-four hours. He'll have the code word. Excellent job, Sidus, There will be a nice bonus on its way for you. Get your retirement plans in place." The last was ironic, as both men knew that people didn't simply retire from the Society's employ; not before they were too old to be of use anymore. Few made it to that age.

"It's a pity that Reigna was lost in the process, but nobody is irreplaceable. The rest don't matter; they had to go in any event after this." Septentrio observed, with Sidus's silent assent.

After speaking to Sidus, Septentrio opened a conference call to the other three leaders.

"Momentous news, my friends. We have the code and it will be broken in a matter of weeks now. As you know, we have been waiting for centuries to get to this point. "

"That is good news, Septentrio. What next?"

"One of my men will recruit two linguists to start work on the translation as soon as the flash drive is delivered to me."

# Chapter 37 – This Must End Now

The next day, Daniel asked Ryan and Emma if they could manage without him for the day, as he had urgent errands in New York. He then drove to the Times to put his resignation letter in the hands of someone who could do something about Kingston. He knocked on Selleck's door.

"Aaron, could you spare me a few minutes?" Daniel asked.

"Certainly! How's our star archaeology reporter doing," Selleck said jovially. Unaware of what had been going on in Daniel's life; Selleck was shocked when Daniel said he was giving notice and handed him his letter of resignation. He was even more shocked when Daniel explained what had happened to Sarah. Before Daniel could elaborate on his grievance against Kingston, Selleck gave him an appraising look and said, "What's the rest of it?"

"I was getting to that. Aaron, the reason I'm handing you my resignation instead of John Kingston is that I'm afraid if I saw him I'd kill him." Selleck's eyebrows shot up, but assuming that Daniel's statement was hyperbole, didn't interrupt him as he went on, getting more and more agitated as he related his evidence.

"I can't prove any of this, and I can't tell you how I know. But John Kingston hacked into my computer shortly after I started this story, and he personally arranged for me to work with Dr. Allan Barry, who involved Sarah. This chain of events resulted in the deaths of Sarah's friend Mark Simms, Barry himself, my grandparents' being taken hostage and now Sarah's kidnapping and injury. If he didn't personally order the murders, he's neck deep into some kind of conspiracy and indirectly responsible for all of it." Daniel had worked himself into a furor, and was pacing the office. Alarmed, Selleck asked him to please sit down and discuss it.

"No, I have other matters to attend to. But if you don't do something about Kingston, I may just sue the Times. I don't want this swept under the rug, Aaron. I want Kingston taken down, where he can't do this to anyone else. In fact, maybe I'll go and kick his ass after all."

"Wait, Rossler, please! There's no need for that. I'll handle it personally. But, we don't want to lose you. Isn't there some way we can work this out?" Selleck sounded sincere, and Daniel answered in kind.

"Aaron, you know I love The Times. I've enjoyed my time here, but my personal life is in Providence. My first priority is Sarah. I want to be with her to support her recovery. I can't be in two places at once."

"What if we fixed it so you only had to be here, say, a couple of times a month? Would you consider telecommuting?"

"That's an intriguing idea that I'd certainly consider. But won't it open a can of worms with other employees?"

"We'll get HR to write up a policy that only you and a handful of others would be qualified for. How about it, Daniel, can we count on you? I'll have HR write up a contract. You'll be a freelance contributor with a regular column. Turn in the column on time, and we won't worry about what you do with the rest of your time. But, we want the scoop on whatever you find, is that fair?"

Daniel emitted a sharp bark of a laugh. "I'm afraid that ship has sailed, I'm not risking anyone else on this pyramid boondoggle. I'm quitting that as of now."

"Fair enough, and I understand though I'm sorry to hear it. Are we good then? Will you be able to get a column in this week, or do you need another week of leave?"

"I'll get it in. And thank you, Aaron."

"Can't let our best talent get away."

~~~

Next, Daniel collected Raj for a coffee break, narrowly avoiding Owen. He hated to hurt Owen, but the fewer people he had to talk to, the faster he could get back to Sarah. Owen didn't need to be mixed up in this business anyway, it wasn't safe and by now it was irrelevant. A wave of frustration and something akin to grief washed through him at that thought.

Raj took the news rather calmly, Daniel thought. He made no objection, even said something about being glad he could get back to his own research. Daniel thought it a bit strange, but then Raj was always a bit strange. He could never guess how Raj was going to react to anything. It was as if the man were of one of his mythical alien races, with different emotions and priorities than Earthlings. The thought amused him, but of course he kept it to himself.

"Raj, I'm sorry I sidetracked you for all this time on a wasted effort," he said, instead.

"No worries, my friend. No effort is ever wasted. I now know much more about cracking an encoded message than I did before. Perhaps I'll find a use for the knowledge at another time."

Satisfied that he had accomplished his errand with Raj, Daniel's next stop was Sinclair's. Once again he was pleasantly surprised that the man didn't object.

"I think that's a perfectly reasonable response to Sarah's kidnapping," he'd said. "Maybe you can take it up again when all this has settled down."

"I don't think so, Sinclair. It's been too traumatic. If I never hear the word pyramid again, it'll be too soon," Daniel said in a defeated tone. Sinclair let it pass.

"Well, I sincerely hope your lovely Sarah remembers you soon. I wouldn't want her to have forgotten me, either! Please bring her 'round for a visit when you can," he said.

Daniel knew when he was being dismissed. A moment later, he took his leave after promising a visit if and when Sarah was up to it. He drove back to Providence with nothing on his mind but Sarah. He would have been glad to know that while he was accomplishing his errands, an indignant John Kingston was being grilled in Selleck's office and later by the police. Selleck had fired him and would be pursuing civil charges if the criminal charges didn't stick.

He would have been less glad to know that messages were flying back and forth in the shared email drafts folder, only to be erased as they were read. But he would learn of it soon enough.

When he arrived in Providence, he went straight to the hospital, where it was Ryan holding vigil at the time. Sarah was sitting up in bed, looking more herself, and his heart clutched at the sight of her. His impulse was to kiss her, but he restrained himself, seeing only a look of pleasant welcome on her face, not the flare of love that he was accustomed to. Ryan left to give Daniel a chance at a visit, and Sarah didn't evidence distress, so Daniel took advantage of his time with her.

"Hi, Sarah. Do you remember me?" he asked hopefully.

"You rescued me from those people," she said shyly. "They showed me your picture, you know. They said you were my boyfriend, and that they'd hurt you if I didn't tell them the formula. Do you know what they were talking about? And are you my boyfriend?

Daniel spoke gently, "Yes, I know what they were talking

about, but you don't need to worry about it now. It's all finished." He didn't answer her second question, because he simply didn't know how to. He thought they were more than boyfriend and girlfriend, but she clearly didn't remember that part. If he told her all of it, would it shock her? Distress her? He couldn't risk it.

Sarah, though, wanted an answer. This man had risked his life to save her, her dad had told her. She liked that he was looking at her with an open expression as she examined his face for any hint of something she could remember. All she felt was that he was very attractive, and she could well have been dating him. She asked again, "Are you my boyfriend?" By now he'd found his answer.

"I'd like to be. We meant something to each other before, and you still mean the world to me. I know you can't remember, but if you'll give me a chance, I'd like to win your trust and friendship again. If you want me for your boyfriend then, well, I'm ready, willing and able."

The phrase stirred something deep in her memory, but nothing solid came to mind. It was a nice answer, though. Very graceful. It didn't presume anything, and yet, he'd told her he was still hers if she wanted him. She gazed at his earnest face and said, "I'll give you a chance."

At the end of visiting hours, the hospital asked everyone to leave, now that Sarah was past any crisis. They felt she needed her rest, and her family reluctantly agreed. Daniel was loathe to leave her unguarded, but he had something to tell her family, and this was as good an opportunity as any. The five of them went to a restaurant that was open late, glad to have a real meal at last, and he broached the subject there.

"I suppose you're wondering why I've called you all together here," he intoned, deadpan. As the others chuckled at the tired and feeble joke, he said, "No, really, I have something to say. I want you all to know that I'm devastated at what's occurred because of my research. I'm calling a halt to it and turning everything I have over to the CIA. Let them figure it out; it's too dangerous for ordinary citizens. I only wish we'd known before Mark's death what the stakes were, and I'd have done it then. I can't bring him back, but stopping now will keep Sarah and my family safe from further attack, and that's all I care about."

What he took to be a stunned silence followed this speech, and he waited for them to absorb it and react. Ryan was evidently going to be the spokesperson, because he cleared his throat. "We know what you've been up to in New York, son, and we appreciate that you've made arrangements to stay with Sarah as long as she needs or wants you there. But Raj warned us about your plan, and we don't think it's the best option."

Daniel's mouth dropped open. "Wh…Raj? How?" He simply couldn't form a coherent sentence, so Ryan answered what he thought were Daniel's questions. "I got a text message telling me to go to a certain email box, and I remembered how you and your friend were communicating in secret. When I got there, I found a message from Raj telling us what you'd been up to, and that you were on your way to tell Sinclair it was a no-go, too. Shortly after that, a message from Sinclair came in saying you'd been there and were on your way here. Sorry to do this behind your back, son, but we wanted to present a united front."

Daniel was still confused, so he just stared at Ryan, waiting for him to continue. Instead, Luke took up the narrative. "We understand where you're coming from, but we don't think you've thought it all the way through. I'd like to point out some things you may have missed."

Daniel opened his mouth to object, but Luke was already ticking off his points on his fingers. "Number one, there is a slight chance that the danger is over or at least diminished but only until they figure out that you have scrambled the data and code. And let me tell you they are going to be very annoyed when they discover that. On the other hand, those people were definitely working for someone else. How will you convince them that you've stopped working on it, and how do you know that's what they want? It's more likely they want the finished product. They could just as well kidnap you or your linguist and force you to finish the job, doesn't matter if the CIA has the code or not. They will want it as well."

Daniel had to concede that the point was valid, so he put on a conciliatory face and started to respond. However, Luke wasn't through.

"In the second place, giving it to the CIA doesn't erase your memory, or for that matter, Sarah's. Whoever hired those kidnappers don't know she's lost her memory. If they still want it, you and Sarah are easier targets than the CIA. They'll still come after you." With a sinking feeling, Daniel realized that Luke was right. It wasn't a solution.

"So, what else can we do?" he asked.

"I thought you'd never ask. You've got a couple of options. You could release it all now, everything you've got. Let the scholars of the world sort it out. There's just one problem with that. You don't know what's there. It could be benign knowledge, or even advanced knowledge that would be of benefit to everyone. But think about it, if your theory is correct and it's impossibly old, it could just as easily be the opposite. What if it's weapons of mass destruction? Or plagues of viruses and or bacteria for which we have no antidote?

"If you release it to the world, bad guys with the resources that you've seen brought to bear against you are the most likely to be able to exploit the knowledge. Do you want weapons of mass destruction in the hands of terrorists? The key to horrible diseases in the hands of people who might release them just to profit from a cure that only they know? It would be like you personally releasing Armageddon." After this long speech, Luke fell silent. Daniel was clearly considering his words, and would catch up in a minute.

"None of those sounds like what we want," Daniel said slowly. "And yet, what choice do we have?"

Luke looked at Ryan, who sighed as he realized what his next words were going to mean for his daughter. "It's the hardest for you, Daniel, but it's the right thing to do. You must see it through. Raj and Sinclair agree, which is why they contacted us. We're here to persuade you to continue your quest. You must crack the code and see what's there. Only then will you know what can be released and to whom. We all need to see that you and Sarah are better protected, but it will never be over until it's available to everyone who can benefit in a positive way."

"But, Ryan," Daniel objected. "We've already seen that we can't be protected. Not even the CIA was able to keep Sarah from being kidnapped. It's simply too dangerous."

Luke said, "Son, did you ever see a Marine pick up a grenade and pull the pin, then realize he didn't have a target?" Daniel nodded, not that he'd seen it personally, but that he understood what Luke was saying. "You know, he can't let go of that grenade until he finds the pin and puts it back in. It's too dangerous. You've pulled the pin on this particular grenade, and until you crack the code, you're going to have to hang onto it for dear life. You understand?"

Daniel was afraid he understood only too well. "So, you're saying, keep on going, then release the information that isn't harmful to everyone at once and get out of the way."

"Correct," said Luke. "Once it's all over the media, it will no longer be of any advantage to kill or kidnap you or Sarah, or anyone associated with you. It will be a *fait accompli,* and the bad guys will just have to compete with everyone else to exploit it."

"Guys, let me think about this. For now I'll tell Raj not to destroy his copy of the database if he hasn't already, and I guess he can keep entering data. But that's all. I don't want Sinclair working on it until I've had a chance to talk it over with Sarah, and who knows how long that will be?" Daniel was reluctantly coming to agree with Luke's arguments as he absorbed their logic. But, if he had anything to say about it, it wouldn't be Sarah or Sinclair taking the risk. Raj would have to fend for himself. For the first time, Daniel had an inner chuckle as he thought of his paranoid friend revealing himself to strangers to save the project that wasn't even his passion.

Luke went on to say that he would ask David to keep his surveillance up, but to back off his insistence on results for a while. Everyone agreed that Sarah needed a chance to recover before they proceeded, and David would have to accept it as well.

# Chapter 38 – Yes, Yes, Yes

Sarah didn't mind his company, seemed glad to have it in fact. By the time she was released from the hospital, she had remembered Luke and Sally as soon as they walked in the door together, another good sign. They got a hotel for the week, leaving Daniel, Ryan and Emma to sort out who would stay with Sarah at her house when she was released.

Sarah was released from the hospital on the second day after that, since nothing more could be done for her physically. Over the next week, Daniel and her parents filled her in on what she didn't remember on her own, the pieces of the puzzle gradually knitting together until she remembered almost everything prior to meeting Daniel, although she still didn't remember him, and had to re-read the paper she'd written in support of her tenure bid several times before it sunk in. Sarah didn't seem surprised that Daniel would be staying at her house and accepted it as just one more thing that she had to re-learn, for which he was very grateful. Keeping her constant company would surely help her remember him.

Daniel had contacted Martha Simms when Sarah's crisis was over, apologizing for neglecting her. Martha seemed depressed, and Daniel couldn't blame her. Especially after he told her that the specialists had cautioned against forcing or even encouraging Sarah to remember recent tragic events too soon. She would remember Martha and Mark, he explained, but not Mark's death. Seeing Martha would cause her to ask and then she'd be forced to confront it. Though her heart was broken, Martha understood, and Daniel promised to stay in touch and let her know as soon as Sarah could handle seeing her. Martha asked just one thing.

"Those bastards have taken everything from me Daniel.

Promise me you'll find them and bring them to justice."

"Martha, I'll do everything in my power, and that's a promise." Little did he or Martha know that most of the killers had already paid the price, though the man pulling the strings might never be brought to justice.

Luke and Sally flew home after the first week, with Ryan and Emma following after another. Watching the two young people together had convinced them that Sarah wasn't distressed by Daniel's company, and he wasn't pressuring her to remember. Now that he was free to stay with her full-time and just submit one column per week for the Times, they were sure he could eventually charm her again as he had the first time. They extracted a promise that he'd keep them posted daily and left her in his care with confidence.

Daniel had found time to contact Raj and tell him that he had accepted the Clarkes' logic; and though the research was off for a while, Raj could continue to input the raw data, as long as he continued to take safety precautions. However, he cautioned Raj that they still didn't know who was behind the murders, as the kidnappers were unidentified not only as to their personal identity, but also their affiliation. Neither Daniel, nor the Clarkes, nor police, nor Agency authorities believed that the dead men and woman were acting on their own. The safest thing would be to lie low, research-wise, until David had investigated more thoroughly and perhaps identified the kidnappers. Besides that, Daniel told him, the recovery of Sarah's memory was his first priority.

Slowly, over a period of weeks, Sarah regained most of what she had lost. The only exception was the pyramid research and falling in love with Daniel. She had obtained disability leave of absence from the Institute, and legal advisers there had offered a generous settlement in return for her assurance that she would not sue because of their security breach. Since Leavitt doubted she could bring a successful suit under the circumstances, Sarah accepted the settlement and devoted herself to the memory exercises that the specialists told her would eventually result in the return of most of her memory if not all of it.

Sarah liked Daniel. He was very caring, apparently wanting to cater to her every need, and, under the circumstances, very patient. Upon her return home, she had found evidence that a man was living with her at the time of her accident, his clothes in the closet and his toiletries in her bathroom. She had no reason to believe it wasn't Daniel. She found him good-looking to the point of distraction. She wanted so much to remember! But gradually, Sarah came to accept that those memories might never return.

And yet, as pleasant as she found him, she could find no spark between them. She knew it made him sad. But he just teased her and said, "This is an extreme way to get rid of me, sweetheart. This selective memory loss is rather suspicious." And then he would grin to make her understand he was kidding. The oddest thing about him was his constant joking, twisting common sayings around so they ended differently and meant something else. It was endearing, although sometime irritating. Once in a while, it was even familiar, as if she had heard the twisted saying before. He called them paraprosdokians, and they were often so corny she couldn't help but laugh.

Sarah's memory might not have been whole, but her body remembered its patterns. She was happy to accept Daniel's invitations to walk on campus and hike some nearby trails. Daniel took her to the highest point in Rhode Island and teased her about how low it really was as he'd done on a previous occasion, and she laughed, but it didn't trigger a memory of him. Daily, Daniel posted updates on one of the hidden email addresses that had been appropriated for that use. Periodically, he called Martha to report on Sarah's progress. It was a remarkably stress-free time, as the specialists had cautioned Daniel not to push Sarah, and even though he longed for her to remember him, he just enjoyed being in her company.

The change wasn't gradual, as he'd thought it would be. One day, Daniel returned from a trip to the grocery store to find Sarah holding her white teddy clutched in both arms. No sooner than he recognized what it was, color flooded his cheeks at the memory of the last time she wore it. His eyes sought hers, and found them smoldering.

"I bought this for your birthday," she said, a slow tear escaping. "You told me once when we Skyped that you hoped I'd bought a white teddy, so I did, for your birthday. Daniel, we loved each other, didn't we?"

"I still love you, Sarah," he answered intensely, fearing that her past tense meant it was no longer true for her, though she seemed to have had a memory breakthrough.

"Daniel," she choked, holding out her arms to him as she dropped the bit of lace into her lap. One stride took him to her, and he lifted her into his arms, holding her closely and murmuring, "my love, my love" over and over again. Her body was trembling, but she lifted her face to him and sought his lips. Their kiss sealed the past to the present, and her mind snapped into full focus.

Daniel sat down on the sofa and drew Sarah into his lap to comfort her as she experienced, and grieved, the past few months in rapid succession. She wept inconsolably when she remembered Mark's death, curbing her sobs only to ask after Martha. Assured that Martha was eager to see her when she was ready, Sarah whispered, "Soon, darling. We're all she's got now." The only memory she was spared was finding Barry, and Daniel was actually glad of that, as were her doctors and her family when they learned of it. She didn't need to ever remember that.

As traumatic as her full memory returning was for her, Sarah was so happy to once again feel Daniel's love surrounding her. She understood that he'd been holding back for her sake, but she felt so much safer within the circle of his arms, and there she stayed as much as she possibly could. She insisted he return to her bed that very night, where she discovered that if he hadn't been such a gentleman, Daniel's lovemaking might have made her remember sooner. Her body responded as if to long habit as he loved her.

If he hadn't been so busy absorbing the emotions of Sarah's sudden recall, Daniel would have been on his knees thanking God for the return of his Sarah. Never had he felt such joy and overwhelming sense of relief. With his nose buried in the gardenia scent of Sarah's hair, he held her close as if he'd never let her go. For a few days, he wouldn't let her out of his sight, following her everywhere like a faithful dog, and even standing outside the closed door when she required privacy.

~~~

Though it had been only four weeks since her kidnap, Sarah felt as if she'd been away on a long trip. She already knew that her classes were being handled by a substitute, and that her tenure hearing had been postponed until late in the semester, but she began to be restless, with nothing to occupy her time now that she remembered everything. Daniel recognized that he needed to provide a distraction, and remembering his vow, began to plan a surprise that he hoped would end well for him as well as Sarah.

When she awoke, Sarah found a breakfast repast of waffles, fresh strawberries and whipped cream, along with mimosas and coffee. "What's this?" she asked. "Did I forget our anniversary?"

"Ha ha, that's my job, and we haven't known each other for a year yet," Daniel smirked. "No, I just wanted to surprise you with a special weekend. Happy Special Weekend," he said, handing her a single red rose from which he'd carefully trimmed the thorns.

"Aw, sweetie, thank you," Sarah cooed, genuinely touched at his gesture.

"This is just the beginning. Eat up, we're taking a road trip," he responded.

Obediently consuming her breakfast but taking time to savor the sweet strawberries, she wondered where he'd managed to get such good ones at this time of year. Strawberries were her favorite, she remembered. In a way it was odd, how sudden realizations like that made her likes and dislikes seem more immediate, where before they were just there and of no particular importance. As if her life had come into focus after being fuzzy for years. It had to be a side effect of the temporary amnesia, she thought, because she didn't remember having thoughts like that before. Sighing happily, she dipped a succulent strawberry into the whipped cream and savored it slowly, completely unaware that Daniel's breath had turned ragged as he watched.

The day was crisp but sunny when, after breakfast and clearing away, Daniel bundled Sarah into the car and tossed in an overnight bag for each of them and their hiking boots into the back seat. Sarah laughed, and said, "I don't even get to pack my own bag? How do I know you remembered everything?"

"You won't need much," he grinned. "We're just going for overnight, and you're wearing the right clothes for today already."

Sarah was dressed in soft brown corduroy pants and a plaid flannel shirt, with a cashmere sweater knotted by the sleeves around her neck. Daniel, in jeans and a plaid flannel shirt of his own, looked like a hunter, or maybe a cowboy, Sarah mused. A delicious one, she thought to herself, lost in admiration of the figure he cut in his tight jeans. What fun, that he had planned a surprise for her. She needed some adventure.

Half an hour later, Sarah waited in the car at a tiny resort near Fisherville, while Daniel went into the office for the key. The silver-haired woman at the counter had to be the one he had spoken to on the phone, so he grinned at her. Her face lit up and she came around the counter, where he made good on the promise of a big hug and thanked her for making their cabin available for early check-in. He could hardly wait for evening, when the bulk of his surprise would unfold. Meanwhile, he had a beautiful woman to entertain and keep busy while his co-conspirator arranged the surprise.

A brisk walk around the lake consumed most of the rest of the morning, and then lunch at a cafe in town that boasted a great seafood chowder. After lunch, Daniel followed Sarah patiently from store to store in the quaint little tourist town, becoming a beast of burden as she bought this and that and handed him the bags to carry so her hands were free to find more. It was a special kind of joy to see her laughing and smiling, the Sarah he'd known before Mark's death gradually coming to the surface. He'd fallen in love with this Sarah, and though he loved her in all her moods, through thick and thin, this happy version was his very favorite Sarah. Watching her was like watching a kitten play. It just naturally made him smile.

When she was tired of shopping, Daniel insisted on taking Sarah to a movie. She was curious; it was almost as if he were avoiding their cabin, but this was his surprise and she would go along with it. They had a choice between a chick flick and an action adventure, and Daniel insisted she pick. Almost as a challenge, she chose the chick flick, but to her surprise, Daniel didn't object. He even gave every evidence of enjoying it. Finally, when the movie was over with the appropriate amount of tears on Sarah's part for the happy ending, they emerged from the theater into the early December twilight. Sarah slipped her arms into her sweater, as the air had grown chilly.

Back at the little resort, Daniel left Sarah in the car again, saying he needed to check something with the proprietress.

"Everything's ready, dear," the woman assured him. "There were almost too many flowers for the available places to put them, but we managed. The champagne is chilling in an ice bucket, and the caterers just brought the food. Your girl is going to swoon."

"I can't thank you enough for helping me pull this off at the last minute."

"You're so welcome. I'm a sucker for young love. Do me a favor, though."

"Anything," said Daniel.

"Bring your girl to the office in the morning. I want to see if she's pretty enough for you."

"Oh, I can attest to that. She's the most beautiful girl in the whole world—way out of my league. I don't have a clue what she sees in me, but I'll take it."

Laughing, his co-conspirator waved him out. "Go, have fun. And come see me in the morning."

"We will."

Daniel pulled Sarah's car up to the door of the honeymoon

cabin and rushed around to open her door for her as she waited impatiently. He had with difficulty trained her to allow him to open doors for her, as she was used to doing it herself. But, she thought it was so sweet that he was old-fashioned that way. However, this time, as he gave her a hand to help her out, he swept her into his arms.

"Daniel, what are you doing?"

"You'll see. Can you manage the key?" Awkwardly, she leaned down to work the big key into the keyhole and twist the doorknob. Her first glimpse into the cabin made her gasp. On literally every surface, fresh flowers were arrayed in glorious abandon. Roses, lily of the valley, tulips, every flower she could name and a few she couldn't, graced the nightstands, the counters, the top of the chest of drawers, and even the shelves on the walls that she thought had contained knickknacks earlier.

"Daniel, how?"

"We have our ways, my dear," he said, in a funny accent, waggling his brows. Setting her down carefully, he put his arms around her and kissed her. "Do you like it?"

"I can hardly take it in! Daniel, what is this all about?"

Barely taking time to swing the door shut, Daniel dropped to one knee, and Sarah's hands flew to her mouth as tears started in her eyes. "Sarah, love of my life, heart of my heart, will you marry me?"

Overcome, all Sarah could do was nod, until Daniel stood to take her in his arms again. Then she said with a tremulous smile, "Daniel, I will marry you, yes, yes, yes." Squeezing her tighter with one arm, Daniel slipped the other hand into his pocket and removed the ring box and pressed it into Sarah's hand. When she opened the box, her eyes went wide and the tears that were threatening spilled over.

"Oh, Daniel," she breathed. "This is the most beautiful ring I've ever seen. It's perfect! How did you know?"

He took the ring and slipped it onto her finger, whispering, "A perfect ring for a perfect woman."

Sarah found the white teddy in her bag, and smiled at Daniel's detailed planning. Trust Daniel to have enough confidence that her answer would be yes to bring along the special touch to start their night of love off right. She called out to him, "Don't you have an errand to do, my love?"

"No...Oh, yes, so I do," he said, grinning, and took himself outside so that his woman could prepare a feast for his eyes.

After a night of tender passion and not much sleep, Daniel presented his intended to the delighted proprietress, who gave them coffee and scones from her own kitchen. Sarah's color was high, whether from being a little flustered by the woman's attention or because her skin was still inflamed from his kisses, Daniel didn't know. But Sarah was always the most beautiful when her soft skin had that ruby glow. He was going to have trouble driving, because he couldn't tear his eyes away from her. That she was his overwhelmed him and kept driving lumps into his throat at the most inconvenient times. Like when he thanked their hostess again for all her help.

"Dear, I was so glad to do it. You let me know when the wedding is, and I'll make sure to have your cabin for you."

"Thank you. We haven't even discussed that, or where we might want to go on honeymoon. But if Sarah agrees, I'd love to spend our wedding night here."

Sarah just smiled and nodded.

When they returned to Sarah's house, Daniel suggested

they call his family with the good news. Sarah agreed that would be a lovely idea, and so it was that they had a long Skype conversation with Ben and Nancy, Daniel's parents, and then Nicholas and Bess. Bess insisted on going out to get Daniel's friends, who were still on guard duty, so they could hear the good news, too. When they saw Sarah, Pierce let out a wolf whistle, while Ellis swallowed convulsively. *Sarah and her effect on the male of the species*, thought Daniel. *I'm going to have to carry a club.*

After that, of course, they had to call Sarah's parents and her sister Meg with the good news, and then Luke and Sally. Daniel's brothers, Aaron and Josh, had missed his call and would hear the news from their parents. The person Sarah wanted to tell next was Martha, so they drove over to surprise her.

As they would have expected, Martha was ecstatic about the engagement, and she exclaimed over the beauty of the ring enough to satisfy the proudest groom and the happiest bride. "When's the wedding, my dears?" she asked.

Daniel and Sarah looked at each other and laughed. "We haven't gotten around to setting a date yet," Sarah explained. When they got home, though, yet another unpleasant reminder of the kidnapping was waiting on their front porch.

~~~

While Sarah was recuperating, Sgt. Jackson had not been idle. It was too much of a coincidence to believe that Mark Simms' and Alan Barry's deaths had been unrelated, especially since the one person who linked them, Sarah Clarke, had been kidnapped. However, nothing had turned up in the evidence to identify the perpetrators.

With the kidnappers' deaths, Simms' and Barry's murders were deemed solved, but unexplained. Sgt. Jackson was livid over the unauthorized action during the exchange, but nothing could change the outcome. As the only two people on the scene who weren't dead, Sarah and Daniel were immediately tested for gunpowder residue and Daniel's car was thoroughly searched. Both came up negative.

No one mentioned the drones, so Sgt. Jackson was forced to conclude that David had managed to get a sniper on one of the nearby roofs. A professional, of course, since no trace of shell casings, footprints, fibers or anything else that didn't belong was ever found despite a massive CSI effort. Jackson was also incensed that David, citing national security, declined to be interviewed regarding his role in the rescue. Everything on the persons of the dead kidnappers, plus everything from their car, was boxed up and placed in the evidence room.

Now, weeks later, Sgt. Jackson wanted nothing more than to satisfy his own curiosity. It was the best he could expect, as all leads, such as they were, had grown cold. Furthermore, he'd never had the opportunity to interview Sarah about what she remembered. As Daniel and Sarah approached in Daniel's car, Sgt. Jackson's lanky figure peeled away from the wall where he was leaning and he raised his hand in greeting.

"Jackson, what are you doing here?" Daniel said, only slightly less hostile than the words sounded. Jackson held up both hands now, in a conciliatory gesture.

"Just wanted a little chat with Dr. Clarke, if that's okay. So I can wrap up my investigation and close it once and for all."

"You'd better come in then," said Sarah, quelling Daniel's objection with a look. "I'm afraid I won't be able to help much, though. I don't really remember anything about the kidnapping until I woke up, which we've worked out was at least 24 hours after it happened. "

Jackson shook his head. "That's about what we've got on the rest of it, too. Two dead victims, no leads, four dead kidnappers and you, Dr. Clarke. Any idea of why someone would want to kill all of those people?" Jackson trailed off, aware for the first time that Sarah was looking at him in consternation. "What is it, Dr. Clarke?"

"You said four dead kidnappers. Daniel said it was all of them, but there were five of them," Sarah explained.

Now both of the men were staring at her. "Are you sure, darling?" Daniel asked gently. "How do you know?"

"When I was in the car, I heard them talking. I knew one was a woman, and all she said was 'shut up', but before that, there were four different voices, arguing."

Daniel turned to Jackson. "One of them is still out there. You can't close the investigation."

Jackson answered grimly. "Damn straight."

# Chapter 39 – It Goes In Cycles

Septentrio stared at his recently-hired linguist in rage. "Are you telling me that everything about the data we gave you is gibberish?" he demanded.

The linguist had never seen such contained rage, and shook in his shoes as he answered. "We can make nothing of it," he said carefully. "It seems to be deliberately randomized. Even a code we couldn't break would be more uniform in, for example, distribution of the individual symbols. We're fairly certain that the problem lies with the data."

For a moment, Septentrio fought his rage, cognizant that his first thought, killing the researchers, would do no good. They'd fooled him this time, but the fact that they went to the trouble to do so meant that they genuinely thought they had something of value to hide.

The tantalizing message on the scrap of paper that Impes had retrieved from Mark's killers confirmed it. Rather than kill Rossler and the woman, or even the data specialist, Raj, it would be better to let them continue to work while he monitored them, or rather, while Sidus monitored them. After the code was broken would be plenty of time to snatch it, and then these troublesome people would be of no further use. At that time, he could exact his revenge.

Though he had reached a sane and reasoned conclusion, Septentrio needed an outlet for his rage. He would make do by calling Sidus on the carpet for the incompetent job he'd done in not verifying that he had a true copy of the data.

"Why am I surrounded by incompetents?" he shouted as soon as Sidus's face appeared in his screen. "Give me one reason why I shouldn't fire the lot of you and replace you with someone who knows his ass from a hole in the ground!"

"Sir, please. I didn't have time to even look at what was on the flash drive before your courier took it. If I had, I would have known. But, there's good news. The woman has recovered her memory and work will resume soon, you have my word on it."

"Bah, your word. No more fuck-ups, Sidus, do you hear me?"

"Loud and clear, sir."

~~~

Sarah had been looking forward to a conference that she had planned prior to the murders, as something normal for a change. Though Daniel insisted on accompanying her everywhere, it still felt good to begin to get back into work mode. Technically, she was still on leave of absence, but she insisted on returning to campus to conduct the conference. The guests of honor were several of her colleagues from the University of Cairo, distinguished Egyptologists she'd met in her studies for her doctoral thesis. Between lectures and after hours, Sarah and Daniel had the opportunity to socialize with these men, and carry on some stimulating discussions.

One of the more interesting of the many discussions Sarah and Daniel had with her friends had to do with the timeline of human history. Without begging the question of what attributes constituted a human being, Ahmed Mustafa, a professor of archaeology specializing in pre-historic Egyptian studies, mentioned in passing some scholars who shared his specialty theorized that human civilization had to have predated the accepted 6000 BC mark, perhaps by tens of thousands of years. The couple were fascinated to hear his thinking on the subject, but Sarah couldn't help asking, "Where is the archaeological evidence, Ahmed?"

"We believe the Great Pyramid is part of it," he replied.

"However, you must understand that we believe the destruction of each cycle of human civilization also wipes out most of the other evidence, such as buildings and monuments. Think of the Colossus of Rhodes, destroyed in an earthquake before the birth of Christ. If a local earthquake can destroy one of the wonders of the world, think what world-wide catastrophe would do."

Daniel's mind had seized on the phrase 'each cycle'. Now, he asked for an explanation of what Ahmed was talking about.

"Before I begin, I must ask if you are familiar with certain scientific facts," Ahmed answered. "You are aware of the precession of the equinoxes, yes?"

"Wasn't that what all the Doomsday prophets were on about a couple of years ago?" Daniel answered. Sarah's expression indicated her confusion, so Ahmed answered by expanding Daniel's statement.

"Yes. Many people in your country confused it with the end of the Aztec calendar," he said, making the hand sign for quotation marks as he said the word 'end'. "However, some of us recognized that the most recent end of the precession was in 2008, and believe me, some of my colleagues were very disappointed that the world didn't come to a disastrous end. Many genuinely expected it."

Seeing Sarah's shock, he went on. "No, my dear friend, they are not, how do you say, crackpots? I must explain another scientific fact. First, let me just say that the precession of the equinoxes is nothing more than the phenomenon caused by the earth's axis describing a circle as it rotates. Because of the tilt of the earth, as well as the gravitational pull exerted by the sun and the other planets, in a marvelous ballet of the universe, our earth is a ballerina, twirling in place, you see."

Sarah smiled, entranced by the analogy. Daniel was

nodding, impatient to hear the rest of the story.

"Now, she does not just twirl, but sways, so that if her arm were pointing upward, it would describe a circle around her, do you see?"

Sarah nodded eagerly, finally able to picture what Ahmed was describing. He went on, "This means that the equinoxes rotate as well, and what I mean by 'cycle' is that the circle takes approximately 26,000 years to complete. During that time, if you were to graph the equinoxes, they would show as the spokes of a wheel. Each spoke will be in the same place every 26,000 years."

Now Sarah had it completely, her agile mind moving on to a conclusion. "If that's the case, how do we know where the circle begins?" she said. "Couldn't we simply pick any given year and say that the cycle was complete, because the equinoxes are now in the same place as they were 26,000 years ago?"

"Ah, I see you have discovered the reason so many Doomsday prophets are disappointed in their predictions," laughed Ahmed.

"Then I don't see what merit this has, vis-a-vis the pyramid builders," she observed.

"But wait, friend Sarah. You have not heard the rest of the story. Do you know about tectonic plates?"

"The theory that the land mass of the earth used to be all in one piece, and that plates below it move?" Sarah ventured.

"Yes, but I must protest the word theory. This is a scientifically proven fact. Once, the entire land mass of the earth was jammed together like a large ball of clay. Imagine how that might have affected the tilt of the axis, the weight of it causing a rotational pull like that of a gyroscope that is out of balance. We believe that this condition of being out of balance is what began to break up the plates, and that it would have had more force as precession of the axis tilted along the leading edge of the bulge."

"So, you mark the beginning and end of a cycle at the point where the gravitational pull is greatest, causing some disturbance of the tectonic plates, have I got that right?"

"Precisely. Naturally, as the plates have redistributed the land mass, the effect is diminished. But, we still have cycles of weather disturbances accompanied by movement in the plates that, while they may be minuscule on a world scale, cause catastrophic events such as typhoons, hurricanes, volcanic eruptions and earthquakes."

"But those occur all the time," Daniel protested.

"Yes, however, on a cyclic basis, they cluster. Each year, the events become larger and occur closer together until, a shift occurs that almost instantaneously wipes out most of the life on earth. We can predict approximately when that will occur if we take note of the clusters of natural events and look back over the past, to see when an event such as, say, the disappearance of the dinosaurs, is large enough to show in our geologic record. That is the end of a cycle."

Daniel sat back, stunned. It made too much sense to dismiss it, but he needed time to absorb the idea and think it through. The burning question was, if this was known, why wasn't it taught in schools, discussed in scientific research papers? Why had he, an investigative journalist with fairly broad knowledge of archaeology, not read or heard a peep about it? Before he could ask the question, Sarah brought up another point.

"Would this explain how it could be that a large animal such as a mastodon would freeze instantly, so quickly that the food in its stomach is as fresh as if the animal had eaten it only minutes ago?"

Ahmed nodded with approval. "Yes, we believe so. Furthermore, we think that the occasional confusion of the magnetic poles is another key to understanding these disturbances, though it happens much less frequently, and is much less dramatic than your popular science fiction writers would have it."

"Well, you have certainly given us food for thought. Could you sum it up for us, in terms of what we're researching?"

"Gladly. We are convinced that the Great Pyramid is a survivor from the last catastrophic destruction of human civilization, built to withstand the natural disasters that would have accompanied such an event. If we're right, then we can think of only one reason for the civilization that came before us to build such a thing, and that would be to record their existence, as well as hopefully their knowledge. Clearly, they were more advanced than we are today. This begs the question of how many times this has happened. In light of recent discoveries of 400,000 year-old humanoid remains bearing DNA that is too close to ours to dismiss, we have to believe that many such civilizations could have arisen and been destroyed."

"How do you account for the last six thousand years, then, when our civilization hasn't been destroyed?"

"I would simply believe that we find ourselves near the beginning. However, we must look a bit further back, because we don't find the evidence of massive destruction six thousand years ago. No, I believe we are closer to the end."

A shiver went through Sarah as her friend said the last words, her knowledge of the end times described in the Bible paralleling some of the events of the times too closely for comfort.

Ahmed ended their meeting by saying, "I am not one who

wishes the secret to remain secret. That makes no sense to me. How is it to open 'in the fullness of time' if we do not at least try to understand it? And, when we understand it will be the proper time to understand it. How can it be otherwise? May Allah grant you the wisdom to complete your mission, my friends."

Sarah stood, and then Daniel, who held out his hand to Ahmed. Ahmed hesitated, shook it briefly, and then touched his hand to his heart. Sarah understood that if she held out her hand Ahmed would be put in an awkward position, so she simply nodded to him. Ahmed said, in English, "Go in peace."

Sarah completed the ritual by responding, "May God protect you." Daniel, having been in an Arabic-speaking region during his time as a journalist with the Marines, spoke a passable Salaam.

Later, at home and with the jamming device deployed, Daniel and Sarah spoke of the ideas Ahmed had put forward. In the light of the partial translation of what they could only assume was a greeting message, displayed as it was in the entrance passageway of the pyramid, it made perfect sense. If it were indeed true, what they were on the verge of discovering could be even more dangerous than two murders, a hostage-taking and Sarah's kidnap indicated; something of such massive danger as to be truly a matter of national or even world security.

This was too big to set aside, and yet, too big to handle on their own. It was time to call in reinforcements, and not just a couple of Marine buddies. Talking late into the night, Daniel and Sarah decided to bring in older and wiser heads, knowing that it was dangerous, but these were people who were already involved to some extent. Tomorrow, they would call Sarah's dad and uncle as well as Nicholas and possibly Sinclair.

# Chapter 40 – We Need Your Help

As expected and promised by Uncle Luke Daniel and Sarah hadn't heard a peep from David since the day of Sarah's rescue. They hadn't been thinking about him much lately as it seemed as if everything had returned to normal. But, in the back of his mind, Daniel did know he would turn up again sometime. So, it came as a bit of a shock when Daniel answered a knock at their door early the following morning, to see David. David had packed up and left without waiting to say goodbye before Daniel or the Clarkes returned to Sarah's house from the hospital after the kidnapping

"May I come in?" David's easy smile disarmed Daniel, who stood aside.

"Of course."

Sarah had come out of her office, curious to see who was at the door. She was searching her memory because the man looked familiar, and Daniel eased the moment by saying, "You remember David, don't you darling?"

Sarah's face cleared. Of course, the CIA agent who had met with them before she was attacked.

"I think so. Nice to see you, David."

Sarah knew from Daniel that David had also helped with her rescue, and that Sgt. Jackson was unhappy about the rest of that scene, with the kidnappers all being killed. Without being able to question them, everyone including Daniel and Sarah was still in the dark about the motive. As had become her habit when events in her recent past were brought up, she stayed silent and let Daniel do the talking. Some memories were very clear, but a few weren't. Daniel had discussed with her the danger that their research had put them in, not to mention the men who had been killed. It was safest for her to pretend she remembered nothing about it and let Daniel take the lead.

"How are you doing, Miss Clarke?"

"I'm doing well, thank you. I've recovered 98% of my memory, but some of what happened is still fuzzy, I'm afraid. The doctors say that's normal with a traumatic brain injury, especially if there was strong emotion at the same time."

Ignoring her conversational gambit, David plowed ahead. "Do you remember whether Prof. Barry was dead when you got to his office, or whether he was shot while you were there?"

"No, I'm afraid I don't, and the doctors say I may never recover that particular memory." Sarah's voice betrayed the agitation that the subject still caused her. Daniel tensed, ready to interrupt if David continued that line of questioning.

"That's too bad. It might have shed light on the murder." David's statement was as calm as if he were discussing the weather.

"Just a minute," interrupted Daniel. "I've got a serious issue with you, David. What happened with the drones and the killing of the kidnappers? That left us with no way to question them about their motives. And while I am at it, I still want to ask you where the heck were you when I needed help to rescue my grandparents from kidnappers? You've got your nerve, waltzing in here and just bringing up traumatic memories for Sarah without even giving an explanation of your own movements. I've got half a mind to kick your ass from here to next Sunday." Daniel had become more agitated as he spoke, the emotion of both the incidents overtaking him by the end of his tirade.

David held up both hands in a conciliatory gesture. "I know how you feel, man, and I apologize. If you'll give me a chance, I'll explain. No need to kick my ass," he added half-humorously. And also remember I have been scarce because Luke asked me to lay off you for a while to give Miss Clarke time to recover."

Daniel gestured for him to sit down, while never taking his eyes off David's face. Sarah seated herself, too, but Daniel stayed standing.

"Remember I told you I thought we had a mole in the Agency? Well, now we're convinced of it, and it appears he has access to everything we do, all our communications, literally everything. I told you my phone was playing up the day you tried to call me about your grandparents, remember? I now believe that he was somehow jamming it. Obviously, he got past Sarah's minders the day of her kidnap, and he managed to get control of those drones, too. It's imperative we catch him, and we will." Daniel paused after this long speech, leaving an awkward silence.

Daniel's reporter senses were screaming. This all sounded highly unlikely, but he wanted to talk to Sarah before he let on that he didn't believe David.

David took up the narrative again. "The thing is, the two of you are clearly targets for this guy. If you were in danger before simply because of what you've discovered, you're in even more danger now because you've escaped his net. He's bound to try again. Hey, what the hell?" he added, as Daniel stepped forward aggressively, fists balled, ready to attack.

Daniel hissed, "You miserable son of a bitch, you knew we were in more danger and you waited over four weeks to tell us? What are you doing about this? You *knew* the mole had gotten past Sarah's guard, and yet you leave her with just that one useless guy sitting in his car two blocks away to protect her? What kind of fucking protection is that?"

Now Sarah jumped to her feet and put herself between the two men. "Daniel, calm down."

"Yeah, man, calm down," David started, causing Sarah to whirl on him.

"He's right, you know," she said between her teeth. "The only reason I'm stopping him from throwing you out of here bodily is that I don't want him arrested for assault. But if you don't explain yourself right now, I'll throw you out myself. Make it good."

Faced with two angry people, David began to backpedal. "No, wait, you don't understand. I've increased your surveillance as I promised Luke I would. There are now four to six people around you at all times. You won't see them, because they're professionals. You wouldn't *want* to see them, because if you can spot them, the bad guys can, too. We want to catch them, not scare them away."

Daniel, still livid, could not control the contempt in his voice as he finally expressed his doubts. "I don't believe you. Why should we believe anything you say? You've always got a pat answer, but your words and our experience don't match up."

Calmly, David answered. "All right, you don't believe me? I'll prove it. You and Sarah recently spent a night in Fisherville, where I believe you became engaged. On your return, you went to Mrs. Simms' house to tell her about it. Sarah has conducted a conference and you both had private discussions with visiting scholars from Egypt talking about human history, I can show you a few pictures if you want. Your grandparents, Daniel, have been staying with your parents in Asheville, North Carolina, and a couple of men who look like ex-military of some sort have been guarding them. Your friend Raj recently moved from a house in Hoboken where he'd gone to ground from his primary residence, I can give you the address if you want. Do you want more?"

'Great,' thought Daniel. '*The CIA knows about Raj's safe*

*house. He's going to kill me.'* Aloud, he said, "Okay, I'll concede you've got more surveillance around us. But so what? This impasse can't last forever. Sooner or later, either your mole, or the bad guys, or you have to make a move. We can't live like this."

David said, "I'm sure you're aware we have continued to investigate the murders as well as why anyone would be interested in your research."

"No, I wasn't aware of it," Daniel answered. "Sgt. Jackson said the investigations were closed, considered solved."

"He may consider them closed, but the Agency won't be satisfied until we know who was behind them and why they were interested. From what our analysts can determine, you may be onto something, Rossler. We'd like your help in taking it the rest of the way."

Sarah looked quickly at Daniel, who met her eyes with a small shake of his head. Then he addressed David, "I don't know, David. We may just want to drop it. Look at all the trouble it's caused, our friend Mark Simms dead, Prof. Barry dead, my grandparents terrorized and Sarah's injury."

"Daniel, I'm going to assume you're a patriot." David gave him a steady look that belied what he had just said.

Daniel answered, bristling at the implication, "Of course I am. But, I'm a civilian. And my first duty is to Sarah. She isn't fully recovered."

David held up his hand. "I understand your misgivings. However, no one but you has even come close to posing a viable theory about why that pyramid was built. You yourself say it couldn't have been when and for the purpose that Egyptian scholars have accepted. Daniel, I'm telling you that national security could be at stake. People high in the Agency have taken an interest, and we'd really like your help. At least say you'll consider it." David's tone turned conciliatory. "You'll have all the help and protection you need. Say the word and we'll get you whatever you require to finish the work."

Daniel was still shaking his head, while Sarah stared at him impassively, maybe attempting to communicate with him through brain waves. David continued, "Think how you'd feel if the wrong people solved the riddles first. If they used it to endanger thousands of people. What if it's the cure for cancer and they only use it for themselves? How can you take that risk?"

Sarah was staring at each man as he spoke, her head turning from side to side as if at a tennis match.

"Daniel," she said. He put his finger to his lips in a shushing motion, thinking for a moment.

"All right, how about this. I propose that you give us some time to discuss it between ourselves and with our group." Without saying so, Daniel had thought of something that bothered him. If David and his team were so diligent, why hadn't he mentioned Sinclair? It was something he wanted to mull over and talk about with Sarah.

"Daniel, time waits for no man. What if someone else solves it before you do?"

"Then you'll have your answers, won't you? Look, let us talk about it in private. I'll phone you tomorrow and give you our answer."

"Make it the right answer, Daniel." It almost sounded like a threat.

After David left, Sarah broke her silence. "Daniel, what's going on in your mind? I could almost see the wheels turning."

"Don't you think it's strange, if he put more surveillance

on us, that he doesn't know about Sinclair, or wouldn't have mentioned him if he did? And what about the fifth kidnapper. He was monitoring those drones. He would have seen the guy get away."

"Okay, and I appreciate you trying to protect me, too. But, Daniel, what if it really is a matter of national security?"

"It could very well be. And I think we should agree to help, but not for the reason you think. David wants our help pretty badly, and I think we need to know what the real motive is. Think about it, though, Sarah. From everything you remember about the CIA, all the revelations that were going down before your kidnapping about our government spying on ordinary citizens, would you really want something of global importance to be a secret known only to the CIA? Besides are we sure we can trust David? Remember we also trusted Kingston and Barry."

Put that way, no, she didn't. Sarah thought it through, and then said, "So we're back to where we were before David came by, only with more questions. I think it's time to call Luke."

# Chapter 41 – The Great Pyramid Speaks Again

Luke listened without interrupting as his niece explained why they were calling. As soon as he heard that they had misgivings about David, he stopped them. "I'll be on the next plane to Providence. See you soon."

Sarah couldn't help but feel like a little girl with a problem and that the adults were on their way. She and Daniel had been muddling through, and there was no question that Daniel was smart as well as courageous to a fault, but she felt they were both out of their depth when it came to the CIA. Luke's help would be most welcome.

For his part, Luke's gut was telling him things that he didn't want to hear. He'd survived his field career in the CIA by paying attention to those gut feelings, though. Something was wrong, here, and he was determined to get to the bottom of it. For that, he needed to be on the spot to talk in person to some people who were in a position to investigate the matter. Once in Providence, he listened again to the whole story, and gave some advice.

"Kids, I agree that you shouldn't trust just anybody, certainly not everybody. But it won't pay to get crosswise with the CIA over this. I think you should tell David you're ready to cooperate, go on about the research as if you have no suspicions, and let me look into it in the meantime."

Daniel said, "In other words, keep your friends close and your enemies even closer."

"Precisely," answered Luke. "I'll get to work on my end right away, and I'll let you know what I find out. Then we'll come up with a plan to rid you of this threat once and for all. Are we agreed?"

"Sounds like a plan to me," Daniel answered, with Sarah's

nod confirming that she agreed.

Later, Daniel called David to tell him they had decided to carry on.

"Glad to hear it," David said.

~~~

Two days later, the couple were in New York to talk with Sinclair and pull the team together to work on the research again.

"Let's talk about the data," Daniel suggested, after suitable social formalities had been met. "Here's where we are with it right now. Raj has entered all the languages you suggested into the database, along with the numerical values for the stones that we established last summer. The numerical values all turn out to be Fibonacci numbers, which we believe can't be an accident. What would you make of it, Sinclair, by the way?"

"Off-hand, I'd say they represent a syllabary."

"Why do you say that?" Sarah interjected.

Sinclair answered, "There are three main types of writing systems, one having graphic representations of words, which could be in their thousands, one having letters, which usually have fewer than fifty, and one that represents sounds, or syllables, that you can put together in various combinations to form the words that people speak."

"Sort of like shorthand," Sarah said.

"You could think of it that way. If that's what it is, you're going to need to find patterns of two or more stones together to form the spoken words. Have you done that?"

"No, Raj wanted to know what to do next, because so far he hasn't been able to find a correlation between the stones and any of the ancient languages we've looked at." Daniel answered.

"That's what I suggest, then, but I may be able to refine the recommendation if I could see the raw data."

"Then let's set it up for you to meet him at his place, where he's got it all on his computer. What do you say?"

"Sounds like the way to do it. When?" asked Sinclair.

"We're supposed to get a date and time from you and text it to him. We were going to do something fun to send him your address, but I guess that won't be necessary now."

"I know," said Sarah. "He'll need to know it's at his place. We can send him his own address."

"Good idea," said Daniel. We'll do that when we get home, so our minders won't associate it with this visit.

Sarah sat up very straight suddenly, and said, "Daniel, have we ever showed Sinclair the original message? The one in the passageway?"

"No, I don't believe we have. What an oversight!" Opening his laptop, Daniel pulled up an encrypted file with the original calculations and the message that Mark Simms' linguist friend had made of them.

"We think this was written in what amounts to clear text, to make sure that someone knew there was more elsewhere, but still keep it secret until something had happened to reveal the code."

Sinclair nodded, following the logic easily. With that, Daniel turned the laptop around and revealed the familiar words:

**[Unknown word] traveler/person/human/man from future. [Unknown word] critical/important/significant [Unknown word] telling/story/message [Unknown word] read/browse/assimilate/learn all/ [Unknown word] everything**

**here/in this place/at this location [Unknown word]**

"Who translated this?" asked Sinclair.

"A linguist at Brown, a friend of Martha Simms' husband. He took off right after we got Sarah back and hasn't been heard from since."

Sinclair gave Daniel a steady look that emphasized his earlier story of people in his acquaintance disappearing. Then he said, "Let me see what he was working from."

Side by side, the images stared back at them from the screen as Sinclair gazed at them for a few minutes, long enough for his guests to become uncomfortable with the silence. As he looked, Sinclair muttered a bit under his breath, then scribbled something on a notepad he got from a drawer in the sideboard next to him. Then he said, "Okay, that's a very rough and literal direct translation, but here's what I think it says.

**We salute and address you, Those Who Come After. All the knowledge we have gained in the Tenth Cycle is contained in this monument. Learn from it and use this knowledge wisely.**

Sarah and Daniel gaped at Sinclair. How had he done that? No unknown words, no hesitation in the choice of words, just a straight message that made the utmost sense given what they had deduced about the interior message. Then, both of them speaking excitedly while Sinclair continued to stare at the images as if he weren't sure of his interpretation.

"Come after what? What's the Tenth Cycle? Oh, my God! It must be an encyclopedia. Wow, what all is in there?"

Out of the indecipherable jumble of questions, Daniel's voice rang out more strongly. "Sarah, what do you know about a Tenth Cycle in Egypt?"

"Nothing!" she cried. "I never heard of anything referred

to as cycles, except what Ahmed told us. What can it mean?"

Sinclair finally came out of his reverie to answer. "I'm going to go out on a limb here. I think Those Who Come After referred to a civilization that the builders expected to succeed theirs. That would suggest that the cycle they refer to is the rise and fall of their civilization. If theirs was the tenth, what's ours? And what does it mean for our view of history?" Daniel and Sarah stared briefly at him, awed by the realization that they were in the presence of a genius. He had hit on the right answer without even hearing about the information they had gleaned from Ahmed, or their own theories, not to mention translating the rough message in a matter of moments. Nicholas was not exaggerating when he told them Sinclair was brilliant.

To Sinclair's bewilderment, Sarah and Daniel stopped babbling questions and rushed into each other's arms. "It's true!" Sarah kept repeating, while Daniel lifted her slightly every few seconds, bouncing her on the floor as he would a child. "Daniel, you've done it! You've proved that the pyramid is impossibly old. Think what it will mean!"

"Will someone please explain to me what's going on?" Sinclair demanded. Only then did the breathless pair sit down and take him through the reasoning that Ahmed had explained to them weeks before during their meeting. A look of wonder crossed his face as he listened and assimilated the reason for their excitement. "We're not the first! Kids, do you know what this means?"

There was no question now. What they'd felt intuitively from the first rough translation was now proven beyond a doubt. Information of great importance was contained within the pyramid. There was no choice but to ferret it out. With Sinclair's blessing, Daniel used his computer to send an email message to Raj using their usual ruse.

'Translation refined. Here's the text: We salute and address you, Those Who Come After. All the knowledge we have gained in the Tenth Cycle is contained in this monument. Learn from it and use this knowledge wisely. Imperative the data entry be finished ASAP. Translation on interior to start immediately.' Just typing the words again gave Daniel the odd feeling that his head was floating, while his stomach, in contrast, was dropping. It made him giddy.

In a car 300 yards away a man put a strange looking device, something like a dish antenna, about eight inches in diameter, away on the back seat of his car. He took out his cell phone and dialed.

"Something just happened," he reported, then listened for a moment.

"No, I don't know what, as usual, I can't hear anything when they're inside. But, they were making enough noise that I could hear the shouting and laughter without the antenna. They were celebrating something. Now it's gone quiet again."

Again, he listened, then responded.

"Okay. I'll stay on watch, but it's just useless trying to hear what's going on inside. Whatever they're using to damp communications is way beyond our technology to break through."

"Okay, I'll call *when* anything else happens."

# Chapter 42 – How To Trap A Mole

Immediately after meeting with Daniel and Sarah in Providence, Luke had that very afternoon flown to Washington, where he had made previous arrangements to meet at short notice with his former supervising officer. He'd been extra discreet the last time he was here, but it was now time to tell the story to someone he could trust to keep it under wraps, while carefully looking into David's activities.

Samuel Lewis, no relation to the dozen or so famous men who shared his name, was that person. A brilliant strategist, he'd risen through the ranks of the Agency rapidly and was widely thought to be the next Director. Even the current Director expected it, and in a surprising twist from the usual rivalry and suspicion, instead gave Sam every opportunity to learn and to shine. Lewis was waiting in his office when Luke arrived and was shown in. He rose, hand extended, and came around his desk to give Luke a familiar hug.

"Good to see you, Luke. How's retirement treating you?" The last was said with a wink, as Lewis knew very well that Luke was still in the game as a consultant. He'd even tapped him for an operation himself once or twice.

"Not too shabby," Luke replied. "But I'm afraid an old friend has gone rogue on me, and I'd like to ask your help in flushing him out."

"One of our active agents?" Lewis asked, with a frown.

"Afraid so. David Johnson."

With that, Luke began to explain the story, beginning with David surprising him in the car a few months before, his strange actions during Sarah's kidnapping, and now Daniel's gut instinct that something was wrong with the man coupled with Luke's own misgivings. As much as possible, he kept the pyramid code out of it. There was no use spreading that any further if he could help it. Lewis was shrewd, though, as well as smart and capable.

"Does this mysterious code threaten national security?" he asked, sternly.

"I don't know what all is in it, Sam, and that's the truth. I'm fairly confident that there are secrets the government is going to want to know. And I'm absolutely sure that my niece and her fiancé are going to do what's right with the information. They're loyal Americans, I'm certain they won't allow it to be used to harm our nation."

"What would you like me to do?" Lewis asked, apparently accepting Luke's assurances.

"Two things. See what you can find out about David's assignment to the case, and arrange for protection for my family."

"I can do that. Tell me who we're going to protect."

Luke listed his family and Daniel's and also Martha Simms, to a low whistle from Sam. "Wow, that's a handful. Okay, I'll contact the FBI for your family, hang on."

An immediate phone call set the arrangements in motion. "Your family will have security at their homes within the hour. Do you need to warn them?"

"No, already did. You know I like to be proactive." Luke grinned, a feral expression that would have been frightening if Sam hadn't known him well.

"Well, so do I. Let's see what we can find out about David's doings." Going back around behind his desk, Luke pulled up David's personnel jacket and read. Then he made another phone call without comment to Luke.

"Sadler, can I see you in my office immediately?"

In a moment a man in his mid-thirties knocked once on the closed door and entered, drawing up short when he saw Luke. His eyes went questioningly to his superior officer.

"Sadler, what do you know about Agent David Johnson and his recent activities?" Sam asked.

"Why, nothing!" said Sadler, surprised. "He's been on medical leave for the last six months or more. Why?"

"I think you'd better look more closely. Tell him, Luke."

The story repeated, a very red-faced Sadler rushed out of the room to issue an order for David to be picked up for questioning as soon as possible.

There was nothing for Luke to do now but wait until he was apprehended.

By early Tuesday morning in Rhode Island, CIA agent David Johnson had been arrested when he tried to meet with the agents he'd been using to trail Daniel and Sarah. None of them were happy to discover they'd been participating in an unauthorized operation, so they weren't particularly careful in their handling of him. It was a very indignant David who faced Sam and Luke in a CIA safe-house interrogation room that afternoon.

"What is this, Sam? And Luke? I'm surprised at you. I've done everything I can for that niece of yours, and this is my reward?"

Sam employed the 'we know what you did, we just don't know why you did it' method of interrogation, methodically telling David what they knew of his activities.

"We know you weren't authorized to run this operation. Who are you working for?"

David sat with a neutral expression on his face, his hands folded and lips firmly pressed together.

Sam continued, "Remember that all those agents you have been using without authorization are also being picked up. We have a few of them already, and they're all upset that you were using them for illegal purposes. They'll cooperate, no question. There's very little we can't find out, even if we don't know the whole story right now. It'll go better for you if you come clean, David." Sam said the last sentence with compassion. David could be facing charges of treason.

Shaking his head in mute denial, David still refused to speak. Softly, Sam began to apply the psychological keys that would eventually unlock the lips of even the most stubborn operative. He was good at it, which partly explained his rapid rise in the Agency. Pulling up the record of David's activities over the years, he casually asked how David would like to roommate with a Mafia assassin that he'd been responsible for putting away. Other cases came up, and over the hours, David realized that he was literally stuck between a rock and a hard place. Finally, he was ready to bargain.

"You know that as soon as they hear I've been turned, my life will be worth shit, right?" he said bitterly.

"I'm afraid that's not our problem, David," Sam said gently. "But if it will help you do the right thing, here, I'll see about witness protection."

"Bah, they'll find me anyway. I'm as good as dead, no matter what. I might as well take them down with me," Luke spat.

Always careful not to give away his own role in anything that would get him in even worse trouble, assuming there was even worse trouble, David began to talk about his employment within a secret society called Orion, where he was code-named

Sidus. He readily gave up the four code names of the leaders, Septentrio, Occidens, Auster and Oriens, but claimed not to know their real names or locations.  He also said that though he wasn't sure, he had reason to believe Septentrio was living somewhere in Germany..

"I've never seen any of them in person. I had dealings mostly with Septentrio, over secure satellite link. Any time there was video, they wore masks and hoods, like monks. I got the feeling they were in a place that was really old; all I could see behind them was stone walls. But I don't know where," he repeated.

"Why did you do it?" Luke inquired.

David sneered. "Why else? You know we get paid shit, working for the government, we have no family life, my wife and children left me because of this fucking job. I'm an outcast and a lonely man. If I don't look after myself, I'll die alone as a pauper. I think this country owes me for what I've sacrificed... I had bigger dreams. They've paid me quite a bit over the years, but this was supposed to be the biggest pay-off of all. I could have retired to some remote island, spent the rest of my life in luxury somewhere warm. That would have been a bit of compensation for what I have done for this country my entire life without so much as a "thank you". This was supposed to be my last assignment."

Sam took up the questioning again. "Tell us more about them, everything you know."

David rambled a bit, but the picture that emerged was of an ultra-powerful, ultra-rich organization with connections in virtually every government, every large international corporation and even global financial powerhouses. In fact, it could be said that the Orion Society *was* the global financial powerhouse, as its considerable assets, carefully disguised, were spread throughout every major banking institution in the world. David had garnered much of this information through his position within the CIA, and the Orion's leaders were unaware of the extent of his knowledge. But not for long, he reflected bitterly, as he knew there were others like him, backups if you will, in the CIA. It wouldn't take long for Septentrio to become aware of his arrest.

Throughout the hours of talking, David grew careless, and mentioned the way Orion Society victims were made to disappear. Sam didn't follow up with any questions; he didn't want David to stop talking. But there were unsolved cases going years back where the victims had been mutilated as David described. Sam wondered how many of them David had been personally responsible for killing.

The most bizarre part of the narrative was when David described what he'd learned of the ritual of 'retirement' of an Orion Society director. He had mentioned in passing that the current Septentrio, his contact, would be beyond the justice of the outside world within twenty-four or at most thirty-six hours of the others learning of his, David's arrest.

"And why is that?" Sam inquired.

"When they fail in a project of this magnitude, they are expected to retire honorably. To them, that means suicide. There is a choice only in the manner of it. If the leader fails to honorably retire, not only he is murdered, but his successor as well. They always do it, not because they care about their successor, but because they can't stand the idea of their family being forever shut out of the society. I'm telling you, these guys have been doing this for centuries."

The last question Sam asked was, "Do you know why they've been so interested in Luke's niece and her research?" David's eyes flicked to Luke, who had tensed at the question.

"It's because of the pyramid code," he said, his eyes steadily on Luke's. "They want the secrets that Daniel and Sarah are about to discover. They have known or suspected for centuries that the Great Pyramid was built with the sole purpose to convey a message to future generations. No one has ever been able to even come close to opening that message; that is, until those two came along and are now on the verge of cracking it. "

When they left David, Sam asked Luke if he were satisfied that his family was now safe. Luke had realized that they never would be safe until the pyramid code was translated and disseminated, as the family had determined weeks ago.

"Sam, I need you to keep those Fibbies in place," he said now.

"Not so fast, Clarke. You owe me more of an explanation if you want me to go out on that limb for you."

"All right, Sam. We'd better get some coffee and take a drive. I'll tell you what I know."

As soon as he had a chance, Luke wrote up the whole incident in the shared email, to let Daniel and Sarah know that one of the heads of the Hydra had been cut off with David's arrest. Unfortunately, everyone knew instinctively that he hadn't been working alone. They must all remain vigilant against another venomous head of the serpent arising. But, at least Luke had convinced Sam that continuing protection was called for, along with giving the man a headache and indigestion that he thought only a stiff shot of vodka was going to fix.

# Chapter 43 – An Honorable Discharge

As David had explained to Sam and Luke, it took less than twenty-four hours for word of his arrest to make its way back to the highest leadership of the Orion Society. It was Auster who grimly called for a face-to-face meeting in Wurzburg. Septentrio knew what this meant, and prepared himself. He insisted his son accompany him to the meeting, without telling him that he would be initiated as the new Septentrio when he, Septentrio the senior, had announced his retirement. The boy was weak, he'd always known. Even now, when the 'boy' was in his mid-fifties, he resisted his father's attempts to marry him to a suitable woman in order to provide an heir. If Septentrio had fathered another child, even a female, this sorry state of affairs would not have come about. It was too late to worry about it now, though. The others would have to see to it that, sexual preference or no sexual preference, his effete son would produce an heir.

Septentrio dressed carefully in his ceremonial robes, and saw to it that his son dressed in the robes that had been prepared for him. Some of the choices he would face would not have ruined the robes in which he carried out his honorable retirement, but he had in mind a choice that would not fail to leave an indelible impression on those he left behind. At the appointed hour, he presented himself to the group, his son by his side.

"What is your decision, Septentrio? Is it to be gunshot, poison, or perhaps you'll open your veins?" Auster's question was a little too glib, Septentrio felt. He regarded her with disfavor, ignoring the horrified expression his son turned upon him.

"Father, what does she mean?"

"This is our way, my son. Carry on the Septentrio role with honor." To the others, he said, imperiously, "Follow me."

Only the local newspapers would report the death of a

prominent local banker, who, in a bizarre turn of events, had fallen from the highest tower of the old castle ruins. No one, not even the man's family, could explain why a man of his years would be climbing and exploring in the ruins. A funeral was duly held and attended by many of the townspeople.

On the same evening of his father's funeral, a short but formal ceremony invested the middle-aged son of the deceased into the office of Septentrio XXXIII. He would be the 33$^{rd}$ person to use the name in the position that spanned more than eight hundred years. An explanation was demanded. The man, long knowing that this moment would come, but not temperamentally suited to the office, struggled to answer.

"My father informed you that something continually jammed the CIA's listening devices, I believe. Before he took his life, Father became convinced that the Rosslers and their colleagues had some sort of advanced electronic device to accomplish this. In any case, they were able to elude our attempts to learn of their activities. In doing so, they made a thorough fool out of our CIA mole. We are making arrangements to terminate the man as soon as possible, but he has disappeared. Another has been dispatched to learn of his whereabouts and make sure he's unable to talk."

"Don't try and make stupid excuses for your father. He made a complete mess of this, Septentrio, and his failure has put all of us in danger. You'd better clean this up and quickly. Have you made arrangements to activate Sidus's replacement? We expect you to travel to the US and take care of this matter personally." Auster's harsh tones suggested that if Septentrio were unable to fulfill these obligations, she would be happy to take over.

Behind his mask, Septentrio paled. In a quaking voice, he answered, "My father made those arrangements as his last act as

Septentrio prior to his 'retirement'. I will do my best to follow through on this assignment."

The others privately thought that there would be yet another new Septentrio before the year was out, but did not voice it. Each was considering his or her nominee, one of the younger sons of their own houses. Clearly, the current Septentrio was unsuitable, and he had no heir.

The next order of business was to discuss which of their operations should be suspended until Johnson was eliminated. He knew too much, including, they suspected, the real identity of Septentrio's father. They were too exposed, and that was a state of affairs that couldn't continue. Each had a prepared new identity to assume in the case of utter disaster, the others not knowing what it was. Certain contingencies had been arranged for them to communicate again when the danger had passed. Everything was in readiness to elude whatever pursuit might be sent after them.

As the meeting adjourned, Septentrio spared a glance at the spot where his father's lifeless body had been found. What terrible thing had he done in a past life to be saddled with this obligation now? In passing, he spat on the rubble that had only recently been cleaned of his father's blood.

~~~

It didn't take long for David to frighten himself to death regarding his fate, and become convinced that if he told the CIA all he knew, he might somehow escape it despite his claim to Sam Lewis. Accordingly, less than twenty-four hours after he'd told Sam that he had no more to say, David sent for him.

"Okay, I've got more. If you'll arrange for witness protection, I'll give it all to you."

Sam spoke slowly, making sure David understood every

word. "I said I'd try, David. I'm not sure the offer is on the table anymore."

A broken and desperate David begged, "Please. Otherwise, it's a death sentence."

Sam repeated. "All I can do is try. And your information will have to pan out before I'll even do that, David. Take it or leave it." *It's a terrible thing to see*, Sam thought to himself, *when a bully and criminal like David gets a taste of his own medicine*. But he secretly relished it. A taste of his own medicine was exactly what David needed, Luke remarked, with Sam's agreement.

It quickly became apparent that no witness protection was in David's future as he confessed everything, beginning with the spying on Daniel and Sarah, bugging their homes, following them and hacking into their computers, even deploying listening devices from concealed places while the couple were out in public. If that had been all, perhaps David could have escaped punishment for his crimes, but there was more.

He explained that it was Impes who was behind the murder of Simms and Barry, revealing the code name of the retired NYPD chief who'd botched his assignments early. He revealed that Sarah's kidnapping was a mistake, but that she and Daniel had both come very close to dying on the day the exchange was made. And that he'd deliberately shot down the kidnappers to keep them from talking.

When Sam asked where to find Impes, David only smiled grimly, and said, "I put him in the Potomac, minus his head and fingers." That sealed his fate. He would never leave prison alive, and according to his own estimation, if he survived a week it would be a miracle.

"One thing that always puzzled us," David asked, now that he'd given away all his bargaining chips.

"What's that?" Sam asked.

"We could never hear what they were saying indoors, and sometimes not when they were out of doors, either. I've never come across anything like it. Do you know what they were using to jam our equipment?"

Sam smiled. He immediately put two and two together. Somehow, and in all likelihood through Luke, they must have got hold of one of those ZeroS devices that top field agents had been using with such good effect for the past few years. He decided that it would be best not to ask Luke about it as he did not want him to have to lie about it. At least it had served the good purpose of keeping Daniel and Sarah and others alive.

David looked at Luke as he said, "I think they've acquired some pretty sophisticated equipment. We never knew everything they were talking about, which is why our moves went so wrong."

Luke kept his face impassive. No one need ever know what Daniel and Sarah had, if he kept his mouth shut.

# Chapter 44 – To The Safe House

Naturally, Luke reported everything he heard to Daniel and Sarah. David's confessions, while not entirely unexpected, held revelations of a conspiracy so terrible that Sarah shook in her shoes when she heard of it.

Their close call was even closer than they'd realized, and it made both Sarah and Daniel extremely nervous, especially when David was assassinated within a week of his arrest. Though he'd told them there was a mole in the CIA that turned out to be himself, David was more prophetic than he'd known. There really was another mole, and his sights were no doubt set on them.

~~~

Together, Luke, Daniel and Sarah came to some hard decisions. Now, more than ever, it was imperative that they get more of the translation done and done quickly. There was no time to waste, as they now knew that the Orion Society would stop at nothing to get their hands on the data, even if they had to destroy Daniel and Sarah along with anyone helping them, to do it. Furthermore, they now suspected there was no one they could trust, at least as far as government agencies were concerned, not to have been infiltrated by the enemy. They were on their own, with the exception that Sam Lewis had made arrangements for FBI protection for their families and Martha, vetting each assigned agent through his own trusted sources. Luke could only hope that no one in the employ of the Orion Society had slipped through.

It didn't take much discussion to determine that their best course of action would be to translate as much as they could, looking for an earth shattering discovery, and then broadcast it to the world, thus making their capture no longer of value to a criminal organization that wanted to maintain a low profile. It wasn't a surprising conclusion, considering that this was the idea they'd had for some weeks now. The question was, where would they be safe for long enough to implement this plan? And who all did they need with them?

After much discussion, it was decided that Luke would call in some favors, which he was reluctant to discuss. One by one, and for various reasons, they had rejected most of the ideas any of them could put forth. They had briefly discussed attempting to set up a safe house, such as Raj had. But then, they remembered that David had known all about Raj's safe house. They had no reason to believe that even with Luke's expertise they would be able to evade another CIA mole. The same objection came up when they discussed leaving the country. Where would they go? Of all the countries that were proposed, the only one that made any sense was Israel, for several reasons.

For one, Israel was an ally of the United States. Most Israelites spoke English, an advantage not found in a South American or Asian country. For another, Israel's not-so-secret service, the Mossad, was the best in the world; even better, some thought, than the CIA and NSA rolled together. However, Luke pointed out that expecting help from the Israelis would require that they have something to trade for it. The initial translation of the greeting message would not be enough. They needed something substantial, something that could be proved out as both viable and valuable.

"Leave it to me," said Luke. "I'll be in touch as soon as I can make some arrangements. In the meantime, pack what you need for a few weeks, as lightly as possible. You're going to have to gather some cash but I need to think about how to do it without setting off alarms."

"I wonder if Raj has any ideas about that?" said Daniel.

Luke remarked, "From what you've told me about Raj, I

wouldn't be surprised. But, you wouldn't want him to be in legal trouble, would you?"

"No, but I'm still going to ask him if he has any ideas," grinned Daniel. Sarah wondered what he had up his sleeve.

"What have we decided about who needs to be physically in the same place for this caper?" asked Luke, trying for the same light mood as had overtaken Daniel despite his very real worry for his niece.

"Well, we obviously need Raj and Sinclair. Sarah and I of course. Martha has a vested interest in the outcome, as well, and I wouldn't want her to be here alone. What about you Luke? I'd feel more comfortable if we had you with us, and I'm sure Sarah would as well."

Sarah was nodding vigorously. Luke said, "I'll be here as long as you need me. So, why don't you get in touch with those people and have them ready to go as soon as I can get back to you?"

With that, Luke left, and Daniel and Sarah drove to Martha's to persuade her to go with them.

"Oh, my dears, I don't understand why you want me along," Martha said, when they'd explained where they were going and what they'd be doing. "I can't help with the translation, I'll just be in the way."

Daniel's concern was that Martha would be vulnerable if he and Sarah disappeared without a trace, she would be all on her own. No one would know for days if something happened to her. He wanted her safe with them so that no harm can befall her in their absence. Rather than say that however, he made a joke of it. "Well if you don't come with us, who's going to keep us in baked goods?"

Martha laughed. "I know very well that isn't the reason. Do you really think it's necessary for me to come with you?"

It was Sarah's turn to exercise her powers of persuasion, though Daniel's were legendary. "Yes, hon, we think it's absolutely necessary. If Mark was here today he would be part of this team and you would have accompanied him. As far as Daniel and I are concerned, you are part of this team and will now be continuing what Mark has started. Besides we also need a mother to look after us. Is there any reason you can't be gone for a couple of weeks without telling anyone?"

"I guess not," Martha said, "since gardening season is over. My bridge club may wonder where I got to, could I just tell one person that I'm going on an impulse trip?"

"Can you resist the temptation to tell her anything else?" Asked Daniel. "It won't be safe for her to know that it's anything but an impulse trip."

"In that case, I can certainly resist the temptation," said Martha firmly. "Is there anything in particular I need to bring?"

"Just bring a couple of changes of clothing, and your passport. Do you have a backpack?" asked Sarah.

"A rather large one, that we used to take on our back-country overnight camping trips," Martha answered.

"That's perfect," said Sarah. "We're working on how to acquire some cash. We'll let you know if we need you to bring some."

"I have plenty in the bank," Martha said. "Mark's insurance just paid out."

The couple then made their way to the library, where they knew they could find pay phones outside. While Daniel called Raj, Sarah called Sinclair. To both, the couple communicated the same request as to Martha, emphasizing that the utmost secrecy would be required.

By sundown, Luke had scooped up Raj and Sinclair in a rented Suburban, and the four were on their way to Providence, where they would pick up Daniel, Sarah and Martha. From there, their destination was a small town on the Canadian border, called Stanstead. The border actually ran right through the center of town, and on the US side, about 2 miles out of town in a secluded spot amongst trees,  sat a spacious safe house that an old Mossad contact had made available on the strength of Luke's assurances that he would make it worthwhile.

At each stop, he took evasive action to make sure he wasn't followed.

For the first couple of hours, the conversation centered on how each person would contribute to the translation effort in order to be as efficient as possible. They were all well aware that they were under a deadline that had no set time…whenever the Orion Society found them, they would be lucky to escape with their lives. Raj was determined to keep a regularly-updated high-capacity flash drive with him so that the data wouldn't be lost, even if they were driven from their safe house by gunfire or other violence. Likewise, Daniel would be in charge of a separate device with the cumulative translations stored in it.

Unbeknownst to Daniel, Sarah's gun was packed in her backpack, along with all the ammunition she had at home. She would not willingly be taken hostage again, and intended to defend herself, along with the older team members, if necessary, rather than run. It may not change the outcome in the long run, but it would make her feel much better if she could take out some bad guys before they were overrun.

Daniel, unaware of Sarah's grim musings, tried to sleep so

that he could take over the driving later on.

~~~

It was four a.m. when the weary group straggled into the house from the large attached garage where Luke pulled up in the Suburban. They quickly spread into the four bedrooms, Luke and Sinclair sharing one, though Luke would remain awake throughout the nights and sleep in the daytime. They had two hours to sleep, then Raj would awake the others and they'd get to work. During the drive, they'd discussed how to blend into this tiny town without attracting notice. It was decided that Daniel and Sarah, as the ones least likely to be needed at any given time, would take turns going about what appeared to be normal business, rather than excite comment by staying indoors with the blinds closed as if they were hiding. Accordingly, they would do the food shopping, spreading their business out among several nearby small towns so as not to have anyone notice they were shopping for more than the two of them. Otherwise, they would have little business in town other than filling the Suburban gas hog, which they'd also do in several different small towns.

The group was strictly off the grid. Cell phones were off and the SIM cards removed, wi-fi disabled on all laptops. They'd sent word to both families letting them know that they'd be unreachable for a while, and that in the case of any problems they would be in touch, otherwise not to worry. Martha and Sinclair had no one to notify, of course, and Raj had arranged for vacation time from the Times, so he wouldn't be missed, either.

# Chapter 45 – The Great Pyramid Reveals

The next few days were a flurry of work, Raj completing all of the data sets in the first group, those that used each Fibonacci number as a skip sequence, starting with the first symbol. He also arranged the entire data set into eight by eight by eight cubes, with no skip sequences designated. Sinclair would use them to start new skip sequences with each successive symbol if he needed to, although the exploration of the sequences in three dimensions would have to wait.

At this point, they all believed that Sinclair wouldn't be able to translate even a small fraction of the information in the time frame they were thinking, less than a week. His focus turned to searching for an index of material. Once they located that, they'd search it for something that seemed more advanced than current science, though still understandable, and that could be quickly proven. That would be the evidence Luke and Daniel presented to Luke's Mossad contact when they asked for asylum while completing the work.

Daniel was also crafting a Times story that hopefully would afford their group some measure of protection by being too much in the public eye to just be killed or abducted. Daniel still hoped to be with Sarah, the rest of the core group and preferably his and Sarah's extended families in a safe place when the story hit. It was going to be controversial, to say the least. He wasn't sure whether he was more leery of bad guys with guns or the academic community.

Sarah started working on a white paper to be used for presentations to scientists and academics and with the help of Martha a few different length PowerPoint presentations to be used when they had to "tell" the story.

~~~

Sarah had told him before they left that she was content they were doing the right thing, no matter what happened to her career because of it, good or bad. In fact, she said, she would never again be able to confine herself to her narrow specialty, with so much material to study. But, she believed that it would be difficult for the Institute or the University to fire her, since she would be a public figure, too prominent, again, to deny her tenure simply because they'd discovered something that was outside the pale of the academic community. If necessary, she'd fight, rather than rolling over and taking it or even pre-empting the issue by resigning. No legitimate field of study should be suppressed because of academic politics. That's what had gotten them into this in the first place.

Daniel thought she was the bravest person he'd ever met. Of all of them, she had the most to lose career-wise. He could always make a living writing, even if he had to turn to fiction. Raj's career would be untouched, since his role was merely data analysis and he'd be able to get even higher-paying jobs when it was revealed. The others were retired. But Sarah had worked hard for her degree and for tenure. To be willing to give it up for something he had brought into her life was beyond what he expected of her. He loved her all the more for it.

~~~

Raj was explaining to Sinclair all the steps he had taken to develop the data set that they would see as soon as he had finished setting up the twin monitors on his laptop. Sinclair, having taken the time since being asked to participate in the project to learn all he could about the pyramid, listened carefully. In a matter of a few minutes, Raj had the equipment connected and was powering it up as they spoke. The two men recognized immediately that they were well-matched in computer skills, despite the age difference. Raj was delighted to be able to say what he did without having to explain why, as Sinclair got it immediately. It was far more satisfactory even than bringing his friend Daniel up to speed, which did require more explanation. With each point Raj made, Sinclair nodded, approving of the process and recognizing that much of the work he would have had to do was already done, thanks to Raj's program.

However, he had an idea to take it further.

"Raj, what do you make of the significance of the Fibonacci numbers?" Sinclair asked, not wanting to step on the man's toes if this was old ground.

"That there is some. I have been thinking perhaps that different messages can be made of these blocks of data, depending upon where we start and whether we read linearly or in a skip sequence." Raj had forgotten the word, but he understood that their thinking was now that each unique stone represented a syllable. Aha! That was it...a syllabary. Now he corrected his statement. "Different messages, depending on how the syllables are strung together into words."

Sinclair had followed it even without the clarification. It was what he'd been thinking. Now the other three got it, because they had talked before about skip sequences, someone having brought up the idea in conjunction with a distantly-remembered conversation about the Bible Code material. But, Sinclair had more to add.

"I'm thinking along the same lines. But, I think we have to start somewhere with a more compact chart of the syllables. Raj, did you run a comparison of the number of instances of each separate formula against the Linear A and Linear B languages?"

"Yes, I did, although Daniel could not explain to me why we should be using a Greek dialect."

"Nor can I. It's a gut feeling, based on the fact that we think it's a syllabary we're dealing with, but that's Linear B. As of yet, no one has translated Linear A. It's an unknown language, called Minoan only because of the location of the first place archaeologists found it. It does seem to share some characteristics of Linear B, though. I'm thinking we can use it as our Rosetta Stone if my gut feeling is correct."

New understanding bloomed in Sarah's eyes, as she was a little more familiar with the scholarship around the ancient languages than the rest. "You're thinking, compare the formulas with the highest number of instances with the corresponding Linear A symbols, and try them as a direct correspondence."

Sinclair looked at her with approval. "Yes, my dear, exactly. Now, when researchers have previously compared Linear A texts with known word values for Linear B, which as Raj said was an early form of Greek, they haven't had much luck. It produces unintelligible words. Clearly, it's a link to a language we don't know, but we have our ways of cracking a language like that if we have a large enough data set. Yours is huge." Sinclair turned to Raj with admiration. "Son, you have done an outstanding job on a very tedious task. Congratulations, your work will probably have been key to our successfully translating what these ancients had to say to us."

Raj, though excitable and demonstrative in the presence of good friends, was more reserved among these near-strangers. He showed his pleasure at the compliment, however, by blushing and lowering his eyes. Sarah thought it was charming. She was beginning to warm to this strange friend of Daniel's.

Sinclair had continued to talk, and Sarah schooled herself to pay attention. "Now, once we have the syllables, we'll have to arrange the data in some way. I suggest that the Fibonacci numbers that are found everywhere in the pyramid are an indication that they should be used somehow, beginning with the fact that the pyramid has eight sides, rather than the normal four."

His words electrified those who heard him. Eight! How could they have missed the significance of that? Of course it meant something! Eight was a Fibonacci number, probably THE most important one. If that were the case, they should arrange the values in their original order, but broken in lines and columns of eight, at least for a start.

Raj's fingers flew over the keyboard as he performed the first task Sinclair had asked of him, that of determining the Linear A symbols that should correspond with the block values as they had calculated them. Hoping that they hadn't performed too many calculations, or followed that notion down a wrong trail, he made the two-step comparisons as quickly as the laptop could work. In far less time than anyone but he and Sinclair expected, they were looking at a chart of about two hundred signs that corresponded with the same number of values in the blocks. However, there were hundreds of signs left over, as well as an approximately equal number of block values. These they would set aside until they had dealt with what was already known. Quickly, Raj added the corresponding signs and meanings from Linear B. Eighty-seven of the signs were syllabary in nature, building blocks of other words. A hundred more were ideograms, signifying objects. Commodities, probably, Sinclair explained, but it gave them a group of nouns--the names of everyday objects--to work with, and that was a start.

Sinclair had Raj add a column with the transliterated pronunciation of the syllables and the English name of the objects corresponding with the Linear B ideograms. The makeshift Rosetta Stone emerged as he watched, fascinated, muttering the Greek sounds under his breath. Time stopped for the others, though in fact the progress was rapid, thanks to the powerful server and Raj's expertise in using the Oracle sort functions. When they came to the end of the known symbols, everyone heaved a sigh as if they had been holding their collective breath. Only Sinclair, his eyes dancing down the column of Greek syllables, was too wrapped up in memorizing the pyramid values associated with them to realize they had reached a climax of sorts.

Raj broke the silence. "What would you like me to do next, sir?"

Absently, still intent on his memorization task, Sinclair said, "Call me Sinclair." Then he looked up, smiled and said, "Sorry, I was woolgathering. What did you ask me?"

"What would you like me to do next?" Raj replied.

"Can you bring up on the left-hand screen the stone values arranged in their natural order, but grouped in rows and columns, as we talked about? And leave this chart up on the other; I want to be able to compare the values with the syllables easily."

"Yes, of course, just a moment." Raj answered, bringing up the base data set on the left-hand screen. He selected a block of about five hundred values in their natural order, that is, as they lined up in the construction of the pyramid, and then gave a couple of new commands. The screen refreshed and in place of the original long column a set of values appeared in an eight-by-eight grid. Sinclair ran his eyes over it, flicking now and then to the left side of the screen where the syllabic comparisons still showed. His eyes widened as he studied, then a grin spread over his face and he exclaimed, "Jaysus!", then immediately apologized when he saw Martha's hand fly to her mouth.

"What is it, Sinclair?" Sarah ventured.

"I know now why no one could make anything of it

before." Sinclair mused, running his finger back and forth over the natural-order text lines without touching the screen.

Impatient, Daniel started to say something, but Sarah put her hand on his arm, seeing that Sinclair was still thinking about his discovery, whatever it was, and would clue them in when he had come to a conclusion.

Sinclair, unaware of the agitation of the others, finished traversing the lines with his finger and nodded with satisfaction. "We always thought this was a progression from early right-to-left writing, like Phoenician." Shaking himself out of his solitary ramblings, he addressed the group. "Or Hebrew. Everyone understands that not all languages are written left-to-right like modern English or Romance languages, yes?" Seeing everyone nod, he went on. "At some point, Greek began to be written in a pattern called Boustrophedon. That meant, the first line was written right-to-left, and then the second went left-to-right, with all the words in a mirror image of how they would have been written on odd lines."

Various expressions met his words as the others struggled to visualize what he meant. In an effort to clarify, Sinclair again pointed at the screen, demonstrating that the words would be read as he had described, first traveling from right-to-left, and then reversing the direction on the next line, so that his finger zig-zagged as it progressed down the rows. Comprehension dawned on each face, seconds apart, as each got it.

"What does it mean?" Daniel asked first.

"It means that when other researchers tried to make Linear A manuscripts make sense, they assumed right-to-left for each line of script, because it was thought to be older than Linear B, and Linear B was still written that way. It was only later, as Greek developed, that their script took on this pattern. But what we have here is proof that Boustrophedon was actually a return to an old pattern, rather than development of the new."

Fascinating as this was, Daniel had a burning question. "But, how do you know that, when you haven't translated the message yet?"

Sinclair looked surprised. "Oh, didn't I say? Sorry. And, forgive me, I haven't fully wrapped my head around the fact that we have a Linear A-like script transliterating the ancient Sumerian, but this first part is an index of the subjects that are covered in the code, and where you'll find each." He pointed to the lines of values, reading now as if it were nothing to him to transliterate twice and then translate as he went.

"See here, mathematics, history, astronomy..."

His words were drowned by the others shouting in amazement. Sarah's scream brought Luke running, gun drawn, to the dining room where they were working, to behold Daniel and Sarah dancing in a circle, with Raj staring at Sinclair as if he had seen a ghost, his mouth open, and pounding Sinclair on the back violently.

"What is it?" cried Luke? His initial impression was that Raj was giving Sinclair some weird kind of CPR, while Daniel and Sarah had lost their minds. Finally, he went to stand directly in front of Sarah and shout in her face. "SARAH!"

That served to bring the chaos to an abrupt end as Sarah looked at Luke sheepishly. "Yes, Uncle Luke?"

With some asperity born of the fright he'd received, Luke answered, "What the hell going on in here? Who's hurt?"

"No one," a calmer Daniel said, taking Sarah into his arms and hugging her tightly. "I'm sorry, Luke. We just had some amazing news. Sinclair here has cracked the code!"

Luke's calm reception of that news served to settle the others down. Quietly he asked, "Well? What does it say?"

Everyone turned to Sinclair, who was finally catching his breath now that Raj had stopped pounding him on the back. "It says there's a library of subjects that the builders knew something about, and it tells how to find the messages. That's as far as I got before the bedlam set in." Despite being manhandled by Raj, Sinclair seemed to have recovered his good nature. "Let's see what we can make of the rest of it. Let me work in peace for a few minutes."

Martha was sitting in a chair tears running down her cheeks as she said to herself, "Mark my dear where are you? How I wish you could be here to see what you have started."

Sinclair noticed Martha crying and walked over to her. He put his arm around her apologizing again for his outburst, but she only shook her head. She didn't ask him to remove his arm, though, finding it very comforting. Since her husband's death, she missed physical contact, and enjoyed every hug she got.

Martha and Sarah decided it was a good time to fix lunch for the group while they waited for Sinclair to announce that he had more translated. Later, munching on their sandwiches and salad as they stood or sat around the dining table, far enough from the computer equipment to keep Raj happy, the others excitedly discussed what the next move should be. Obviously, there must be more to the message as it was currently arranged that Sinclair hadn't had the chance to see. Raj had only selected a small sample, after all. From time to time one or the other of them paused in their thinking and talking to look at Sinclair in awe and remark again how amazing it was that he could just perform all those mental gymnastics, reading it as if it were written in English. Daniel, realizing that Sinclair had memorized the values and their corresponding syllables in less than half an hour, resolved never again to judge a person's ability to assimilate new information by their age. Even if Sinclair was a genius as he and Sarah had decided, it was a remarkable achievement.

Modestly, Sinclair waved away their awe, and said, "I'll admit that it would be easier if we did some more comparison charts and wrote the syllables in Arabic script."

Raj answered, "That's no problem. I'll do it while you are eating." Setting his lunch aside, he went back to the keyboard and entered a few more commands. "Do you want the Sumerian form of the Arabic script? It is the most ancient I have loaded in the database."

"Yes, that will do. I suspect we're dealing with something even more ancient, which is what made me think to use Sumerian as I pronounced the sounds we related to each value. What a jumble though! This will turn the linguistics community on its head and wipe out several theories of how language developed in the region."

Looking at Sinclair, Daniel said, "I'll bet everything you need to prove it is hidden somehow in that code. How fast can we translate all of it?"

Sinclair shook his head. "Not fast. I mean, it won't take long to translate enough to convince even the worst skeptic that we're onto something, but to get it all done...it just depends on how much there is. How many Fibonacci numbers have you determined to be represented in the stone values?"

Daniel looked to Raj for confirmation before answering, "As far as I know or recall, all of them are Fibonacci numbers."

Sinclair gave an exaggerated slump, as if the idea were overwhelming, then straightened with an excited gleam in his eye. "In that case, using each number as a skip sequence, there could logically be hundreds of different texts in the same stones. Of course, it would require the use of a computer to arrange the stones in such a way that the texts would all make sense, and we're talking about a more than 6000-year-old civilization, so most likely they didn't have anything like our computers. But even a few different starting points or skip sequences would represent hundreds of hours to translate, if I'm working alone. Have you considered bringing in another linguist or dozen?" Sinclair asked, with a whimsical smile.

Daniel's answer was more serious. "No, we actually hadn't thought that far ahead. Bad oversight again. We'd better keep at the first message. I mean, finish the one you started, and meanwhile Raj could create reports for the next several numbers as skip sequences and you could take a look at the first few lines to see if we're on the right track."

Daniel's suggestion met with the approval of the others, so Sinclair asked Raj to print out what he had and then create the next couple of thousand rows, or however many it would take to exhaust the data, for him to work on when he finished the first set. After that, Raj would use the next Fibonacci number to create a report that would pick out every thirteenth value and so forth, working his way through the entire sequence until the numbers grew too large to make sense for the volume of data they had.

Soon the room fell mostly silent, only now and again one or the other making a remark, as Sinclair worked with Sarah hanging over his shoulders and Daniel reading upside down from across the table. Raj continued to set up sequence reports until he grew tired of doing it one by one and wrote a program to go through the steps. It was when he remarked that the data set seemed to be shrinking with each iteration of the program that Martha, who displayed astounding general knowledge for someone who did a degree in home economics more than 30 years ago and have been a housewife most of her life, had a brainstorm.

"Of course! As the Fib numbers get higher, we skip more and more symbols. The higher we go, the shorter the text will be that corresponds to that number in the sequence!"

"Begorrah, she's right!" exclaimed Sinclair, looking at Martha with not only surprise but respect and prompting Sarah to snigger. "What?"

"I just love it when you go all Irish on us," Sarah teased. "I can't resist a man with an accent."

Sinclair shot a good-natured grin at Daniel and said, "Better watch out, Danny Boy, I'm beating your time with your girl."

Daniel answered with a grin of his own. "Speaking of beating..." Prompting Sinclair to hold up his hands in surrender. The comic relief served to break the silence that had prevailed since the last spate of conversation.

Daniel was the one to ask Raj what number he was working on.

"One-hundred and forty-four," was the laconic answer.

"Hey," said Martha. "Let's see what that one says."

So far, the initial sequence, the one that used all the stones without skipping any, had revealed nothing but a list of subjects with corresponding numeric values that they couldn't quite see the reason for, and Sinclair hadn't reached the end of that grid yet. Martha's suggestion was tantamount to saying they should skip to the end of the book to see how it turned out, but the others were eager enough to get more information that they all agreed. Quickly, Raj printed out his latest grid and they all held their breath as Sinclair began to translate.

"Ye who have found the key, hear our chronicle. Know that in the year... of The Tenth Cycle" Sinclair stopped, puzzled. "There's what may be a numerical notation here, but I don't understand it."

"Maybe they give a clue later on. Let's go on and figure out when later." Daniel said.

"Okay. In the year unknown, the Supreme Council of Knowledge, commissioned the least of their number, I, Zebulon, to build this monument and record our history for Those Who Come After. In all the cycles, this has never been attempted before."

"Holy shit!" Daniel exclaimed, prompting a quelling look from both Sarah and Martha.

Another little commotion ensued but Sinclair held up his hand to calm them down before they went completely off the handle. He went on after the interruption. "We of the Tenth Cycle believe that we have achieved more than any Cycle before us, and, knowing our fate, wish to leave evidence of our knowledge. With this knowledge, perhaps you, our children, may continue our progress and stop the cycles of destruction that have held our kind to less than our full potential for ..." Again, Sinclair paused, "Some number again, I can't make it out. Then, 'years.' Good heavens, this is maddening."

Daniel looked up at the others. "This is already explosive information. There's some sort of cycle of destruction, just as Sarah's friend Ahmed and his colleagues believe. We need to find out where we are in it. Sinclair, as you read on, do you see anything that gives a clue as to how to read these numbers?"

"Not yet, but let me keep reading. 'We leave this monument for your enlightenment. However, our leader has decreed that it must be coded in such a way that it may not be read until you have achieved a measure of civilization to equal our own. Know this: if wars still disturb the peace of your world, you will not be able to escape the destruction that will come in the fullness of your cycle. You must cease fighting amongst yourselves and work together on the answer. Only then will mankind achieve the shared knowledge to avoid the same fate as those who have gone before you.'"

As Sinclair's voice trailed off, the others looked at each other in consternation. War was definitely a part of their world, and no one saw a way to bring it to an end permanently. In fact, these five people couldn't see a way to end any small skirmish, much less the wars that dotted the globe in every corner. Their mission had just become larger than they had ever dreamed.

Sinclair was saying that he wanted most of all to understand the numeric notation, so they'd know when and how long the Builders' civilization had lasted. They could no longer refer to them as Egyptians, nor did anyone believe they were Minoans. That time sequence wouldn't work at all, despite the similarity of the language as Sinclair had worked it out. Even Sumerian didn't quite fit. Builders it was, at least until they discovered somewhere in the record what they called themselves. Daniel had suggested Cyclers, but everyone thought he was joking, and he didn't correct them.

Knowing they couldn't translate even a significant portion of the material, much less all of it, Sinclair resorted to skimming the first few lines, whatever it took to get the gist of the subject matter, and then labeling the printed data cube with the Fibonacci number that indicated the skip sequence. As Sarah picked up a few of the pages Sinclair had laid aside, she had an idea.

"Hey, guys? What if the numbers in the index are the same as these Fib numbers that indicate the skip sequence?"

Daniel was thunderstruck. Of course! Eagerly, he joined Sarah as they started notating an index of their own and comparing it to the presumed numerical symbols in the translated index. It soon became clear that Sarah had been correct. What a simple solution! By the time they were finished with what had been done so far, both marveled that they hadn't seen it before. Sinclair, though he continued to translate, looked over at their progress from time to time. When they announced that they thought they had it, he took the pages and looked them over.

"No doubt about it! Where's that section we read about when they started to create the record?"

"It was skip sequence one-forty-four, wasn't it? Sarah said.

"Yes, that's it, now where did that go?" Finding the page he wanted, Sinclair looked back and forth at the symbols representing the numbers they had. Then he took a fresh page, wrote the symbols from the year that dated that section and the Arabic numerals they represented below them. When he had finished, he pushed the paper toward Daniel and Sarah, an awestruck expression on his face. With trembling hands, Sarah picked up the paper and read the number.

"Twenty-five thousand, nine-hundred and ninety-two. Oh, my heavens!"

"What," Daniel said, having misunderstood what he heard. "Their civilization is about six hundred years older than ours. Can they have made that much more progress?"

"No, Daniel, *thousand.* Nearly twenty-six *thousand* years of unbroken civilization. You're thinking twenty-first century, and forgetting that we're counting from the birth of Christ, not from the beginning. I make it nearly twenty thousand years older than ours. I can't imagine what they might have known." Sarah sat down abruptly, the shock of the enormous number fully sinking in.

Martha said in a very soft voice betraying her bewilderment, "In six thousand years, we emerged from the Stone Age, began living in cooperation and specializing our work, learned to communicate with each other, fought wars, learned how to fly and how to make electricity an inextricable part of our lives. We can't even begin to assimilate all the knowledge we have, much less what would have come out of such an old civilization. Think of the progress we've made in just the past hundred or so years, and how rapidly it's advancing in the last fifteen."

Sarah said with a flash of humor, "How about a shot of tequila?"

Daniel laughed. "Sometimes too much drink is barely enough," quoting one of his favorite sources, Mark Twain. If there were ever an occasion where too much was barely enough, this was it.

The others, each reacting in his own way to the astounding number, were brought back to the present by the laugh that Daniel had provided. Sinclair suggested that a round of Irish coffee was in order. Only Raj, who was not familiar with the drink, demurred. But Sinclair insisted, and explained how it was made, then adding, "Only Irish coffee in a single drink provides all four essential food groups, alcohol, sugar, caffeine and fat."

Raj laughed, wrinkled his nose, and then said, "Oh, what the hell. Why not?" Sarah laughed at the familiar idiom pronounced in Raj's lilting accent, and went to the kitchen to help Martha fix the drinks. Fifteen minutes later, they all sat around the table, Raj moving from behind the computer to a spot where coffee could not be spilled in the keyboard, enjoying their drinks and discussing what the revelation would mean and how to publish it.

# Chapter 46 – Daddy Would Have Been Proud of Me

In Würzburg, Septentrio the younger paced back and forth in his father's study. Before his death, his father had warned him that the other members of the group would be watching him carefully, waiting for him to make a mistake. As he paced, Septentrio kicked at a piece of furniture that was in his way. The conflicting feelings he struggled with kept him enraged, and he was having a difficult time controlling his temper.

For over forty years, his father had belittled and berated him for his sexual preference, told him he was weak, and proved it by having him beaten often until he gathered the courage to fight back. After that, several times a week, Septentrio would go to his bed only to find one or more women waiting there for him. Time after time, the women would humiliate him for his rejection of them, and he had no doubt that his father had ordered them to do so.

As a consequence, Septentrio hated his father fiercely and would gladly have murdered him himself. And yet, his hatred, with no other outlet, was now directed toward the people he blamed for his father's death. Daniel Rossler and Sarah Clarke. Even now, their detested faces smiled and mocked him from his computer monitor.

His brief from the other members was simple. Deal with Sidus and his traitorous actions, and find Rossler and Clarke before more harm was done to the interests of the Orion Society. The first was easy, he had only to activate their backup mole in the CIA system, and extract the information about where David was being held. It was a pity they hadn't time to deal with him as he had dealt with Impes. After his henchmen had shot their way in to the safe house, Septentrio personally put the bullet in the brain of the fickle David.

It would have pleased his father, Septentrio reflected, to know that he was both ruthless enough and clever enough to have the traitor killed while in custody of the CIA. Probably surprised the hell out of him, too, if the truth were known.

Septentrio code-named the new operative Latet, and took great delight in tormenting the man with the fate of his predecessor for grievous errors. Unlike his father, who knew just how to motivate without wrecking his assets with fear, the current Septentrio was a petty, bitter man. He would bully his assets into obedience, and never know why he couldn't keep loyal employees.

However, Rossler and Clarke had disappeared without a trace. Septentrio wasted no time in tracking down their known associates, only to learn to his frustration that Rajan Sankaran had also disappeared, as well as Sinclair O'Reilly. He even went personally to the home of Martha Simms, finding her gone as well. Clearly they had all gone somewhere together; however they had dropped off the grid as if they had never existed. No charges had been posted to their credit card accounts for several days, their cell phones were turned off and none of their cars had been spotted anywhere that might have recorded their license plate numbers.

Reaching out to his CIA, FBI, and NSA contacts produced no better results. The Rosslerites had disappeared like a needle in a haystack. A quick reconnoiter at the homes of the extended families found them heavily guarded but still no sign of the researchers themselves. Septentrio's mood was so foul that he had half a mind to wipe out the families, along with their minders, but logic told him that this would not help gain the cooperation of the researchers.

The only clue that showed the Rosslerites had left behind was that, curiously, each missing person had withdrawn large sums of cash on the same day that they all disappeared. The only logical conclusion was that they were prepared to stay hidden for quite some time, and may even be making plans to leave the United States. Infuriated, Septentrio set a trap that he knew would foil their plans.

Through his CIA contacts, Septentrio floated the rumor that Rossler and Clark, aided by Sankaran and O'Reilly, were potential terrorists with links to Al Qaeda. Photos and faked transcripts of their meeting with the Egyptian scholars gave rise to the assumption that they were conspiring with Egyptian radicals. Within hours, APB's had been posted for all four of them and with that, their faces broadcast over every news outlet as armed and dangerous. Suddenly the group was the object of a worldwide manhunt.

At the same time, the Orion Society, not wanting them to disappear in the hands of some law enforcement group, offered a reward among their underground network for the capture of the researchers, to be paid on receipt of all members without harm.

# Chapter 47 – Let's Show You What We Have

As soon as the initial giddiness had settled down, Luke knew it was time to arrange for his Mossad contact to make a visit and see what they had to offer for the group's safety. He spoke briefly to Sarah, explaining his errand, and slipped away unnoticed by the rest. Luke made his way to the Canadian side of the border and found a pay phone that accepted both currencies. He placed the call.

The next day, half an hour before the stated six a.m. meeting time, Akiva Beckman arrived with a crew of technicians outside the safe house. There, they quietly activated with remote control devices the permanently-installed listening devices in all the rooms, being thorough in case a word or two whispered in the bathroom or elsewhere could shed light on Luke's mysterious request. Beckman, a consular agent with the Rhode Island assignment working out of the Boston consulate, would have been the appropriate person for Daniel and Sarah to speak to in any case. However, Beckman was Mossad. His status was known to certain CIA agents, Luke among them, in an open secret that allowed them to work together whenever any operation required cooperation between the two agencies. Otherwise, the CIA turned a blind eye to Beckman's activities, trusting from past association that they were not aimed at harm to the United States.

Promptly at six that morning, Akiva presented himself at the front door of the safe house. In the doorway stood a tall, well-built man in his early thirties. He extended a hand to Akiva and drew him inside, where several other people waited despite the early hour. Akiva's dark, curly hair framed a high forehead and sharp brown eyes, adding to the pleasantness of his angular face and engendering instant trust among the researchers. Smiling, he introduced himself.

"I'm Akiva Beckman," he announced. "But if we are to be friends, you may call me Beck."

Sarah was charmed, and Daniel, considering the man too old to be a rival, felt comfortable in his presence also.

"Beck, thank you for agreeing to see us. The lovely lady with me is my fiancée, Dr. Sarah Clarke, aka Sarah, and I'm Daniel." Indicating the others as he spoke, he also introduced Sinclair, Martha and Raj. Luke, the man already knew of course.

"Well, then, shall we sit down and discuss why I am here?" Beckman led the way to comfortable seats in a spacious living room, explaining that this was a house where his consulate brought those who sought his help to enter or re-enter Israel, there to await permission if they had nowhere else to go.

"All right, my friends, may I call you by Daniel and Sarah? Both names with long tradition in my culture," he added with a smile.

"Please, let's don't stand on ceremony," Sarah responded.

"Daniel and Sarah, then. Why don't you tell me briefly how I can help you?" Akiva included the others in his request by giving each a short but steady look, but Daniel was clearly the leader, and to him he addressed his remarks.

He warned Akiva, "This is a long story, but I can tell you in a nutshell what we need. Then maybe you can ask the questions I know you'll have, rather than hear it from the beginning."

"That will do for now. Please, proceed."

Daniel drew a deep breath, and said, "In a nutshell, people are trying to kill us, we have reason to believe our own government, or people working for the government, as well as an international group of very powerful people with bad motives are involved. What we need is asylum."

It was nothing less than Beckman had anticipated, though stated more bluntly, so he betrayed no surprise. Instead, he said, "I suspect that before a decision can be made, someone is going to have to hear the whole story, but why don't you expand on that just a bit."

"Before we reveal the reasons, we understand that you will not speak of this to anyone, not even your government, if you can't assure us that our request will be granted, is that correct?" Daniel had come armed with his anti-listening device, and belatedly wondered if he should have brought his digital tape recorder, too. Then, realizing that having a recorded assurance meant nothing to bullets, he accepted Akiva's answer. Trust was beginning to come hard, but they were desperate.

Akiva nodded, and said, "You have my word. My association with Luke here is valuable to me. I would not lightly jeopardize it."

Satisfied, Daniel went on. "Okay then. What I'm about to tell you may seem unbelievable, but we can back it up. Please try to keep an open mind." After taking a deep breath, he plunged into the core of the story. "Without going into how all of this came about and the steps we've taken to get where we are with it today, we've made a discovery of historic importance. You could say it's world-changing. Our government, your government, every government in the world is going to want the information, along with many powerful corporations. Along the way, our research has prompted someone, we're not certain who, to kill two of our associates, hold my grandparents hostage and kidnap Sarah here. Four kidnappers were killed when we retrieved her, and we've just learned that there was a fifth who evidently escaped. We're about ready to reveal the information, but we'd like to be somewhere safe when we do. After searching for options, we settled on Israel as the safest place, assuming we can get official protection."

Akiva heard the claim with evident calm, but now asked, "May I know what the discovery concerns? Just in broad terms, if you will, please."

Daniel looked at Sarah for agreement, and she nodded. "You may be aware that both scholars and crackpots have had theories about the Great Pyramid at Giza, Egypt having more significance than meets the eye. We've proved it, and in the process have found a record from an ancient civilization that predates all accepted theories of the history of humanity. As I said, we have proof. We can back it up. Just what we've translated so far indicates that they may have been far more advanced than we are currently, and the extent of the record indicates it may be all laid out in a way that we can understand and apply."

Beckman's mouth had opened in astonishment. This was completely unexpected. Attempting to maintain a professional detachment, he asked, "What proof can you offer? This is an extraordinary claim, and if it's legitimate, I think I can assure you that my government will be willing to help you, in return for access to these records."

Daniel had come prepared for this question. He said, "Sarah?" signaling her to bring out one of the documents she and Martha had prepared, then continued as Sarah handed them to Akiva.

"The first page shows what we had discovered at the time of our colleague's murder. The second, the more accurate translation by our linguist. Take a look."

Akiva scanned the first page, noting that whoever had translated it hadn't known what some of the--words? symbols?-- meant.

**[Unknown word]** traveler/person/human/man from future. **[Unknown word]** critical/important/significant **[Unknown word]** telling/story/message **[Unknown word]** read/browse/assimilate/learn all/ **[Unknown word]** everything here/in this place/at this location **[Unknown word]**

He read aloud, getting only to the word 'future' before his eyes flew to Daniel's. "What does this mean?"

"Read the next page," Daniel urged. "All will be explained."

The next page had the complete translation of the full text, including the numbers that had eluded Sinclair on first reading. Put together, without the hesitations as Sinclair translated and the interruptions of the others exclaiming at each new sentence, it was even more impactful.

"In the year 25,992 of the Tenth Cycle, the Supreme Council of Knowledge, commissioned the least of their number, I, Zebulon, to build this monument and record our history for Those Who Come After. In all the cycles, this has never been attempted before.

We of the Tenth Cycle believe that we have achieved more than any Cycle before us, and, knowing our fate, wish to leave evidence of our knowledge. With this knowledge, perhaps you, our children, may continue our progress and stop the cycles of destruction that have held our kind to less than our full potential for two hundred and sixty thousand years."

Then he repeated slowly in utter astonishment, "Two – hundred – and – sixty – thousand – years!" Akiva repeated in an excited and high pitched voice with emphasis on each word. Akiva's reaction, a profane exclamation, was blasphemous, creative and so foul that Sarah and Martha blushed and Daniel's hands formed into fists. A shaken Akiva apologized and said, "You could have warned me."

"I guess I should have." Daniel remarked.

"You understand that this will negate the entire history of my people," Akiva accused.

"No it won't," Sarah argued. "The history of your people in our cycle is intact. It is only what went before that's different, and that's the case for everyone. However, we understand the explosive nature of this discovery. It's what convinced us that it's too dangerous for us to be here, or anywhere else that our enemies can penetrate, when we release the news."

Daniel continued, "We have a record of the steps and methods we used, but briefly, it culminated in our linguist making several translations, all consistent with what I've told you and what is stated in this document. At the moment, he's searching the records for a sufficiently advanced piece of scientific evidence that can be corroborated. As soon as he finds it, we want to be ready to release the news of the discovery, and obtain help in translating and utilizing the rest of it.

"As for access, we plan on giving that freely as public information. Obviously, we'll need to get wide consensus on restricting access on anything that might be used for great harm. We haven't quite sorted that out yet, but in any case it's premature. Only a tiny fraction of what's there has yet been translated."

Beckman could hardly contain himself, the thought that with control of this information his country could at last be secure from the enemies that surrounded it. But, he must give these Americans the assurance that his government would cooperate, and then make the arrangements to do so. It would take finesse. Perhaps there would be an opportunity for their own linguists to find something of advantage that only Israel would know of. In any case, the cachet associated with sheltering the people who made such an important discovery should be enough to secure their entry and shelter in Israel. He stated only a portion of these thoughts, though. "I think I can assure you that my government will cooperate with your request. It may take a few days to make the arrangements."

Daniel answered, "Do you intend to phone someone? We've been avoiding that, because we know the NSA, at the very least, is listening for keywords. Can you make sure you don't mention our names, or the pyramid?"

"I'll use a scrambled phone, of course," Beckman assured him. "Please don't worry, we know how to get around your NSA."

Daniel wasn't sure how he felt about that in general, but was reassured for the issue at hand.

"I believe I can assure you that my government will be happy to host you and protect you while you complete your task," Akiva repeated. "However, I must warn you that we cannot protect you while you are on US soil. Until I can make the arrangements, you must understand that you are on your own. Is our hospitality in this safe house adequate for a few days?"

"Very much so," Sarah replied. "Thank you for making it available to us."

"How many of you will be visiting my country?" Akiva asked delicately.

"Just five of us. Uncle Luke will stay here and see to the safety of our families," she replied.

"Very well, I'll make the necessary arrangements." Half-bowing, Beckman excused himself and left, getting into a dark panel van. Inside was a technician with a set of headphones on his head and a chagrined look on his face. "What is it?" Beckman asked.

"Akiva, I don't know why, but I couldn't hear a word of your conversation."

A speculative look came over Beckman's face as he wondered if these people had already made use of their new discovery to create something that would jam state-of-the-art bugs. Now that would certainly be something his government would want. If it could defeat Israel's advanced technology, it must be very good indeed.

After he had returned to the hotel where he was staying, Akiva contacted his superior officer in Mossad headquarters, where it was now late in the afternoon. "You're not going to believe the conversation I just had..." he began.

# Chapter 48 – You Have Been Cleared

Shortly after Akiva left, Luke took a call. None of the others paid much attention until Luke's sharp voice broke into their thoughts.

"How the hell did that happen?" He demanded.

After listening for a moment, he said, "All right, we'll be on the lookout. Are you sending more guards?" He listened for a moment more, then disconnected the call. Finding the others all staring at him, Luke said, "I have some bad news."

Various expressions of dismay went around the group, but Luke continued, "David is dead, one gunshot wound to the forehead, in his sleep."

No one was going to mourn David, at least no one in the present company, but the question on everyone's mind was the same as what Luke had asked. How the hell had that happened? David was in CIA custody. Luke explained that the guards at the safe house where David was being held for questioning had been taken out as well, leaving the way open for the assassin to get to David. Lewis, who had called Luke personally, was livid. Not only was their witness gone, but three of his hand-picked men were in critical condition and one dead. The only explanation was that there was indeed another mole at CIA headquarters.

Agitated chatter broke out as the research group questioned Luke as to their continued safety under the circumstances.

"Lewis is sending for more CIA guards to join those who are watching already," he said.

"How do we know one of them isn't the mole?" Sarah said, frightened.

"We won't have to worry about it very long," Daniel

soothed. "Akiva promised to get us out of here as quickly as possible." Nevertheless, the group was less than productive that day, concerned that they had nowhere to hide and nowhere to go and that time was running out.

In fact, they were already out of time, but they didn't yet know it.

~~~

Daniel and Luke had finally managed to calm the rest of the team and they were making good progress with the translation of the index, when another interruption rocked the group. On the second day after Luke had learned of David's death, Akiva returned unexpectedly. He brought the news that an all points bulletin had been issued for them and that they were no longer safe in this small town where new faces were easily noted.

"The word went out that you're associated with Al Qaeda," he said. "It was done so well and so professionally that I almost believed it myself, especially when I saw pictures of Sarah smiling and laughing with a couple of Egyptian men."

"Oh good grief," Sarah said. "Those were a couple of scholars that I've known for years. I have no inkling that they are associated with Al Qaeda, and all we were talking about was the theory among some Egyptian scholars that human history has gone through a number of cycles."

"A picture is worth a thousand words, especially if one or two of those words are Al Qaeda. It doesn't take much to strike fear into your countrymen and anger into the hearts of mine," Akiva said. "But, I checked with my agency, and they cleared you."

"They what?" Daniel asked. "What do you mean, they cleared us?"

"It turns out that we have been tracking your activities as

well," Akiva said. He had the grace to look ashamed as Daniel and Sinclair both exploded with oaths of dismay. Sarah and Martha just looked at Akiva emotionless – no swearing or outbursts could shock them anymore – they were becoming immune to that. Nevertheless he went on, "I have clearance, you will be welcome in my country, and my government has pledged your safety, but first we must smuggle you out of the US."

"How do you propose to do that?" Daniel said, still seething at the notion of a foreign government tracking his activities. Raj was right, he reflected. Everyone has been watching us, there's no such thing as privacy anymore.

"Leave the details to me but be ready to go at any time after darkness falls," Akiva said.

While the Rosslerites once again packed up their meager belongings, including only the external hard drives and flash drives with data and programs copied from Raj's laptop, Akiva made a visit to an old friend. With him, he carried the passports of the four team members and Martha.

Beckman walked into the office of his old friend Bernie Cohen, captain of the Canadian border patrol station in Stanstead. Beckman's team had use this crossing several times over the previous years, assisted by the Jewish head of station whose sympathies lay with Israel. Whenever he could get away, Akiva indulged in the rustic pleasures that Bernie enjoyed; fishing and a good Scotch. Today he carried a brown paper bag in one hand while the other protected the five passports concealed in his pocket.

"Shalom Aleichem, Bernie," Akiva said, placing the brown bag casually on Cohen's desk.

"Aleichem Shalom, my old friend. To what do I owe the pleasure?"

"Ah, my friend you wound me. I am here merely to greet an old friend as I was passing through." As he spoke, Akiva placed the five passports on Bernie's desk and spread them out. Bernie flicked his eyes toward the dark blue folders and raised one eyebrow. From his drawer he took a self-inking stamp, and drew the first passport toward him, placing an entry stamp upon the appropriate page. The two friends continued their casual conversation as he repeated the process with each of the other four.

"Have you had any good late-night fishing?" Akiva asked as he slipped the passports back into his pocket.

"What would you consider late at night?" Bernie responded.

"Oh, anytime after, say, ten p.m."

"Oh yes, the fishing is great after ten p.m.," said Bernie.

"I'll have to try it. Where would you suggest I go?"

Bernie named a spot a few miles out of town, and the two exchanged goodbyes when Akiva stood to go.

"Mazel tov," said Bernie, wishing him good luck with a wink, as he put away the brown paper bag in his lower desk drawer.

Akiva turned up again at the safe house at about dinnertime and gratefully accepted Sarah's invitation to stay. After dinner, he handed each person his or her own passport. He then instructed the group to be ready by nine-thirty that evening, when he and two of his men would pick them up and take them to the border crossing where he expected to be able to smuggle them out of the United States and into Canada with no further trouble.

~~~

All was in readiness when Akiva and his two men arrived to transport the team to the border crossing. It was a moonless night, quite chilly. Everyone but Martha had on dark down jackets. Martha had brought her ski gear, but the jacket was white with pink trim. Akiva regarded it with disfavor, and asked if she had another. Martha responded that she had not expected to play cops and robbers when she purchased her fashionable jacket. Akiva shrugged. There was no help for it, Martha would be a liability in that jacket but the others refused to leave her behind.

Akiva and Luke rode in the front seat of one SUV, with Sarah, Daniel and Raj in the back. The other two Mossad operatives drove a second SUV, with Sinclair and Martha. While they were in town, the drivers maintained normal driving procedure, but as soon as they had reached the outskirts, they doused the headlights and continued with nothing but the parking lights to guide them. Sarah was nervous; it was too dark a night to be driving unfamiliar roads without headlights. She could only hope that Akiva knew the roads.

Moments later, Sarah's question became moot as a roaring noise approached. Before she could ask what it was, Daniel shouted, "Sarah, get down!" Seconds later, brilliant white light illuminated the interior of the SUV as the helicopter overhead spotlighted them. Akiva shouted in Hebrew into his radio, and the SUV following them quickly turned off even their parking lights and left the road for the cover of the hedgerow. Inside the lead SUV, pandemonium broke out as a tracer round flew in Raj's window and out the other side. Daniel flung himself over Sarah, while Raj, being smaller, slid off the seat and crouched on the floor board, wondering if this was going to be the day he has always feared.

Akiva stepped on the gas, and began weaving, as Luke pulled out a fearsome looking semi-automatic weapon and returned fire at the helicopter. If Daniel had seen it, he would have admired Luke's ability to hit his target with the car weaving as it was. The helicopter prudently backed away and Akiva began shouting for his passengers to gather their stuff and be ready to dive out of the car when he stopped. Each time the helicopter approached again, Luke fired a burst at it, until Akiva found a densely wooded area in which to ditch the car. Everyone tumbled out, clutching their belongings, and ran, following Akiva.

He led them through the dense woods and to a small cabin where he had them wait while he collected the others. Sarah clutched Daniel and sobbed with worry for Martha.

As soon as the helicopter lost the lead SUV, it returned to the area where the pilot thought the second car had dropped out of the chase. Because the cover was not as dense, he located the abandoned car immediately. On the off chance that the occupants were still hiding there, he sent several rounds into the stopped vehicle, and was gratified to see two people scurry from the back seat and run. To his astonishment, one of them was wearing a bright white jacket, fully visible even on the moonless night. He had orders to bring back his quarry alive if possible, so he maneuvered the chopper to cut the figure off from deeper cover.

Martha was paralyzed by the racket the chopper was making and the fear of the bullets she expected any moment. In her too-visible white jacket, she knew that if the occupants of the chopper wanted to kill her, there was no way she would escape. Suddenly, shots rang out from her left, pinging off the chopper audibly. In response, it rose, and from nowhere, Sinclair appeared, throwing his own jacket over Martha's shoulders. Sinclair put his arm around Martha forcing her to duck, and ran with her to the deep cover only yards away. But the chopper was back, and bullets began to fly, causing Martha to scream.

As they gained the cover of the dense bramble of wild

cranberry bushes, the two Mossad operatives went on the offensive with their semi-automatic weapons, finally chasing the chopper away, at least for a while. The four remained where they were, unsure of their location, until a commotion from behind them revealed Akiva.

"Follow me," he said. "Mrs. Simms, you must not let your jacket show, or they will spot us immediately."

In response, Martha shrugged out of her jacket and allowed Sinclair to help her on with his again, though she protested that he must be cold.

"I'll be okay," he said.

Martha, Sinclair and the two Mossad operatives followed Akiva more than a mile through the cold woods, until they reached the cabin where Sarah and Daniel awaited anxiously, along with Luke and Raj. Once they were all inside, Akiva made certain that the windows were tightly covered before lighting a gas lantern he found on a shelf in the cabin.

As soon as the lantern flared to life, Martha noticed some blood stains on her blouse. When she looked around the room, she saw that Sinclair was nursing his left hand with his right and demanded to see it. Reluctantly Sinclair presented his hand for her inspection.

"You're bleeding!" She exclaimed.

"It's nothing," he said. "Just a flesh wound."

"I've heard that one before," she said. After a pause, she added, "In a Monty Python sketch."

Despite the tense situation, that drew a laugh from everyone, no one's heartier than Sinclair's. Akiva searched the cabin for a first aid kit, and insisted that Sinclair bring his wounded hand to the kitchen sink where the lantern revealed that, rather than a flesh wound, it was a through and through hit to the fleshy part between his thumb and forefinger.

"Thank God it missed the bones," Akiva said. "We need to disinfect it, and that's about all we have the supplies for."

Martha dressed Sinclair's wound, while Luke and Akiva consulted a map that Akiva drew from one of the pockets and his fatigue pants.

"It looks like we've made it across the border," Akiva said. "You have about a three mile walk across the fields to reach the nearest small town. Luke and I will go back to Stanstead and I'll call operatives in Canada to pick you up."

A brief consultation revealed that Sinclair felt he could navigate by the stars and the group decided as a whole that it would be less dangerous to attempt to cross the fields in the dark where the helicopter would have less chance of locating them than during the day. They could always lie down in ditches or under trees if they heard the helicopter approaching, so that even the searchlight would fail to reveal them. The only trouble, was that Sinclair had no jacket, having given his to Martha. Martha tried to give it back, but Sinclair wouldn't hear of it. Eventually Sarah had the bright idea to search the cabin for anything that would help, and they found an olive drab wool blanket that Sinclair could drape around his shoulders.

Luke hugged Sarah tightly, shook hands with the men, and kissed Martha on the cheek before making his departure with Akiva. A few minutes later, the five researchers departed the cabin also, after Daniel made sure that everyone knew the code words in case they were separated.

Akiva led Luke and his other team members back to the lead SUV where he radioed his Canadian counterpart to be on the lookout for the researchers as they entered the small town where someone could pick them up. They then dropped the two operatives off at their abandoned vehicle, and both cars made their way back to Stanstead.

It didn't take long for Daniel to notice a faint track across the fields which he thought may lead to the little town they were making for. The sky was beginning to brighten as the time for sunrise drew near, when he saw armed men in the distance, apparently moving toward them. As they had planned, the group scattered to both sides of the track each person finding cover as they could. When the armed group grew close Daniel could hear one of them saying, repeatedly, "Tenth Cycle." This was their codeword that these were friendlies, so he answered, "Rosslerite," and revealed himself to the men.

As soon as they saw that Daniel was safe, the rest also came out of cover. The men who had come to meet them offered water and food in the form of protein bars, and then positioned themselves before and behind the researchers, to escort them back to town. However, before they reached the town proper, they broke away from the trail and led the Rosslerites to a barn where they had concealed a van. They were soon on their way north to Highway 10 where they turned west for Montréal and an El Al flight to Israel.

## Chapter 49 – Welcome To Israel

A man who bore a remarkable resemblance to Akiva Beckman met the group as they deplaned, introducing himself as Baruch Beckman. "Brother?" questioned Daniel.

"Yes, Mr. Rossler. Akiva is my older brother. Welcome to Israel. Come with me, please."

They gathered their carry-on luggage, one bag containing a diplomatic pouch with their precious electronic devices in it, and followed Baruch to an area next to Customs, where most of their fellow passengers were undergoing searches of their baggage and short interviews to determine if they would be granted entry. El Al was one of the most secure airlines in the world, with armed sky marshals undercover on every flight, and most of the pilots having military experience. It was even the only airline so far to be equipped with infrared countermeasures systems, to combat the threat of anti-aircraft missiles. The Rosslerites, however, were traveling under diplomatic credentials arranged by Akiva. Neither their personal bags nor the diplomatic pouch would be searched, on orders from someone high in the chain of command. The names of their high-level protectors were not revealed to them, but everything had been arranged in the most luxurious manner possible.

After bypassing Customs, Baruch led them to a sturdy-looking seven-seater SUV and saw them safely ensconced in the back seats, their luggage stowed expertly, before he took the front passenger seat and directed the driver to an address in the city. He then turned to face them over his shoulder. Daniel noted with relief that the driver kept to the right lane, having decided he had driving dyslexia when vacationing once in Indonesia.

Baruch was giving them some information, to which Sarah had been paying close attention. Shaking himself to dispel the flight fatigue, Daniel now did the same, along with the others. "We have secured a large estate for your use. You will have a household staff to attend to shopping and cleaning needs. The estate is walled. Mossad agents will patrol the perimeter, so you have no need to be concerned for your safety. Do you have any questions?"

"Only about a million," Daniel answered. "This almost sounds like we are to be prisoners. I hope I'm wrong."

"I'm sorry if I made it sound that way," Baruch responded. "Nothing could be further from the truth. Our government wishes to extend to you the same courtesies we would extend to any important guest whose safety has been in question. Think of the head of a minor country, for example, who has been deposed by violence."

At this statement, Daniel and Sarah turned awestruck faces to each other, as did Martha and Sinclair. Raj seemed to take it in stride; he was just happy there was no one shooting at him from helicopters. Head of a minor country? But Baruch was still talking. "That said, I urge you to voluntarily stay within the walls of your residence as much as possible. We will endeavor to protect you, but our country is besieged at all times by our enemies, and those may be your enemies as well. As soon as the news of your discovery has been made public, malevolent forces will be seeking your whereabouts. When they discover that you are in Israel, certain assumptions will be made. At that point, we will ask you to consider the lives of our agents who protect you, and stay safe within the walls."

The initial headiness the group had felt on being informed of their living arrangements waned with each sentence. In fleeing the US, they had been concerned with their safety and that of their friends and loved ones. Now it seemed that a small army of strangers were prepared to lay down their lives to ensure it. It was humbling and dismaying at the same time. Any thoughts of tourist activities fled, leaving in their place the knowledge that the enterprise could not wait for rest and relaxation, nor any personal consideration. It was paramount that the public announcement be made as soon as possible, and work begun to unravel all of the secrets hidden in the blocks of the Great Pyramid.

However, at that moment, even more important was letting their families know that they were safe. They were sure that the Orion Society had discovered they'd flown the coop, so to speak.

"Baruch," Sarah said, in her most persuasive and feminine tones, "would it be too much to ask for you to contact your brother and ask him to let our families know we're safe?"

"Of course not, ma'am," he replied. "I'm sure it can be arranged. I'll check with Akiva," Baruch answered with no elaboration.

"Thank you so much!"

Martha then said, "Sorry to be so demanding but I am worried about Sinclair's hand. Would it also be possible to arrange for a doctor to have a look at it and give it the proper treatment? He was wounded during our escape the night before last and I am worried complications might set in."

Though Sinclair tried to wave off the attention, he was secretly pleased. In the past few days, this lovely woman had proved intelligent, resourceful, and caring, not to mention a great cook. Not since his wife had passed had he met such a paragon.

Sarah sat back to watch out the windows as they traveled through the unfamiliar but somehow familiar city.

Sarah's mental impression of Israel was always informed by pictures of the Holy Land in books she had read as a child. It came as a bit of a shock to see modern buildings instead of clusters of adobe. Throngs of people of diverse ethnic heritage traveled the sidewalks, swirling and rushing, passing buildings that might have been constructed in mid-twentieth century standing cheek-by-jowl with brand-new steel and glass structures. In many ways, it reminded her of New York, and she mentioned that observation to Daniel.

Baruch, anxious to show off his city, said, "Yes, you call New York the Big Apple, am I right?" Receiving nods, he said proudly, "Tel Aviv is the Big Orange." Sarah choked back a giggle, not wishing to offend the man. She wondered if he was also proud of the filth and trash in the streets.

# Chapter 50 – Let's Go For A Swim

There was no time to waste now. The attack as they left Stanstead had shaken them all badly, so in spite of jet lag and the distraction of the beautiful villa the Israelis had put at their disposal, the five of them got right to work. Raj and Sinclair were in charge of continuing to extract and translate the data, while Daniel and Sarah polished the article he would publish in the Times when a suitable verifying fact had been found in the coded material. That left Martha at loose ends, but she was soon busy organizing the household and directing the staff in keeping the four comfortable as they worked long hours.

Before an hour had passed, a doctor arrived to take a look at Sinclair's hand, over his protest that it was all right. The doctor agreed, praising Martha for the first aid she'd applied, but handing over a course of antibiotics and some strong pain-killers in case Sinclair needed them. Martha looked on closely and promised to make sure the wound had proper care. Sinclair, though he protested the doctor's attentions, found himself rather pleased that Martha was so eager to take care of him.

At noon, Martha invited the others to join her for lunch and a tour of the hexagonal villa, where she'd been exploring all day. Each wing was dedicated to a different type of room; six spacious bedrooms, each with its own bath, in the wing adjacent to the entry and leftward down the hall that connected the entire structure. The grand tour continued from where they were, the informal dining room being part of what Martha called the utility wing. In addition to the dining room and kitchen, there was a laundry room and a room containing the trappings of infrastructure such as the water heater and a panel that controlled the air conditioning system, along with various storage rooms that they didn't look into.

That left three segments of the hexagon to explore. The first contained several rooms devoted to entertainment, from a state-of-the-art theater room to a music conservatory that boasted a baby grand piano, several guitars, and a few instruments that Daniel assumed were native to the area. A very formal large parlor was there, along with a more informal room that Daniel would have called a family room, with seating groups, a television, and stereo system.

Next came a wing devoted to rooms that were outfitted as offices and conference rooms, of which Daniel, Sarah and Sinclair had already appropriated two for their use, one for Daniel and Sarah together and another for Sinclair.

Finally, the last segment contained several rooms with an enormous array of electronics equipment. Daniel pulled up short, amazed. He turned to Raj. "Did you have all this brought in?"

"No, I assumed you did," Raj answered. One room had two computers with the exact specifications they needed to deploy the entire project that was waiting on the external drive in the diplomatic pouch, along with various peripherals. Cables snaking through the walls revealed that the two rooms on either side of it contained mini-farms of cubicles, each with a computer on the desk, all apparently networked to the two servers in the central room. "This is going to be perfect!" Daniel crowed. "Man, I can't wait to fill these rooms with researchers."

They proceeded down the hall, Daniel explaining to Sinclair what they were thinking about handling all the new information.

Sarah had hung back with Martha, interested only in the fact of the computers, not the details. "Martha, are you sure you're going to be okay here with us? I mean, we practically kidnapped you, insisting you come."

Martha gave her a sweet smile, with a bit of mischief behind it. "It's okay, dear. At least you brought along someone to entertain me. "

Sarah's laugh rang out as she tucked her arm through Martha's. "Well, there is that."

The men were several yards ahead of them, and now stared back down the hall, wondering what was so funny. Seeing the women arm in arm, Daniel said, "We're probably better off not knowing."

Sinclair said fervently, "You can say that again. I have to tell you, son, I'm quite taken with the lovely Martha, but she scares the hell out of me."

"Oh?" said Daniel, surprised.

"Yeah. I haven't met a woman that charming, except for your Sarah, of course, since my Emily passed. And I'm not sure I'm willing to give up my golden years to another woman."

Daniel nudged him with an elbow. "Come on, live a little! Besides, we're planning to keep you busy through your golden years. You'll want a woman to go home to after a hard day's work translating and helping to run the world's most exciting non-profit organization."

"Hmmph, we'll see about that." Sinclair answered.

Daniel only smiled. He could already imagine what Sarah would say when he told her about this conversation, though he should probably leave out his part in it, or be ready to dodge some flying object.

Martha explained to the others that she had taken the liberty of instructing the staff where to put everyone's luggage and that they'd be taking their meals communally in the breakfast room. Hearing no objections, she beamed at the group and showed them the intercom that would summon them for dinner later, then showed each party to their rooms to freshen up. Raj was heard to mutter that he had work to do, but everyone ignored him and thanked Martha for her thoughtfulness in making herself useful to the group in a way that she was most suited for. Sinclair was elaborate in his praise, turning Martha's soft cheeks a becoming shade of pink.

~~~

Sarah occupied herself in unpacking, with Martha chatting comfortably from her perch on the foot of the bed. They had packed only their backpacks when leaving the US, which left everyone with a limited wardrobe. On the other hand, it appeared she wouldn't be going anywhere, so there would be plenty of time to acquire anything else she needed. Disappointed that neither she nor Martha had packed a swimsuit, she looked through her clothes to find something that would serve the purpose, but found nothing. There was a size difference anyway, Martha being several inches shorter than Sarah, and carrying a bit more weight around her middle, though she was still slim and fit for her age.

"I know," Sarah said. "Baruch told us to call him if we needed anything, and that the household staff would take care of shopping. Let's send for a swimsuit."

"Oh, I couldn't dear. That's frivolous."

"Martha, I refuse to swim alone, and the guys are busy. We need swimsuits."

Her objections overcome despite continuing protest, Martha finally told Sarah what size she wore and the type of swimsuit she'd prefer, a conservative maillot if possible, and even better if it had a bit of a skirt. Baruch told Sarah to speak to Rachel, whom she would find in her office off the kitchen, and it would be taken care of. Sarah and Martha found the dignified head housekeeper right where they'd been told, and explained their request.

"That is easily done," the woman said in a heavy accent. "Do you also need water shoes or sandals?"

"That would be great," Sarah answered. "A pair for me, too, I didn't think of that. And beach towels?"

"You will find those in the small cabana next to the pool," Rachel said.

"Perfect. Thank you Rachel."

"It is my pleasure."

~~~

The second day in Tel Aviv found the research well under way as Raj and Sinclair had managed to set the project up before breaking for the night. Sinclair's directive was to fully translate the index, and try to make sure that they had the numbering system set up correctly. They were going on the assumption that the numbers associated with each subject in the index referred to the skip sequence to find it within the massive data set. But, Daniel hadn't realized just how many ways there were to start the skip sequence, much less how many directions to run. Even beginning to extract the knowledge of the pyramid record was going to take an enormous effort. Sinclair needed help, and before they could get him any without causing problems down the road, they needed to get their foundation in order.

Accordingly, he was on a house phone to Baruch shortly after Sinclair left him, inquiring after the attorney they'd asked to be on hand.

"I can have him there any time. Is there anything in particular that you need him for?" Baruch asked. Instantly, Daniel's hackles rose. Surely it was none of the other man's business. Then he realized that perhaps the question was aimed at getting them an appropriate specialist.

"Yes, we need to arrange to set up a nonprofit foundation," Daniel said, hoping that would be enough of an explanation. He didn't want to go into their plans for the discoveries, fearing that Israel would withdraw its support if someone guessed that there would be no favoritism in the distribution of the knowledge.

"Very well. Will four o'clock be satisfactory?"

"That's fine," Daniel said, already beginning to think of the questions to ask the attorney. Sarah, impacted by jetlag, was taking a nap when she was awakened by Daniel gently shaking her shoulder. "Wake up, Love, the lawyer will be here any minute."

Still in a sleep-induced haze, Sarah sat up in alarm. "Lawyer?"

"Shh, Love, it's okay. The lawyer to help us with our questions about the foundation. Do you need some coffee?"

"Oh, yes, Daniel, that would be perfect," Sarah said with relief. When she tried to recapture whatever it was that had alarmed her about the word lawyer, it was gone. Nothing, probably. She was just muzzy from sleeping in the daytime. Before Daniel returned with the coffee, having endured a scolding from Ilana, the cook, for not just calling her to bring it, Sarah splashed cold water on her face, changed into fresh clothes and considered whether to put on makeup. No, she thought, I'll do without. Daniel always told her he liked her best that way, anyway. He complained that when she had her 'war paint' on, she looked like a caricature of herself. What a tribute to my skill in applying it, she thought with a hint of asperity. But then, he looked gorgeous without makeup. Why did women feel they had to wear it?

Just then, Daniel returned with her coffee, saying, "Drink up, Love, the lawyer will be here in five minutes."

"Oh, Daniel, would you find Martha and tell her I won't be able to swim with her until later?"

"Sure," he said. "Hey, we should all have a swim before dinner."

Ten minutes later, the lawyer greeted and introductions out of the way, Daniel, Sarah and the attorney, Mikhail Benjamin seated themselves around a conference table in one of the smaller rooms.

"How can I help you, Mr. Rossler?" Benjamin asked.

"Have you been told anything about why we're here?" Daniel countered.

"Not really. Only that you are a guest of our government, under the protection of political asylum. Do you require some assistance in defending yourself against your country's accusations?"

'No, nothing like that," Daniel laughed. "At least, not yet. What we need is assistance in forming a non-profit organization, preferably in the United States, as that's our home. Unfortunately, we had to leave before we could get it started."

"I see. How much do you know about forming a corporation of any sort in the US?" Benjamin asked.

"I know we need a business plan, a structure, some money for filing fees, and some sort of description for the business," Daniel said. "What else?"

"Forming a non-profit is similar, except that you also need a unique and easily communicable mission."

"I think we can handle that," Daniel said dryly.

"And, you must have sufficient funds to start up before you can begin fundraising."

"Again, not a problem. At least, I think it isn't a problem. By the way, we need to establish a bank account here, if Israel and the US have banking agreements. Can you ..."

"Yes, there is no reason you cannot have an account here, but I must warn you that it will be scrutinized by both our government and yours."

Sarah spoke up. "Mr. Benjamin, I assure you we are not tax evaders nor terrorists; nothing illegal will be going on. Neither government will have any reason to be upset with our transactions. But if it will help, we're prepared to explain any transaction we make. It will be quite transparent publicly, in fact."

Daniel was nodding. "We'd like to make it a corporate account for the foundation. But which comes first, the account or the foundation?"

"The foundation. Do you have a business plan?"

"Not really. We need to get a steering committee in place before we decide what to do," remarked Sarah, not noticing that her imprecise observation gave the wrong impression.

Benjamin's face showed his distress. "You do not even have an idea of what you want to accomplish with this foundation?"

"Oh, yes," chorused both Daniel and Sarah. Daniel took it from there. "We'd better tell you what it's all about, then you'll see the dilemma. I trust we're under attorney/client privilege? Or does that exist in Israel?"

"That's a complex question. The short answer is, as long as I am in the process of providing professional services, I'm prohibited from disclosing information you provide. However, there are certain exceptions related to judicial proceedings."

Daniel held up a finger, indicating he wanted to mull that over. Sarah was also trying to sort it out. Clearly Daniel was about to disclose the pyramid records, which apparently they'd need to do before this man could help them. But, under what circumstances might they find themselves in an Israeli court of law, with the need to keep it secret? She could think of several, none of which applied if they were going to disclose the secrets to the world soon anyway. She shrugged.

Daniel reached the same conclusion, although he was less sanguine about the short term than Sarah. But, they had put their safety in the hands of this government, and at least one government official already knew why. Nothing ventured, nothing gained was his final conclusion. He marshaled his thoughts so as not to waste much time in the explanation.

By the time he was finished, it was a thunderstruck lawyer who stammered out his response. "Th-this is the m-most extraordinary thing I've ever heard! Are you sure?"

In answer, Daniel pulled copies of the translations, the same documents he'd showed to Akiva a few days ago, from a manila folder and handed them to Benjamin. Upon reading the second one, Benjamin turned white.

"And you have reason to believe that you can translate these records? And use the information?" he asked incredulously.

"Absolutely. We can already authenticate them. In fact, the man behind that second translation is even now working on the index of subjects the records contain. Would you like to meet him?"

Wordlessly, Benjamin nodded, still staring in fascination at the second translation. Daniel looked around for an intercom and went over to see if he could raise Sinclair on it. After a few attempts, he found the correct button and asked Sinclair to join them. Rising to meet his friend, Daniel introduced him to the lawyer, who also rose and extended his hand.

"Have a seat, Sinclair. Can you briefly explain to Attorney Benjamin how you came to translate this message?" Daniel said, indicating the paper on the table.

"Sure, and why not," lilted Sinclair. As succinctly as possible, he outlined the process, which Benjamin followed carefully. Then Benjamin nodded that he understood.

"Thank, you, Sinclair. Mr. Benjamin, do you think we'll require Sinclair's presence any longer?"

"No, not at present, thank you," the attorney said.

When Sinclair had left, Benjamin drew a deep breath. "Well, this is going to be the highlight of my career. I suspect that your foundation will change the course of human history."

"I certainly hope so," Sarah muttered.

"Let's draw up a simple corporate structure, with the ability to expand it if need be. As for a business plan, the simpler we can state it, the easier it will be to follow it, not that it will be a requirement to do so. I'd say something as simple as, "The purpose of the business is to cause the translation and utilization of all relevant records contained in that code found in the Great Pyramid at Giza and discovered by Daniel and Sarah Rossler. What do you want to call the foundation?"

"Wait," said Daniel. "We're not prepared to make all the decisions right now. We've got other people to consult. Just tell us what you need us to provide for you to draw up the papers, and we'll work on it today and tonight. Then, if you would please, come back in the morning and we'll have it for you."

"Very well," said Benjamin. He left them with a list of what he'd need to put in the application, and left, promising to be back early the next day, a Monday.

Sarah knocked on Martha's door and widened her eyes in surprise when the older woman opened it dressed in her new swimsuit, a navy blue maillot with a pattern of small white flowers, draped in a criss-crossed V-neck across the bodice and with a flirty little ruffled skirt playing around the tops of her thighs. A smaller waist than Sarah had realized Martha had nipped in between the curves.

"Martha, you look sensational!"

Martha blushed and drew her in so she could close the door. "You don't think it's too low-cut?" she said. "I really wish I could have picked out my own suit."

"Don't you like it? Wow, Martha, I didn't know you had such a great figure," Sarah giggled.

"Stop it, you'll make me too self-conscious to wear it! No, I like it. I just wish it were a little more modest." Martha lamented.

"Martha, it's not like they brought you a bikini. It's fine, trust me. In fact, you look stunning. Meet me out by the pool in ten, okay? We can get a swim in before dinner after all."

Sarah flew swiftly through the halls, running on tiptoe so Martha wouldn't hear her, to invite Daniel, Raj and Sinclair to join them. "Hurry!" she admonished the men, then ran to her own rooms to suit up and get to the pool in the allotted time. She was neck-deep in the warm water, concealing her deep recovery breathing, when Martha appeared in a long white caftan over the navy suit. Sarah crossed her fingers under the water, hoping that Sinclair would make it to poolside before Martha doffed the cover-up and entered the pool.

"How's the water?" Martha asked.

"A little warm, actually," Sarah said. "I was hoping we could cool off a bit, but the sun has really heated it up."

"What are Sinclair and Daniel doing?" Martha said, starting to pull the caftan over her head. Her head was still tangled in it when Sinclair's deep tones startled her.

"I don't know what the boy's doing, but yours truly is looking at a beautiful woman!" he exclaimed.

Sarah giggled as Martha visibly jumped, hastily pulling the caftan the rest of the way off and giving Sinclair a wild-eyed look before diving into the pool from the side. When she came up, she saw Sarah giggling. Martha swam over to Sarah and whispered in her ear, "I'm going to turn you over my knee if you pull a stunt like that again." But her broad smile let Sarah know that she was already forgiven. Sarah turned her attention to her Daniel, just coming out to poolside. His chiseled chest never failed to make her thoughts turn to private moments, and she briefly regretted that they had company. But a quick glance at Sinclair in a pair of neon green and orange plaid trunks that covered his legs to his knees startled a laugh out of her and saved her from the embarrassment of further ogling her man.

"That's quite a fashion statement," she called, causing the others to turn and look also. Sinclair struck a pose, then belly-flopped into the pool, a plastic bag wrapped around his hand to keep the bandages from getting wet, splashing everyone else. Raj, dog-paddling earnestly, set his feet down and stood to shake himself off in indignation. Sarah thought rightly that they were all going to have a lot of fun in this pool despite the serious nature of their sojourn, a small compensation for being cooped up behind the walls.

Everyone either swam or paddled about splashing the

others for about half an hour, until Rachel appeared, dispatched by Ilana to announce that dinner was ready.

At dinner, Daniel asked the others if they would mind working through the evening, explaining their plans to form a foundation and planning to include the folks at home, as many as he could gather online, via their shared email. It would be a little awkward, but there was no time to wait and gather physically. They needed at least the preliminary decisions made tonight.

"Sinclair, we're going to ask you to head up our science division as Director of Research and Development. I think you should sit in on board meetings, even though I don't suppose it's appropriate for you to have a vote on what your department will be assigned to. Can we count on you?"

"I thought ye'd never ask," rolled the thick brogue that Sinclair sometimes used to mask emotion. "Sure, and I'll be proud t' serve."

"Raj of course as CIO looking after all our technology requirements," Daniel proposed.

The final order of business was to formulate the statement that would serve as the mission statement of the business plan. After much haggling, and major contributions from Martha, who was surprisingly the one experienced non-profit board member, they had a statement that all could endorse:

*The goal and objective of the foundation is to:*

*Undertake, encourage and support worldwide archaeological research including but not limited to conducting research about the Egyptian and other pyramids wherever they are to be found and to share the knowledge gained through its research activities for the common good of all people.*

Posting it on the shared email account for the votes of the

others, everyone retired for a well-earned night of rest, expecting Benjamin early on Monday morning to retrieve the information they'd compiled for him.

# Chapter 52 – One Battle In The War

While these events were taking place in Israel, Septentrio had flown personally to the US again, to sort out the disastrous raid on the Canadian border town that had left his organization in shambles. Acutely aware that it was his neck on the line next, he set out to intimidate the remaining undercover agents with temper tantrums to travel immediately to Israel to kidnap the pesky researchers that they couldn't seem to stop or capture. Behind his back, the CIA operative who'd taken Sidus' place, code named Latet, got in touch with Auster, who consulted with Occidens and Oriens before placing a video call to Septentrio.

The latter was indulging himself with a massage, having, as he thought, put the plan in motion to capture these upstarts once and for all. Irritated at having his relaxation interrupted, he snapped into the phone, "What!"

Auster's voice came through, instructing him to take the call on video. Septentrio thought a bit of display of his contempt for the woman was in order, driven by the ill-temper that had gripped him for days. In nothing but the towel that covered his lower body, he activated the video feed.

"What do you want?"

Auster's sneering face made Septentrio think a second time about revealing his soft, doughy body to her, but it was too late now. "We have heard that you've ordered teams to Israel to capture this research team," she began mildly.

"Yes, and they'd better make short work of it, or they'll answer to me," he declared.

"The others and I believe this is the wrong approach, Septentrio. Why don't you go home, and we'll sit back and see what happens. Some organization will end up with the responsibility of deploying the information, and it will be easier to infiltrate that than to go up against the Mossad in their own country. It's over, we lost for the moment, but we'll win in the long run."

"But what about…" Septentrio couldn't bring himself to utter it. His father's death was still too recent, his conflicted emotions too raw, to discuss it. Besides, he'd been trained to understand that they never discussed it once it was done.

"You've just taken office, Septentrio. It was your father who botched this mission, and we've exacted our price for that. Go home and wait." Auster rang off without further conversation, and Septentrio resumed his position on the massage table.

"Start over," he instructed the masseur.

Auster reflected afterward that the son was a considerably worse liability than the father. Not for the first time, she cursed the setup that left her just one of four and not the most powerful one at that. She'd like to see that sniveling weakling begging for his life, but now was not the time. It was too soon after the power shift caused by his father's death. Later, she would seize control. In the meanwhile, she would set up stumbling blocks for him.

# Chapter 53 – The Rossler Foundation

Mikhail Benjamin sat at the conference table in a larger room of the villa on Wednesday morning, facing this time not only the principals of the foundation, Daniel and Sarah but also an attractive older woman who was apparently already named to the board, and the intense fellow he'd met before, the linguist Sinclair O'Reilly as well as a shy looking Indian man, Rajan Sankaran. All of them were maintaining polite manners, but the atmosphere in the room ranged from slight tension to confusion. And it was all his fault. He should have given them the other document first, the one that was drawn up as they asked, or at least warned them that he had a suggestion.

Rossler stated the question that Mikhail had known was coming ever since he heard Sarah's gasp as she read it over. "I don't understand," Daniel said. "Didn't we say four board members, with one position rotating among our family? This says twenty-one."

"Please, if I may explain," Benjamin responded.

"Please do," said Sarah in her best professorial tone.

"I have another set of the documents, drawn up as you requested. But I spent some time thinking about how to set it up in such a way that it will best serve your goals and objectives, and I therefore offer this document as my recommendation and best advice. You have given me to understand that this is perhaps the greatest scientific discovery of all time," Benjamin started, then hastily corrected himself. "Of our time, our cycle if you will. It seemed to me that a broader base of representation would be needed. The East has a highly diverse political climate. How can an Arab board member represent Israel, or vice versa?" He spread his hands in silent supplication for understanding. It was something he believed passionately, and hoped to persuade his clients to believe as well.

Martha looked at the young couple and said, "He has a point. More would be better. It will make Board meetings a little tricky," she smiled, "But maybe there's some technology that will make it feasible."

"Of course," Daniel answered automatically. "Video conferencing, no problem. Why were we thinking the lower number in the first place?"

"We were tired," Sarah inserted. "We should have waited for the jet lag to pass."

"No time to wait. Do we have consensus?" Seeing the nods around the table, Daniel said to Benjamin, "It seems we owe you an apology and a thank you. Twenty-one it is. Care to have one of the positions?"

A heady mixture of relief that his presumption had been accepted and terror at the prospect of being one of the board members almost overcame the young attorney. "No! I mean, thank you very much, but I don't feel qualified. I suggest you endeavor to sort all the nations of the world into seventeen politically similar groups, each to be represented by a board member to be elected by the heads of state of those countries."

"You've given this a great deal of thought," Daniel observed.

"Yes, sir. It is just a suggestion. All of this is just a suggestion. As I said, the other documents are ready if you wish to revert to your original plan."

"No, I think it's a good suggestion. Do you have the groups in mind?" Sarah asked.

"No, ma'am, I haven't gone that far, although certain groupings are very natural."

"Why twenty-one, then?" Daniel said.

"Oh, why, isn't that obvious? It's a Fibonacci number, and the number of the members of the Supreme Council of Knowledge in your translation."

Thunderstruck, the other four looked at each other, before bursting into spontaneous applause, much to the young lawyer's discomfiture. They considered it unnecessary to run this change past the rest of the families, feeling certain that it would be well-received. Daniel and Sarah signed where Benjamin indicated they should, and he departed to post the package by overnight express mail to Luke Clarke in Boulder.

Sarah said, "I suppose we'd better get busy and finish that white paper."

"Right, but can you handle that on your own? I've got a set of questions and answers to write up for Selleck, and a press release announcing the formation of the Rossler Foundation."

"Daniel?"

"Yes, my love?"

"I'm so very proud of you. And I love you with all of my heart." Daniel stood and pulled Sarah out of the chair beside him, wrapping her in his arms tightly and kissing her thoroughly.

"Sweetheart, I love you, too. And I'm equally proud of you. Now, let's go change the world."

# Chapter 54 – Breaking The News

Because there were some leading physicists in Israel, Raj and Sinclair were focusing their attention on anything that appeared to have anything to do with energy generation or particle physics. These were areas where science had advanced to the point of understanding something likely to be radical and mind blowing, but hadn't yet solved the problems. Within a few days, they had uncovered something about fusion.

Baruch was summoned, physicists who were sworn to secrecy until the major announcements were made arrived at the villa. The translation of the fusion data stunned them, but they rushed to replicate the instructions on a small scale. This alone was going to change the world, as plans for larger scale pilot plants were available in the records. Soon no one in the world would lack for abundant, clean, ultra-cheap energy. Although they hadn't yet proved anything on a grand scale, the physicists involved were unanimous in agreeing that the previously-unknown technology would work.

Now there was nothing to stop the group from making the announcement. Daniel called Luke on the secure phone and arranged with him to fly to New York the next day and go to meet with Aaron Selleck. Then Luke phoned Selleck, asking to meet with him the next day at ten a.m. on a matter he couldn't discuss over the phone. Recognizing Clarke as Sarah's last name, Selleck became excited to hear news of Daniel, who'd disappeared. He agreed to meet.

At ten o'clock the next morning Luke was invited into Selleck's office as arranged, the two men shaking hands and introducing themselves. At five minutes past, Luke's strange looking phone started ringing. He answered and after a short how-are-you-doing-and-is-everyone-still-ok said, "Ok giving the phone to Aaron now."

"Daniel, good to hear from you!" said Selleck. "Do you have good news for me?"

"I do indeed," Daniel said. "How would you like to take a little business trip to Tel Aviv?"

"Rossler, what have you been smoking? Tel Aviv? What's there?"

Daniel laughed. "Don't worry Aaron, I didn't smoke anything, there was no time for it, and I don't do that shit anyway. I am really in Tel Aviv and I need to talk to you urgently and face-to-face. So please hear me out."

"Ok, I am all ears," said Selleck.

"You know, Aaron, I've always trusted you, and you and the Times have been good to me. I'm about to return that favor. There's a big, big opportunity here, for the Times and for you. Most probably the biggest opportunity the Times has ever had. But only if you can keep it secret until I give the word."

By now, Selleck was on the edge of his chair, thinking *spill it, already*. But he could hear that Daniel was serious, and that he wouldn't be rushed in the conversation. Nevertheless, he said, with a bit of impatience, "Okay, I get it. So what do I have to do, and what is it that I need to keep secret?"

Having had a bit of practice, Daniel was now able to give a succinct introduction that was sufficiently convincing, followed up with a peek at the translation of the passageway greeting that Luke showed him at Daniel's direction. He began with telling Aaron that they had broken the code they'd been looking for, and that the information was explosive. Luke peered at Aaron closely as Daniel made these revelations, and as he betrayed nothing other than intense interest, judged him ready for the kicker.

Daniel said to Selleck to ask Luke to give him a document which Luke handed to him.

Selleck began to read. His eyes widened and he turned white, alarming Luke. As Aaron finished the reading, color flooded back into his face and he clutched at his chest and dropped the phone on the desk. Luke sprang from his chair, "Mr. Selleck, are you all right?"

"Yes, just let me get my breath."

Luke grabbed the phone and told Daniel that Selleck looked bad for a minute, but that he apparently was going to be okay. "Just give us a minute so he can recover," he advised.

Daniel wondered how many more reactions like this their announcement was going to cause over the next few days after it was published.

Selleck had the phone back. "Jumpin' freakin' Jehosaphat, Rossler is that for real?"

"It's for real, Aaron, and that's just the tip of the iceberg. It's only the greeting - the amazing thing is that they included an entire encyclopedia, complete with index. We're waiting until some of the advanced science our linguist has discovered in the records can be confirmed, both to validate the story for the Times and to quell the inevitable outcry. You know that people will be screaming 'hoax' as soon as you publish this. We have to have our ducks in a row to prove them wrong."

"Agreed," said Selleck, beginning to recover a little from his shock. He opened his drawer, retrieved a prescription bottle and put a small pill under his tongue. "It almost gave me a heart attack, and I was kind of prepared. I can just about imagine what the churches and the evolutionists are going to say. This may be the only time they ever agree. What do you want specifically,

Daniel?"

Impressed by Selleck's immediate grasp of the situation, Daniel said, "We're prepared to give you the exclusive plus ongoing publishing rights. But I think you will agree that this is far and away beyond my contract with the Times. We've used our own resources and time on discovering it."

"Agreed,"

"Okay, I'd like you personally to write it up. I'd like you to come and interview us here in Tel Aviv, and I believe that the story will be one-hundred percent guaranteed to earn you, personally, a Pulitzer."

"Why aren't you going to write it yourself, Daniel?" Aaron said, fearing he knew the answer. He was right.

"Aaron, I have to resign from the Times, I'm sorry. This is so big that we have already set up a non-profit organization to continue study and control as well as we can how the information is used. We plan to distribute it as widely as possible, so that everyone has a fair chance at benefiting. Plus, we feel that doing so will allow the cooperation the greeting mentions to happen, and sooner rather than later. I'm afraid I'll be too busy to discharge my duties to the Times.

"Nevertheless, we'll need startup funding. I'm asking you to see to it that the Times gives us generous compensation for the exclusive and ongoing rights."

Now completely calm outwardly, though adrenaline was coursing through his veins at the thought of a Pulitzer for him personally, Aaron responded. "All right. When I see you I we can talk money but rest assured if this is what you say it is, money is not going to be an issue."

"Let me know your flight details," said Daniel. I'll make

arrangements for someone to meet you at the airport and bring you to us. Have a safe trip."

The following day, a much disoriented Selleck flew to Tel Aviv on El Al. He was met by a fellow who looked like no one would mess with him, and delivered to the door of a large walled villa. He could get used to this! Inside, Daniel greeted him, with Sarah and a couple he didn't know right behind him. Of course, Raj he knew. To Raj he said with a smile, "Nice holiday spot you picked, Raj."

"Am I finally going to get more of this wild tale you warned me about?" he teased Daniel.

"Probably more than your heart can take. Did you bring your little pills?" Daniel retorted.

"Yes, but it won't be that much of a shock this time," he said.

"Don't count on that. You are planning to stay a day or two, aren't you? Let's have something to eat and if you would like to have a quick swim to cool you down. We can go to the conference room afterward and get started. Leave your bags here, someone will collect them and take them to your room."

Selleck was too curious to accept the offer of a swim first. "No, thanks, but I'm on pins and needles about what you have to tell me. I'd rather get started right away."

Daniel had prepared a Q&A document that was well-organized to tell the story in chronological fashion, leaving out the murders and Sarah's kidnapping, because they didn't want those crimes to overshadow the importance of the discovery. As Aaron went through the questions, with Daniel and Sinclair answering for the most part, he jotted down phrases next to the answers that were on the pages. Before they were an hour into it, he knew that this was going to be the most sensational story he'd ever worked on. Ever seen, even. If this didn't give the Times a shot in the arm, nothing would.

No one could refute the science that was coming from the coded records; not only the clean energy from fusion reactions, but in just a few short days, one medical researcher had instantly cured the colds of several volunteers, using a formula for a pleasant-tasting potion found in the medical codes. He considered that substantiation enough considering that even with our advances in medicine doctors still couldn't cure a cold, only treat symptoms.

After several hours of questions and answers spanning two days and a pleasant evening's swim the night he stayed at the villa, Aaron flew home. The group had admonished him that, while he could publish everything else they'd given him, he couldn't reveal their location. He promised them a story worthy of their accomplishment, to be published in two days' time.

Before he left they talked money. Selleck offered them $3 million for the exclusive and ongoing rights, confirming that he was authorized to commit to that amount. He arranged then and there that the money be transferred into the name of the Rossler Foundation.

After Selleck left, and while everyone else returned to trying to occupy the long hours of anticipation before the announcement, Daniel sent a message to the family back home. 'Be sure to watch the major news networks two days from now. All hell's about to break loose.' A chorus of 'way to go', 'congratulations' and 'go Rosslerites' responses came through from Jacksonville to Asheville and Boulder. The family was on board, and it was about to get very exciting.

Luke, however, had something else to say. 'Expect an

angry call from the President, or at least from someone high in the government, Daniel. You guys might want to put your heads together and think what you'll say when he demands you return to the States or hand over that data."

"Good idea,' Daniel responded. 'We'll do that tonight.'

~~~

**WORLD HISTORY ALL WRONG - THE WORLD ABOUT TO CHANGE**

"In the year 25,992, the Supreme Council of Knowledge, commissioned the least of their number, I, Zebulon, to build this monument and record our history for Those Who Come After. In all the cycles, this has never been attempted before.

We of the tenth cycle believe that we have achieved more than any cycle before us, and, knowing our fate, wish to leave evidence of our knowledge. With this knowledge, perhaps you, our children, may continue our progress and stop the cycles of destruction that have held our kind to less than our full potential for two hundred and sixty thousand years."

Thus read the message to us from our forefathers, left in an obscure code in the blocks of the Great Pyramid of Egypt. Previously thought to have been built approximately 3,500 years ago, we now know that it was in fact built much earlier, although the date has not yet been established.

In the most earth-shattering, far-reaching and life-changing archaeological discovery of our current civilization, Daniel Rossler, an ex-NYT journalist and Dr. Sarah Clarke, a recently-tenured young professor of the Joukowsky Institute for Archaeology and the Ancient World, in Providence, Rhode Island, has turned the world as we know it on its head.

The couple, assisted by brilliant IT specialist Raj Sankaran and world famous linguist Sinclair O' Reilly as well as several of their family members, have discovered a hidden message in the blocks of Great Pyramid of Egypt at Giza.

Not only will their momentous discovery destroy the theory of evolution; it is expected to send current historical and academic thinking into turmoil. Among the discoveries: the ancient Egyptians did not build the Great Pyramid; the real pyramid builders were from a civilization predating ours by perhaps more than 30,000 years. This discovery has proved that human civilizations go through cycles of birth, growth and destruction lasting about 26,000 years each. We will not know for certain until more translation has taken place, but it is believed that our current civilization represents the eleventh cycle. Human beings indistinguishable from ourselves and civilizations much more intelligent and advanced than ours, have inhabited the earth for more than 260,000 years.

More important than the historical facts about the builders is the fact that a civilization preceding ours has left us their combined scientific knowledge, gathered over their 26,000 years of development.

Although to date the Rossler Foundation's research has just scratched the surface, they have already unveiled the existence of an extensive library of information consisting of hundreds of thousands of what we today call "books" and "records". The records, which are expected to eventually run into many millions, cover subjects ranging from fusion technology to medicine, astrology, politics, religion and other technologies which we currently still relegate to the science fiction realm.

For example, schematics for a breathtaking Star Trek-type medical device resembling a handheld scanner that can scan a patient's body in a matter of seconds, spitting out DNA data, vital signs information such as heart rate blood pressure and oxygen levels in the blood, as well as giving immediate warning of more than 500 diseases, even cancerous cells and the onset of conditions known to cause dementia, has the medical scientists involved jumping with excitement.

Initial evidence from the records suggest that people of the tenth cycle were living normal active healthy and productive lives up to 180 years on average.

A team of world-renowned physicists have already verified and confirmed some of the fusion technology discoveries that promise a clean and cheap energy source for everyone on the planet.

This gigantic unearthing is bound to not only jolt science and politics but also religion, academia, economists, evolutionists, intelligent-design proponents, historians and many others who will have to account for this information or rethink their current positions.

It is already abundantly clear that positive as well as potentially serious negative implications for the human race are in the cards.

The authors of the message made it very clear that the information is being entrusted to its discoverers to be used for everyone's benefit, to improve our lives and enhance our society. The Rossler Foundation has already pledged to honor that trust by seeing to it that the information is distributed in a fair and responsible way to all nations.

The NYT has negotiated the exclusive and ongoing rights to publish the research findings of the Rossler Foundation. We have assigned a special section in this paper to keep our readers up to date as and when new information becomes available. Please see Page B1 for more on the remarkable discoveries already available for further research, courtesy of the Rossler Foundation.

The editors of the New York Times encourage human beings of all walks of life in all nations, to stay abreast of and assimilate this knowledge, which is certain to bring about, as Huxley termed it, a Brave New World; hopefully this one a utopia instead of the dystopia envisioned by Huxley.

~~~

The all-caps headline, a departure from the Times' regular look, screamed at early-morning commuters two days later, true to Aaron's word. Expecting some clever trick to be revealed, many read the story. More than a few realized that their lives, in fact, everyone's lives, would never be the same. The majority didn't understand the impact at all, until the radio and television news media began to pick it up and tell them what to think.

The Times story recapped the sixteen months of research that had led to the discovery of an ancient encyclopedia. The revelations therein ripped the lid off every scientific and historic discipline there was, throwing academics of all stripes into panic and dismay, except those who pronounced it a hoax before they understood it had already been validated and proved. They would be the first to fall as the world adjusted to the new reality.

The Rosslerites, as all members of the foundation would eventually be called, watched with their hearts in their mouths as news media all over the world began to pick up the story the Times had published that morning. It hardly seemed possible that they could have managed everything within that time, but there it was, a secret no longer.

Sinclair had several monitors slaved to the server and showing different TV feeds from around the world. On one, the Pope was downplaying the discovery, saying it was too early to draw conclusions and that the Church would be involved in studying the facts as they were revealed; meanwhile, people should remain calm. Behind the scenes, one Cardinal was heard to joke to another, 'Too bad we no longer have the Inquisition.' The Pope, however, a saintly man who nevertheless was an adept politician, was already thinking that the Church should have a representative on the board of this Foundation that the story mentioned.

Another feed showed a number of oddly-dressed people cavorting on top of a skyscraper as had been shown in the film Independence Day. Closer inspection showed them to be wearing makeshift antennae or other trappings of people who believed in, almost worshipped, extraterrestrial life. Daniel half-expected Raj to be among them until he realized that of course Raj was right by his side, shaking his head at the foolishness. Everyone knew aliens didn't alight from a UFO and say 'take me to your leader.' Still, he expected contact to be soon in coming, despite Daniel's little joke. He was still smarting under that one, when Daniel had laughed and pointed at the screen showing the alien-welcomers, saying 'What do you call a tick on the moon? A luna-tick!" Everyone had laughed then. Now Raj knew what they truly thought of his obsession, but he would show them. They would all apologize soon.

Still other feeds streamed the news from governing bodies, including the US Senate, all showing a great deal of consternation and bombast as the members debated what this announcement would mean for their respective countries. They couldn't see, but could imagine the same sort of frenzy occurring anywhere that people had a stake in the status quo: governments, industry, universities, churches. No one would escape the consequent confusion.

Daniel was rather enjoying the chaos, while Sarah, with her hand pressed over her mouth, worried that riots may break out. Sinclair was busy keeping the feeds alive, some of them pirated, and Martha with tears in her eyes silently spoke to her deceased beloved. "Mark, I wish you were here to see this. You started a revolution, my darling."

# Chapter 55 – Absolutely Not Mr. President

Earlier that morning in Washington, at about the same time as the media began to pick up the Times story, President Nigel Harper strode into the Oval Office for his morning briefing. A contingent of aides and advisors were on hand just outside the door and waiting for their few minutes of precious time with the Chief Executive, but first Harper would scan the security briefing and anything else that his staff had deemed important. A quick perusal of the summary, prepared two hours before from overnight news items, convinced him that not much had changed overnight. Until he read the NY Times clipping that was at the bottom of the stack.

The headline was intriguing, clever of them to grab the attention that way, he thought. As he read, though, and realized that the article was serious, color drained from his face. Barking the names of his Chief of Staff and one or two aides, the visibly-disturbed leader of the Western world demanded answers.

"What the hell is this? Did we know anything about it? And if not, why not?" Aides scrambled while Phil Bertrand, Chief of Staff, tried to calm his principal.

"Mr. President, I don't recall anything in any briefing about this. But I'll get the Directors of the FBI and CIA on the line at once, and see if they have answers. Is there anything else?"

"You're damned right there's something else. I want to talk to these people...yesterday! Get them on the line."

"Um, Mr. President, I, uh, I'm not sure we know how to contact them." Bertrand had never had to make such a statement in his life, and hated that he was making it now. During a crisis was not the time to have the President lose confidence in him. He looked up to find Harper's eyes boring into him.

A deceptively quiet sentence escaped Harper's clenched teeth, "I suggest you figure that out." It would have been better, Bertrand thought, if he had yelled. When Harper got quiet like that, heads tended to roll.

"Yes, Sir," he said in a crisp voice. "You'll have it as soon as possible."

"That had better be sooner rather than later. After you get that, call the Speaker of the House, the Senate majority leader, the Secretary of State, and the Directors of the FBI and CIA. They're to be here in three hours for an emergency meeting, no excuses. And send in the Press Secretary."

Bertrand left the Oval Office as if shot from a slingshot, and jerked his thumb back toward it as he made eye contact with the Press Secretary. He didn't envy the woman who was about to enter the lion's den.

"You wanted to see me, Mr. President?" she said, steeling herself for a tirade. But, Harper had managed to calm himself for this conversation.

"Margaret, we need a response to this, am I right?"

"Yes, Mr. President. The sooner the better."

"Announce a press conference for four this afternoon. Prepare something generic that says we're looking into it, everyone stay calm. I'll use that if I haven't found out something more substantial. And have some writers on hand just after lunch. I've called a meeting for ten-thirty, and by noon we should have some idea of what's going on."

"That sounds like a good plan, Mr. President."

"That's why they pay me the big bucks," grinned Harper, a multi-millionaire in his own right who had taken a substantial pay cut to become the President of the United States.

Bertrand, meanwhile, had rousted the two Directors and within the hour discovered that Assistant CIA director Samuel Lewis already had some information about the Rosslerites, and indeed had known something of the story that was causing such a ruckus. After calling Lewis and dressing him down for not alerting the President, Bertrand demanded that Lewis locate the Rosslerites and make arrangement for the President to contact them right away. Lewis called Luke, who called his old friend, who contacted Akiva Beckman. Assured that the information would be kept strictly confidential, a phone number in Israel was passed back up the same line, eventually reaching the Director of the CIA, who promptly made his way to the Oval Office with it.

"Where are they?" the President demanded.

"Israel, Sir," answered the Director, who was a little worried about his job, since he had known nothing of all this. He was going to have to clean house the first chance he had, because evidently his people had been playing fast and loose with their brief. They weren't even supposed to be running operations within the borders. He especially needed to talk with his Assistant, and by Hector, the man better have a good explanation for keeping this under his hat.

"Why the hell are they in Israel?" Harper barked. "Aren't they Americans?"

"Yes, Sir. Apparently they had some concerns about their safety."

"All right, I'm going to want the whole story in a minute. But first, I need to call these people. Bertrand, get in here and help me with this damned phone system."

~~~

Into the sound and fury that reigned in the server room

came the old-fashioned ring of a land-line telephone. Everyone looked around for the set, which no one had used in this room since they arrived in the villa. Not finding it, they spread out, but the ringing stopped. They were all unsettled about the missed call until Daniel spied Rachel running down the hall with a handset in her outstretched hand.

"Mr. Rossler, it, it, here..."

Daniel took the set, frowning with bewilderment at the agitated housekeeper. "Hello," he said.

"Mr. Daniel Rossler?" queried the voice on the other end of the line.

"Yes."

"This is the President of the United States of America. You seem to have dropped a bombshell, young man."

Daniel almost dropped the phone. The President! Calling personally...and how had he obtained this number?

"Yes, Mr. President, so it seems."

"I trust that you and the lovely Ms. Clarke are loyal citizens of your country?"

"Yes, Sir."

"May I ask why you chose to make this announcement from Israel?"

Daniel's blood chilled a little when he realized that the President obviously knew their location. If the US knew, then so did other countries, maybe some that weren't so friendly. Not to mention the Orion Society. Carefully, he answered, "Mr. President, I'd like to respectfully refer you to the head of the CIA for the answer to that question."

"Are you implying that the CIA has been involved in

something that gave you reason to believe you weren't safe?"

"Yes, Sir, Mr. President."

A heavy sigh was transmitted across the line. "Very well, I will speak to them. But I'd like to congratulate you on your discovery, and say how proud I am that Americans were the ones to break the code."

"Sir, it took a great deal of effort, and not all of us are as American as you seem to think. Our data analyst is a naturalized citizen, but was born in India. I want to emphasize that we feel the discovery belongs to the world, not just the US."

"I'd very much like to have a conversation with you face-to-face, Mr. Rossler. May I send Air Force One to bring you home?"

"Mr. President, thank you very much for the offer. But, for reasons I'll be happy to explain in person, we are not prepared to leave our present location. We're under the protection of the Israeli government, and that will stay the same until certain arrangements can be made. We're willing to meet with you, but only on our terms."

President Harper's voice was a little colder, almost dangerous, when he responded with deceptive mildness, "And what would those be, Mr. Rossler?"

"Mr. President I don't know if you are aware what has driven us into this position. If you will allow me I will give you a very brief overview. I hope you will be able to understand our caution."

"Please go ahead. It seems to me there is lot I don't know that I should have known," said the President, looking across the room at Bertrand who appeared very uncomfortable.

"Mr. President some of our friends and colleagues were

murdered during the course of our research, my grandparents were taken hostage and Dr. Clarke was kidnapped and almost killed. For most of this time we were under the so called protection of a CIA agent who we have now learned has been working for an international organization with malicious intent.

"For the last few months since our friend Dr. Mark Simms was killed we were under constant threat, right up to the last day in the USA, when we narrowly escaped with people in a helicopter shooting at us, trying to kill us and wounding one of our team members in the hand. If it were not for the help of our current hosts we would all be dead by now.

"We want to know why, and we want the killers and perpetrators found and punished. It's our understanding that the CIA agent who was presumably protecting us and was recently killed while in CIA custody has been working for a secret organization called The Orion Society. What can you do to help us find our friend's murderer? Finally, Mr. President it was a big shock to find out that this CIA agent was actually just waiting for us to translate the code and then kill us as well."

"Rossler I swear I knew nothing about any of this. I am shocked and ashamed to learn that we could not provide you the protection you and your group needed when you needed it. I promise you I will investigate this and heads will roll.

"Having said that, I still have to meet with you and your group and I now understand why you don't want to leave Israel. I am happy to listen to your conditions."

"As I said, we won't leave safe haven. You'll have to come here if you want to talk face-to-face, otherwise it'll have to be by video hookup. Whatever the format or the venue of the meeting we'd like you to bring some people with you. The head of the CIA, because we've got some questions for him. Leaders and opposition leaders of both houses of Congress. We won't give this information to one political party, or even one country, alone. It needs to be distributed fairly and in a balanced way."

"Go on." If Daniel noticed the ice dripping from the President's tone, he didn't remark on it. Instead, he went on, improvising as he spoke. "We'll have the meeting recorded, and both your party and ours will have copies so the record can't be misinterpreted after the fact. Sorry, Sir, but we have prior experience of what happens when you can't document something. Nothing personal."

"No offense taken," came the dry answer.

"Is there anything else?"

"I can't think of anything at the moment, Sir."

"I'll be in touch."

Daniel let out a breath he didn't know he'd been holding after the call was disconnected. The others were all looking at him with curiosity, having heard only part of the conversation, but enough to understand what had just happened.

"Well if Mohammed won't go to the mountain, then the mountain must go to Mohammed. It looks like we may have some high ranking company very soon."

In Washington, an irked President Harper called his Chief of Staff back into the room. "Who are these people? How did they get the protection of the Israeli government? Why could we not protect them? Why is the CIA involved and not the FBI? Why is it that they seem prepared for every eventuality? Get the FBI on this immediately. I want full background reports for everyone involved and you better make sure you don't miss anything I am supposed to know about them."

"Yes, Sir."

It was a testament to the seriousness with which the President took the situation that only three days after the phone call, Daniel received another from the Chief of Staff, detailing the plans. With the cooperation of the Israeli government, the President would make an official visit, concealing that he would be meeting with the Rossler Foundation. Over the course of several days, he would be wined and dined by the President of Israel and he, along with the leaders of the Senate and House of Representatives, would meet with leaders of the Knesset. All to put up a smoke screen for their meeting, which would take place in the villa. Before the President arrived, though, a team of Secret Service agents would scour the villa for weapons, bugs and anything else they might consider dangerous.

The Chief of Staff gave Daniel to understand that the whole charade would be tremendously expensive, apparently in an attempt to intimidate him. Daniel let it roll off his back. The meeting was to take place on a Thursday, the soonest that all arrangements could be put in place. What Bertrand didn't tell Daniel, was that the President's staff, courtesy of the FBI, now knew everything about the Rosslerites, right down to the color of Sarah's underwear, the recipe for Martha's oatmeal cookies and Daniel's first grade marks. And what Bertrand didn't know, was that one very important trait of Daniel's was somehow missed; his legendary powers of persuasion.

With little to do, now that the secret was published and they were just waiting for the right time to go home, the group persuaded Daniel to request some entertainment from Baruch. The women wanted to see Jerusalem, in particular. Sinclair wanted to interview several linguists at the university, with an eye to hiring help as soon as their non-profit status came through. Accordingly, Baruch was notified, and came through with flying colors. Tours and shopping trips were arranged, all under the still-watchful eyes of his agents, but everyone agreed that the threat had become moot when the secrets were published.

Evenings were spent in the swimming pool, but even soaking until they turned pruny left several hours to fill. One night, Martha asked if anyone could play any of the instruments in the music room. Sarah was hesitant to confess to it, but she was a near concert-quality pianist. Daniel played passable guitar. Martha declared 'live karaoke night' and organized the whole evening, asking each member of the group what they'd like to perform and downloading sheet music from the internet if they asked for it. When it came to Sinclair, he declared that all he knew was Celtic ditties, but Martha said he'd have to participate, so he named one that was a particular favorite, The Old Dun Cow. Innocently, Martha agreed it would be fine.

When the evening came, everyone was in fine spirits, particularly Sinclair, who'd imbibed some liquid spirits in anticipation of his performance. Sarah played and sang beautifully, offering her namesake Sarah McLaughlin's Arms of an Angel. Because she was so good, the others balked until Martha threatened to withhold her special surprise, an apple pie that she'd persuaded Ilana to allow her to bake in the kitchen. Then, they each sang in turn, with either Sarah or Daniel accompanying them on their respective instruments. Finally, it was Sinclair's turn. Somewhat red in the face from fortifying his courage, he began, a cappella because no music had been found. The song was hilarious, telling the bawdy story of a pub that caught fire and how all the patrons took the opportunity to go to the basement and drink all the barrels of beer. By the time he'd sung four verses, everyone was joining in on the chorus, especially on the repeated 'McIntyre':

*And there was Brown upside down*

*Lappin'' up the whiskey on the floor.*

*"Booze, booze!" The firemen cried*

*As they came knockin' on the door (clap clap)*

*Oh don't let 'em in till it's all drunk up*

*And somebody shouted MacIntyre! MACINTYRE!*

*And we all got blue-blind paralytic drunk*

*When the Old Dun Cow caught fire.*

The last verse brought the house down, everyone declaring the evening's entertainment the most fun they'd had in many months. Sinclair forgot himself and seized Martha for an exuberant kiss, which, to the amusement of the others, she returned before pounding on his arms to let her go.

~~~

On the appointed day, a cavalcade of black SUVs with tinted windows and no identifying marks arrived at the gates of the villa wall, and was duly ushered in by Secret Service agents who had arranged with the Mossad guards to be inside for the day. One by one, they discharged their passengers under the watchful eyes of more agents. The passengers were shown into the villa after each was obliged to show identification, even though the agents checking them knew the four men and one woman on sight. Finally, a slender man whose relatively youthful face belied his silver shock of hair emerged and was greeted at the door. "Welcome, Mr. President. Everything is in order."

On hand for the meeting were the guests; President Nigel Harper, head of the CIA Westley Parkins, and the requested heads of both the leadership and opposition of both houses of Congress. In addition, behind the scenes were the Chief of Staff, on hand to smooth any difficulties, and a supervisor for the army of Secret Service agents who swarmed the place. The regular villa staff had been replaced by a hand-picked butler and chef, who would serve lunch to the party when they took a break.

Daniel, as host of the meeting, deferred to his President to begin, after introducing the Rosslerite party and in turn being told the names of the politicians and CIA head.

"Well, Mr. Rossler, first let me say again that we are all very proud that Americans, even those who have adopted our country," he said, with a nod toward Raj, "have made such an important discovery. We're also proud that, rather than profit tremendously yourselves, you have pledged to the world that these discoveries are to be distributed fairly."

"Thank you, Mr. President," Daniel said, as CEO and spokesperson of the Foundation, unless someone else's expertise was needed or they were addressed specifically.

"However," Harper continued, "For reasons of national security, we must insist that you turn all of this over to your government."

Daniel began to shake his head in unison with the rest of the team, but the President wasn't finished. "Mr. Rossler, think for a moment. This is far too big for a small group of individuals to handle. You're going to need money, resources, that aren't available outside a major government entity. Furthermore, I understand that the first thing you've released is the plans for a fusion generator. Don't you realize how dangerous that could be in the wrong hands? You're out of your depth. You'll all be well-compensated for your roles in the discovery; in fact, name your price. Every man has his price."

Shock ran around the half of the table occupied by the Rosslerites. This wasn't at all what they'd expected, to be insulted, although Raj and Sinclair each thought they should have seen it coming. Daniel struggled for an answer that wouldn't be considered rude, then decided that since the demand was rude, he needn't bother to mince words. Looking around at his people, he saw that they were as irritated at the President's high-handed speech as he was. A small smile played around his lips as he thought of the answer he'd like to give, an expression he'd picked up from an Australian colleague while he was embedded with the Marines in Afghanistan, "Mate, not as long as you got a hole in your arse."

However, he curbed his whimsy, answering instead, "Absolutely not."

Now it was Harper's turn for shock. As President of the United States, he was not accustomed to being thwarted in such an abrupt way, though the media often had harsh words for him. His eyes narrowed, and the Congressional members of his party waited in anticipation of the firestorm they could see coming. The opposition party was rather enjoying the President's discomposure, but they, too, expected cooperation in this matter. Sarah regarded her fiancé with an odd expression as well, making a mental note to ask him what he was smiling about.

"I beg your pardon?" The President feigned that he hadn't heard, or hadn't understood. His words were intended as a mild threat.

"We will not turn over any information to one country alone, Mr. President. I thought I made that clear when we spoke on the phone."

"Young man, do you understand that we can and will get it, with or without your cooperation? Surely it would be best for you and your colleagues to at least benefit financially from your discovery. How can you speak for them? Put it to a vote."

Daniel looked at his colleagues, who were all shaking their heads. "We already have, Sir. I think you can see their answer. Mr. President, all of us love our country. We want to go home. But, we will not be intimidated, nor will we stray from our course. This knowledge belongs to the world, and the world shall have it. That includes the United States, but it isn't for her alone. I must warn you that if you force our hand, we have already prepared to publish the methods we're using and the raw data to the internet before you even leave this compound.

Daniel was playing the biggest bluff of his life while continuing, "The information is all in the hands of our lawyer with instructions to push the "publish" button if we don't reach agreement today." The team saw that and played along with poker faces and nodding heads.

"Every country in the world, including some neither of us wants to have it, will be able to translate the records and use them as they see fit. We don't want to do it that way, we have a plan in place to distribute it fairly and responsibly. We will not be intimidated by you or any other government, and we won't allow this to disturb the balance of power. We're happy to work with you on a solution, but not one that sees the US as the sole owner of these records. They were left for the entire world."

Sarah, gazing with adoration and pride at her Daniel, thought he'd never looked so noble. His chin raised in defiance, a spark of righteous indignation in his eye, he looked to her more Presidential than the President, who was dressed and pampered like an actor. She glanced at Harper to compare again and noticed he was visibly deflating, his shoulders drooping and a resigned look on his face. She thought, good heavens! Daniel has just handed the President a large slice of humble pie, and it looks like he's going to eat it!

Daniel had stopped speaking, and a long, uncomfortable silence ensued. Finally, the President spoke. "Gentlemen, and Ms. Speaker," he said with a hint of some dark humor, "it appears the jig is up." To Daniel and the rest, he said, "I'd hate to have to play poker with you, Rossler. I apologize if I came on a little strong, there. It was the consensus of our party," indicating the members of Congress, "that we attempt to simply seize the information. Given your response, and the fact that you have political asylum here and it would be extremely embarrassing to try to extract you, we concede your conditions. There is no question that the United States must be part of the solution, not part of the problem. Tell us what your government can do to help you."

The reversal was so swift that Daniel was once again left reeling. Again, he looked at the others in a silent request for help, and received encouraging nods and smiles. "Well, Sir, if you put it that way..."

Hours passed as Sarah and Daniel and Sinclair showed them how they had translated the code and what they had discovered. The outsiders couldn't quite get their heads around the facts; that some tens of thousands of years in the past, a civilization more advanced than ours had existed and been destroyed so utterly that only the Great Pyramid at Giza remained. That within that pyramid were secrets that would revolutionize science, beginning with nearly free, clean energy and including the likelihood of unthinkable medical advances. And that, along with the science that would greatly benefit mankind, would come revelations about the history of mankind that were likely to topple churches and historians alike. They sat stunned as the presentation finished.

Bertrand the head of the CIA, was consulted as Martha, Daniel and Sarah related the events of Mark's murder, Barry's murder, the elder Rosslers' hostage taking, Sarah's kidnapping, as well as their escape from the USA. Sinclair asked about the Orion Society, and Bertrand's face darkened. His opinion was that if they were involved, it was a good thing that the group had been as careful and secretive as they were. Bertrand's gaze came to rest on Raj, who paled and resolved not to ask about Area 51 after all. He was still leery of these people, and coming to the notice of the head of the CIA was the last thing in the world that he wanted. After consulting with the President in a separate room, Bertrand assured the party that if they would agree to return to the US and set up the foundation there, he and the President would personally guarantee their safety and the safety of their families. Lewis had briefed Bertrand on the rogue agent, Johnson.

The meeting was punctuated by a sumptuous lunch prepared by the President's own chef, before all the details were settled.

After lunch, they got down to the business of negotiating what role, if any, the United States government could expect to play in the work of the Rossler Foundation. Martha and Sarah had put their heads together, and now requested permission to present their suggestions. The Foundation was seriously underfunded, having only the three million dollars that the New York Times had paid for the exclusive story in its coffers. They could use either more funding or help in fundraising.

The Congressional party held a quick conference and announced that they would cooperate in introducing a bill which would provide permanent funding, though it couldn't for a variety of reasons be the only monies that came in. They suggested that the President speak to other heads of state to provide some funding as well, both to prevent the appearance that the US was receiving special treatment and to spread the burden of what looked as if it could become an expensive operation.

Daniel mentioned that they intended to seek the philanthropic assistance of a wealthy benefactor, and received assurances that names of such people would be made available to him, as well as letters of endorsement from the President and others.

It was only after discussing the fantastic sums needed that the President thought to ask what they intended to do with it all.

"We need to hire an army of translators to start with," Daniel stated. "Sinclair, do you have a presentation ready?"

"Sure, and I do," Sinclair affirmed.

"Roll it," said Daniel.

The President's party watched with open mouths as Sinclair's presentation made it clear to them just how massive the data was, and how much information it could hold. It then went on with a slide show of the index, and what he'd translated so far.

Into the silence, Daniel spoke. "We have every intention of exploiting this information for the good of mankind. With that in mind, we need scientists to interpret and replicate, historians to make sense of what must have happened, and above all, as I said before, an army of translators. Sinclair has done a phenomenal job, but he's only one man. It would take him several lifetimes to translate it all. We need physicians to compare symptoms and understand what diseases we now have the cure for." He trailed off, almost overwhelmed himself at the magnitude of the task.

Now, the President spoke. "Rossler, you do realize that some of this information could be very dangerous in the hands of some parties, do you not?"

"Yes, Sir. It's one of the reasons why we have chosen to appoint a board that will fairly represent all political persuasions. The Board will see to it that dangerous information is suppressed unless and until other information is translated that ameliorates it."

"I'm glad to hear it. I wouldn't want a country that we're now at war with to have the secret of fusion weapons, for example."

"I understand, and neither do I. However, I'd rather no one had that information, not just countries that harbor terrorists. Mr. President, in some parts of the world, *we* are considered the terrorists." Daniel asserted.

Now Sarah spoke up, the dire prediction of the greeting always on her mind. "Mr. President, one other thing is of urgent importance. We have to determine where we are in our cycle. And if the secret to ending war is in those records, we have to find it as soon as possible. Whatever destroyed the civilization of the Tenth Cycle, and presumably those that went before it, could still be in operation in our civilization."

"Agreed. All right, I see your point. Now that I've guaranteed your safety, are you prepared to come back home and get started?"

Daniel grinned. "Articles of Incorporation were filed in Colorado several weeks ago. All we're waiting on is 501(c)3 status."

"Young man, I think I need to appoint you to my negotiations staff. I'll see what I can do to speed up that approval. The IRS owes me one. I'll try to get that pushed through for you within the next forty-eight hours."

With that, the meeting was adjourned, but it was now late enough that the President's staff had taken it upon themselves to prepare dinner. The entire party retired to a large salon next to the formal dining room, there to have cocktails while waiting for dinner to be served.

Daniel and Sarah were standing to the side, watching the others interact. Sarah asking Daniel about that smile. When he told her she broke into an uncontrollable laugh hitting him on the arm, "Daniel Rossler I hope you were not contemplating actually saying that to the President were you?"

Before Daniel could answer, President Harper who has made his way through the others to join them said, "Rossler, I'd like to congratulate you once again. You and your team did your country proud, not only by making this discovery, but by planning a fair and balanced way to share it. Speaking not only as your President, but also as a human being, I'm proud to be a part of it. But I have one condition."

Daniel raised one eyebrow, thinking that they had already hammered out all the conditions. "What would that be sir?"

"I'd be honored if you and Dr. Clarke would join Mrs. Harper and me at the White House for dinner from time to time. We'd love to have a personal update of your work, and Dr. Clarke, I know my wife will be as excited to meet you as I have been to make the acquaintance of your outstanding team."

Color flooded Sarah's face, as she stammered an acceptance in behalf of both of them. Unless she had mistaken the intent, she and Daniel had just been invited to become friends with the President and First Lady of the US!

"Oh, by the way," Harper said. "I understand that you two are engaged? You make a very nice couple. Without being presumptuous, may my wife and I look forward to an invitation to the wedding?"

~~~

For Harper, it remained only to meet with the Israeli president. He owed a debt of gratitude, and it never hurt to strengthen the relationship between the two countries. Accordingly, after a comfortable night's sleep at the US Embassy, he presented himself to the formal meeting that had been prearranged. In flowery diplomatic language that was nevertheless sincere, he thanked Israel, and its president personally, for the staggering effort and care they had extended to his citizens. Assuring him that the US would ensure that the discoveries made would be shared equally with Israel, and that anything that posed a danger would be carefully considered before it was released to any country, President Harper exhibited his statesmanship. However, when Harper offered compensation for the monies expended in the operation, a gratified head of the Israeli state clapped him on the upper arm and said, "It was our pleasure." Thus, an obligation was incurred by the US, and Israel was assured of a place in the new world, whatever that would bring.

Three days later the Rosslerites arrived at JFK in great secrecy away from the prying eyes of the press and taken to an unknown location, where all their family and closest friends were waiting for them.

## ~ The End ~

# Remember Your Free Gift

As a way of saying thanks for your purchase, I'm offering you a free eBook which you can download from my website at www.jcryanbooks.com

## MYSTERIES FROM THE ANCIENTS

### 10 THOUGHT PROVOKING UNSOLVED ARCHAEOLOGICAL MYSTERIES

This book is exclusive to my readers. You will not find this book anywhere else.

We spend a lot of time researching and documenting our past, yet 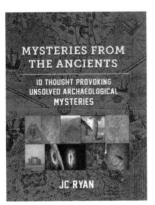 there are still many questions left unanswered. Our ancestors left a lot of traces for us, and it seems that not all of them were ever meant to be understood. Despite our best efforts, they remain mysteries to this day.

Inside you will find some of the most fascinating and thought-provoking facts about archaeological discoveries which still have no clear explanation.

Read all about The Great Pyramid at Giza, The Piri Reis Map, Doomsday, Giant Geoglyphs, The Great Flood, Ancient Science and Mathematics, Human Flight, Pyramids, Fertility Stones and the Tower of Babel, Mysterious Tunnels and The Mystery of The Anasazi

Don't miss this opportunity to get this free eBook now.

Click Here to download it now.

# Thank You

Thank you for taking the time to read my book. Please keep in touch with me at www.jcryanbooks.com and also sign up for special offers and pre-release notifications of upcoming books.

# Please Review

If you enjoyed this story, please let others know by leaving an honest review on Amazon. Your review will help to inform others about this book and the series.

Thank you so much for your support, I appreciate it very much.

**JC Ryan**

# More Books In The Rossler Foundation Mysteries

## THE TENTH CYCLE

**A CONSPIRACY THRILLER**

**THE TRUTH ABOUT HUMAN HISTORY IS ABOUT TO BE REVEALED**

**WILL WE BE ALLOWED TO KNOW THE TRUTH?**

The First Book in the Rossler Foundation Mysteries "THE TENTH CYCLE" is a full-length novel, a provocative techno thriller about human history, conspiracies and an ancient society with power and money that will stop at nothing to reach their sinister goals.

**Amazon USA** - http://amzn.com/B00JMV358M

**Amazon UK** - http://amzn.co.uk/dp/B00JMV358M

# Ninth Cycle Antarctica

WAS THERE A HUMAN
CIVILIZATION IN ANTARCTICA
IN THE PAST?

WILL WE EVER KNOW?

IS THERE AN ANCIENT CITY
UNDER THE ICE OF
ANTARCTICA?

The Second Book "Ninth Cycle Antarctica" is a full-length novel, a stimulating thriller about an attempt at uncovering true human history in the face of adversity and is a follow on from **The Tenth Cycle**.

**Amazon USA** - http://amzn.com/B00K8LRTLE

**Amazon UK** - http://amzn.co.uk/dp/B00K8LRTLE

# GENETIC BULLETS

**A CATASTROPHE OF BIBLICAL PROPORTIONS 35,000 YEARS IN THE MAKING.**

**THE WORLD WE KNOW IS ON THE VERGE OF DESTRUCTION ...**

**THERE IS NO ESCAPE. OR IS THERE?**

The third book **GENETIC BULLETS** is a full-length novel, a stimulating medical thriller about genetic engineering human persistence and resolution in the face of destruction.

**Amazon USA –** http://amzn.com/B00M0DQGXU

**Amazon UK -** http://amzn.co.uk/dp/B00M0DQGXU

# THE SWORD OF CYRUS

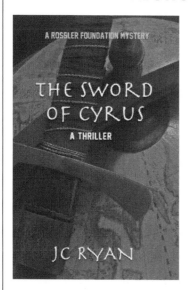

**200 MILLION SOULS ARE SCREAMING FOR REVENGE.**

**THE SWORD OF CYRUS WILL EXACT THAT REVENGE**

**THIS TIME THERE IS NO ESCAPE.**

The fourth book **THE SWORD OF CYRUS** is Book 4 in the Rossler Foundation Series, a full-length novel, a stimulating techno thriller about the danger of nanotechnology to human existence. This book is a follow up of **Genetic Bullets**.

Coming in October 2014     www.jcryanbooks.com

Printed in Great Britain
by Amazon